Celosia's Web

By Maja Fagras

Project Manager: Maja Fagras
Author: Maja Fagras
Editor: Floyd Largent
Cover Art: Mackenzie Fagras

Printed in the United States of America.
First Printing April 11th, 2021
ISBN 9780578894553

Library of Congress Cataloging-in-Publication Data
Names: Fagras, Maja, 1991-author
Title: Celosia's Web
Identifiers: TX 9-402-528

majicmedicinals@gmail.com

IG: @majafagras.author

I dedicate this book to every seeker on their journey.
May it always surprise them with unexpected good fortune
or lessons well learned.

Layer 1: Izar Begiratu; Aurkitu (To Look; To Find)

ying between two mountainous regions, the Basque nation makes a small, triumphant stance upon Earth's surface, nestled in the western Pyrenees Mountains between France and Spain. Here a story is told, although it is not the beginning, nor the end. The humans inhabiting this beautiful refuge hold onto the most ancient of European languages -- or at least, the last surviving language of its kind. And it is known that the structure of one's language shapes the perception of one's experience. Some languages have tools to express emotions that other languages do not. Certain concepts do not exist in some cultures, because the language lacks words for them. Through the lens of a language, conscious thought is shaped, giving the experience a ceiling to rise up to and stop at.

The Basque culture, for example, has words for experiences beyond this reality. The Euskara language makes room for the mystical and magical. It is the ancient ceiling to which their cultural consciousness rises.

Being such a small community, throughout history the Basques barely maintained the footing to stand as their own country. Their recognition as a separate nation waxed and waned with Spain. Despite the ongoing conflict, their language was their biggest strength, unifying them and their culture. This is important to note, because this sets the tone of this particular reality.

In the early 1900s, as the times of dictatorship blossomed, most of the Basque people were quite conservative. Many Basque people were Catholic, and led simple lives. Be that as it may, anciently and more traditionally, Basque people led lives similar to those of pagans, feeling that the dogma of Catholicism was connected to Spain and its rigid politics. The non-dogmatic Basques also led simple lives, but rather ones that were more reverent for the land and the spirit within it.

Geographically speaking, the land itself was a small territory, so small that there were very few valuable resources to let the Basques survive as an independent nation. They maintained their small economy by fishing, whaling, shepherding, farming, and producing iron. For centuries, the Basque people had a practical yet adventurous way of surviving. Enticed by the sea calling them from the northern coast of their territory, they were in constant exploration and communion with the water. The Basque people were master builders, creators of great wooden ships that brought them into the mystery of the unknown. They made their way to Iceland as well as North America well before Columbus, whaling off the shores of what would become Quebec and Labrador. The hunger for new resources and knowledge coursed deep into their lineage. They always were and always will be explorers.

Their shores, facing west toward the Atlantic Ocean, were sheltered in the foothills of the Pyrenees mountain range. This geographic seclusion, kept their culture tucked away from the rest of the growing world. Ancient language and blood lines remained relatively contained throughout the ages, which may be why there is a concentration of RH-negative blood amongst the Basque people.

In understanding the setting, this layer of the story can fully unwind. The story drifts towards a bay ten kilometers north of Guernica, settling on a rural farm where the Kerbasi family lives. A married couple, Bolivar and Lila, were anxiously awaiting the arrival of their firstborn child. Giving birth at home with a midwife, Lila Kerbasi was a self-reliant and natural woman. She was confident and good-hearted. To the untrained eye, Lila might be mistaken for Pagan, because it's an easy way to address a branch of beliefs that are not widely understood.

The year was 1922, and in the crisp coldness on the evening of January 28th, her child was ready to exit the comfort of Lila's womb. Some say that the way a person is born displays the soul's personality, and that anecdote was proven correct for this child. The evening was exceptionally clear, the wide-open sky inviting in the cold air. A fierce and consistent wind seeped through the cracks in the windowpanes of their farmhouse. The walls were strong and unyielding, muffling the wild, swirling charge. This holy laborious process was candle-lit, illuminating the moments of peace, as well as the moments of frustration and pain.

Her midwife was concise and relaxed. With a grounded determination, Lila's gaze was equally present, and yet far away in a land of vision. While squatting low and moving through her birth process, she felt the child's head work through her pelvic bowl while she pushed. On the final push, the small boy arrived and was lifted up by the midwife. He had a calm and cool expression, crying only a few exasperated sobs of relief before he fell into a focused observation of his bodily senses.

He seemed to be suspended in a liminal place, as if deciding something, with his face gradually losing the purple color associated with birth.

As the midwife finished toweling off the child, she checked the vitals on both Lila and her son. After his circulation was encouraged by the midwife, he was satisfied and fell into a deep sleep on his mother's chest. Lila lay there examining her child. Her bewildered expression was placed upon a beautiful, long, oval face, which was framed by striking angular cheekbones. She smelled of grace, lilies, blood, and sweat.

Lila's ice-blue eyes turned to stare mesmerized out the window, into the clear night of the black Moon. She attempted to keep her concentration on the sky, not the pain. The midwife was busy, and set to continue her job by methodically administering stitches to Lila's labia. This stung a lot, as the midwife did not have a high-grade topical numbing ointment. So Lila continually brought her attention away from the pain and back to sky. The stars were so prominent, illuminating the sky while the Moon was in hiding. With an epiphany in her eyes, she spoke the name "Izar" softly as her palm firmly rested upon the back of her child, keeping him close to her.

A magnificent sight for a fly on the wall, to witness her wild hair and her glistening body. As she lay testing the name Izar on her child, she repeated it in a melodic lullaby. The name Izar, meaning star, felt perfectly suited for him. The boy child snuggled in closer at the sound of Izar, giving a sign to Lila that his name fit properly. She fed Izar with her breast; after some failed latches, he got a proper hold and drank.

Satiated and warmed by the magic of breast milk, he fell into a deeper rest. It was obvious that Lila loved Izar immensely, knowing that his soul had a special gravity to it. He carried a wisdom with him from somewhere far away, perhaps the stars. Izar stirred slightly in her arms as they lay lost in a haze of loving; the two souls were kindred, and their reunion sacred.

Bolivar came in when the child was sleeping and his wife was ready for him to enter the space. He brought Lila hot tea and sustenance, and set it down on the nearby night stand. He teared up at the beauty of their newborn son and his wife nestled into the bed, kissing both of their heads.

Time passed. Izar grew into a toddler, and then a child. Lila noticed he was unusually self-aware; his beautiful silver eyes would shift and expose a deeper, more passionate gaze than those of his playmates. Eventually, it was clear Izar did not particularly like to mingle with the rambunctious souls of others his age.

His mother was not concerned about his precocious nature, trusting her child's intelligence and intuition -- although she was hoping this difference did not isolate him in the future. His passion and intellect led him to gravitate towards town elders, older children, animals, and his most cherished thing, the natural world.

He was clear with his words as soon as he learned them, and used them carefully; he preferred eye contact far more, as if speaking through his eyes instead. Idiosyncratically, when he peered through those almond doorways to the soul, he would search as if he were reading a long-winded cryptic poem or counting the threads in a sweater. He stared carefully, being sure not to miss anything. Most children lost interest and couldn't maintain the eye contact, so they shied away from him, leaving Izar alone and confused.

Most facets of Izar's character were peculiar, but they were never ill-mannered or obnoxious. You could sometimes spy him speaking out loud to himself, sweetly articulating a conversation. At first it was curious to listen to him from another room, but when Lila and Bolivar asked him who he was speaking with, his answers would vary. Responding clearly, he would name off creatures from the elemental kingdom -- faeries, brownies, elves, singers -- or he would state actual names.

Bolivar, his father, was closed off to topics of an ethereal nature, but Lila was a believer herself, and was decidedly not concerned. On the contrary, she was proud of his special gifts, as he often knew things he shouldn't. Lila witnessed her son predict the arrival of news or house guests on many occasions.

As he grew older, his conversations with the small beings waned, and his curiosity for the tangible world waxed. He was determined to find out how things worked. This energy was helpful in keeping the farm and household functioning. Lila and Izar spent most days in the garden near the oak tree. Given that poverty was escalating in Spain, Lila and Izar grew most of the food they ate, as well as the herbal medicines they drank. There were markets and neighbors to trade for goods they did not produce. It was a time when self-reliance kept the community alive.

Bolivar, his father, was often away, even with the surge of new politics and social change in the economy. He kept to tradition, and did what his father and his father's father did: he made his living on the sea, fishing. Bolivar was most often to be found in the mist and cold spray of the Atlantic, hunting mostly for the cod and anchovies that went coursing through the shallows of the Bay. Bolivar was charismatic and had the leadership skills to run a big crew of sailors; a voice so clear and convincing that even a siren would hear his persuasion and climb aboard. As a leader in his community, he brought abundance and stability to many families. One could always expect to hear Bolivar praising the victorious days of old, stories about whaling out on the sea.

When Izar was a little older, his family and he sat around the kitchen table, listening to these tales. "....My father's father, traversing the Atlantic in nothing but a whaling galleon, made his way to North America! Up to the Labrador's Red Bay..." Bolivar dramatized the stories of his forefathers with great enthusiasm. This was the story of Izar's great-grandfather's greatest catch, back in those days when whaling was still profitable and legal.

They were all stories that Izar had heard many times, but Bolivar always told them as if no soul had heard them before. The classic story put Izar into a pensive and almost lucid state. Half listening, he sat chewing on greater concepts, ones of empathy outside himself, contemplating his great=grandfather's hunt for the whale. How would it feel to be hunted for consumption? And when great-grandfather made his catch, how did he feel? Were his hands trembling with death? The thought of premeditated murder and conquest made Izar feel ugly about the world, but he also thought of the wealth it brought his people so they would not starve.

This stream of thoughts triggered an epiphany regarding life's paradox. "I am the hero and the villain; life eats life, my life eats life, and that life will eat my life..." Izar said this out loud without thinking about it.

"What's that, my boy?" Bolivar stroked his beard with his thumb and index finger.

Startled by his father's redirection, Izar shook his head while smiling, saying, "Nothing, Papa."

But Bolivar had heard Izar, and responded with his own wisdom, "It's true, the cycle of life is continual, Izar -- as far as I have seen, anyhow. If you zoom in on one piece of the cycle, rather than the whole circle, it might look as if destruction is all that exists." Wrinkling his forehead, he took a deep breath and a deep drink form his mug. He gave Izar a silent, curt nod, and his body leaned sideways to seek the audience of Lila. Izar was left savoring his father's insight. Bolivar lived in a stasis, liberated from the existential questions. He was a good man, but he didn't concern himself with things he could not change.

Bolivar's wisdom and sacredness was within his daily routine. He didn't consider himself a spiritual man, just a man who woke at sunrise and enjoyed his peace and coffee while reading the wind and honoring the Sun. Which was fitting, as he had a huge, fiery heart like the blazing Sun itself. The spirit of the Kerbasi family was brightened when Bolivar was home.

Upon Bolivar's arrival from long journeys, Izar would watch the stiff, broad-shouldered man slowly melt in the presence of Lila. Bolivar would stand still in that familiar doorway, frozen in reverent eye contact, his wide-set green eyes meeting her icy blue ones. Lila had a way of bringing him to a humbling, grounded stasis.

When they came inside together, entering the main room, he would remove his cap, emancipating his wild dark locks, casting them out in all directions. Despite the state of his hair, his beard was trimmed to perfection, as it always was. The man was never seen with an unkempt beard; he took great pride in its maintenance.

When the whole extended family gathered in the main room, they would listen to him speak in his sailor-slurred dialect of Basque, describing his trip and any news from abroad. After a few mugs of wine, everyone had to lean in and do a little guesswork to follow his tales. As the night crept on, everyone consumed more wine, and with that buzz there were rumbles of laughter and animated movements that made the home feel full. On such a day when Izar was confident and warm with wine, he was brave enough to ask Bolivar a question he had been chewing on. "Papa, when can I join you out on the ocean? Will you teach me?"

Bolivar turned towards Izar glossy-eyed, and leapt to his feet! "In the coming years, Izar, you will be old and strong enough to join us on the boats. I feel excitement for our voyages to come!" Bolivar sang out, while patting his son enthusiastically on the shoulder.

Bolivar was like the hearth of the home, brightening the political despair that Lila, her sister Emma, and Izar's grandfather were steeping in while he was away. Effusing a captivating and hopeful gravity, Bolivar pulled his family back into orbit about him, where they were safe. Izar loved this theatrical and lively energy his father brought; he admired and respected him greatly. But Bolivar never truly opened the doors of his soul to Izar. His father was guarded, and maintained a level of concealment that fueled a confusion and hurt in Izar. Perhaps Bolivar was subtly jealous of the connection that Izar shared with his mother. He was a good father, a good man in his community, but Izar could sense that Bolivar was cryptic. His true emotions never spilled over the edge of his soul. Inside him was a vast uncharted space; perhaps it was the sea. If Izar listened closely enough, he could hear the echoing, tolling bell of a lighthouse.

In the fullness of time, Izar grew old enough and sturdy enough to go fishing with his father; he was 14 on his first voyage. Bolivar saw this occasion as Izar walking into his manhood and becoming strong. However, upon Lila's request, Izar was not allowed on any voyages beyond the Bay of Biscay. The thought of his mother at home, abandoned, did not sit well with Izar or Bolivar, so they were happy to comply with her wishes.

The ocean was vast, and it captivated Izar's heart; he understood why his father loved the sea so much. Bolivar was pleased when Izar was keen and able to stay calm against the sea's wild heart, and follow his commands. This gained him respect with the crew, but he was still too young to be truly seen as a crewmate. When the weather was calm, he concentrated on processing and storing the fish, so it was ready for production at a facility in the port. Izar did a lot of grunt work, mopping and cleaning, paying his dues to prove himself to his father, as well as to the crew. He was eager to soak up all the ocean's secrets, to learn all there was to learn. Luckily, he already knew his knots and boat verbiage, so no one had to spend time explaining the details. This was a relief, because there was one thing certain: you did not want to disappoint a sailor. They were harsh when it came to the job, and as on any boat, the men drank, smoked and swore like, well, sailors. Izar partook in smaller doses, because if he declined he would have felt a great deal colder and less accepted. He was still on the lanky side, growing to 1.8 meters as fast as he did. This lack of insulation made life at sea very stiff and cold without a little drink here and there. When the voyage was over, Izar was glad to return home, but was excited for the next one.

The Kerbasis lived a simple life in the country and did not have a radio, so they were often separated from the day-by-day political news. However, this did not protect them from the harsh reality of war. In 1937, the Fascist leader of Spain, Francisco Franco, utilized allied forces and slowly conquered the Basque territory. He banned the Basque people from speaking their ancient Euskara language; to do so was illegal, and punishable by law. Despite this command, some Basques still spoke Euskara in the secrecy of their own homes, in full commitment to keep their culture alive. Franco's goal was to dismantle the strength of the Basque independence, and have them merge fully with Spain.

This same year, 1937, during the conquest of the Basque territories, the town of Guernica was bombed by German bombers who were allied with Franco during the Spanish civil war. Izar and his family lived outside of Guernica to the north, almost on the bay near Urdaibai biosferako erreserba. To their great fortune, their home was untouched; but the skies were filled with ash and blood that Monday, April the 26th. It was a travesty, a cruel atrocity fueled by unreasoning distrust against the Euskadi, that took place in early afternoon. Every Monday, when the seasons were right, Guernica served as a convergence place for farmers and crafters to sell their produce and wares. Many civilians met with an untimely death that day while picking out the freshest greens and hunting for the best of last season's potatoes. Bombs fell from above and struck the farmers market square. Those lucky enough to escape a direct hit scrambled away in fear, their ears deafened and ringing. Those survivors were stained forever by the horrors of war, and for what?

Guernica was a civilian town, once considered a spiritual mecca by the surrounding villages. Many Basque locals came to visit

"Gernikako Arbola," a sacred oak tree that symbolized freedom. Despite Franco's efforts, the tree survived the bombs, and many locals saw this as a sign of hope, proving That their flame as a people could not be extinguished by such monstrous acts. But despite their symbol of hope standing tall, there was still much bloodshed. Humans were used as pawns on that farmers market Monday; used in a propagandized military game to gain territory and power. The bombing was a pure display of flaunting power, and controlling others with fear. The insanity of the tactic inspired many artists to create memorials to it, raising awareness of the atrocity, adversely spreading and advertising news of Franco's handiwork. Some of artists were commissioned by questionable sources.

Izar saw an article in the newspaper about Pablo Picasso and his painting, Guernica, called "Guernica and the evolution of consciousness." The painting is an abstract grayscale composition with limbs and symbols that merge together, representing the cacophony and fallout of the bombing. It is not a painting one walks away from feeling inspired; no, it displays a dark despair about human nature. The paper was mostly filled with information relating to the Spanish civil war and all the travesties that came with it. This was not good for the economy of the Basque people. The chaos and destruction caused a temporary social rearrangement, and dismantled the commerce and local production of goods, which led to much poverty. Izar's hands trembled from a deep pit of anger, the news paper falling limp in his grasp. How could such injustices be justified by those in power?

Izar, angered by the paper, tossed it into the fire hearth and watched it blacken. He knew, that Franco's terrorism was part of a greater conspiracy that one day he would have to face.

Izar, left the farm house and looked up the hill at his mother, and he saw her weeping into her hands for the innocence that was taken. Her hair, loosely tied, fell over her face in sections while she sat under the garden's oak tree upon the wet spring grass. Lila had always sold her flowers and herbs at that market in Guernica. She was there at least once a month, and had gotten to know many of the vendors and farmers who assembled there to create a community. They were kind and humble people, honest and hardworking. Now many were dead.

Izar approached her slowly, and knelt by her side, "They will pay for they have done Momma, even though it is not fair, I am glad you were not there that morning."

Izar pulled strands of his mother's hair back, and held her shoulders. He remembered going there with his mother a number of times as a child, helping her preserve and protect her delicate flowers for transport and sale. The notion of mass murder chilled a place inside him that he hadn't known existed. It also kindled a fire in his soul that felt ancient and angry.

That year saw more shadows in his peripheral vision, especially after the bombs fell. All the collective fear coalesced as a food source for the shadows of darkness -- food that allowed them to grow and replicate. In times of tyranny, a town could bustle in the Sun with laughter and music one moment; the next, it could lie in ash and ruin. Izar knew the world was changing, and that life would be different.

Isolated in the thick air of grief, Izar would sit alone in his room and drift off to his one prized music record. This rare object was a gift given to him on the spring equinox, a month prior on March 21st, by his mother's friend Elenuta. They had met at the market years before. Her intuition, like Lila's, guided her to skip the Market on that fatal day. She was a marvelous woman, a nomadic Romanian gypsy who had traveled across Europe collecting and trading all sorts of magically strange objects. Her soul was clearly old, that much was obvious; her eyes could see through stone and lies. Izar loved when Elenuta came to visit, for she brought with her a mutual understanding. She saw Izar and his depth the first moment she looked into his eyes.

Back in March, on her last visit, it was chilly and damp outside. So they sat in the living room with the fire rolling steady while sipping tea and exchanging small tidbits of personal news. Elenuta was not a traditional woman; she had no husband. The way she cultivated male companionship was abnormal for the times, giving her personal news stories an air of flair, scandal, and electricity.

After the laughter settled and the red on Izar's cheeks dissipated, Lila left the room to refill the teapot and make a trip to the outhouse. When she exited the room, it felt suddenly full of a foreign thick energy. Elenuta asked Izar to come sit closer. Setting the fire poker back on the hook, he left his perch on the bricks to kneel beside her. She held onto Izar's wrist and inhaled a gasping breath. Her eyes glazed over, and she faced him directly and spoke.

"I see your soul's colors. You have a gift of sight that comes from both your lineage and your soul. Do not be afraid of what you see, for you are not mad. You came here with an intent purpose; do not lose sight of that. You will find what you came here looking for. Trust the trees. Do not get caught up in the grief of war; it will shroud your compass. When you find what you seek, your job is to protect, for you are the pillar." Elenuta closed her eyes and nodded off, her shoulders slumping. She inhaled sharply again, her eyes flaring open, normal and clear as they had been before.

He nodded slowly and swallowed the lump in his throat, wishing to ask her so many questions as tears swelled in his eyes. He felt that someone had finally looked at him for the first time as the wise being he was. Elenuta smiled softly at Izar, and spoke: "I am never sure what will come through me, but that may have been one of the most urgent messages I have ever delivered. I hope it made sense to you. I can scarcely remember what was said." She laughed quietly, raising her eyebrows and letting go of Izar's wrist.

Izar nodded, wiping away the tears rolling down his face. "Elenuta, words cannot express what doors in my heart your words have opened. These were doors that have been shut longer than you know. I feel somehow more awake." Izar held his chin high, grateful for the recognition.

Lila entered the room, with a tea tray steaming with hot drinks. Her knowing soul felt the energy shift in the room, and she smiled at the two of them. She said nothing about it, though, and with that, the moment passed and the air became thin again.

Breaking the silence, Elenuta said, "Lila has told me you have an old record player you mean to fix. Is this true, Izar?"

Izar nodded. "Yes, but I haven't started yet. It has taken the back burner, as I don't have any records to play."

When Izar said this, Elenuta's beautiful face gleamed with a secret about to be revealed. Moving some items around in her basket, she pulled out a record in a thick paper case. Displaying it to Izar, she winked, "This is a doorway."

Elenuta stood up from the olive-green chair she had been sitting in and handed Izar the record. When he moved to embrace her, he realized how much he towered over her, so he squatted awkwardly to make himself a more reasonable height to give her a hug. Izar was mindful of the discomforts that others experienced.

He did not feel romantically attracted towards Elenuta, because she was twice his age. However, after he backed away, he noticed the beautiful woman she was. She was wearing dark green velvet and wool that complimented her hazel eyes. Her style was both regal and bohemian. Her adornments and perfume were well suited to her wild and poetic soul. Izar took his record and left the two women to get started with their equinox ceremony, the one they performed every spring.

Izar could not discover the sound of the music until he mended his phonograph. When it first arrived in his custody, it was broken. It took time to figure out the machine. He sat with it for many hours, tinkering with the wires and replacing some of the smaller conduits with parts he scrounged from elsewhere. After a few failed attempts, he restored the machine to its purpose.

"It's alive! Again," Izar said happily, laughing to himself when he got the needle to lower, feeling rather pleased with his accomplishment. Clapping his hands once in excitement, he set out to test his record. Laying the needle down with measured precision, Izar's eyes were level with plane of the record. They sparkled with the hope, waiting for the music to strike. When the initial fuzz of the recording filled the speaker, Izar sat himself upon a rug on the floor. His eyes were fixed on the ceiling as he listened as the soft fuzzing whirr stirred into music. He listened carefully and thoughtfully, remembering Elenuta's words. Yes, this is a doorway, but to where? He wondered.

There were instruments he hadn't heard before, strings whose melodies bent and slid across space. Chanting that sounded like the split of a single cell. Beginning on one note and then fracturing into multiple ones, the sounds spread apart to harmonize. This was the beginning of a new favorite pastime for Izar. He was blown away by its peculiar, hypnotic qualities. Lying down. he would listen with his eyes closed, breathing slowly, until he would drift off into a place where his body could not follow. Most often, he felt as if he was a fish on a line, being pulled upstream. It was never unpleasant, but instead felt warm, like love. He didn't feel time in this place, but when he was there, listening, he felt closer to what he was looking for.

The wars crawled on, and cruel Franco stayed in power, controlling their religion and language, even banning traditional Basque names for newborn children. Things were bleak, and Franco sent Basque men to fight with the Germans in what was soon called World War II. Monsters working with monsters. Izar felt helpless, knowing all about the struggle and suffering throughout the continent and beyond, feeling it deep inside, in a place he could not articulate. Worse, he evaded the draft through no attempt of his own, as there was no official certificate for his birth. He felt guilty, yet relieved.

Projects kept Izar's head clear as the years rolled on. He learned to work with wood and metal, each day growing more confident with his skills. Resources for his projects were limited, but Izar was clever in procuring supplies, and he didn't always follow the rules. He had a moral code that understood the bigger picture of right and wrong, but there were some rules that felt right to break -- especially when those rules were created by people with no moral compasses. The paradoxical way of the world was hard on Izar, for it was ironic and hypocritical, entirely against his nature. He coveted the words Elenuta had shared with him on that solstice. They served as his motivation, his mantra for survival, keeping his unknown purpose alive.

Another way Izar found peace within a wild world was by working with plants. His greenhouse was his church, his place of peace and worship. "Kaixo," Izar whispered to his seedlings in his greenhouse. With the sound of his voice, every tiny stem seemed to surge a millimeter taller. With swift, clear aptitude, Izar began pruning a small shrub that was being stored in the greenhouse for the winter.

The shrub was hypericum, or St. John's Wort, in its dormant phase. There were no yellow flowers budding or blooming, just the leaves holding their positions and waiting patiently for more Sun. He didn't make many cuts on the plant, but Izar felt that the roots needed more energy during their wintering phase. So he nipped at the dying stems.

He also plucked a few leaves to basket for drying. While doing this, he hummed a lullaby with a low baritone vibration. He smiled and remembered gardening with his mother; it was his favorite activity, soaking up knowledge of the cultivation and harvest. Lila had taught him to hum the lullaby; she told Izar that the plants felt safer to grow when that lullaby was sung. Izar always kept that sentiment close to his heart and sang to the plants.

Light on his feet, Izar moved from shelf to table, addressing the seedlings and plants in accordance to their need, Using water he had collected from rainfall with a system of catchments and filtration of different-sized gravel and charcoal. The greenhouse spanned about 12 meters by 12 meters, with the water catchment outside of the greenhouse. It was a reasonably tall structure, a square building with a pyramid top. Izar had started building the greenhouse when he was nineteen. He began by digging into the earth a couple of feet, to let subterranean temperatures allow for a longer grower season. The floor of the greenhouse was recessed a meter; it took him hours of digging and shaping to achieve a level floor that he would later top off with gravel and stone. Using metal for the frame, he welded a square foundation that he secured with cement in each corner, where the poles extended into the earth.

Once his foundation was set, he could move forward with procuring pieces of wood and glass. Now he had a visual reference, and the spatial awareness of what he needed. He needed enough to fill all the walls and the pyramid ceiling. None of the glass would be from the same source, and none of the pieces would be uniform in shape. He would have to get creative. Even his father took interest, and would bring home a selection of random glass panels from nearby ports when he returned from each voyage. Merchants often had selections available from old homes, churches, and hospitals. After the bombings, many buildings had to be torn down, and the glass was salvaged. Everyone in the outskirts of Guernica caught wind of Izar's need for glass, and many people brought him pieces to work with. This helped quicken the construction process, and once he had all the glass he needed in his possession, he began to construct the wooden frame piece by piece, like a puzzle, using the odd-shaped glass as his guide. When there was a spot where no glass would fit, he filled the spot with wooden shutters for ventilation.

He enjoyed constructing the abstract puzzle; it challenged his mind and made him more flexible. This process took the better part of a year. His favorite piece of glass was given to him by Elenuta, his mother's psychic friend from the market. She presented him with a circular piece of stained glass that depicted a beautiful faerie poised atop a mushroom. It was vivid in the light, and it cast hues of purple and lavender. Small reflections of colored light bounced around their faces as they marveled at it.

"It is wise to pay homage to the creatures of nature, as they tend to what we cannot. These are a realm of beings who seldom pass into our world, but adorn it with their mark of beauty," Elenuta mused as she lightly touched the leaf of a nearby plant, admiring its structure. Izar took the glass with an intrigued and serious expression, grateful for the insight and the magnificent gift.

"Thank you, Elenuta," he said solemnly. "This piece will be the focal point of the greenhouse; I shall cherish it. You have keen eyes for fine things. I admire your talent for picking suitable gifts. You are welcome to any herbs you would like when my project is complete. I will grow something special for you, if you like."

Elenuta nodded. "There is a plant I wouldn't mind you growing for me. I wonder if you could start a jasmine vine for me? I also love the Roman chamomile you grew last year; mine always turns out so lanky and limp, but then again I'm always traveling, and perhaps I'm not the best plant mother," she said, winking with a sheepish grin.

"You did trade for a lot of mugwort and passion flower," Izar pointed out, recalling the last growing season. "I'll be sure to grow those again, too."

"Ah yes, that combination was perfect for a dreaming blend I prepare as an herbal decoction," Elenuta remembered as she tapped her finger to her temple. She smiled and bowed her head towards Izar. Turning, she made her way up to the house to join Lila for some tea.

Izar was left marveling at his new circular piece of stained glass, finding the faerie form sultry and mysterious, her energy perfectly depicted by the artist. With timeless beauty and eyes bearing secrets, she sat upon her mushroom with poised invitation. He shook his head, calming his erotic thoughts, and set the glass down. He configured the rest of the greenhouse walls, keeping that special piece in mind, Wanting to pay homage to the faeries facing eastward, at sunrise. This would project the mystery of the Sun's morning light directly through the glass.

When the walls were completed, it was time for the roof. He stabilized it by setting a beam made from a pine log in the center of the floor to reach up and affix to the central point of the pyramid. He secured that pine pole with a perpendicular crossbeam and then used angular cross-braces to stabilize the whole structure. The swirls and knots of the beam told stories of a life long lived, and now it stood majestically, sanded down to a smooth finish. Inside, he built tables and shelves to set all his seedlings upon to germinate. Above the tables, off to the right, he hung a wind chime that would drift between the cross-breezes of the ventilating windows. The soothing tones of a well-made wind chime would likely convince his plants to grow fuller and taller.

The building was a sight to see upon completion, and it attracted many people to their herb garden and farm. It was a work of art as well as a tool created with specific intention. Visitors would marvel when they came to purchase or trade for herbs, leafy greens, vegetables, stone fruits, and grapes, depending on the season. Most often, the whole setting would expose a hidden joy in people, like letting a bird out of a cage. More often than not, they would find themselves singing or humming as they walked the property, while looking for what they wanted. Izar enjoyed observing this in people. It brought him small, joyous moments of satisfaction. Although Izar felt content, he knew deep down that there was something he had yet to find, especially when he thought of what Elenuta had said. Sometimes he wondered if he had made it all up. While looking into the eyes of others, his hopes waned. He wasn't even sure what he was looking for anymore; nor did he to begin with, if he was honest. He could not explain to anyone with words what he sought. He always thought he would just know when he saw it.

The seasons drifted on, and Izar grew older, becoming more of a man, his voice deepening even more than before. Bolivar took him out on more fishing trips in the winter, because Lila didn't require as much help with the farm and garden. Lila would have an empty look in her eyes whenever her son and husband left. Izar, hugging his mother tightly, said, "See you in four days; we aren't going out very far," with the confident voice of utter reassurance. Lila smiled, and then made a serious face. "Bolivar, keep your men safe," she commanded. She kissed her husband on his cheek near his ear, then walked outside to go into the greenhouse, leaving the men stiff in their winter gear at the front doorway.

Bolivar, sensing Izar's inner conflict, chimed in, "She'll be all right, Izar; she knows as well as I that we need the money, and that we must go."

The Sun was shining bright as they set out. Izar could see his mother in the greenhouse, basking in its trapped heat, light of different colors bathing her face. It seemed as if she were talking to someone, but it was too far away to tell, and Bolivar had a long stride to keep up with. As they made their way closer to town, they managed to hitch a ride in a neighbor's truck to get to port. It was a short ride, but the men were grateful to keep their shoes dry as long as possible. It was nearly the end of January, growing close to Izar's 27th birthday, and the streets were practically made of mud.

Normally, January is the coldest time of year in Basque country, but this year it hadn't gotten too bad. The Sun had come out between showers more frequently, the blankets of thin clouds moving along swiftly. This was a plus, because it meant that the trips out into the sea and mist would be a lot more comfortable than they had been in seasons prior.

When they arrived at port, the men worked together to get the old boat unhitched from the dock. Two men raised the anchor, and after that, she was set to drift out to sea with a surprisingly quiet, purring motor.

The crew totaled seven, counting Bolivar and Izar. The men slurped hot coffee they had brought from home in tall green thermoses. Their coffee scented the air, mixing pleasantly with the smell of old fish and salt. Heading northwest directly towards Iceland, their journey began. Their destination was the outer edges of the Bay of Biscay.

For the last eight centuries, the Basque people had hunted the North Atlantic right whale and the bowhead whale. Their methods were cruel and often utilized the bond between a calf and its mother, first attacking the calf to attract and kill the mother in her state of protection. This method led to a precipitous decline in both species, and there had not been a whale sighted since 1901. Thinking of this made Izar's heart ache as the shore faded into the distance behind them. His ancestors had depleted most of the whales in this region. Bolivar and his crew fished for cod, anchovies, and sometimes shellfish, if there was a big surge of them in the Bay. The fish market was one of the few economies left in these perilous, impoverished times.

Days at sea were filled with grueling work, and talk of dreams for when the war was over. In the evenings, before Izar went to the quarters below to sleep, he would lay on the main deck to view the sky. Immersed in the calm night, the sky stretched around the water's edge like a tight shirt over a pregnant belly. The stars were so vivid, their depth was not perceivable; it felt as if he could reach out and touch one. Patterned sloshing served as a mild reminder against the boat's hull, as if to say, "You are still on a boat, you haven't floated away."

Listening to the sounds, Izar watched his breath dissipate among the magnificence. You couldn't see the beginning or the end. These nights transformed Izar; experiencing the vastness of the ocean stirred a motivational force within him, urging him to accomplish his true purpose. It reminded him of something, like a dream long forgotten, as if he had laid in this very position looking at the stars long ago. He laughed, unsure how long ago that could be when he was barely 27. Nonetheless, in this expansive setting Izar found a deeper connection to himself.

One night, out of the corner of his eye, he spotted orange meteorites in a cluster, blasting past the sky. Little tails of blue and silver seemed to wisp behind them. The event lasted long enough to take a few deep breaths, and then they were gone. After this, he sat up, feeling that it was time to go below to sleep. As he stood up and gathered his blanket, he heard a low, deep sound... or did he feel a rumbling? It was tough to tell on a metal boat. Looking over the edge of the boat he saw ripples in the water, growing in density and speed. Rising up from below came a dim silver glow, a translucent body of light. He watched this light break the surface and zip into the night sky. In its wake it pulled water and all kinds of matter from the sea, which splashed onto the deck. There was driftwood, seaweed, and

rubbish among it. After the sea settled, there was nothing to be seen
but the rhythmic water.

Izar did not have to battle disbelief or confusion at this sight;
he knew there were all kinds of mystical happenings just past human
perception. He smiled and whispered "Kaixo," to the dark waters,
hoping the creature could hear him. When he glanced down, he saw
that upon the deck where the water had splashed, amongst the seaweed
and rubbish, sat a small lump looking very out of place. He bent down
to get a closer look, though in the dark of the night it was hard to make
out the details of the misshapen thing.

Deeming it safe, he tentatively picked up the cold, wet lump,
and felt that it was no more the size of a plum, with ridges and patches
that felt like tiny barnacles. Shifting his grip on his blanket, he
pocketed the lump. When he made his way below, he realized how
tired and sore he was. Despite his curiosity, there would be more
clarity of detail in the morning's light. As he lay his head down, he
smiled again at his gift from the silver light, and slipped into a sleep as
deep as a coma.

Mentally, rousing the next morning was effortless, although his
body was stiff from sleeping in one position. Izar did a quick routine
of stretches before he met up with the crew for coffee. Most of the men
were no doubt still half-asleep on whiskey's lullaby.

During Izar's stretching routine, his breaths were matched
precisely with his movements; or at least that was his goal. He aimed
to stay present in each movement. When he fell out of focus, he
flowed back into it. He felt the wellness within him when he achieved
union of breath and movement. This was something he had discovered
in his time spent alone; he understood how breath was helpful to the

body. Most people teased him for his strange routines if they ever had the pleasure of witnessing them. Izar would stretch whenever it felt like his body required it; he was unrestricted by societal normalcy. He would stretch whenever wherever, at times gaining quite the audience.

Finally, feeling focused and awake, he headed towards the shed, or that's what the boys called it. It was where they made meals, played cards, and enjoyed coffee. Being so small, the little room was thick with the smells of coffee and liquor. Izar poured himself a cup of coffee and went out onto the main deck to examine his sea gift before the day's work began. As he pulled it from his pocket to examine it in the light, he realized it was almost a square, like a small box with barnacles covering half of the surface. It felt hollow, and looked overall unnatural. He was not sure what it was, but it carried an energy that felt like a small planet with its own gravity. He knew that it came to him for a reason, and that he would keep it with him wherever he went. Mystery solved, he put it in his pocket and set to his tasks on the ship.

Izar had a logical simplicity about himself, and moved through his tasks diligently, mopping the fish scud and guts with pride. Nearly full grown, his height was closing in on that of his father. He stood tall and broad-shouldered, down to a tapered waist. His legs were long and sturdy, toned while lifting crates of anchovies and cod. Each step was measured and placed rather than the mindless stomp of a brute. His jawline was square and strong, holding his smile in a perfect placement. His hair, like his father's, was dark and curly; and his beard, already filled in, was maintained with perfection -- like his father's. He looked rather dashing on the boat, even in a knit hat and fisherman's gear.

Knowing himself to be an attractive man, he was confident, but not arrogant. He knew he was attractive because his looks did get him attention and trouble from women. He felt that most women found interest in him due to his appearance only. They didn't bother to hear his soul, or know how to connect with him in a way that felt meaningful. Not to say that he thought himself too good for anyone's companionship, but he simply didn't feel anything for most women. He had tried courting many for an evening, but never felt any spark; nor did he see what he was looking for.

On one occasion, he set his silver gaze to drift out the window, while the woman he was with raved on about the United States and its music trends. Not that what she had to say wasn't intellectual or artistic; rather, it just sounded far away somehow, as if the two of them were inhabiting slightly different realities that barely overlapped. The woman became frustrated; she got up and left, but Izar didn't notice until she was across the cafe and stomping out the door. He did not chase after her, nor did he even stand. His torpor set silent eyes to observe him from the little tables scattered about the room.

This occurrence had garnered him a reputation in the town, one that made him more of a curious prize to be obtained than anything having to do with his true character. Avoiding the complications that going to town often brought, he stayed at the family farm a great deal of his time. He had grown tired of sloughing off flirtatious invitations with cool and non-apologetic explanations. Removing the fantasy and hope from a woman felt like dropping a net full of fish onto a boat's deck. That instant sense of gravity, dismantling the tapestry of fantasy that rumors of his nature had spun, was not something Izar liked doing... but he became used to the process.

After his arriving home sea, his 27th birthday came and went. It was this birthday that triggered him to seek new adventures. He went venturing away from the farm more often. He would pack lightly with enough supplies and clothes to last a couple of days, and head towards the port town where his father's ship was to find a ride. He was looking to head northeast to another port town, Bayonne. The fish production facility had a delivery route to Bayonne. Izar knew some of the drivers, because his father's crew did business with them selling fish.

So one crisp morning in late spring Izar prepared for an adventure. At six in the morning, Izar hitched a ride with a middle-aged delivery man named Etor. His kind and tired eyes counted the truck's load, being sure that his delivery was accurate before they left. Unwilling to speak in Euskara, as he had lost his parents in the bombing those ten or more years ago, he spoke in Spanish instead. Franco's handiwork had done its job with Etor; he wore fear like sweater, woven from the trauma and loss of his family. He spoke Spanish when discussing the agreement for the ride, and didn't use Euskara save for a few quiet words to himself in the truck. The drive to Bayonne took four hours. In payment, Izar helped Etor for an hour, unloading the crates full of fish into the market's back entrance. After this, Izar walked with his pack towards the foothills of mountains, and the forests that peppered their base.

He discovered that being in these forests brought him a sense of homecoming. Determined to find the source of that familiar feeling, he ventured there as often as possible. The forest was a place where he could be himself freely, and use his gifts without anyone watching. As a seer, Izar was blessed with the gift to perceive the dimension just beyond his own. Lila and Elenuta were among the few individuals that he was able to share those experiences with. Speaking about his experiences helped him understand them, but he only had truly mystic experiences when he was alone. This made being alone more desirable.

As a child, Izar was aloof to the abnormality of his ability to see into the next dimension. It took him some embarrassing incidents to understand that not everyone was able to see as he did; nor did everyone believe.

Izar's gift allowed him to see that, despite most people's lack of awareness, the spirits in the dimension beyond were, ironically, very integrated in human reality. There were creatures that lingered in the corners of a rooms, as well as those that skipped through a field of flowers. Small Light Singers breathed life into the bloom, and helped the seedlings sprout. But not all beings were simple and sweet; there were also lugubrious beasts that followed humans about that were impatient and bitter, looming shadows that ensured bad luck to perpetuate their aggressive energy. It was clear to him that there was much he didn't know about the complexities of this other world.

Now that Izar was older, slipping into the state of seeing took practiced focus; he had to ground his body with laborious exercise, or concentrate in stillness with his record.

Every time he made trips to the forest, he felt his lung capacity for air grow. His breaths were slow and deep, consuming the airborne biodiversity. In the corners of his vision, he spied subdued cool-toned lights zipping through the trees. The avidity of their movements left a pleasant sound trailing behind them, hushed, like a soft whispering and drag of an owl's wings in flight. For most people, these sights and sounds would rouse panic or have them dropping to their knees in prayer, but not for Izar. He felt at ease and unassailable when he was in any part of the forest along the Pyrenees Mountains. Comfort wrapped around him like a warm blanket; there was a safety to it he could not describe, as if nothing could harm him within its boundaries. Not to say that the forests did not harbor any shadow, or creatures of trickery, as they certainly did. He could feel their eyes on him from time to time, but he felt untouchable somehow.

The particular forest he was headed for was the Irati Forest. The route he took required him to backtrack southeast a bit, but in the town of Bayonne, there were always a few cars headed into the foothills away from the coast. Positioning himself so he was on the main road out of town, he walked with his thumb out, hoping a car would stop and give him a lift. Locals were typically gracious, and were delighted to give Izar a ride. His kind eyes and handsome face made for easier travel via hitchhiking.

The sky was blue and the Sun was warm on Izar's face; his pack strapped across his back, and he felt good about today. He knew he would find the most perfect ride, though it would take time. So he grabbed a small pad of paper from his pocket, and wrote some random thoughts that came to his mind.

He wrote: Astra inclining, sed non obligant. Izarrak gurekin joaten dira, ez dute lotzen. The stars incline us, they do not bind us. He mused of his destiny, and the fated path he was on. Eventually, Izar grabbed the attention of a smaller faded red car that was puttering along. An older woman dressed in many colors smiled and motioned for Izar to climb in. He was feeling bold this afternoon, and he spoke his greeting in Euskara to see if she too, was Basque: "Kaixo."

To his relief, she responded in the uniting language, and he sat with his pack in his lap and closed the car door. The car smelled like dried flowers and dust. Izar looked at the woman's leathery hands as they lightly gripped the wheel, with the perfected ease that comes with old age. She had gardener's hands, rough with gloveless weeding and pruning. Izar was glad they would have mutual interests to casually speak about to pass the time -- topics on gardening and how the season thus far was faring. It was late June, so naturally, most of the flowers were blooming and the temperature was perfect.

"Thank you again for picking me up. My name is Izar."

She responded with a nod and shared her name. "I am Antonia. So, where are you headed, anyways?"

"Antonia -- what a nice name, flowing like a song." Izar repeated it, melodically, to explain. She smiled at this and nodded. "I am headed for a camping trip in the Irati Forest. Do you know of it?" Izar asked.

Antonia swallowed hard, and raised her eyebrows. "It's a lovely place, but it's haunted, you know; strange spirits gather within its boundaries. Are you sure you want to go to that one?" Antonia shrugged and peered over at him, unsure if he knew what he was getting himself into. "I am headed in that direction, and I will drop you off, but I urge you to reconsider. Strange things have happened to men who venture into those woods alone."

Izar, not wanting to offend the woman, put on a look of surprise and careful consideration, but in his mind he was relaxed and relieved that she knew of the forest and would take him there. He explained, "I am seeking a specific herb that I hear only grows there; my mother thinks that the herb will sell well. I must go for the sake of the farm." He tried to sound humbly noble; he didn't love lying, but he thought it would make things easier and end the conversation.

Antonia nodded, with understanding eyes; times were hard for farmers. The wealth was spread thin. "Well, how brave of you. Just be careful out there."

The car sputtered along for 37 minutes, give or take, and they shared stories about gardening and techniques for healing the soil. Good conversation always made time pass with ease, so the ride felt fairly quick.

Antonia slowly transitioned to a stop and explained that the trail into the forest was just beyond the bend. She also gave him a bag with a few snow peas and dried figs from her property, and she wrote down her address for him if he needed somewhere to stay on his return journey, in case anything went wrong.

Izar smiled, sincerely appreciating her kindness. Waving as she drove off, He stood for a while, stretching his body from the long day of sitting. His heart was warm and he had good feelings of brightness and protection. Eager to taste the woman's Adriatic figs, his favorite variety, he grabbed one from the bag she had given him and took a bite. When the skin cracked, the sweet seeds spread with sugary stiffness; it was truly a divine fig, perfectly dried.

Also thirsty, he gulped down half the water from the canteen he had filled before he left. He hadn't realized how dehydrated he had become. The small snack and hydration brought him back to life, and after everything was packed away, he set his bag by a rock and he walked into a bush to relieve his need to urinate. After strapping his pack to his back, he made his way to the trail.

The river Barranco de Loibeltza was visible from the trail, full and flowing. It was beautiful, as well as cold from the mountain run-off. He followed it until he found a smaller river that fed it from a higher source; upon finding this, he knew it would lead him up into the mountains and deeper into the forest.

The rivers and creeks are the visible veins of the planet, and following them felt like following the nourishing sources of life. This smaller creek led him into a forested place, where oak trees were clothed with lime-green moss. Thick wet air hung like secrets untold, and walking through it left his face moisturized and dewy. Watching the trees while he walked, he admired their stoic nature. They were scattered around the landscape with surprising distances between each one. He was relieved that the forest was not too dense, as denseness made it easier to get lost and not see animals coming. The tree species varied slightly; mostly there was oak, pine, and beech. The pines and beeches stood loftily above the oaks, creating a layered ecosystem.

The creek that surfaced and submerged itself along the landscape of the forest led him to a beautiful pool. The pool felt safe, like a haven for refuge, a place for quiet contemplation, and napping. Above this pool the sky was open. A break in the upper canopy of the forest's enclosure brought clarity and new information with it.

With the angle of the opening, this area got sunlight showering through from the late morning till the heat of the day, whereupon the Sun made its way behind the cover of the canopy. From when he arrived in the area, he got to bask for four glorious hours.

The Sun nourished a medley of wildflowers and shrubs, creating a landscape of colors that was not common in the shaded forest. There were royal blue, periwinkle, yellow and pink flowers scattered everywhere the sunlight touched. The foliage was also brighter and wilder than under the cover of the forest. Izar marveled at the lush shades of green.

He felt inspired, and sitting on a nearby log, he took the notepad from his pocket and repeated the words he had written earlier, speaking them out loud as if to a small audience: "Astra inclining, sed non obligant. Izarrak gurekin joaten dira, ez dute lotzen. The stars incline us, they do not bind us. When he finished he heard a twig snap, and he looked up, seeing a familiar creature scamper off under the cover of some nearby shrubs. It was a small rabbit, and easily startled creature.

Izar began truly looking around, really focusing his energy into a state of stillness. He closed his eyes and breathed long and steady breaths. When he opened his eyes, he saw small dancing lights that zipped around and through the pond, an oasis of vitality that this Sun pocket created in both worlds.

To add to the beauty, wind swept through channels of trees from inside the forest; it also swirled down from above, where the clearing was. The breeze was a relief; it cooled the sweat on his brow, and felt sweetly sensual. It seemed as though the wind was passing through him. Relaxed and feeling deep gratitude for finding such a place, he laid down amongst the flowers and napped.

When he awoke, it was nearly dusk, and he arranged his sparse camp gear so he would have a view of the stars when night fell. When it did, he was not tired, but lay with his face up to the stars, his breathing become a rhythmic comfort. He spied the Moon slowly making its way up past the tree line. It was a half- Moon, giving off a fair bit of light, but not enough to overpower the stars. He wondered about the Moon, and marveled at how quickly it appeared to move in the sky. Hairs on the back of his neck raised; he felt a haunting feeling emanating from that half-illuminated world. He stared at it for some time, wondering where that feeling was coming from.

Suddenly startled by a memory of something, he quickly moved his hands to check his pocket. To his relief, when his hands felt the reassuring lump, he knew his gift from the sea was still there. That lump in his pocket fueled a mysterious drive. The object wasn't special in a worldly value way, but he didn't go anywhere without it, for it was his talisman, bringing him luck and perhaps guiding him to what he was seeking.

Layer 2: Celosia the Mage

Being neither here nor there, there exists a plane that is the seam in the fabric of all things; or perhaps it is the thread itself. Welcome to the plane where the sound waves feel like palms on velvet, soft and breathy, like a moth flying past your ear.

Within this dimensional plane there live two conscious souls: Celosia, and the tree Nami. The landscape and structures, typically assumed inanimate objects, are all beaming with life, in their own layers of awareness.

A large and singular cave sits within a small mountain formation, its structure comprised of garnet and quartz. Bold and sharp, standing with stark abstraction against the ambiguity of its surroundings, the larger faces of the cave are comprised of clear quartz that bear streaks of golden rutile, angular and frozen in time, like fine superb splinters. Each face of the structure meets equally to its next face, forming a clean geometric shape.

Ornately carved red garnet serves as the entrance, translucent and smooth. Along these smooth entrance walls are many glistening dewdrops hanging with no sense of gravity, giving the appearance that the walls are faceted with many tiny illuminated diamonds. Each individual drop sings a constant and hushed tone in harmony. The combined buzz makes the air between the walls feel thick, like a swarm of bees in a blooming tree. Gatekeepers, scanning every molecule that passes through their entrance, only allowing for harmonious visitors.

It is an elaborate system for a singular cave located in a realm that is not a planet nor a star, but a fractured plane somewhere between space and time. Perhaps it is a projection, a dream dreamt by someone long ago.

As it is not a planet, nor a star, there is no Sun; instead, the light in this plane comes from an electromagnetic field. Thus, light does not emit from a single point, but rather it hovers as a mist, flowing above like an aurora borealis. This field contains information from the cosmos, filled with updates riding on waves, sharing stories of the evolution of all things. It is similar to a seed containing a blueprint for growth, for the data for the cosmos lies inside the field.

In this plane, the above is not exactly a sky with a predictable color or consistent texture; there is neither a Moon nor a Sun. However, there are moths that fly in patterns to suggest they have already made it to their light; and drawn to nothing, they are free to just exist.

Being neither here nor there, this plane serves as the seam in the fabric of all things... or perhaps it is the thread. It is like the ambiguity of a dream, where small details are continually shifting: the size of someone's head, the color of an object, or the sense of time.

Above the caves' quartz faces, there is mycelium, and then dirt, feeding the roots of Nami, a wise and ancient being. She is a giant, undying tree, unbound by the pretenses of time and genetics, has lived for eons upon eons. In any given moment, she can shift her appearance, taking shape of any tree species in any growth stage -- from a weather-worn trunk at the end of its life, to a limber sapling bowing with the wind.

It is a rare treat to witness her form as a wisteria tree, her trunk twisting and weaving at a low stance, much like a dancer passionately holding a lunge, her branches winding up and out from her center, extending only to blossom back down into dangling, rich-colored ropes of petals. She is fond of the loose and wild tendrils that are free to move with the slightest wind.

Her purpose is not fully known, but it is said she acts as a conduit for the planes of the electromagnetic web, creating a language through shapeshifting, her expressions relaying the overall tones of existence. In other words, she is the caprice of the cosmos, titrated and translated into an infinite dance.

The web she translates is the beginning and scaffolding of all existence; and after it was first woven, Nami came to be. Perhaps the web was lonely, or felt no recognition for its simultaneous chaos and beauty, so it manifested a friend, an observer. There is no way to know how any of it came to be; that would give away the mystery that drives us all. Also, nothing can be known for certain.

Celosia is the one who dwells in the cave. Her soul is tasked with witnessing Nami and altering the web. The web, divine and infinite, is not always perfect, as all beings within infinity have the capacity to exhibit free will, and that can lead to chaos. Celosia and Nami together are like secluded computer coders, assess and address abnormalities that lead to malformed imbalance. It is an unbiased system that has kept the universe stable.

Celosia, humanoid in form, was never born in the traditional sense of creation, and she was never physically small or had to grow. All it took was one moment for her to arrive; and poof, Celosia manifested in the plane. Her sense of origin was complex and hard to describe; she simply was and is with no memory of "before." Despite the mystery, Celosia and Nami are two souls bound by heart and wisdom. Connected and kindred, they simply exist and fulfill their roles without bias.

Their plane of existence is hard to find, not bound by time or matter. Needless to say, they don't get many visitors, but it is not impossible to have them. It simply takes a skilled soul to find such a place. A place that is neither here nor there; in fact, it is probably too soon to fully mentally grasp its whereabouts or why-abouts.

Celosia, consistently assessing the web uses ceremonial visions to visit worlds in galaxies far away through the eyes of others, investigating and learning. Her most recent vision was quaint and yet exciting. She awoke peering through the eyes of some sort of insect, sitting upon a plant stem bobbing in the wind. Through the strange lens of the bug's eyes, she saw an enormous, blasting fire tearing through the atmosphere of the planet, illuminating the sky with catastrophe, as large rocks with flaming capes came barreling down all around. The insect was clutching onto this slightly drooping stem with its delicately barred arms and legs. As the rocks hit, being in such close proximity, the insect was obliterated along with the lush surroundings. The air was filled with ash, and all became dark and gray. when Celosia awoke, she was gasping for air. She felt as if she were being blown to bits herself.

After a vision, she reflects on its message and looks to see if the web requires any manual adjustments. Like an old-fashioned telephone operator, she will calmly redirect lines to change the flow of energy and move it into balance. A ghostly infinite loom that is visible for her to read. When imbalanced, there are noticeable bends and breaks, twists and knots. The mending process is continual, and a rather thankless task, and perhaps even pointless; but Celosia exists, and the visions arrive again and again.

With cyclical work there is often an order of operations, and recipe for magic, this keeps Celosia busy. In some sense, it is a surprising form of entertainment for her, a dream-theatre, if you will. It is how she learns and interacts with the world. As living with a single tree can have its lonely moments.

There was one vision that changed the way she experienced her life in the plane. It was her most cherished vision, occurring after she ate pomegranate rubies from Nami's limbs. They were deeply red and sweet. This vision unlocked emotions in her that swirled with delicious delight. After consumption, her eyes closed and she passed into another world. When she opened her eyes, they were not really her eyes; she was experiencing the scene of another's life.

On this pomegranate journey, she saw soft leather shoes on the feet of a man walking lightly upon a brush-covered woodland. His dark hair, shoulder length and tousled with loose curls, caught golden light pouring in from above, through gaps in a canopy overhead. His cheekbones were angular and his nose slender like a poet's. His mouth held secrets, wound up in the corners, that curled up into the faintest of smiles.

Celosia swooned at the sight of him, especially with his strong, square jawline, cutting the air like an axe. His features were held in an expression of ease as he made his way closer and came into greater focus. When he caught sight of the viewer, she saw that his eyes softened, and yet his gaze intensified. It looked like the gaze of a mother who had spotted her child after momentarily losing them in a crowd.

Approaching the viewer swiftly, and just short of an embrace, he smiled and sat down upon a nearby boulder. He began speaking to the viewer with a melodic deep voice; it was soothing. He was humble and confidently reciting an insightful thread of thoughts; there was a force within his words that could have melted ice, or soothed a wild lion. His eyes gleamed a charcoal-silver, looking from the page to Celosia, or whomever Celosia was within. Celosia can still remember some of his words... "Astra inclining, sed non obligant. Izarrak gurekin

joaten dira, ez dute lotzen. The stars incline us, they do not bind us."
When she could feel the vision slipping, Celosia tried to stay, as if
trying to grab a fistful of water.

But alas, she awoke beneath Nami and wept for the feelings
within herself. Wishing to go back, she ate every damned pomegranate
on the tree before Nami had to cut her off. She knew better than to do
so; it felt greedy and futile. Knowing she has never visited the same
host body more than once.

That vision had a lasting effect on Celosia, staining her soul,
like ink on skin. The vision almost created a sense of time, time that
didn't otherwise exist. Now there was before the vision, and after it.
She will not let go of that man, his words, or the depth of his eyes.
There is nothing to be done, no knots in the web, no bends nor breaks.
It had felt as if he was lost.

Consecutive moments come and go.

After the pomegranate vision, Celosia finds herself walking
along the white sand, staring out into her liquidous abyss. An abyss
resembling a giant opal that has yet to solidify. Scattered pockets of
wild colors, like many tiny nebula floating at varied depths. Celosia
squinting, watches the nebulas bob and float, wondering what exists
beyond the edge. The horizon appears to continue on until twisting
and turning into the stars and the space between them.

She notices that behind her, Nami's roots have descended long
and low to the door of her dwelling. This gives indication that there is
an awaiting vision within her sap, bark, fruit, or foliage.

The ritual is second nature, and Celosia does not waste
moments. Staring at the rock wall, Celosia moves swiftly, she begins
to crawl up the rock face to reach the roots. Each arm displays her

muscles, which are boldly defined, as she uses all of herself to gain elevation. Despite this exertion, not one bead of sweat nor exhausted breath is displayed.

Her body, fluid like those within dreams is limber, lean, and humanoid in form. When she reaches a wide enough ledge to perch on for harvesting the roots and sap, she sits squatting with an intent gaze. She takes her small, thin blade of carved clear crystal from her waist strap, and as the transpiration from the spongy pores of the roots hits the open air, its redolence sinks into her nose. Celosia sits stunned, momentarily hypnotized, sweet and pained; bitter and splendor shroud her mind as she feels its impending message. Drinking in the information, she fights to focus and wraps her fingers more firmly around the blade's handling side.

She glides the knife across the palm of her left hand, leaving a shallow and neat diagonal line. A golden metallic liquid full of pigment begins to pool above the fresh slice; as the bubble of liquid grows, it gives off the sound of swirling metallic bowls letting off cyclical ringing. Hearing these metallic sounds, Celosia smiles to herself. Murmuring a ritual of thanks and grabbing hold of a nearby root with her bleeding palm, she presents her offering. Then, swiftly, she cuts off a few root tendrils. She is also careful to collect the oozing sap on the blade's edge, as that will be useful too. Ease surrounds Celosia, her diligence and care, will even inspire a blade of grass to stand taller.

Harvest complete, Nami breaths out one large, enigmatic sigh, and like the recession of a strong wave, her roots recede up towards her trunk atop the cliffside. Celosia leaps down to the white sandy beach bearing the plant medicine in her hands, making her way to and through her cave's entrance.

As she passes through the small hallway, familiar liquid droplets buzz as if to say hello. Smiling, her eyes calibrate efficiently to the abrupt shift in light as she walks deeper into the cave. Celosia's long legs take stride with clean and crisp intention. All of her muscles working together, her feet greet the familiar floor. Unlike the stone entryway, the main room's floor bears a different covering that is interactive, alive, and soft. Short sturdy moss, carpets the ground, welcoming and instantly comforting Celosia's feet. Relieved, she sighs out, "Sveiki, palaimink tave šioje pilnatėje." Listening, the moss expands in response to Celosia, becoming more invitingly velvet.

The whole cave responds to her greeting with a small gust of wind, with the scent of lilies in its wake. The cave, far from inanimate; is an entity unto itself, free to interact if so inclined. Responding to the warmth of Celosia, as if it is only complete when she is inside.

The language, she spoke comes from a vision she had on Earth's Lithuania, during a full Moon lit gathering. The women draped in many blankets and shawls all greeted each other, exclaiming "Sveiki, palaimink tave šioje pilnatėje -- Welcome, bless you on this full Moon." Borrowing the phrase, unconcerned with its contextual accuracy, Celosia is tickled by the sense of tribalism it brings; connecting her to something more communal.

While crossing the main space, Celosia's eyes look for a place to set the medicinal bits of root. She eyes the shelf directly to her right, where a few of her tools are stored. Picking up a ceramic bowl, she places her fresh harvest into it, along with her sticky knife. Relaxed, knowing and feeling fully safe and in the swallows of her magical space, she takes one distinctly deep breath and closes her bright silver wide-set eyes. Eyes that are a shade of silver that earth's spectrum has never known.

Upon opening her eyes, Celosia's face displayed a serious curiosity for the roots she held in her hands, the weight of her impending journey was becoming more tangible. Shaking her mind free of that heaviness, she sighs, placing the bowl down.

In preparation for her ritual, Celosia prefers to cleanse herself of any excess energy. Moving across the cave, she approaches a familiar set of carved stone steps. Above, steam swirls from the top of the stairs, spreading out like ghostly arms of invitation. The monolithic bowl of broth awaiting her is abundantly filled with warm element-rich liquid. Naturally flowing and filtering up from the unknown womb of this plane. The tub, her muse, seemingly ancient, looks as if it formed naturally, layer by layer. The walls of the tub were banded and polished smooth, as if the rings of Saturn had been cut with scissors and sent to soar, inscribing the inside of the tub with its strong and structural stripes.

The lower wall of the tub, beneath the water level, is a dark green; and as the rings wrap upwards, the bands transcend into shades of blue that soften into transparency at the top of the basin.

Standing at the clear edge of the basin, Celosia removes her light garments to reveal her naked body. Coy curves and sharp shoulders were stark juxtaposing the steamy mist. Her ash-lavender skin shimmers with golden iridescence. Creating the illusion that her skin breaths, and perhaps it actually is.

Celosia steps off into the water, without hesitation to temperature, she submerges her body in its entirety. Inside this womb, Celosia neither hears nor sees anything, no voices and no visions; she is free to sink into the substantially deep waters, and detach from all her great responsibilities. She need not hold her breath, for she exists without that limitation.

Within her basin she collects all parts of herself, she is a cosmic medicine woman, a weaver and watcher who is has a great deal of responsibility. Her gratitude for her basin is vast, for it is the only place she has where she can enjoy pure solitude and reprieve from visioning. It is the only place where she is free to have unadulterated quiet.

While under the liquid's seal, Celosia is suspended in reverie feeling the illusive nature of timelessness. When the moment strikes, Celosia knows when she is ready to emerge from the water. Rising up she breaks the calm surface, combing her hair back with her fingers, she sings softly to herself while moving towards the edge of the basin.

Her hair, sleek and dark with moisture, hugs the shape of her head, highlighting her sharp cheekbones, and eyes wider-set. Her brows are dark and full, showing no hints of concern or tension as she places her hands on the clear edge to hoist herself upwards -- suddenly, a sensation overcomes Celosia, and her hands slip from the edge of the basin. A vibration surges from her abdomen; the sensation is foreign but not painful. The skin of her belly tightens as the sensation rises up into her chest. She is dumbfounded, still and unsure.

Feeling a sense of violation, Celosia closing her eyes, sinks into the water. Beyond her will, a vision arose while in her tub, impossible, she thinks. In the soft focal point of her minds eye, she sees a powder- blue line plunging through a dark blue cosmos cloud, heavy with purples and wisps of magenta; again, she hears ringing like spinning metallic bowls. Curious where the blue line leads to, she follows it through the cloud. She sees it continue onward, and when shapes become clear, she sees herself in her basin, as the powder-blue line leads directly into her abdomen. Puzzled, under the water she waits for the vibration and vision to end as it should, but to her amazement, the dull roar in her belly does not subside. One part of her feels violated and bombarded by this unavoidable presence; while another part of her feels truly alive and caught up in the mystery. And then, as suddenly as it came the sensational vision leaves, while a pair of silver eyes trace past the scene in her mind, leaving her submerged with nothing but stillness.

Celosia stays beneath the water for stretch of moments. Collecting herself and subduing the shock. Eons could have passed, or perhaps seconds, until Celosia felt ready to surface.

Upon exiting the monolithic bowl of broth, Celosia eyes were staring wide and unblinking. Each stone step bore a steamy footprint as Celosia moves down the stairs. When she walks she appears to float, over to a curly piece of wood that holds blankets and shawls. Celosia finds a peach colored shawl to drape over herself. She had seen the shawl on a beautiful woman during a vision; that particular reality had a fine and creative sense of fabric. In admiration, she wanted to have one of her own to wear. All she had to do to obtain the shawl herself was to clearly imagine the object in her mind's eye, and poof -- there it was. And when an item becomes obsolete, it disappears.

Sufficiently draped in the shawl, she moves to "summon" a fire for her ritual. Sitting down on pillows and furs, she stares into the smooth, soot-free hearth, inviting the fire to arrive. Concentrating with her hands placed over her belly, the glow of fire's first light illuminates the delight in her eyes. Even though she is bewildered at what had just occurred, she knows she must carry on with her ritual as planned.

Moving forward, she diligently sets into a flow of small tasks, in preparation for her journey. From the wall, a cool spring of water pours out like a small fountain; the pool below is a skinny stream on the ground. The stream's flow is directed away from the main space, down deeper into the cave.

Filling a stone pot with the water, Celosia sets it to boil by hanging it above the fire. As precise as spider limbs spinning a web, she cuts the roots into tiny, non-uniform pieces. While waiting for the water to boil, she stares into the flame and its ultraviolet hues.

The water begins to bubble and is ready for the plant bits. The once hardened resin and roots, melt into the water as she stirs. Like calligraphy, her motions are artistic with each lap of her blade around the pot. Now that all ingredients are simmering, she sits observing the pot and thinking of those silver eyes and their familiar haunting stare. Almost warning her, with an urgent expression. As the pot begins to steam, it infuses the dry air of the cave with a bitter-sweet scent, rousing Celosia from her distant thoughts. The mixture in the pot is ready to drink, and Celosia ladles herself a cup of the warm liquid and doesn't bother filtering out the root bits.

Holding the cup close to her lips and nose, the bitter scent makes her salivate. The clay cup feels warm and heavy in her hands as she wonders if the silver eyes will appear again. Shaking off the thought and tipping the thin edge of the cup to her lips, she drinks the brew. Gulp and zoom, she is aloft and off, her body sinking back into the pillows and furs beneath her.

There is not much sensation from Point A to Point B; in a blink, she simply arrives in a new reality. Before opening her new set of temporary eyes, Celosia is surprised to find that she is fully inhabiting another being's body, engaging with all the sensations: sight, smell, touch, taste, sound, and telepathy. She has never had the full sensational experience of embodying another being. As she stands within the host, she tunes in and collects the information surrounding her. The body she is inside of is very tall and soft with fur; the space she is occupying is cool, and fills her with sterile comfort.

When she makes a 360-degree observation, she sees that one: she has immaculate core strength lending to fabulous balance. Two: she is within an egg-shaped room filled with sleek white opalescent technology. Flat pieces of glass that stand quiet and naked, displaying nothing. The decor in the room appeared featureless, which was likely implicit cf its sophistication.

On the wall beyond the white sleek instruments is a huge oval viewing window, with glass that appears to fuse without a seam to the white, glossy walls of the egg, almost as if the white walls have faded into transparency in the shape of an oval. While caught in the awe of the view, a voice calls from behind her, sounding somewhat urgent and familiar. "Captain Malva, I have brought you the Tribe's Weaver upon your request. I thank you for your patience with my delay; it took me longer than expected, as Hatch 211 is shut for the reserves program." Celosia noted that this one is handsome and humble; a true honest soul. As Celosia listens, she can hear beyond the words and isolate the tambour of love in his voice.

Smiling salaciously and blinking slowly, Celosia gives the man a nod, unsure of what he meant. She is enjoying this interaction with another living being. She waits till the man leaves, and savors every detail of his face. These beings are feline; tall and humanoid, but definitely feline, like the little cats she has seen on earth.

When the door closed, she had hardly noticed the Weaver's presence, as she was mesmerized by the interaction. When Celosia turns to acknowledge the other being in the room, her eyes soften. The Weaver is clearly older and wiser, although her body and features have not degenerated much compared to the young officer's. The depth in her icy blue eyes is what gives away her age and accumulated wisdom. It is heavy, like a lead sinker on a fishing line, almost creating its own gravitational field.

The Weaver gives Celosia a knowing look, and says in an elegant and steady voice, "Celosia, welcome."

Celosia is a bit shocked to be called by name, but listens as the Weaver continues. "It is my understanding that Malva has intentionally sent for your presence to inhabit her body. We were not certain it would work. She has been preparing for your arrival for some great time."

The Weaver pauses, and leans in as if to smell her; and then she goes on. "Malva feels connected to your soul through the web; she has told me she can follow a chord to your plane, but has had trouble accessing clarity with you, so she summoned you. We do not know how much time you'll have here, so we should get to it."

Celosia nods and responds via telepathy, as speaking is not something she often does. "I can see how my inhabitance in her form is unlike most visions I undertake, and I am willing to see what can be seen and listen to what can be heard."

Shifting seamlessly, the Weaver responds, also with telepathy: "Malva is the Captain and prominent figure in our tribe, Avior. We hail from a tangible Moon of a gas giant orbiting the binary star system of Sirius. We have been involved with a vexing issue in our galaxy. Long ago, we responded to an evacuation that took place on Earth. I myself was incarnated on Earth when the evacuation happened." The Weaver's mental voice has become strained, as she shook her head slightly from side to side.

"It was a terrible day, with much chaos. The Earth's Moon, you see, was once a living, conscious sphere, serving as a portal and a gatekeeper for her realm, allowing souls to incarnate and experience their biological library incased in the prism of duality. Earth's Sun and the once-luminous Moon were in harmonious union, broadcasting the prism and its duality-light within the dark, and the subsequent dark within the light." The Weaver has a distant sparkle in her eye, as if remembering her times on Earth, and its majesty. Shaken from her reverie, she continues her telepathic speech.

"A virus of sorts had taken hold, one that has the potential to infect the galaxy further. The Moon spirit tried her best to cure it, and shut down her portal in hopes of halting its spread. But alas, her efforts have only slowed the problem." The Weaver clears her throat, and begins using her voice to speak out loud.

"As a result of that process, the Moon spirit has disappeared, gone quiet. Earth's Moon now appears to be a barren orb. The Avior people can feel dark energy growing each day with more potency, as if shadows are drifting past our peripheral vision. There is a lingering sense of darkness that is waiting so quietly that one could forget that it was there," the Weaver says, with a chill in her voice.

Crossing her arms behind her back, her hands holding opposite elbows, the Weaver takes a few steps towards the wall as if deciding something, and then turns back to face Celosia.

"We wish to serve the greater expansion of this galaxy, and the Milky Way is our home; we are a part of it, and do not wish to see it fall out of balance. Our mission has been to observe and use our technology and intention to aid everyone on Earth by providing light codes and information. Currently, we have moved our ship closer to

Earth so you may see for yourself, and gaze upon the fields around the planet; perhaps you can see something informative that we cannot."

Celosia, wide eyed and processing, filtered the Weavers words into understanding. She bows her head in the direction of the Weaver.

After this acknowledgment, the Weaver continues, "It's a lot to swallow, but I'm sure you have tasted this energy from your plane, through a fragmented vision." The Weaver pauses, allowing Celosia to absorb the fast-paced download. Celosia nods, as she has felt the dark energy, during many visions to Earth's plane. It is dense, and yet it is exciting and different.

The Weaver looks thoughtfully upwards and speaks again. "We are aware that the higher vibration you hail from can create a fragmented comprehension of Earth's density and duality."

Celosia, did struggle to understand Earth's density, even though she had seen it many times. Shifting the conversation, Celosia spoke, "Where did the Moon spirit go?"

The Weaver walks over to place herself in front of the viewing window, and as she moves, her modestly cut, green one-piece suit billows famously. The Weaver stands on her two legs proud and tall; the essence of her confidence could be bottled into a perfume for those with a wavering sense of self-esteem. Her long silver hair is woven into a few even and clean fishtail braids that mimic the arc of fish bones. She is stoic and staring out past the glass, failing to answer Celosia's question. The Weaver lets out a sigh that parts the curtains to expose her soul's true concern.

Turning, the Weaver sent a steady gaze with grave concentration into Celosia's eyes, "We are grateful for you, for coming all this way to see... With the Moon dark, we can no longer incarnate through the Moon. Some high-frequency beings can transpose themselves by will into Earth's plane, but many beings are unwilling to take the risk."

The Weaver adjusts her head into a tilt, to articulate, "The people of Avior are collaborating with ethereal energy and technology to send some of us down there to see what is happening, but we only have prototypes, and we are unsure of the success rate. Most importantly, we do not have a prototype for the extraction process, and any souls brave enough to go will not have a way back. Our people feel passionate about this, as many people from our tribe are having terrible visions. We can't help but wonder what will happen if we do not intervene." The Weaver rubs her temples with one hand, taking a big breath in.

"I have always heard rumors of your existence, out there living a life in the seam of reality. We have only respect and gratitude that you have arrived here. It is our hope that your ability to affect the web can help. Our people value your soul and the responsibility you bear. I bow my head to you in gratitude." The Weaver bowed her head, and lingered in that position.

"Forgive me for my intense amount of information, but I do not know how much time which we have together."

Nodding, Celosia replies, "I understand, and can sense from being within Malva's form that there is something amiss and lingering. I am willing to see all that I can regarding this galaxy; I can later address and alter the balance of the web if it makes sense to do so." Celosia steps closer next to the Weaver, to look out through the glass herself, observing the solar system.

While gazing straight ahead, the Weaver states crisply, "We are just adjacent to the Moon, and flowing along with its orbit process; as you can see, Earth is right there." Celosia could see a plane with its swirls of blues and greens, an enigmatic beauty that was also somehow tormented with conflict. The white, swirling clouds drifted slowly across the atmosphere.

Celosia, closed her eyes and opened her inner sight. Being within Malva, there is an obvious limitation to her powers. Despite the difference in potency, she can still see the faint gridded web around the planet; it appears like the geometric structure, the Icosahedral shape to be exact. This shape uses many triangles together to create a sphere.

These lines forming triangles pulse with light racing up and down, like fireflies on a track. The grid feels covert and protective, giving off the energy as if to say, "What grid? I don't even exist, don't mind me." Concealment is often a mischievous act. Being the same geometric pattern as the shell of a virus, it likely serves the same purpose. Within the shell of its geometry it creates an untouched atmospheric basin, allowing for replication to take place. Celosia feels the heavy force and its ill intent.

Somehow, it all feels familiar to her, the dissonance echoing. Opening her eyes, Celosia feels she has seen enough, and seals the image of this web to her memory, like a hound with a scent. The room is refreshingly white and soft, in full juxtaposition of what she just saw. The comforting, stable presence of the Weaver helps center Celosia. Leaning in, the Weaver's gaze is level to her own, knowing eyes to knowing eyes. Without a word or thought shared, they both lightly leaned in so their foreheads could touch; eyes closing, they simultaneously open their inner sight. With the warmth of a grandmother, wisdom and love surged into her, and Celosia unglues herself from Malva's body and reality. Drifting back to her corner of the universe, she sees a pair of silver eyes viewing her as if she were a comet passing the night's sky; and then all vignettes to black.

Celosia knows she is back in her cave, but she doesn't open her eyes right away; lingering in the blackness is relaxing, and she wants to savor the details, wanting to keep all events and images straight and preserved in her memory.

The medicine of Nami plays the role of an odd, eccentric teacher, liberated and surreal, giving lessons in small and seemingly unrelated segments, but what just occurred is very different from all the other visions from Nami. She has never been summoned, nor recognized at all when she travels. Many times when she arrives in an experience, the beings around her feel that there is something new in their midst, tickling intuition and making hair stand on its end. But never, ever has she had full motor control, or recognition, something completely different was unfolding.

The vision with the Weaver was so real and so interactive. Celosia felt a great sense of meaning and validation from the words of the Weaver. The corners of her mouth curled up to bask in the gratitude others may feel for her responsibility. Although everyone has a role to play and some form of responsibility, it is still nice to be seen.

She lay soaking up all the details and despite her recognition, she was truly disturbed by it all; the darkness surrounding Earth. It stirred many questions within her. How had she not known of it sooner? How did anyone know who she was? Can her web-work even help against such an ominous force?

Finally, done with her unanswered questions, eyes open, she stands up and knows she needs to visit Nami. Perhaps she will share some wisdom on the situation.

Grabbing a blanket, Celosia leaves her cave. Walking towards the trail leading up to Nami, she soaks in the light from above, nourishing her skin and soul while universal information transfers into her -- a systems update of sorts. With the sand transitioning to stone beneath her feet smooth and sturdy, she progresses up the mountain's path. Narrow and zigzagging upwards, the path opens up on the crest of the slope and then flattens out to a clearing.

Once atop the bluff, Celosia takes in the view of the vastness extending into the stars. To her right, far, far away, tiny comets with tails glowing orange make steady headway across her line of sight. 'Tis a good omen to see comets in a pack, rolling through space, like spotting buffalo in the hills of the Dakotas. Nodding her head in gratitude for the sight, she comes to find that Nami is quaintly vibrant but not loquaciously so, almost as if she is holding a secret that she is waiting to share. Her bark healthy and bright, she takes the form of an orange blossom tree with a healthy green jasmine vine climbing up and around her trunk towards the canopy, which is full and thick with leaves and flowers.

Eyes brightening and skin dancing with golden movements, Celosia feels scintillation in the air. Aromatic ardor pours pleasantly from the central nectarous point in each blossom; the balance of the fragrance is precise. The light and brightness of the orange flower compliments the low floral notes of the jasmine; two opposite and equal forces colliding for the sake of beauty.

Fallen blossoms also cover the ground beneath, so when she lies there surrounded by them, she is engulfed by the fragrance.

Spreading out her blanket, she smiles and greets Nami, their souls dancing in recognition and togetherness. Nami, like a grandmother, has provided a place of safe wisdom and unconditional love. Laying on the blanket on her side, knees bent in a comfortable fashion, Celosia has a view of the petals falling slowly down to the ground while, in the distance, comets passed slowly. With all the fragrance and comfort, she weeps lightly and knows not why. Perhaps for the beauty of it all and her place within that, or maybe she weeps for something else, erupting from a source that lies untapped beneath her calm demeanor.

Though feeling a great depth and tasting many flavors of life, Celosia has rarely had an emotional experience in regard to her own self. She has seen enough of the universe, of its love and passion, cruelty and ingenuity. She has tasted the spectrum of emotions; although, out of all of her visions, she has never seen anyone like herself, alone, save for Nami.

That discovery has been slowly gnawing on the edges of her soul, pointing to an unavoidable loneliness. Despite Celosia's thorough understanding of connection, knowing that separation is an illusion and that all is simply one and made of the same fabric, she is also aware that the unity divides into this tangible chaos of infinite realities that are intentionally separate. The paradox of existence is hilarious, in all its synchronized chaos. Just because one is aware of it does not change the terrible loneliness.

With all the emotions from her recent journey inside of Malva and the responsibility that will likely unfold from that encounter, Celosia exhausts herself and falls asleep beneath the orange blossoms and jasmine vine.

Layer 3: ιός the Nameless, the Shapeless

A deflated being drifted aimlessly through space, depleted by the longest, farthest, and most grueling journey it had ever been on. In a way, this being had no choice in where or why it was going; it was seeking somewhere new to call home. Shapeless and fragmented, it floated through space with the momentum from the blast. Home had been pulverized into rubble and dust. In fact, the being was shapeless, itself made of rubble and dust, cast off into space on a pilgrimage. Just before the blast, the being recalled a vacuum, a blackness, and a great wild light, With no inkling as to why, or even how long ago it had occurred... as it had been set adrift for what felt like forever.

In space, the light spectrum varied; there were pockets of nothingness, voids that lacked even stars and starlight. It was dark, it was cold, and it was lonely. Eventually, starlight became visible again, and this was a monumental turning point for the being, as it was no longer alone.

In the small streams of light from the distant stars, the being recalibrated to the shift. This light was so distant the waves did not reflect any color. However, if the being had had a mirror, it could have finally seen itself, its shape. The being was a giant dust cloud, made up of tiny floating particles with small uniform gaps between each speck. The dust cloud compiled and held conscious thought and awareness; it was alive in its own right.

As the cloud floated, it thought, "I yearn for that which allows me to grow, and rebuild myself. I will never decay or die in the vacuum of space, but I may go mad with this isolation. Perhaps I can shut down my conscious thought and conserve sanity. If I'm lucky, when I come across a planet or a dying star, I will wake up." It hesitated, and thought of its origin before turning himself off. The details were fuzzy, but he remembered how it felt, and it felt good to remember the distant feeling of power one more time. Before he could think another thought, he shut down.

While drifting without thought, the dormant cloud joined the migration of a couple of asteroids while in his prison of the drift. Held in the same velocity, the being almost didn't exist at all in the dark; there were no dreams and there were no sounds, no thoughts.

It took many, many celestial cycles for the stars to align, and for the being to awaken. He awoke when his cloud struck some object, and his system for sensory disruption activated his conscious mind. He woke to a sensation of being stretched to the apex of his elasticity; it was rather startling and rather fast. As luck would have it, he was being pulled into a black hole with a group of asteroids. The temperature rose rapidly in comparison to the stark cold of space. Colored lights danced, displaying patterns in every direction. Each tiny particle compiling the being was visible in the light of the black hole's intense magnetic field, revealing that he was a crimson red and metallic. There was no telling where this singularity would take him. Time would shift and space would bend, making everything irrelevant. He could end up anywhere within spacetime; it was even conceivable that this portal could take him back to his home before it was destroyed. This black hole could also kill him, obliterating his mind. Black holes are mischievous tools of the universe, and the only consistency with them is that they will transfer and transform matter. It is not clear whether an individual black hole spits matter out in the same location every time, or if the route is specific to the matter traveling through it.

One thing was certain: there was a strange polarity within this tunnel that charged and surged, and those forces managed to rearranged some small, elemental particles within the cloud-being, altering him ever so slightly. When he emerged from the other side, it was clear he was situated in a star system in which planets and moons were orbiting in a collective patterned dance. The being was pulled into an orbit alongside the smallest planet, which was icy and cold in appearance. It was making the largest and slowest orbit out of all the synchronized participants. He wondered how he could propel himself towards the planets that were making smaller orbital patterns. Again, he would have to wait, patiently, as the momentum of velocity in space was a cruel joke.

While the being waited, he began naming things around him, and ultimately decided that he too needed a name for himself. When the sound ιóς came from his awareness, he decided then and there that ιóς would be how he could reference himself as separate from the rest of the universe.

Creeping round with the orbit, next to that little planet, ιóς waited, observing the cycles and personalities of these magnificent worlds.

One perfect moment arrived, and ιóς began to feel the gravity of another mass making its way near. ιóς had very little mass, and he could be easily swept up in another's wake. To his great fortune, something like that was happening. When the giant mass moved past him, he was swept along by the object, dragged in its magnetism. ιóς did not recognize the type of object pulling him along, but it was making a direct path towards the third rock from the central star that was the focal point to which all structures in this system paid cyclical homage.

Before long, ιóς and the object pulling him slowed with the planet's pull. He was so close to what looked like luscious life, yet the universe was the mastermind of cruel jokes. Once again he waited, orbiting in a velocity he could not control. But at least this time, the view was dynamic and stunning.

ιóς enjoyed the view from his place above the atmosphere. He could see a marvelous small Moon that sparkled like a refracting feldspar. This Moon emitted a light-blue glow that seemed to send some kind of electric signal to the blue-green globe it orbited. They appeared to be very interactive. The small Moon felt as alive as the planet, and the giant star at the center, full of fertility and love, also beamed out its consciousness.

He had nothing to do but observe it all while he waited. Every so often, the Moon would pulse with a golden light, or maybe it was silver. The light seemed to send down visible currents on a wave across space and into the planet, and on down into its core. Some great form of life and consciousness dwelled here, that much was clear. This all gave him such hope for a new life. With this hope, ιóς was content to watch the orbits and wait.

It did not take many cycles of orbit before luck struck again. A meteorite collided with ιóς. Soon, they were headed towards the green and blue planet, pushing through the atmosphere! Finally, ιóς had arrived within the potent sphere of life he had been watching for so long! His sensorium was overwhelmed and overloaded when he crashed into a great blue sea. The meteorite, pinning ιóς along with it, sank down into the liquid water at a rapid speed.

On this planet, gravity allowed his light particulate body to sink with the rock to what seemed like the edge of space again. It was dark and cold, but luckily it was not lifeless. "This feels ironic," ιός thought, with a vibrant sense of humor. A magnificent pulse of bioluminescent light highlighted the ribs of a very strange fish. ιός was mesmerized; he knew not what the creatures on this planet looked like, but he knew they were vital, and for now that was all that mattered.

ιός made it to the rocky bottom and waited for a long while, observing the marvelously strange beings that existed in the waters. They had unique rhythms and tactics for survival.

Then the monumental fated action commenced: ιός was touched by a dark and ancient creature with small black eyes and many rows of teeth. It was on this day that the creature's smooth and muscle-dense body rubbed itself onto the ground that ιός was lying on.

When this happened, ιός seeped inside of the being like water into a sponge. He was alive! This was a vital life force that he could hitch a ride inside of; he was finally free. He didn't even know he could do it until it was happening.

Like a parasite, he could infuse his will and essence into the creature through skin contact. ιός took over the animal completely in the span of a week, learning how it moved and how it hunted. He was satiated by blood, and by eating the living. Sometimes he would even feed off carcasses of the dead, decaying sea creatures. He was able to move freely and explore. ιός didn't yet know the names for things, but he was inside a shark, a six-gilled sleeper shark, otherwise known as a Greenland shark -- moving slowly and patiently along the ocean floor.

Layer 4: Malva - Cohesive

Conserve your energy, Malva. Stay seated." The Weaver leaned in with concern, while maintaining an expression of calm composure, her perceptive eyes looking into Malva's. "I'm not sure where you went, but you are back." She used her careful hands to feel the vitality of Malva's lifeforce, and was pleased with what she felt. Then she stood up, straightening the creases in her garments. Walking across the oval room, she asked Malva if she wanted something to drink.

Malva replied with a soft voice and a tired nod. "I feel very thirsty and cold. I would appreciate a warm drink very much." Sitting up a little straighter on the floor of the egg-shaped pod, Malva lucidly blinked her eyes, taking slow, deep breaths. "How long was Celosia here? It was almost as if I saw her enter my body, while I went to a different place altogether... it was timeless, and I can't be certain how long I was unconscious." Malva looked as if she were trying to hold onto the details of an old memory, slightly squinting her eyes.

The Weaver spoke with vague clarity: "She arrived, and I managed to deliver the message to her cleanly. Celosia made it clear she understood and was willing to help." Standing tall and poised, she had busied her hands by preparing the beverage on a nearby counter. Using telekinesis, the Weaver heated the liquid with her mind; steam swirled up from the wooden mug, emitting an earthy aroma with spicy notes. Quietly, the mug floated across the room and set itself gently onto the pod floor next to Malva; who smiled graciously at her old friend.

The Avior all had some degree of telekinesis; some individuals were stronger or more skilled, but very few could heat a drink so effortlessly. Malva lifted the mug and took a sip; when the warm liquid made its way into her body, her soul seemed to properly seat itself inside of her body, like a foot filling in a snug sock.

"Did you get a read on her energy signature? Were you able to track it?" Malva asked, with clear hope in her voice.

"I haven't had a chance to check our systems yet. The broadcaster you're wearing has yet to be downloaded into the database. When you finish your drink, let's take a look. I know that technology seems like the only option, but you know my opinion and feelings about the use of technology for something like this," the Weaver lectured.

Malva said nothing, just continued to sip from her mug, imbibing the herbal medicines of her home planet with contentment. A few drops spilled past the rim of the mug onto her long-sleeved jumpsuit. As they fell down her suit, she moved them along with her mind, and lifted them into the air and back into her mug. She was careful to say nothing, in full reluctance to the Weaver's comment.

Her outfit was stark against the white surroundings of the room, dark navy blue in color with a velvety texture. the design was simple, without any embellishment save for the slender, deep-V neckline that exposed her midline all the way to her hips. The dark velour hugged her tall, lean body. Practical by design, it was a simple suit with just a few pockets.

Upon finishing the contents of her mug, she felt ready to stand. Bringing Celosia into her body took a great deal of psychic energy, but was by no means dangerous or beyond her skill. Anticipation built on her face as she unlatched a metallic bracelet from her wrist and placed it on an oval glass plate no bigger than her palm. She began an activation process with her telekinesis, and the technology sprang to life with a soft whirr. A holographic wave pulsed upwards from the plate in concentric rhythm as it analyzed the bracelet's data.

Malva was watching the waves as if she were holding her breath. The Weaver spoke, breaking Malva's trance: "I have no doubt that a congruency exists between your signature and Celosia's. I know you have felt a connection to her since you were a youngling." The Weaver, smiling, sifted through her memories of Malva from long ago, her eyes twinkling. Clearing her throat, she came back into the present. "Call me old-fashioned, but I have my apprehensions about using technology to send souls to Earth. I know we need to mitigate this dark force from the inside, but it just feels so reckless. We still don't have the technology to recover the soul. It is a potential suicide mission."

Malva responded, eyes fixed on the holographic waves, "I understand your apprehension, and I have my own concerns about our mission. But we have a willing candidate," she raised her hand, indicating herself. "The process has been perfected; our technology will never match the finesse of Fengári, but it's something. We may actually be able to end this age of darkness on Earth and keep it from spreading." She looked up pointedly, matter-of-fact determination written all over her face. "Besides, if Celosia decides to go, it will only be her and me. In that case, we will need to use very little technology. That is why I'm so interested in the data. If I can prevent the Avior from going into the unknown, to potentially never return, then I will do that. I will go myself." Malva took a deep breath, the significance of this mission weighing heavily on her.

The Weaver looked down and swallowed her opinions, knowing full well that her wisdom was not always welcomed or acknowledged.

She also knew that Malva was right. Malva had been too young to travel to Earth before Fengári went dark; she never knew what it was like to visit Earth that way. Indeed, around half of the Avior had never been to Earth via Fengári. Most who had not gone were curious, and willing to attempt find out what the darkness was, despite the increased risk. The Weaver, having lived a long time, had known Earth and Fengári intimately. This was a very important factor in her understanding and growth. Her heart had ached the day that Fengári went dark. She was there the day of evacuation. It was a sudden jolt to ripped from earth so suddenly, only to wake amongst the chaos. The Avior tribe assisted with the evacuation to the best of their ability, but nothing could be done to stop the will of Fengári. It was quick, she shattered herself into tiny specks of dust, while a dark cloud began shrouding Earth. You could no longer enter into her, only stand on her colorless, bland surface.

In the aftermath, the Weaver could barely hear the Sun's telepathic voice, like muted, echoing calls of anguish. Ílios was in a tranced rage at the loss of his one love. The waves emanating from his inner soul lashed about on his surface. It was impossible to communicate with him, though the Weaver could sense his thoughts of self-destruction and prayers of hope. If one could see him in an animated form, he would appear as a madman, rifling through books thickly laden with small text, his eyes scanning desperately and unyieldingly for something priceless that was lost.

After witnessing Ílios so bereft, the Weaver slept in her ship for many days; partly because she was deeply sad, and partly because she wished to find Fengári in her dreams, somewhere out there in the deep darkness.

"These are shrouded times, and I know that this problem will not be easily solved," the Weaver stated. Malva was multitasking, and only half hearing what she was saying. The glass screen sitting in front of Malva like a window began filling with data and images of wave patterns. Malva's eyes scanned the data with precision; then she looked dumbfounded, and placed her free hand on her head and ran her fingers through her hair. She sighed airily and smiled ever so slightly. Attracting the Weaver's attention, she waved for her to come over and take a lock. Meanwhile, Malva sent a telepathic message to her Lieutenant, Vivet, to join them in her office.

Malva smiled because she had verified what she already felt to be true: her soul was linked with Celosia's, and that meant they both could go to Earth.

Like humanity, the Avior lived on a planet in the Milky Way. From Earth's solar system, their stellar system was just visible in high-gain telescopes as a faint, distant star located just to port of Orion's belt, between the primary constellation and the Sirius binary. However, their world existed in a higher realm than Earth's humanity, the molecules oscillating at a higher quantum frequency than those of Earth. The environment in which they existed was fueled by three small suns, and there was never a sense of full night on their planet -- only either full daylight or variations of twilight. The sky laced the planet with an ambient sense of ease, a gradient of colors that were always shifting and displaying in wild, vivid patterns. On the surface there were many small bodies of water rather than one large sea, as was mostly the case on Earth. The Avior enjoyed the water and its sentience. It was clean and safe to go into.

Being of a higher vibration, the felinoids had little conflict with other lifeforms, both on their planet and in the surrounding galaxy. The

Avior prided themselves in their knowledge of the various forms of life in other realities. This was how they had gained knowledge of Celosia. They were communal and open; it was rare that they paired up for long, and they all took responsibility for raising one another's children. There were a few who did take union and remained that way, but it was very rare that an Avior made such a long-term bond.

Malva was born to one of the tribe's healers, who had matched DNA with one of their master builders to create her specifically. Her gestation took only two months, for in higher dimensional realms, the gestation period is dependent upon the soul that incarnates into the body. Some Avior babies developed in three months, while some needed many more months than that. Although with their own sense of time, what is the concept of a day? The Avior month could be equivalent to an Earth year; there was no exact science to determine their perception of time as opposed to humanity's.

Malva looked a great deal like each of her parents, with her mother's white fur with black spots on her outer arms, shoulders, back, and the sides of her face. Her spots were shaped similarly to a Terran serval's. Her hair was long and dark like her father's, and most often she wore it tied back into a simple braid. Her eye color was uniquely her own, from neither her mother nor father; the striking silver color came from her soul's origin. The Weaver had sensed a wise and active force within Malva the first moment she had seen her silver eyes.

The Avior were gifted with extremely long lifespans, with very few signs of aging; and as such, they were open to exploration and discovery. Equipped with space travel technology for a hundred thousand years, they traveled off-planet often, exploring the Milky Way and beyond. They were curious about all there was to see and learn in the universe, and no matter how long they were gone, they always returned home to relay what they had found. Some found love and connection off-planet, and it was socially acceptable for them to pair with other species. Although bearing children outside species was impossible, they were allowed to freely be who they needed to be.

Existing as they did in a higher dimensional frame, the Avior were more aware than most of their molecular connection with their homeworld. They knew at a deep level that they were made of the same star-stuff as their own planet, which in a sense made them one with it. One benefit to this was that when residing on their home planet, they had the ability to teleport themselves anywhere, using the congruency of the mineral makeup in conjunction with telepathic intention. Wherever the consciousness moved, the body would rebuild itself with the surrounding elements from the planet itself, effectively creating a new body every time. The previous body was automatically disassembled and returned to nature.

While it was theoretically possible, teleportation within a space vessel had its complications and dangers. Although one could argue that the ship had been built with materials from their home planet, it was not the *same* as the planet, and not all the elements found in the homeworld were present in a ship. Unsure of the outcome, the Avior refrained from off-planet teleportation. If anyone had ever tried it, they had never come back to speak of their success.

The wiser members of the tribe could sense the wisdom and strength in Malva soon after she was born. Her development of psychic abilities and telekinesis was rapid, and soon exceeded the skill of many full-grown adults. She took interest in social structure, technology, and addressing issues with positive solutions. Her passion was clear. Malva was given tribal responsibilities at a very young age, when she worked with the healers alongside her mother. Malva also had a talent for navigating and piloting Avior surface ships and starships. She was trained thoroughly in the basic function of the tribe's technology and engineering, and took to it easily.

Some of their aerospace technology had been a gift from other colonies of felinoids, as well as beings of other races. Conflict between the Avior and other peoples in the galaxy was essentially nonexistent; by the time of Malva's birth, there had been a very long era of peace and innovation among the Avior and those allied with them. As Malva gained age and experience, their aerospace technology made leaps and bounds of its own, as the Avior integrated their telekinesis and telepathy into the energetic fields of their machines.

Every Avior had skills in different areas, a diversity that had been one of their tribe's greatest strengths. Some were best at working with water, while others were better at working with heat and kinetic energy. Some felinoids worked with Earth and minerals, while others favored the dance with etheric energy and air. Their talents interlaced, and most could work with all the classical elements on a basic level, though very few could master more than one. Malva's tribe was currently comprised of 12,991 Avior, and of those, only eleven had mastered all the elements telepathically. It had been no surprise to the Weaver that Malva would take her place as one of those eleven beings when the time was right. The Weaver had keen observation and discernment skills, her icy blue eyes penetrating straight to the soul. She watched Malva age, witnessing her talents ripen.

Beyond her mastery of the elements, Malva's biggest strengths were her control over her emotions and her ability to see the bigger picture.

When Malva was younger, there was a photon belt was passing near their planet's atmospheric envelope, and the quanta sparkled like glitter in the far distance. The Weaver was sitting on the edge of town, admiring the photon belt's interactive colors of lilac purple, heavy with swaths of cream. Plumes of dark purple churned low on the horizon. With her head tilted upwards, rejoicing life, she saw Malva in the corner of her vision, heading off on her own. Curious about where she was going, the Weaver cloaked her biofield and carefully followed Malva into the lush valley outside of town. She made sure to keep some distance between them.

The wind was blowing, carrying with it ribbons of bioluminescent particles. The ribbons danced around Malva's poised form as she advanced deeper into the vegetation. Her calm energy was tangible, and sent plants to swaying in unison as she passed.

Keeping her distance, the Weaver focused on concealing her aura from telepathic acknowledgement in order to remain hidden. Her intent was not malicious. She needed to be certain and aware of what heights Malva's talents were rising to, solidifying what she already suspected, which was that Malva was to become one of the Eleven. It was tradition that once such mastery was gained, the Avior was summoned to train and join the Council of Eleven.

It was one of the Weaver's duties to keep an eye out and listen for any whispers of the rising skill of an 'Eleven'. The Avior had lost a member of the Council a long time ago, and there had only been ten on the Council since. It was worrisome to some members on the Council that this depletion had persisted for so long; they feared that a mutation of the Avior genome was taking place, and there would be fewer of them as time wore on.

The Weaver, however, was not worried, and assured them that another would arrive in their natural time. She was curious why Malva had thus far concealed her mastery and gifts. She did not flaunt or present them to anyone. She often ventured into the wilderness to practice her talents in solitude and secret. This was not the first time the Weaver had followed Malva into the wilds.

Malva made her way through the foliage, admiring the scent of each plant, breathing in their terpenes. She was walking with no hesitation, as she knew where she was headed, and she walked on for some time. She climbed up the face of a boulder and over its ledge. When she reached the top, she followed a hidden trail that switched back and forth among jagged rocks.

The Weaver wondered why she did not teleport to wherever she was heading; perhaps there was something necessary about the journey. She thought this too soon, for Malva's form disintegrated before her eyes as she stood between the columns of a natural stone arch. The Weaver immediately teleported to the place where Malva had disintegrated, hoping to sense her direction or match the destination. Catching a destination was like reading coordinates; she found that Malva was *inside* the jagged rock. The rock was hollow, and inside there was a pocket of crystals growing upward and stalactites hanging from the ceiling. The Weaver could not follow her there, as that would give her away; instead she took a seat and closed her eyes. Focusing on Malva's location, she used her light-body to enter the walls and sit on the far side of the enormous geode.

Malva was performing a routine of stretching and inversions, using the crystalline structures to assist her. Afterward she stood still and closed her eyes; the crystalline forms began to grow, oh-so-slowly, and all points stood erect and then all tilted slightly to the right, creating a circular basin for her to use to send energy in one direction. Ribbons of etheric wind swirled around Malva's right hand, and she sent it into one of the crystalline pillars. Each tip pointed to the next, and when one was fed etheric energy, it was poured into the next one and then the next. This energy poured into each pillar until the power flowing through the structure became a sealed vortex.

Malva removed her hand from the crystals, sat in the center of her vortex, and expelled a sound similar to a roar. What happened next was unclear to the Weaver, but it was certain that a small beam of light came from Malva's heart and shot directly upwards. Her light-body didn't leave her form, but the cord was something the Weaver had not seen before; it stirred great curiosity within her. After some time, the cord dissipated, and Malva opened her eyes. After some deep breaths, she laid one hand on a crystal pillar and released the etheric wind to roam free again. She smiled as it passed her, to go wherever etheric energy goes.

She then stood and took a strong stance, setting the pillars back to the placement they had originally assumed. Turning towards the Weaver, Malva titled her head and smiled. "I can sense that you are here with me, Weaver, despite your cloak. I can smell your scent. You smell sweet like tumbarrow root, and spicy like crandike bark." With that she teleported back to the arch outside between the great rock and found the Weaver's body sitting there, waiting.

When the Weaver arrived back in her body, she breathed a big sigh. Malva said with understanding, and also slight annoyance, "I know it is your role to listen for the Eleventh, but please do not share what is not yours to share."

The Weaver replied, sounding thirsty, "Your talents have grown to heights that amaze me, and perhaps would set others into a state of distress. It is my duty to be certain of what you are capable of. I will not share what I see, but I implore you to consider stepping forward."

Mollified by the Weaver's words, Malva smiled. "I just wanted to explore my talents without them being shaped by training, to explore my gifts before indoctrination. I will come forward at your side someday, but I will not expose the level at which I can call the elements. I do not wish to raise any eyebrows, or give reason for anyone to fear me. I know my intention is pure, and I plan to keep it that way."

The Weaver stood to look eye-to-eye with Malva and nodded; then, together, they teleported to a place where they could enjoy food and warm herbal drinks. When they arrived, they sat in hovering cushions that were like lily-pads curved for back support. Malva's eye were wide and distant; something must have happened, wherever she had gone. She seemed thick with thought. The Weaver took it upon herself to order for both of them, although she would always order triple the drinks for herself and double the food for Malva.

"Do you want to talk about what you saw or where you went?" the Weaver asked, crossing her legs.

Malva blinked a few slow blinks and cleared her throat before she responded. "I saw her. I saw her plane. It was thin, like paper." She paused. "I have been practicing this form of travel for a while now, in that cave, and I have been getting closer and closer to finding Celosia. Today I finally made it there. The visit was brief, and I didn't have the ability to speak, but I was there." A grin slowly crawled onto Malva's face, her head shaking in wonder.

The Weaver, wide-eyed, took many gulps of her drink, "Celosia? The cosmic web-weaver? That is curious indeed." The Weaver eyed several felinoids who had entered the space and crossed the large outdoor patio they were sitting in. "If you don't mind me asking, why Celosia? Why seek her out?"

"I have many dreams about her; she comes to me often, whispering things. Her eyes are silver, like mine. In these dreams, it feels like there is something she wants to tell me. I feel connected to her somehow," Malva said, wrinkling her nose. "I know it is a little strange that Celosia would be visiting anyone, and I myself wonder why, but still, I am compelled to find out." Malva began eating her plate of fruit, completely focusing on chewing and experiencing the flavor.

The Weaver nodded, drinking more of her herbal tea, taking in the information and staring off into the distance. "You have always been precocious. This is strange indeed, but I am by no means surprised. Thank you for sharing; I won't ever repeat it." The Weaver tapped her temple lightly with one finger, smiling. "I must say, I wish I could see what you saw."

The two women ate and drank, enjoying the simple colors in the sky and the marvelous people-watching. People-watching was quite entertaining at this spot, as it was a fairly popular place to gather. It was known to more than just the felines; many different races came to enjoy the food and drink. They observed as beings came and went with all different energies, guessing at where they were headed next.

It had been a long time since that moment in the geode cave, that day Malva first had made contact with Celosia. Since then, she has risen in the community and followed her path to take her place in the Council of Eleven. All was flowing along as it should, with relative normalcy... until the dreams of the Avior tribe started to shift toward darkness.

Now Malva and the Weaver sat in the starship, observing the results of the data-dump, sketching out a plan of action, their eyes wide with amazement and their mouths slightly open in surprise.

Layer 5: Fengári - Wisdom and Placement

Planet Earth, a biological library, served as an interactive learning experience. Its purpose was to teach the lesson of duality. Upon that sacred rock was beauty, density, and limitation. All this was made possible by the active collaboration of the Sun and the Moon. The two spirits projected a dualistic prism of light to create a basin for souls to experience and grow.

Not only did they orchestrate experience, the duo were affiliated with the Royal Orbit, an ancient installation of beings who built galaxies to watch them evolve. As Keepers, they were in charge of maintaining the cycles required to keep their biological library alive. This included humans, animals, plants, and minerals.

The ancient mother, Fengári who was the Moon, exuded energy that was both loving and sensual. Her soul, gifted with keen perception and compassionate wisdom, soothed all those who came to her. Her signature was an energy thick as stone and smooth as silk. To be around her was as soothing as drinking a warm, creamy cup of chai on a cold day.

Upon looking up at her from the Earth's surface, you would see a giant sphere of feldspar, refracting and translucent. When gazing up to see the magnificent wonder, it would sparkle and appear fluid, mirroring the oceans below on Earth. Floating suspended in orbit, her surface was bright amidst the backdrop of the dark, starry sky.

The Sun and the Moon worked together in rotational unison, like lovers. Ílios, the fatherly Sun spirit, was hot and charged, a catalyst of life, unable to be visited by many beings due to his sheer nuclear heat. But Ílios often incarnated onto Earth's surface to observe it up close, and of course, find Fengári.

In his deity-form within the Sun, he was masculine, and in every way opposite to Fengári. He was of enormous size, and charged with the energy to build mountains and shake up landscapes. Sharing his bounty of radiant light, he kept living beings alive and warm.

His love for Fengári had been burning ever since they came to be, though they did not embrace in their heavenly form often, or talk about what they were having for dinner. Their union wasn't about the physical connection of literal togetherness. It was larger than that. They had a mission, and its perfect execution was the symbol of their love. When Ílios incarnated on Earth, however, he did not mind meeting Fengári there and practicing what they preached. There was no mistaking him when you came across him on Earth. His richly green eyes and his ability to lead were notable, and made him easy to find. He was a master of the cycle of birth and death.

Within the Moon, Fengári's spirit appeared wispy, and as if made of liquid. Her limbs always connected to the walls and floors of the

Moon, like the fruiting body of a mushroom connected to the greater mycelium. Radiating a soft glow, she was graceful when she moved, her long legs blurring like two small waterfalls.

Fengári's colors were variations of shimmering sea-foam green. Her icy blue eyes peered keenly from her elegant face. Her manifested form within her Moon served to physically greet and welcome the souls who wished to enter her portal. An interfacing platform for organizing trips to Earth, the Moon was the key facilitating portal to gain entry.

Beings from all around the cosmos could arrive and travel through her portal to incarnate upon Earth. Life plans and bodies were crafted and executed. An Earthly experience was where souls could learn and taste the limits of density and duality. Beings could incarnate into etheric elemental forms, plant life, animal life, and human, all participating in the harmonious and challenging cycle of consumption. This was the way the plane had operated for a very long time; clean, advanced technology was available, and all categories of forms were synergistic. There was life and there was death, but it was not cruel.

Fengári's portal was a travel destination for curious and brave souls from throughout the cosmos, a platform to learn and grow. Each lifetime upon Earth can vary in length, but for most souls, the time spent on Earth was a relatively tiny blip in the grand scheme of infinity, an experience with many flavors and layers. The souls were guided by the Moon spirit; she was their shaman, their facilitator for this cultivation process.

The order of operations was systematic, but not rigid. There was an initial assessment, an initiation, and a ceremony of sorts to send a being through the portal. With Fengári's integrated knowledge of the stars and the vibrations they created, she could calibrate a time for an individual soul to arrive that was in alignment with their personal learning and growth. This calibrated selection process was not left up to the Moon spirit, and each being had a final choice in their journey; although it was wise to follow her advice, as Fengári had a gift, like a scale, of weighing where a soul lacked enrichment.

Each soul emitted a sound signature, a specific scent, and Fengári would find a place in space and time where that signature would prove as a match for the balance -- like surrendering to an ocean wave and flowing with its current, a key in a lock, or dancing your way through a crowd at a concert, Fengári would align a soul to arrive in a time where their energy was congruent.

Perhaps the soul would incarnate as a human, growing in a womb and being birthed on the Solstice. Or perhaps as a sea turtle hatching during a full Moon, or arriving on Beltane as an elemental nymph governing a river and its ecosystem. Maybe even existing as magma, rolling and pushing its way through the Earth's underbelly. Her ability to give a soul the experience it required was impeccably accurate, and many souls returned from their death hoping ride the ride again. Others could not manage the limitations of form, and by will would simply leave if it was unbearable. Souls were never trapped or bound by the wrath of a god should they need to eject, to abort the mission; it was their choice to make.

Fengári had no need for slumber or normal sustenance. Able to split her consciousness, she could be in many places at once -- as an incarnation on Earth, existing as the Moon, and then again as the shaman within the Moon. The only fuel she required came from fulfilling her purpose, the love exuding from Ílios, and water; she drank an immense amount of water wherever she was.

Ambiance and minimalism were second nature to Fengári inside her Moon. The decor was simple, light walls that matched the outer face of the Moon, and one large, circular cream-colored floor. The floor met the frame of a magnificent portal that shimmered like liquid glass; the frame was sturdy, woven with thousands of thin strands of polished silver. It was statuesque and prominent, the only focal point in the room.

A variety of beings came to incarnate, both material and formless. The process for either kind was similar, but not the same. Here is a story and example of the formless, and how their arrival looks:

One random moment in time, a light drew near the Moon's surface. All it took to enter, was to draw near, like passing through silk hanging on drying lines in the wind. Once inside, there was only the one big room and Fengári's form. Her greeting felt corporeal and simultaneously ethereal. She reached out to touch the light and read its energy with closed eyes.

"Hmm, ahhh. I see you wish to be alive but not human; I can feel this resistance like cold steel on naked flesh. But your soul lacks tangible understanding, and does not know the true feeling of being in a material form." The light being moved slightly, unable to articulate a response. The Moon spirit continued to read its energy, holding her arm outstretched, which also connected into the floor like a slender waterfall. Her hand moved to what could have been the central point of the light being, and she imparted an image and a feeling to it, transposing words into feelings, trying a different form of communication. After this she waited and felt for a response; after all, every being was different.

The light being responded, and Fengári knew what was next. She took something from within her own torso area; the flowing matter could have been part of her body, or a long silk robe. It didn't matter. Producing a small pair of scissors, her eyes gleamed with purpose. Presenting the old, tarnished silver shears between them, Fengári cut around the being with precision and speed. While doing do she hummed one long note. When complete, the scissors dissolved back into her robes slowly, like a rock sinking into mud.

"If you are ready, you may walk through the door. Given your apprehension, I will impart the gift of memory, so if you find Earth overwhelming, you may leave at any time. However, if you feel content, then follow the cycle of this short life you will live through to its end." With that, the being floated to the glassy portal and sank into it.

After a strong sensation of speed and visual patterned fractals, it awoke, struggling its way out of a breakable membrane. All six of its legs were thin, working in harmony to crawl out. Ingrained with a genealogical memory to chew and consume the surrounding matter, to store energy, the caterpillar knew exactly what to do: to eat the leaves it had hatched upon.

The light being had the gift of memory, so it was aware of its previous existence. This was only a partial distraction from the experience. It did what felt natural, and it lived upon the leaves of the citrus tree it was hatched upon. The caterpillar grew and consumed continually until it knew the next phase of its life: the metamorphosis of the caterpillar within its chrysalis. It found itself a curled, dried leaf that was connected to a stem. Next it set to work expelling a silk thread to encase itself for a long resting phase. Inside the cocoon, it experienced the process of biology, function, and the unfolding of transformation, the physical organism growing and shifting with time, moments and sounds shifting around the outside of the protective layers of silk. These sounds were amusing and lucid sensations for the light being. There was bright light with warmth and a darkness that brought chill; it switched back and forth in cyclical patterns. After some time, the transformation was complete, and the need to crack free was upon the light being, curious for the next phase to come. The light being followed along with the genetic will of the form, and made its way out.

Unaware of the names of things, the being existed, propelled by a need to survive and follow function. One fuzzy leg at a time, the small creature labored to break free. At last, an atlas moth clung tightly to the cocoon it had broken from and let everything expand and settle, exposing its red torso and copper-colored wings with white spots. With time and energy gathered, flight was the next phase for the small creature; without being taught, it took to the air, fluttering in the night sky, looking for a mate. It knew it needed a mate to continue the cycle, so it looked and presented a scent for another moth to become attracted to it.

The light being consciously sat as a passenger in this vehicle, observing the will of nature from the eyes of the moth. Its life, lasting only two weeks after becoming a moth, ended after laying eggs for the cycle to begin again. The light being felt the body's energy falling, and with that sensation, it was back in the colorful tunnel of fractured light. Once again, the light being was within the Moon, entering through the portal. It sat there for a long while, absorbing all the sensations of density and form. There was a sense of exhilaration and elation within it; the experience invoked a deeper curiosity and willingness to see more. In time, after digesting the experience, the being would be back to see Fengári, and taste yet another lesson of duality.

Fengári's portal room was always available, and she was always waiting expectantly. She could accommodate and send many souls at once, but she could only stretch herself so far; she was not infinitely capable. But she *could* bend and space and time with her parallel rooms, stacking them like the many pages in a book. So in the Moon, there lay many sleeping beings beneath webbed blankets, waiting for their souls to return.

Sensing a being's arrival, Fengári stood ready. A feline arrived at the outer surface of her realm in a simple but tangible craft. She entered through the surface, and once inside, the felinoid displayed a look of wonder and familiarity. Able to speak, the feline introduced herself: "I am the Weaver of the Avior tribe. I feel great appreciation to be here to experience a lesson in density."

Fengári smiled, and with a whooshing movement, was suddenly just inches from the Weaver, her ice-blue eyes kind and ecstatic. Standing closely, she raised her left hand and embraced the back of the Weaver's heart, her palm flat against her spine, pressing firmly. They stood thus for a moment. The Weaver felt waves of emotions she had never before known, and let them flood through her. While this was happening, Fengári watched, listened, and felt through the palm of her hand. She cocked her head and then touched the Weaver's forehead with her other hand.

Laughing a soft and joyous laugh, Fengári asked "What is it you wish to learn? For I can see some experiences that will suit you, but it feels like you have a specific curiosity."

The Weaver opened her eyes and spoke softly. "I seek to learn the scale of emotion, and I do not wish to recall the memory of my life as a Weaver, nor do I wish to remember the experience I have when I return; I only wish to gain the insight. I trust your age-old wisdom and guidance for this journey. I am filled with building excitement, and perhaps some nervousness."

Without further prodding or conversation, Fengári nodded one quick nod, and pulled her scissors from a place beneath the silken waterfall drapery of her form.

When transposing a soul from living biological forms, there was a different cutting technique than that for light beings; and every soul requires different alterations. After the cutting was complete, the Weaver, like a ghost, stepped forth from her form and walked into the shimmering portal, while her body was left with just enough soul energy to sustain itself. Fengári summoned white root-like tendrils to lift and cradle Weaver's form, moving it gently to its resting place off to the side. White roots shifted and wove to become a swaddling blanket that covered the Weaver up to her chin, like tucking in a child for bed.

Fengári made sure the Weaver's body was covered and properly settled with the delicate sparkling blanket. She laid a palm to the Weaver's forehead; the body's eyes fluttered lightly, and until her soul returned, the body would rest.

Meanwhile, the Weaver's soul made its way through the portal. Barreling down a tunnel of fractal light, she became rainbows and sounds, until suddenly she breathed in a giant breath and began her journey on Earth, without memory and without knowing the purpose of her life in that new form.

The Moon spirit did not perceive time in a proper line, but she was in tune with the linearity of Earth's time. She always knew how long it would take for a soul to undertake their journey, though she would sometimes be surprised when they exited earlier than planned. But

Fengári was not surprised when the Weaver breathed back into her
body on the dot, as expected; she awoke in her feline form, lying there
with eyes wide in awe. Indeed, she laid there for some great time,
taking in the expanse of her previous form and reintegrating with her
life as an Avior, like waking from a dream.

Fengári approached the Weaver and removed the webbed blanket,
pushing it back down for the white floor to absorb. She again touched
the Weaver's forehead with her palm, and smiled down at the Weaver.
The Weaver smiled and looked far away, trying to hold onto her
experience and savor each detail, but knowing its memory was fading
quickly and she would soon forget it completely.

Standing to leave, the Weaver bowed in appreciation and exited
the Moon to her ship outside, where it had been sitting idle, anchored
and waiting for her return. She was changed, and her soul was
enriched; she knew she would return again for another journey in the
future. Powering up her ship with her hands, she shifted away from the
Moon and zipped through spacetime to get back to her home planet.

This harmonious process existed for eons, serving uncounted souls
throughout the cosmos, delivering perspective and growth. But a day
came when everything changed, when the harmony was stripped away
and the system was compromised. This occurred when the being ιός
arrived and began his cultivation of cruelty and chaos.

Layer 6: Celosia - The Arrivals and the Exit

Celosia wakes beneath Nami, her petals of floral delight dried and blowing away off the cliff's edge. Stretching her body with pleasure, she holds long, exaggerated poses that give her body vibrancy and length. Her skin's hue has changed; now she is more periwinkle than lavender. Her eyes, silver, calibrate Nami's details into focus. Nami is no longer an orange tree; instead she is a small grove of aspen trees growing from the same roots, with leaves in a state of perpetual fluttering, like paper-doll children giggling with secrets. There is a solid stream of etheric wind rustling through the trunks of her grove.

The trunks of aspen trees typically grow straight, but her trunks are all twisted around one another, each trunk connected to the next one -- as if a giant started weaving each trunk as a section of a braid, but the task grew tedious and the large being lost interest and wondered off.

Celosia can hear something, but is not sure what it is, so she places her ear upon the one of the trunks. She hears words, clear as day. "Celosia, in gratitude I call upon you for aid. I would like to commune with you directly, as I have before." While the voice speaks, her inner sight projects images of crystalline shapes and a massive wind turbine. The voice is clear and sturdy, the voice of a woman, one she has heard before... or is it after?

Celosia's sense of time is fractured compared to most of the cosmos. Her memory does not line up congruently with others, yet somehow it does. It is very possible she has communed with this being before, but that has yet to come and simultaneously already is.

Filled with curiosity and purpose, Celosia knows she must deepen this vision. She pulls her knife from her leg strap and slices a small line on her shoulder; it oozes that familiar golden liquid, running slowly due to its heavy viscosity. Celosia sweeps it up with her fingers and makes a symbol on Nami's trunk with it, low at the base near the dirt. The bark splits itself open beneath the symbol and exposes a current of sap, which Celosia lets collect on the edge of her blade. She chants:

"Nami, please guide me; I feel this great wave coming, and I need guidance. I thank you."

She stands poised, balancing her sap on the blade as she jumps from the cliff's edge. In no time, she lands with sturdy legs slightly bent at the knees, displacing the shock. Her body is truly amorphous and made of light; her capabilities to perform physically demanding stunts are boundless, and would defy most physics in other realities. Oftentimes there is no rush to go anywhere, so she doesn't always exercise her abilities to move quickly; but in this case, there is immediacy expressed in the clear voice in the trunk, and she is listening.

Once inside her cave, she heads straight for her bath. The cave greets her with the scents of copal and baking bread; this is a pleasant mélange full of opposition and balance. Even though Celosia doesn't eat food to survive, she enjoys the sensations of the olfactory system, and the magnificence of its ability to trigger memory. Every reality she has ever visited has been woven with mysterious scents that have given her peace.   Celosia gathers in the scent information as she sinks into the heated waters of her basin, and cleanses herself of any emotional charge she has gained from her nap on the cliff's edge. It all falls away from her body with a force like gravity, and she feel lighter, lending to a buoyancy that is slowly pulling her back to the surface. While rising up wet and fresh, Celosia wills the fire in the corner to join her. In the quiet of the cave, a single crack splits the silence and the fire lights itself in response. Celosia dries herself next to the warm violet light of the fire, and wraps her shawl around herself.

Setting about her usual tasks of water and pot, chanting and focus, Celosia makes calm haste in preparing her brew. It is not long before she sits ready with her cup, drinking the warm sweet vision liquid. She closes her eyes and is surprised she does not fall into a veiled place of vision. Instead, a great violet light shines from of her cave's entrance. Her reality shifts into a more dreamlike ambiguity; it is very slight, but a shift has occurred. Remaining seated, Celosia holds her breath while she waits and watches. A white feline with a single dark braid makes her way into view. The being is in awe, but doesn't look alarmed. She bears an expression of reverence and peace, and Celosia knows her to be Captain Malva, from her most recent spirit journey.

Celosia's face must display shock, like a child caught raiding a cookie tin, because Malva stops and bows. "May I enter your safe space further, to join you at the fire?" Malva asks with her arms slightly held upwards.

Celosia gives a slow nod in response, knowing she isn't in any danger, as her dewdrops guard the door with pure discernment.

Malva comes closer, taking in the scents and the sights. Celosia rises as she approaches, and they stand eye-to-eye at the same height.

"You are welcome to sit with me here, but there is more space in another part of this cave that may accommodate the both of us more comfortably." Celosia gestures to the feline, who is truly a beautiful creature.

Thinking for a moment on this invitation, Malva agrees that more room may feel more appropriate and appreciated. Celosia doesn't often have company, as not many beings make it to her reality, but despite the rarity, she prefers to bring conversation and meeting into her living space rather than her medicine den.

Malva is enamored by the sight of Celosia, observing her every move, her grace and serenity. Celosia leads them both farther into the cave. Malva is filled with safety and certainty, feeling more like herself than she ever has before, as if this is a reunion of sorts. She notices that the floor is thick with cashmere-moss, soft and dry beneath her feet. To her right, a stream of cold, fresh water flows alongside the moss; it looks ankle-deep and gives off the impression that it is a joyous little body of water, just glad to be flowing along. This stream adds humidity to the air; in each breath there is depth, crispness, and laughter.

Small, luminous mushrooms line the path where the wall meets the ground, lighting the way in their mysterious glow. Malva hopes she never has to leave; she feels foolish, childish, for her unforeseen giddy excitement at the knowledge that she has made it all the way to Celosia.

After some time following the luminous mushrooms and the stream, a golden light becomes brighter as they breach a bend in the hallway's path. A vast opening greets them, filled with a vast expanse of plants, flowers, and trees of unnamable species. They twist around and pepper the whole space, which doesn't appear to end. There is an endless sky, colored like the petals of an African violet, with tiny specks of sparkles you have to squint to see. Golden light beams through the branches and leaves, which are moving slowly, as if breathing. Small orbs bob through the violet expanse, casting the golden light and its subtle movement.

Celosia's grin is contagious as she bows and raises her arms as if to say, "Welcome to this humble place." She guides Malva on a slow walk through the plant life while moths and a variety of other winged creatures bounce through the air, flitting and fleeing from one moment to the next. Malva reminds herself to focus, as she may not be able to stay for long, and after all, she did come with a purpose, and must communicate her message. She opens her mouth to speak and is immediately cut off by Celosia. "Do you enjoy the life you're currently living? What is it truly like to consume sweets?"

Completely caught off guard. Malva laughs out loud. "Did you say sweets?"

"Yes, sweets, the flavor of sweets and chewing them for fun, and so on." Celosia touches her own lips and looks as if she truly would love to chew a sweet treat.

Malva laughs again, and this time responds, "I do enjoy many moments of life, but there are other times when it is uncomfortable, and I feel neutrally apathetic about it. As for sweets and chewing, yes, I quite enjoy the sweet fruits of my home planet. There are many ways to enjoy them; we could speak of each way in detail, but I just don't think it would do the experience justice." Malva smiles and winks.

Celosia nods seriously, deep in thought, considering her response.

"Celosia, I came here with an intent, and I must share it while the moment is here." Malva clears her throat and gets to it. "I have always felt an emptiness, a void within me that isn't fulfilled by my world. I have always suspected I came from unusual origins. I have applied myself to magic and science, disciplined myself. Eventually, I discovered I could record my own energy signature and project it out into a galaxy mapping system. I used harmonic frequencies with the signature, and also found different dimensions as well." Malva pauses, to see if Celosia is following; and although she is looking at a moth, her ear is attentive.

"It took me some time to program the system correctly; despite my people's reputation for advanced technical knowledge, I myself struggle with fully grasping its language. When time passed and my project was complete, I found you in the data. I saw that we were linked somehow, and seeing this, I understood how to use my true gift, to actually locate you. While locating you, I wear a device to track my body's frequency and location, and log that data. Like a tuning into a broadcasting radio wave. I'm not sure if I'm making any sense, but I do have a point."

Celosia reaches out and touches Malva's white, furry hand. They both stare down at their touching hands, noting the difference of texture and color side-by-side. "That was a lot of information, I realize," Malva says. "I hope you understand."

Celosia looks as if she is concentrating so intently that she is counting the hairs on Malva's hand. She is actually reading the energy signature of the feline's soul, with eyes like a microscope. Celosia appears frozen in time while she sinks into a different state, where she sees all the subatomic particles that coalesced to create Malva, small specks that dance in sporadic cycles, like billions of bubbles in a champagne flute. She compares the dance of Malva's bubbles to the dance of her own. Phase One of the bubbles' movement is near-identical, like a solid drumbeat repeating itself. The difference is that Celosia's signature has an extension to it, a secondary layer, as if a violin solo mingles with the solid beat of the drum.

Their souls resonate on the same base signature; this is certain. Celosia feels a wave of realization flow over her, and emotions rise up along with the realization. Celosia blinks, recalibrating to her typical sense of vision, and she explains what she has just observed to Malva, who stands listening intently and proudly to hear the news, feeling suddenly less alone in the cosmos.

Malva and Celosia share the same soul. This was what she was trying to explain with her story, but she is glad Celosia has her own way of seeing it.

The mood in the air is bright, and the space responds to their feelings. The sky changes, producing beautiful webs of lightning. Striking the sky in alternating patterns, the colors are in an unknown spectrum to which no description could do justice. The lightning is like an omen, blessing the epiphany-like the nature of their encounter. Flashes of color-tinted light reflect onto their faces, while they sit soaking up the information.

Malva breaks the silence. "I have been having visions, visions of you and of a planet in my home galaxy, since long before the people of Avior took notice. There is something happening on Earth; it was clear when Fengári went dark that something was amiss, but I am certain there is a darkness there that someone must address. I sense such maliciousness." Malva cringes in the retelling.

"The reason I came to you is because when I sent a broadcast of my signature externally into time and space... it not only extended to you, but also into the density of Earth's dimension, like a fruit on a skewer, connected by a signature represented as the skewer, where various versions of us are the pieces of fruit. I was able to map out our signature's path and follow it upwards to you and manifest myself here." Malva realizes how much content she has shared, and places her hands at her temples and takes a deep breath. Malva's expression is both determined and overwhelmed.

Celosia responds after a long pause, as if allowing the rustling of the leaves to add their own wisdom and opinion. "I suspected as such. It is becoming clear to me that my own energy is involved with Earth somehow; however, when I investigated the web I was confused as to what I was seeing. My -- *our* energy signature is singular and also layered simultaneously. I knew that a signature could be shared throughout dimensions, the same soul split in simultaneous existences. But I did not know whether the souls could cross paths and be aware of themselves. I am grateful and relieved to meet you, as another me," Celosia says, her head shaking lightly in surrendered amusement, now certain that anything was possible.

Relieved to be understood, Malva's face slowly drifts into a smile, and she opens her arms to embrace Celosia in a long, meaningful hug, the kind of hug you might give to the younger version of yourself if given the chance to go back in time -- a hug that translates a shared knowing and acknowledgment of deep appreciation. The beings embrace for some time, psychically transferring eons of information to one another. Their combined energy field is strong, and the force they create is tangible, a reunion of self that is holy and strange.

Celosia breaks the silence and speaks softly, her words lightly whirring over the fur on Malva's shoulder. "You are me, I am you—" Celosia releases Malva and gestures that they continue to walk onward through the hearty flowers and foliage.

"Celosia, I would like to send our energy down into the Earth. My tribe has crafted a technology that can broadcast a signature into Earth to incarnate there; however, there is no way to recover the soul... we have ideas and theories, but none of our tribe's members are willing to risk that sort of mission. We are also uncertain about the technical details of pairing with a body and landing in a specific timeline." Malva pauses, and bends to smell a flower as if to clear her thoughts. It is a powder-blue velvety blossom that unfurls by untwisting itself. The smell is of honey-smoldering sweet grass, an unexpected but pleasant scent.

"Peculiar place this is; I am fond of its oddities," Malva says, marveling at the surroundings.

"Yes, this place has an eccentric will of its own," Celosia shrugs.

"Celosia, with your connection to the web, do you have any insight on what will remain of you after a descent such at this? Sending apart of yourself to Earth?"

The question lingering, Celosia is quiet and concealed in her thought process. She stops walking as they approach a circular enclosure. The boundary of the circle is formed by large, pale-pink crystalline formations, like a miniature Himalayan Mountain range. Along the base of the pink stone is a green vine that has spread itself into beautiful knots, like a crown around it all. The ring is fairly large, with a diameter ten times Malva's height. The floor inside the ring is pure gold, with a carving in the center. The carving is of geometric shapes, and from the vantage point where Malva stands, she cannot decipher any specifics. The top of the wall comes up to Celosia's chest, and between time Celosia is suddenly perched atop the ledge with her feet hanging inside. Malva use her arms to push up onto the wall and seat herself.

Celosia breaks the silence, but her eyes remain uncertainly calculating, "I believe I can separate myself and remain here fully conscious, because in some sense, it already is and already has been done. We are already living the aftermath of me splitting my soul, in a sense. Although I will not be able to perceive the experience easily; I haven't perceived you until now that I know of." Celosia shrugs. "I trust that I can land safely, and I do not fear the choosing of a body or timeline; I feel that with the web's help, I can navigate my way once the process has begun. I am willing. Celosia speaks with fascinated wonder in her eyes, her face still, while her hair spins wildly in the wind that only seems to be swirling around her. Malva feels no wind on her own body.

Celosia continues, "This ring we are sitting upon, is new. I have never seen it before, and yet—-" She trails off. "My cave is always fluctuating and shifting, and this ancient device is implicit of our impending descent. I suppose this is how it all begins, the tool I use split myself into pieces in order to broadcast them... it has arrived due to our need of it. I know that gold is highly conductive and it flows beneath my flesh; Its almost as if the disc is calling me." Celosia looks as if she understands what needs to be done, because it was always going to happen.

Malva nods at this, and with a soft flicker, her solid appearance begins to soften, and her comprehension becomes more abstract, as if in a dream. Celosia doesn't skip a beat and announces, "I will feel it when you are accessing your technology, and I myself will be here in this ring awaiting the process. I am so glad you came here. I gather that I will be in communion with you, one way or another."

With that, Malva becomes soft as mist and blows away in a sporadic current of wind. Celosia sits alone on her ring's edge, gazing into its center curiously, contemplating and breathing in the aroma the cave effuses. On this occasion the cave has chosen the pleasant scents of steamed jasmine rice and simmering burdock root.

While she is lost in the sensation of the scent, the golden platform suddenly spins into currents beneath Celosia's dangling feet. The currents move in a directional spiral towards the center of the golden floor, where the carving had been visible.

At the apex of the swirling floor, a translucent egg begins to form, like a tornado made of flexible glass. After the shape stabilizes in size and density, the whirring sound steadies. A shadow appears inside the center of shape; it is hard to perceive full details through the opacity of the tornado, but Celosia squints to see. Unable to make any sense of it, she leaps down onto the golden floor and the egg becomes quiet and slows into stillness; when it ceases spinning, the walls melt like ice in the desert.

The figure that was kneeling inside faces Celosia. He has skin like a dark, starry night, including nebulae and star systems, as if he were airbrushed with the living scenery of space. The void and depth of the darkness between the stars is magnetic. When a shooting star zips across his chest, Celosia gasps.

His muscles are well-defined and wrapped perfectly around his form. Masculine and poised, he is a picture of absolute male beauty; there is even something like hair falling past the striking line of his jaw.

Humanoid in form, like Celosia, this stranger has a great amount of energy lying beneath his skin. He stares at Celosia with a set of silver eyes, and Celosia holds his gaze, as well as her breath. He feels familiar to her; there is a kindness flowing from him, as thick as the gravitational pull he wields. Celosia holds her footing firmly and dares not move toward him just yet.

They stand wordlessly for what might be forever, until he breaks the silence: "Do you remember me?" The starry man takes a step forward and pushes some of his hair back from his face, tucking it behind an ear. The hair refracts light; a mixture of platinum and golden strands, glimmering with the glow of her cave.

He pauses after his first step, as Celosia has not responded to his question. Her soul is pounding, and the golden sap running beneath her skin is ringing like cymbals, louder and louder, resounding in one giant climax of sound. With that burst of sound, Celosia is suddenly flat and horizontal upon the golden floor.

In no time, he is down next to her, feeling her energy, checking to be sure she is all right. He places his hand on Celosia's brow, and her eyes part to open, her eyelids fluttering like a bird's wing. When open, her eyes are wild with confusion. Memories of visions come flooding into her mind's eye, *These familiar silver eyes,* she thinks, *and the familiar touch of his hands...*

Celosia's eyes are looking directly into his, and she opens her mouth to utter, "I do not know where I know you from, but I feel deeply certain that I do. How did you arrive on my disc?" She states as her eyebrows crease into a frown.

They move swiftly to a seated position, while his hand slowly sweeps away from her face, moving to gently rest on her hand. Celosia, although startled by his touch, does not want him to stop touching her. He knows this somehow, and continues to do so.

He says, "You once knew me as Eithar, from a place far from here. I feel as though I have been eons searching for you, but the time I have spent searching is relative. Traveling through dimensions and wormholes of space is full of disillusion and warped perception.

Remembering you took focus and will, and in some places, all I could recall was the sound of your frequency signature. There was no why, when, or who." Eithar shuts his eyes and bows his head, processing his journey and arrival, clearly weary.

Celosia presses her free hand onto his chest and feels for his frequency, hoping some memory will spark to life. There is something of a song in him, a river dense with current; melodic and slow, Celosia finds herself dropping into her mind's eye. From there, she examines the web and sees light-blue threads weaving around the being, like a loose layer of lichen on a tree. Celosia follows some threads coming off him; one leads to a place beyond form, and others to lush environments blooming with life, color, and sound. What catches her attention is a thread that leads directly into Earth, weaving through and around it. With that, Celosia snaps back from her mind's eye, and says nothing. When she tries to move, she finds she cannot; and the more she touches him, the more she is unwilling to let go. So they sit there in silence, except for a light nervous humming from Celosia.

Moments pass, and things must be accomplished. Malva is creating the channel for travel, leaving it open for Celosia to descend into Earth's frequency. Her journey must ignite soon, and Celosia can't help but wonder if Eithar is somehow tangled up in her mission to Earth as well. She has seen his eyes so many times when having visions taking place on Earth that it is hard not to draw conclusions or make guesses.

Shifting abruptly, she looks directly into his eyes and speaks. "Eithar, I have seen your eyes before in visions, and your touch is a comfort that I have never had in this place. I wish to know you. But I am in the middle of something beyond myself, and I must see it through before we can begin to assemble this puzzle."

Eithar, eyes flaring with muted passion, says in a hoarse baritone, "I will not part with you, unless it is upon your request. My journey to find you is complex, and I'm not even sure what order it is in."

At this, Celosia is already standing; and circling Eithar while facing him, maintaining eye contact, she makes precise steps that cross at the ankles. Appearing like a curious cat surveying a potential threat.

Without a word, she begins to leave, leading Eithar wordlessly off of the golden disc and past the rose-colored stones. He smiles, as if he can hear her thoughts. When her feet meet the greenery, she steps lightly, and Eithar follows. He shadows her back through the foliage and towards the stream that flows against their direction of travel. The light becomes dark and the air thick when they enters the caves path. Quickly, they find themselves at the edges of Celosia's agate basin, the warm water spring. The cave makes no fuss of the new being, but it does alter its scent to dried leaves, acorns, and leather. It is subtle, but Celosia notices the fragrant shift, and she cocks her head at its familiarity. Celosia looks at Eithar, shakes her head, and steps into the water; he follows wordlessly.

For Celosia, this is a test, to see what happens to him beneath the waters of the cave; if there be anything to expose, this will be the time. When they crash into the depths and darkness of the water, it is hard to see him fully, but his arms hold hers at the wrists, gently but firmly.

In the quiet of the water there is only one sound that echoes clearly, symphonic and wistful. The music she had heard from him before is now layered in and merged with her own song, and admittedly it is dynamic, and amongst the most beautiful sounds she has ever had the pleasure to hear.

In the rhythm of the song he breaths, while he pulls her closely in the slow drag of the water. They float suspended in a tangle, his cheekbone pressed into her temple where the end of her eyebrow leads into her hairline. His skin is cool to the touch, but not cold. The delicious combination of the sounds their souls make together is hypnotic. Again, Celosia is faced with a pair of silver eyes, but this time it is no vision; they are tangibly connected to a body, and right in front of her. Eithar certainly passes the test, and the mystery of his arrival and instant bond with her should concern her; but instead she is calm, enjoying the indulgence of the moment, of several consecutive moments.

Below the water, time is nowhere to be found; the life and death of a star could pass, just as easily as the brevity of a butterfly landing upon a flower. Being with him under the water is easy and full, well-rounded like a plum, juicy and ready to fall from a branch.

Celosia knows this time must end. Soon she will descend to Earth, and hopefully, some part of her will remain here and be able to learn more about Eithar and their connection.

It is unclear what will happen to her sense of self when she descends. *What will happen to Nami? I must see Nami before part of my soul is cast away.*

Like necklaces in the jewelry box, Celosia is unsure how to untangle from Eithar; it takes a second, but when she does, she rises to the surface, shattering its glassy stillness. Dripping with steam and swirling with water, she stands at the stair's edge and motions for Eithar to follow her. Wordless, he obeys; and like Celosia, he grabs a blanket to dry off with. Celosia is moving quickly, and her appearance is fragmented. Never has she felt so rushed to do anything. Eithar struggles to see her in linearity; she is here drying her hair, and then there across the cave, draping her shoulders in soft fabric.

Remaining observant and quiet, he follows the sporadic trail she leaves. Passing through the cave's main opening, the droplets of discernment along the cave walls swirl up off the stone and swarm Eithar. Like a glittery school of fish, they swim around him, synchronizing around and then *through* his body. Eithar stands frozen as they make their movements; like a twisted horn torus field, they twist around and pierce painlessly through his chest.

After a few rounds of this pattern, the droplets complete their task, and with a snap, cling back onto the stone walls. Eithar turns to face Celosia with a wild, brilliant grin that shines brightly in the dark hallway. Celosia can't help but smile back at him, but she keeps herself contained.

Finally, they are out upon the sand in the open space, the endless soupy galaxy above. Eithar takes Celosia's hand, and she stops to looked at their paired hands with deep curiosity, and meets his eyes again. She then points upwards to the distant ledge. Understanding, with no time passing, Eithar and Celosia arrive swiftly upon Nami's ledge.

Blinking off the change in scenery, Celosia's focus adjusts. What she sees is a magnificent oak tree, curved and twisted. The base of its trunk is anciently thick and covered in moss. Nami is breathtaking, but her branches are shaking, each tiny leaf shuddering. Celosia and Eithar watch while she shifts again, and the tree begins to split at the place where the branches stretch out from the trunk. The split advances all the way down to the roots; then the two halves of the great tree fall onto opposite sides of the ledge, landing with shattering force. Celosia is startled but does not move; she only watches with keen eyes reflecting the uprooted, split tree.

After a few moments, a fire sparks and heat accumulates under the scattered limbs oozing with sap; soon the whole tree covered in flames. Celosia's jaw loosens slightly as she watches Nami's display.

When nothing but charcoal remains, she kneels and picks up two small, dark lumps of charred wood. All that remains of the grand oak tree, the fragments in her hand still retain the heat from the fire. She ritualistically uses her knife to shed some of her golden blood, and lets it drip into the ashes. Eithar, without a word, holds out his own arm as well, to join in the ritual. His blood, platinum in color, soon rolls down his arm to mingle with Celosia's. The two liquids mix easily and are consumed by the charcoal and ash.

Moments later, in that very spot, a small sprout breaches the soot and reaches upward with one swift motion. Nami is restored to a fresh, living tree, her light-green limbs twisting around Eithar and Celosia as if to embrace and acknowledge them, joining them all in momentary union.

Nami is limber again and full of life. Seeing this peace and rebirth helps Celosia feel more settled and relieved somehow, as if Nami is showing her that even in death and chaos, there is always more life waiting to bloom. Celosia knows it is time for her to go down to the cave, and then down to Earth. It is all happening so fast. With Malva's and Eithar's sudden arrival, this mission to Earth has gone far beyond random chance or coincidence; there is something grander than herself pulling her to the blue-marble world.

Celosia bows to Nami. "I am going on a journey, Nami, but I suspect you know that already. Be well; hopefully I won't really have to leave you at all." Celosia stands erect, and takes a deep breath before she turns to make the descent back down the cliff face, with Eithar close behind her.

Moving quickly, they look like a flash, charcoal held closely in the palm of her hand. When they walk back towards the cave's entrance Eithar stops Celosia, looking into her eyes. "Are you really leaving?" he asks, looking at her as if she were a mirage in an everlasting desert, overcome with thirst, filled with hope and simultaneous defeat. In his eyes is the untold story of his journey before arriving to Celosia's cave.

All she can do is nod, and motion for them to continue into the cave. Her face is calm, although internally, questions are reeling through her mind at a million miles an hour.

Walking towards the fire and stream, she gathers up a mortar and pestle from a shelf and places them on the floor near the fire. When Celosia and Eithar sit around the fire, it grows in size and candor, an inviting lavender hue.

Celosia puts the charcoal from the oak tree into the lava-stone mortar. The pestle is made of similar stone with a wooden handle, and she uses it to lightly tamp the charcoal into smaller pieces. After everything is small and manageable, she focuses, working the pestle in precise, circular motions. Soon, she has fine black powder that shimmers in the firelight. Eithar watches with amusement and sits still, his thigh pressing into Celosia's; it is a subtle contact, but it seems to go without saying that it is soothing for them both. She stretches her arms and readies a pot containing stream water over the fire.

When both of them have a steady gaze on the pot, waiting for the water's surface to crack with heat, Celosia speaks quietly. "When this elixir is done brewing, I will take it with me to the golden disc you arrived on. From there, I will make my descent to Earth, and I do not know how much of me will remain here, if any at all." She sighs, and massages her forehead. "Will you be joining me? If I recall correctly, you mentioned that you would not leave unless I requested that you do so. What I desire is for you to join me. It is also possible that some part of us will remain here after the ceremony. I just don't know what will happen." She is aware that this is a big ask, such a selfish desire to bring him along. She was embarrassed -- no, *shocked* when the invitation fell out of her mouth, as she hardly knows Eithar. But she does know that she doesn't want him to leave.

Eithar looks over his shoulder and spots two ceramic cups on the shelf where the mortar and pestle were stored. He stands and quickly retrieves them, with care, each step measured and poised for his great stature. He sits back down, and places the cups before them, looking steadily at the now-simmering pot.

"I will go as you go," he says, "If you show me the way. I have come this far to find you; I cannot face loosing you again." Eithar keeps his eyes steady on the surface of the water in the pot, watching it dance lightly and cheerfully. Celosia collects the black powder and disperses it into the simmering water, then stirs the contents with a wooden stick. Removing the pot from the flame swiftly, she places a lid on top to let the spirit of Nami mingle with the heated stream water. Soon it will be ready, and they will fill their cups.

Celosia looks at Eithar from the corner of her eye and slowly turns her head to face him. "So, you have lost me before?" She smiles, and then decidedly frowns.

He nods. "It is complicated, but yes, many times."

Celosia replies, "Vague, but I suppose it would take a lot of time to tell the tale. Well, to shortly settle some matters, I have always had an empty space inside of me where I feel memories should be, but they just aren't there. I have no memory of you, and yet, my soul recognizes yours. And I hope to one day regain those memories. This descent is a guessing game; there can be many outcomes. Perhaps we will lie crumpled on the golden disc in a slumbering void of dreaming; perhaps we will lie consciously dedicated to the dream of our experience on Earth. We may feel nothing at all and remain whole, or maybe even disappear..."

Celosia trails off. She can't help but feel filled with discomfort and slight excitement for the change.

Eithar nods with a heavy heart and smiling eyes. "Weaving through this universe, this multiverse, is always a leap into the unknown. It can be beautifully surprising, confusing, and even painful; but if there is one thing I have learned, it is that nothing is ever lost or destroyed." As the words leave his mouth, the concept echoes through the cave; this proclamation comforts them both.

With cups filled to the brim with black, hot, silky liquid, they follow the stream down the hallway towards all things green and living. The cave sends a wind that blows up against their back from behind; the wind is cool and smells of moss, fresh sap, candle wax, and linens. The cave's wind communicates a message of farewell through scent.

That wind carries them all the way to the rose-stone walls. The golden disc is humming, a sound so high-pitched it is barely audible. Shadows are cast onto the faces of Celosia and Eithar in the shapes of tropical leaf patterns, the light behind the tall, hanging foliage piercing through sporadically. It seems many of the lights orbs are pleased to gather near the portal disc, no doubt to witness the impending event. Celosia is going on a journey, so naturally all the elements of the cave coalesce to see the moment transpire.

Two pairs of feet step softly but resolutely onto the golden disc. Looking like warriors with cups of tea instead of swords or weapons, they valiantly approach the center of the disc. Celosia sits with her spine connected to it, knees bent and feet crossed at the ankles. Eithar sits behind her, his chest lined up with her back. He presses himself so closely to her that there is no space between them. He is her shield, the whole backside of her protected and stabilized by his bold and peaceful presence. Celosia feels at peace with him behind her like this; her breath catches and then releases as she sinks into the warmth and safety of his body. Against him, she looks like a lavender sunset in the depth of his cosmos skin.

"Find clarity in your mind's eye. I will find the tethers to Malva and then Earth, and once I have full hold of those tethers, I will drink my cup to completion. As I drink, you will also drink."

"Yes, without doubt," Eithar says, his response physically resonating through Celosia's back.

Sitting on golden disc, it begins to spin and vibrate. Celosia and Eithar begin to hear their frequencies' melodic union ringing louder and louder, moving towards crescendo. As the sound builds and the tethers located by Celosia merge with them, they each lift their arms and drink the silky black elixir in one large swallow.

When the cups roll to the side, Eithar wraps his arms all the way around Celosia, and he kisses the back of her head. From here, everything vignettes to black, and once all is black, a burst of light swirls like a tunnel, pulling them both in like a vacuum. At this point, their frequencies crescendo, breaking into fractures of light and sound. Beyond a distant echo, there is only stillness.

Celosia and Eithar remain on the disc, Eithar with his arms wrapped tightly around Celosia. They sit motionless, as if sleeping upright.

Layer 7: Eithar Foraging for Pieces

To know Eithar, and to understand why he ended up in Celosia's cave, we have to crawl back through his story. The Universe as we know it is expanding and swelling, filled with star systems and infinite potential. Within this timeless inhalation of the universal breath there lives all that can possibly be. Infinity implies that all, and I mean *all*, potential exists. This is a heavy and dizzying concept that removes the head from the body: everything that ever has been, is, and will be. Perhaps the universe will soon be ready to exhale, and all the stars and space between them will contract and implode into its next breath. Pressure and release.

In a system far from Earth's galaxy, there exists the realm of ancient deities of the Royal Orbit -- those who create the galaxies and govern their systems, like Ílios and Fengári of Earth's prism, but on a larger, more formless scale. Vast and limitless deities, those of the Royal Orbit are responsible for orchestrating advanced systems of biology and formation, creation and evolution of light and matter -- like mothers forming children in their uteruses, orchestrating organs, tissue, and importing souls from the web-like multiverse. Among the Royal Orbit, there are sanctions ruled by no more than three beings; too many cooks in the kitchen can get a little hectic.

To tell their story well, personification is necessary to distill the concept of their essences. Eithar, known for being a straight-shooter and true to his word, was accompanied by Althea, known for her kindness and her extraordinary vision of the grand scale. They built a galaxy system together: nothing too gaudy or extravagant, but mindful and organic. The system consisted of many stars and four interacting binary systems with orbiting moons made of diamond. The two often had their disagreements, which unfolded into dynamic discussions, very diplomatic in nature. Compromise nearly always led to creations both of them could admire. They were true equals, but opposite enough to build dimension into their relationship.

Although highly-evolved souls, they learned the lessons of responsibility often. Take, for example, the time Eithar wished to create giant winged creatures that he called Kitsunes. He seeded them on an inhabited planet in one of their systems. Blinded by the grandiose structure of the creatures, he lacked the foresight to see how they would affect the existing ecosystem. He made the moves on the project before discussing it with Althea, which wasn't uncommon; the two often nurtured small projects with little interaction or approval. However, when the Kitsune hatched from their eggs, Eithar knew he had made some huge errors in his impulsiveness.

He busied himself with figuring out a way to solve the problem without destroying them. Nothing got by Althea, though; she could read the difference in the ecosystem with just one air sample. Her reaction was cool and aloof, waiting to see if Eithar would come to her with his mistake.

In time he did. Granted, it took a few cycles of biological reproduction of the species before he came to her, desperate for a solution for the chain reaction he had created. Eithar could not hide his mistake for long, nor would he. Althea and Eithar experienced time differently than their systems. A generational cycle of life to death among the Kitsune equaled perhaps a day in their perception.

The Kitsune were vicious. Their exoskeletons were comprised of layered scales, metallic crimson discs that were cool to the touch. The scales were made of a pliable metal similar to gold, but much lighter. During flight, their scales ruffled like delicate wind chimes, or the ankle bracelet of a belly dancer.

Eithar's design was mostly for Althea, as sounds, above all else, were her greatest of pleasures. Pure delight swelled within her when she heard the tones created in their worlds, especially the sound of the Kitsune. Beyond the sounds they made, Kitsune truly were a sight to behold. A Kitsune had a flat, heart-shaped face that sat like a mask on its rounded skull. The "mask" was furry white; against the crimson metallic scales of its skull and body, the contrasting boundary in textures and colors made it all the more striking. Four eyes of green, like swirling ferns, vibrant and keen, contrasted with the white fur.

Yes, they were esthetically pleasing; but were they sane? No. There was a major dysfunction in their behavior. Kitsune had an underdeveloped sense of familial and tribal bonding, which led them to mutate and reproduce asexually. When they produced an egg, it was left to fend for itself, as the parent would move along after leaving an egg behind.

A Kitsune was not a balanced creature; it brain's processing centers was overdeveloped in its drive for survival, which was also responsible for its drive to dominate specific territories. These two poorly developed elements, when combined, made for a huge ecological mess. Kitsune were also very large, and through their size alone quickly became the top predators on their planet. Instead of a slow evolution, like many of the creatures Eithar and Althea had influenced and created, these Kitsune demons separated, pillaged, and multiplied with immense speed.

Many local ecosystems began to take hits from these devastating beasts. Their saliva alone was so acidic it was wreaking havoc on the trees the Kitsune roosted in.

Althea, all the while keeping an eye on the situation, had come up with a few alternatives in her lab. But her lab was more like her internal drawing board; a space of her own design, it was her den, her cave. It was where she birthed her creations and thought about solutions to problems such as these.

Despite the very real devastation the Kitsune created, it was always difficult to end the life of any creation. Instead of death, Althea preferred to implement a change somehow: a forced mutation, or an evolution of sorts. She could inoculate a change using altered bacteria or viruses, and shape the beings' electromagnetic waves. She knew she needed to balance the control center of the Kitsune, and give their prey a fighting chance to survive.

The control center in a Kitsune was a flexible crystalline column that extended up the center its body. It was the main "hard drive" for all the functions that the animal needed to live, and it was in that column that Althea decided she would implement change.

Eventually, Eithar came to Althea plain-faced and despondent, embarrassed by his mistake. Althea was loving, not the sort of soul who would rub salt into a wound; instead, she felt that everything that happened was inevitable, so why get flustered? Reassuring Eithar that his creatures were above all beautifully creative, she assured him that the imbalance could be repaired, and immediately went to work with her plan to circumvent the issue.

While Althea walked him through her solution, Eithar was lost in her silver eyes. Like his own eyes, they were inviting and intelligent, masterful and wise. In a hypnotized state, he listened to Althea, reminded often of how perfectly paired they were -- how much he loved her. In these situations, they further built trust and vulnerability; mind you, it took literal eons to get there, but they did cultivate it. Eithar was humbled and able to listen to her wisdom; beyond love, there was respect, and following that there was trust.

The decided jointly that an introduction of a gene-edited fungal organism into the Kitsune population was the best option with the least amount of casualties. The fungus was sourced from the vegetation that was a primary food source for the prey of the Kitsune demons. When introduced, it worked to enhance spinal activity in the regions that controlled breeding and nesting. Very precise molecular understanding was Althea's forte. The original malformation only took one generation to correct; soon the mannerisms of the Kitsune shifted, and they were nesting in pairs with hermit-like personalities, which reduced the rate of their wild roaming and reproduction. This restored some balance to the ecosystem. Further down the evolutionary road, they might require more tampering; but for now, there was a symbiotic flow.

Eithar was not as gifted in the intricacies of symbiosis as Althea; he had more strength in design and creativity -- whereas Althea's strength lay in the details, the tiny particulates and their interactions. She was superbly mindful of the impact of life. This made them an ideal pair; they were without a doubt a known pair among the Royal Orbits, often an inspiration of teamwork, as not every system was ruled with such moral taste. In fact, other galaxies were built deliberately to thrive on chaotic destruction... but this is the balance of infinity.

Everything in their galaxy was rolling along systematically; to them, much of it was about enjoying and observing the machine operate. In their most recent observations, the stars surrounding the planets were transforming, headed to their expirations, as all living things must transform through death. Althea enjoyed watching magnificent fuming gases explode with color, but now they were intriguing because they were the flares of change and death.

Althea became greatly internal while watching these deaths, and a tolling bell rang in her. Some part of her fracturing, she fled without word. She spent most of her time dissolving into the interstellar wind and swirling about the galaxy. She felt the need to clear her mind and fully accept that there *was* a cycle, not only for her galaxy, but for her as well. Something rang deep within Althea, an internal clock of sorts, and she knew that in time, transformation through death would also be coming for her. But how would she know? Would she have to initiate it herself? These were all questions and concepts swirling along with her bodiless journey through the void of her galaxy.

Eithar knew that something was wrong; he missed Althea and could not find her, he could only feel Althea's existential tumbling. This made him feel loss, a feeling he had no concept of until it happened. Planetary seasons passed, and it completely wrecked him, tormented him, and led him to feel more of his darkness than he knew existed. Disappearing without explanation was unlike Althea; was it something that he had done?

The binary systems moved slowly through their oblong journey, and Eithar found himself wondering the surfaces of the planets in search of Althea, but he would not find her there. All he would find was her delicate handiwork, twisting codes of creation that were so unique. While on one planet, he took form of a shadow, and followed a deep crevasse. He sat atop a metallic ribbon that stretched across the planet. It looked as if it were frozen in mid-flight, some sections bunched up like ribbon candies. Eithar enjoyed staring down into the abyss of the crevasse, not quite remembering what was beneath it. Slowly, like a sun rising, he heard subtle growing tones; or was it a fragmented song?

Watching, he saw that from the crevasse a vine, violet and smooth, climbed with many limbs, each tendril echoing a tone like wind-chime pipes. When it breached the edge, it settled into a spot next to the ribbon and coiled itself into the shape of a blooming flower. The stationary pose of the vine allowed for its song to be clear and congealed.

Althea had created these beings to soothe creatures. Her concept was one of a magnetic empathy that would draw the vines near excessive disruption, where they would then instinctually emit a frequency that would mend those disruptive patterns. She called them *Celosia*. Eithar noticed a flock of Celosia sweeping in from all directions and planting themselves around him. While he was weeping, as much as shadow can weep, the Celosia played their mending song for him. Surrounded by these sounds, he was closer to Althea; he could nearly smell her in their vibrational ringing. The little vine creatures certainly worked. They managed to help Eithar process his feelings, and move him into a new headspace.

Althea did not intend to be space wind forever; she just needed to seep into the feeling of death and what it all meant. Despite her deep satisfaction with her existence and placement in the Royal Orbit, she was certain there was more or less beyond the edge of her soul, and she was now set to find out what that was.

Althea eventually shifted back into solid form, small pixels clinging together like magnets to mold her vivacious deity-form. Soft and curved lines built her structure, although her body was more like a giant sparkling blanket that could wrap up into form. She was always wrapping and then unwrapping to extend out like a floating, sheer cloud. She was ready to find Eithar, so she set to calling out to all the beings among their galaxy to put word out she was looking for him. Luckily, he was quick to be found, for he had been searching for her for so long, and most of the beings were eager to help. They were also incentivized, as the seasons had gone colder than normal, and everything was less bountiful without the love of Eithar's and Althea's union.

Eithar was not angry at Althea when he saw her; instead he crashed into her, splashing tiny pixels all around. They collided so deeply that they merged. One of them had been blue, the other red; they were now floating as one, in a purple cloud with tiny specks of blue and red hanging in the field around them. To anyone looking up from the planet beneath them, they would appear as a spectacular lavender aurora borealis dancing in the sky, invoking reunion and joy.

Althea had missed him so; and it wasn't until she had spent the time apart from him that she realized that he was a part of her forever.

Eithar had so many questions racing around, so within their purple mist they manifested into small humanoid forms and lay tangled on a pillow of their own violet dust, communicating with breath before attempting to do so in lingual concepts. Their breaths contained questions in them, excitement, fondness, wrinkled brow lines, hurt, and most of all relief. Eithar's hand swept around the back of her neck, and he held his palm over the curve of her lower occipital as they lay tangled. When ready to speak, Althea began, "I did not include you in my thoughts and feelings. I should have made them known to you before I left, and for that I apologize to you. Hurting you was not my goal, but a product of my own unraveling."

Eithar nodded at this silently, accepting her sentiment. "Perhaps when you unravel, I unravel too, and I did. I will admit, I found darkness and I felt pain; balance was lost. More than this, I am curious what you felt, that led you to hide in a such a way?"

Althea melted and reformed, sitting farther away, her hands fidgeting. "Our stars are dying all around us, and this transformation through death is also coming for us... or maybe we are coming for it. Either way, Eithar, I feel that when this galaxy dies, I too wish to dissolve with it and begin again. Here at the top, in the Royal Orbit, it is starting to feel like the bottom."

Eithar was astonished, his face sharpening and softening in confusion. "Where exactly does death live? How do you envision the process? I mean, do you see yourself going alone as you did before?" he asked with vacancy cast across his face, as he slumped into Althea's lap.

"I am not asking you to end who you are now, but I invite you to come with me. When I was away, I observed our brightest and largest star, Nagda 3147, the one you designed, the biggest feat of our galaxy." Althea was growing bigger, with animated limbs, as she emphasized its mass.

"Well, something is different with its death process than with that of our smaller stars, which only contain hydrogen and helium. Nagda 3147 contains most of the elements. Its fusion is even condensing into elements denser than iron, which is not normal; the pressure of the fusion is compacting the density right into the core. This process has been underway for quite some time, from what I can tell. The sheer weight and compaction of the mass in the core of Nagda 3147 will cause it collapse inward on itself, and then, I believe, to implode beyond the ability of even light to escape."

Althea stood. "We have made a major oversight that will affect our whole galaxy, and I feel its divinity. Nagda 3147 was always destined to be this way, but it is unclear how it will affect the galaxy during its further evolution. It may act as a gravitational vacuum and pull in the surrounding stars and planets. In time, it could devour our entire galaxy, and I feel the process has already begun..." Althea looked off in the direction of Nagda 3147.

Eithar's face displayed shock, with the sudden weight of their creation's mortality heavy in his heart. He stood and stiffened, slowly bringing his particles back into himself. "I have failed us with so many of my ideas; and now that the end of our creation is near, it rests heavily within me. What can we do?"

Althea gave him a menacing grin, and looking straight into him, she said, "Firstly, declaring failure is premature; there is potential in this chaos that may lead to something new and unforeseen. Secondly, I find it perfectly crazy. We can hop in the implosion and discovery what it is we have created! Death, rebirth, or transformation, it would be an awfully delicious ride. And it is time sensitive. I know that I will explore that implosion, whether you join me or not."

At this concrete statement, Althea's line was drawn in the sand and her mind was set to ride the implosion. Eithar, however, had a clear conflict with either idea, and either way it was possible to lose her. "Althea, how much time do we have before the jump?" Although he asked as if he were jumping too, he was unsure if he wanted to. Could he wait and watch and somehow help if something were to go wrong? His thoughts reeled into the infinite possibilities of outcomes.

"Did you hear me, Eithar? We have one binary orbit; we will have to watch it closely near its last phase, so we do not miss the kick-off." A binary orbit was the time it took for a star to rotate around the stationary planet and its small Moon. This was a very short time, maybe a week.

Eithar was listening, but he wasn't really hearing; his mind was filled with equations on when Nagda 3147 would transform and change everything, and bent on wondering at how death arrives for everyone in its own unique way. *How will it arrive for Althea and me?* he thought. Althea was one half of their whole, and he was unwilling for that union to be severed. Would they find each other, would they remain intact... or would they be lost and scattered forever?

Eithar needed more time, more time with Althea and his own struggle with change and transformation. But Althea had already immersed herself in the process of change. She sat with herself and came to a place of peace and excitement.

All he knew was that the implosion was drawing nearer each moment. And it terrified him.

Layer 8: ιόσ Becoming More

The ocean was cold and dark, but it was no matter for ιός; being a shark, he felt no such discomfort. In fact, he felt right at home. Hundreds of years passed while he gained strength and understanding of the form he had taken. It was rewarding and primal. He could travel a great distance, hunt, and scavenge for the edible creatures, dead or alive. His body was strong and sleek, his mind attuned with the flesh of the creature.

Sharks and a few other creatures of the ocean have the ability to read the electromagnetic waves carried through the conductive substrate of salt water. Pores along ιός's face would take in the surrounding data. These pores were connected to a gelatinous channel which was in turn connected to an organ responsible for processing electromagnetic currents, similar to the way eyes process the spectrum of light waves.

Within a one-mile radius, his pores could detect the racing heartbeat of a fish, the fluttering of a scuttle, and even the slinking movements of oceanic vultures picking flesh from the dead. To a human, the ocean would appear to be cold and quiet water, devoid of life; but to ιός, it was an elaborate and vibrant orchestra of sensations, infusing him with the cycle of life. A game of territory and survival.

Hunting down the source of electromagnetic waves took very little time. He was efficient, and in that there was power, and in power was the glory of the kill. ιός was not certain when his life in the shark form would end; in fact, it rarely occurred to him that a predator might come for him. The lifetime of a Greenland shark can surpass two hundred years; despite their significant size, their longevity is due to their slow and conservative mannerisms.

ιός had grown to be eight meters long and had lived for 400 years, which was nearly double the average lifespan of the Greenland shark. He didn't know it yet, but his presence in the shark gave off an affect, cellular regeneration and of some sort. Despite this extension, he could not make a body last forever, and the shark was slowly falling apart. In his lifetime, he experienced mating with a female shark only twice; each time he bit into her fin and held on while the instinct of nature overtook him. Overall, it was a fairly thoughtless process, action only. There was no curiosity or care for the offspring, for the male does not stick around for the rearing.

A rare moment of lucidity overcame ιός after he had fertilized one of the females. "Hmm, the process of continuation and sharing of genes, continuation... this must mean there is a time when I will die, or at least this body will," he mused while swimming away from the disgruntled female.

This conscious thought gave a shock to his whole nervous system, as he rarely had inner commentary or logged observations concerning his experience. Rather, he survived presently in the primal form and function of it all, wholly existing as a shark. It was like method acting; to truly understand the shark, he had to fully become the shark. Now that he was on Earth, he was in no hurry to do anything but learn; he had spent too much time alone in the darkness of space.

Genetic continuation is a fascinating quality of Earth life. From the coral reef and tiny fish to the whales and the sea lions, all creatures have a way to begin again and recycle their genetic information. As if temporarily split open by this epiphany, ιός experienced a content and connective moment with his oceanic home, admiring the fine-crafted handiwork of the details; everything had a purpose and a place.

The moment passed, and two years rolled onward with no further commentary. On a spring morning during a full Moon, ιός swam loftily along in the dark, mysterious waters, particulates and microorganisms hanging quietly in the individual beams of light shining down from the surface. He found himself lucid and conscious with thought on this day, looping on complex queries of his own origin and how he came to be. "Where am I from, and how did I survive? Who am I? The observer inside the shark, or the shark itself? I am aware that I am both a shark and the mind within it. How do I continue to survive? Can I reproduce myself?" Questions poured from ιός into an unanswerable void. He continued on in this headspace for the better part of a day, uninterested in food or the kill. These troubling thoughts ate away at him instead.

Why could he not remember much at all from before the blast and ash? After the emotional wave had crashed? No answered within him surfaced, so he gave up and lost his sense of lucidity, and swam on as a shark once more.

All the conscious thoughts and questions had led him off his usual course; he was swimming along in a different current altogether. He was out of his usual territory.

It was on this spring morning when ιός found himself in new warmer waters. He felt vulnerable, and this emphasized how aged his body felt, how it was falling apart. Instincts to disappear and die somewhere far away had begun to take over. So he swam, following the signal to warmth somewhere closer to the surface.

After miles in this action, ιός spotted what appeared to be a whale floating on the surface, piquing his curiosity. He swam closer to investigate.

The whale was large, brown, and unlike any other whale he had seen. There was no electromagnetic signal coming from the form, so perhaps it was dead and therefore food. Upon touching his nose and teeth to the belly of the creature, he found it was unmoving and the flesh hard; his teeth merely scratched along the surface with an unpleasant sensation. He circled and circled the creature; little did he know there was great commotion above the surface. In truth, the whale was a ship inhabited with humans, humans entrenched in disagreement.

ιός did not know why he circled and followed this creature; perhaps because it challenged his alpha instincts, surpassing his own size, and exhibited resilience to his attacks. He followed the boat when it was dark and when it was light; he did not rest. As if a great force within him was guiding him, he was magnetized and knew not why, nor did he even think to ask himself why. He just swam.

Meanwhile, above the surface, a crew of nine adventurous men from a place near what would one day be Jerusalem rowed in unison. Two men took to adjusting the sails, and one man took the main routing oar. Tired eyes and weathered skin revealed that they had been at sea for a long time. Rations had run low, and that was displayed in the structure of their faces, angular cheekbones pulling skin taut like sails.

The crew members had all spotted ιός stalking them, giving some members of the crew anxiety and triggering superstition. The old shark, nearly as long as their own boat, drifted alongside the vessel, sometimes surfacing and other times swimming deeper. Unsettled by the shark's general ambiguity, a few of the crew spoke of attacking it with spears or harnessing it with ropes. The fear the shark's presence sparked an argument among the men, who were tired and malnourished; of course, it was exasperated by extreme the extreme pit of hunger gnawing within them.

The scuttle and aggression was extinguished by the leader of the crew. He was even-tempered, able to keep his men calm through a storm or through a tough time with low rations. He could dilute the testosterone of his crew and command peace without being aggressive. He watched and he waited, noticing the subtleties of the shark's movements, his eyes scanning for potential danger. After observing the creature, he resolved that the sea had given them a guide home, and decided it was a good omen. As days passed, the men began thinking of the creature with less skeptical fear-based concern, and saw it as a reflection and momentum towards home.

Breathing and moving as one, their rhythmic grunting became the music that drove them. The wind was lighter than normal, and to gain speed they had to row.

They had only some days left until they reached land, now almost all the way across the Mediterranean Sea, sailing from the west headed east, their vessel due to reach a land that would one day sit between Israel and Egypt; though those names had yet to be born, and for now only small nomadic tribes moved with the seasons and survived there.

The year was roughly 16,000 BC, and the innovative hunter/ gatherers on this boat were founding a village, rooting down and building structures, building a new way of living by staying grounded in one spot, inventing agriculture and even building towers into the sky. The land's climate had become more hospitable over the last 100 years, resulting in an ideal environment for this nomadic tribe to settle in.

Their leader was a large man, tall and lean, built like hard steel. His skin was dark and his features angular, though hidden beneath a wildly protective beard that nearly connected to his sharp eyebrows. His facial hair worked to absorb the harsh, salty winds at sea. They called him Jushur, and he was a stoic man, full of pensive thought and reason, more intelligent than any other man in his tribe. Though he was brave and courageous, he did not boast or flaunt this quality; he did not see it useful to overextend his energetic resources. Like most of his crew, blowing their own testosterone.

Night came, and most of the men slept, while a few took watch in turns. The sail slightly slackened, so the boat was set to a slow drift eastward, steering with the main oars. Jushur dreamed of his beloved and their child. Small waves that lapped the boat's curve delivered those dreams to drift softly in the night.

Below the boat, ιός was weary, half-asleep and half in pursuit of this unusual creature. He knew that soon his body would pass, and the need for a new one would quickly arise. He did not know why he was blindly following this thing for such a great distance, but without hesitation he kept swimming, his mind shut off. He moved fluidly along with the pace of the creature, and could almost taste the dreams drifting from it, pouring out like a mist from the surface. They puzzled and motivated him to continue. ιός began to sense the electromagnetic pulses of food and creatures all around, gathering that a reef was nearby and the water was shallowing.

"The shore!" a hoarse voice called out from a man on the oars. All the men were lifted and set to motion with more strength and stamina, yearning to touch the land once again. Each person set to a task as the shore approached and Jushur guided the master oar and called out orders. As the boat kissed the sand, it made a pleasant sound, *shvvvvuh*. The crew leapt from the boat and began pulling it with ropes, readying it to be dragged up onto dry sand. Jushur had his eyes on ιός, who was lingering in the shallow waters, looking nearly dead, his body scarred and pieces of flesh sloughing off. It tore at Jushur's heart somehow.

Standing at the rear of the boat, keeping the back oar lifted while the water got shallower, he looked back at the creature. When the crew had the boat ashore, wedged with wood, Jushur waded out to the shark, which appeared nearly dead, his long body nearly limp and flailing in each wave that rolled to shore.

Jushur reached down and blessed the shark with his palm, pressing flat on the shark's back near the fin. "For our safe return to shore, I thank you," Jushur said wholeheartedly. For Jushur had thought the shark a blessing from the sea, a guide bringing them safely back home.

Little did he know what lay within the shark. Through his palm he could feel that it was not yet dead, and through his palm he felt a great warmth and an electric shock from the creature. He stood there connected into the feeling, mesmerized by the pull of gravity, as if he might sink into himself and pour out through his palm.

After a long 48 seconds, he came to, feeling dazed. He pulled his hand away while keeping his eyes on the shark as he backed up towards the shore to join his crew in celebration of their return to land.

The great shark's heart stopped the moment Jushur's hand left the body. Now dead, it was on its way to decay, becoming a part of the cycle of the ocean. As the day set into evening, small creatures made their way to the Greenland shark to feed and help with decomposition, and that was that.

Layer 9: Celosia - A New Name, A New Face

The Kingdom of the Fae, the elementals, the nature spirits; all are names describing the same dimension, and the beings within it. The realm is ethereal. The planet Earth is suspended in many dimensions, like pages in a book. Each page has an independent identity, but collectively, they comprise Earth. The most dominant plane of existence, the one humans occupy, is ruled by time and linearity. Meanwhile, the Fae Kingdom exists in a dimension that runs atop and parallel to the density of Earth. Beings who walk upon Earth require specific conditions for the veil to become thin; only in such alchemically rare moments will fragments of the Fae Kingdom appear to those who exist in Earth's density.

It is said that when Fengári created her prismic land with Ílios, her favorite creation was the elemental kingdom. This ethereal dimension was her pride and joy, her energy anchored into its sacredness. It is certain that among the Fae she exists like a whisper surrounding all things, infusing her wisdom and connectivity directly into the world she helped create.

Elementals catalyze all living systems of biology, encoding seeds with a plan for survival and growth, strategy and instinct. The Fae are the essences within the water, wind, fire, and stone. They are the magicians and the scientists, living alongside time, choosing to partake at their will, following the cycle of the elements that govern the natural world. If all nature was destroyed, the Fae Kingdom would surely decay into smithereens.

Within the elemental "species," there are levels of social hierarchy and creatures; there are the compassionate empaths, regal elites, those filled with lightness and laughter, as well as those who find joy in being tricksters and lingering in the shadows. There are many flavors in this dimension, many ways to be, bodies amorphous and unrestricted by specific forms. Immortality is common, and if not that, there are extremely long lives. Education systems exist, but are abstract. Rules can be broken, sometimes without consequence; there is law, and no law. In short, it is a dynamic place where dark and light dance with one another. It isn't all frills and sparkles, as most would assume.

To describe the beauty would not do it justice, as such sights cannot be squeezed into words. However, there are luminescent veins of light running lightly through all things. There are magnificent structures of all shapes geometric, spheres and pyramids covered in plant life or made of water; these structures have their own arrangement with gravity. Some structures, monuments of nature, float and sometimes move to different locations, while others remain in place. An alluring sky provides a constant air of mysticism, as it always displays the stars on a backdrop of soft sunset colors.

Beings of all colors and forms are consistently phasing in and out of stones, air, fire, metal, and water. Some formless beings lie within plant medicine, their essences ready to be called upon by the mortals consuming it, acting as spiritual guides, imbuing knowledge of the plant kingdom and its bounty. Even the fungi impart such lessons. Depending on the place of its cultivation, the experience may reflect the surrounding nature, or the way it grew, allowing for different aspects of self-reflection to occur, activating diverse sensations in the body.

The variety of Fae in the spirit realm are linked to the elements and environments that exist in the human realm. Water beings are sensual empathic souls, who can be found churning in the pools underneath waterfalls, becoming the small rainbows in the mist, and folding within the belly of the Earth in the caves and catacombs. There are those of wood and Earth, the elven humanoids, who are regal, poised, and have the power of sight. They dwell in the trees and forests, as well as meadows and valleys. Some species find the elves repulsively pretentious and serious, but when you truly know them, it is easy to see that their seriousness does not come from a place of judgment -- it comes from a place of calm, honest literalism.

There are beings of the fire and electricity, those made of lightning, magma, and plasma, filled with inspirational charge. These beings are less cultivated in dwellings or groups; rather, they are nomadic, and freer from linear thought.

Most of these beings were placed here by Fengári, and many of them stayed for a long time. Celosia's arrival, however, was of pure and independent entry, a rare feat to accomplish. Her etheric soul shooting down from a place so light and lofty that her purity and soul's energy directed her into a placement in the Fae realm. She incarnated into the Irati Forest, at the base of the Pyrenees Mountains.

Celosia's soul entered as fragmented light, crashing into Earth's dimension. Her soul was faint as she magnetized into a seed buried within the wet soil. With soft awareness, she swirled into the small and yet vast little kernel, infusing herself into the program of the acorn, joining its blueprint for life, as if she were water filling an empty channel. As her awareness anchored, she became the force that drove the sprout through the soil and clay towards light. There was pressure and strain, pushing her way upward.

As the light of the Sun touched the face of the tiny sprout, Celosia's form began to take shape, growing with each breath. Each tiny molecule of air buzzed as if it knew her by name. Her frequency rang like a bell throughout the oak forest, relief sighing through the branches, and even the sunbeams bowed slightly. There was quiet laughter rolling in from all directions, on bubbling water in a small creek, over the boulders, and through the upper canopy of the trees.

All the surrounding elements greeted her and made themselves visible, welcoming her presence into their land. A few voices murmured gratitude and excitement. After the rush of excitement, a being stood before her in the flesh. This being bowed, and gestured to the others to make space and breathing room.

Elegantly structured, the humanoid being before her felt long-lived like a statue. Stoic eyes were steady on her, their head slightly tilting and then straightening. Celosia examined their form, which was androgynous, extremely tall, and lean, with silver skin. The being was well dressed in what looked like a periwinkle satin suit, loose yet tailored to its lanky body. They bowed to Celosia.

"I am Beaudry," said the silver being. "Welcome to the realms of the Fae. Do you know where you are, dear?"

Celosia looked around, gazing off into the land behind Beaudry. Assessing her surroundings and new form, she sniffed herself, wondering what the smell was. Still in shock from the arrival process, her mind and energy was reeling; she felt dizzied and confused. She only managed to nod at Beaudry and tilt her head inquisitively at him, as he had to her earlier.

"This is an oak forest at the base of a mountain, mistress. We collectively, as incarnates, govern these elements; we are a part of them. I myself am the keeper of the mountain; my soul has been with this mountain willingly since its tectonic birth. Being a part of Earth through this realm has been my honor and pleasure."

"However, now is not the time for a detailed history lesson; you have just arrived, and I gather from the look in your eyes that you understand what I'm saying, and possess a knowing from far away."

Celosia nodded at this, showing she understood, as she shifted weight from foot to foot.

"Is there anything we can call you by, a name?" Beaudry asked, his voice as soothing as Roman chamomile.

Celosia shook her head, then bowed her head and spoke with a raspy whisper. "I do not recall my name."

Beaudry smiled calmly. "It would be my honor to bestow a name upon you."

Celosia looked up again at the sky hanging in twilight, with stars spread thick like silver craft sparkles spilled from a malfunctioning shaker. She smiled wistfully, knowing that out there somewhere was her true home. With sudden epiphany, she looked down at her form, assessing who, or rather *what*, she was now.

Beaudry laughed a deep, clear laugh that caused pebbles and rocks to vibrate at their feet. "You are of the stars, as I was long ago."

Beaudry's eyes squinted, as they thought long and hard searching for a name. He scanned the whole of her, as she stood unsure a doe just born. Breaking the silence, he tested a name, "*Indra*, is a name that I feel will suit you well, if you will have it?" Beaudry stepped closer, locked into her, and lightly brushed the edge of her jaw, measuring and assessing her form.

Celosia turned away with shyness, but nodded in agreement to the name. As she agreed, the wind stirred greatly at their feet and spiraled around them both. Beaudry began to chant, speaking softly but clearly as if to an audience, but it was not in the language he had just been using with Celosia. In fact, Celosia was not sure how it was they were communicating, nor the language. All of the information given to her by Beaudry had been assembled and conveyed with perfect comprehension, but the chanting did not register, and felt truly foreign.

Despite not understanding, Celosia gained confidence and stood poised, knowing that she was in no danger from Beaudry. The wind was becoming stronger with the continuous chanting. At its peak, the wind blew through her form, charging all the tiny particles that composed her. Celosia waited for Beaudry to finish and the wind to settle, and eventually, all became still once more, and Beaudry bowed for their finale.

"I have informed the land that you, Indra, have arrived to this forest, coming through to this realm in a seed, which is divinely rare. You are the first foreign soul of the stars I have encountered in quite some time, and I find this all doubly special. You are a lady dryad of this forest, a tree nymph, an oak dryad. We would be delighted if you imbued your gifts here into the fabric of our ecosystem." Beaudry stepped over to the sprouting oak and cast a circle around it with their fingers, drawing a clear mark in the soil.

"This tree is a very important part of your life here; it is your anchor and life source; it lives as you live. When the tree is alive, you can pass into the adjacent dimensional layer, the realm of the humans and animals. You can walk among them if you so choose; so long as the tree lives, its roots tether your soul to walk in both realities. I warn you against staying in the human realm too long, however, because it is best not to meddle in human affairs."

Indra stepped sideways and said softly, "Thank you for your welcome. I am not accustomed to such things-" Indra's stared off trying to recall, "—I feel I have forgotten something very important. My mind is like mud clouding water."

Indra hadn't noticed while she spoke that Beaudry had a few quiet tears streaking down their face, lines of silvers marking their path. "I can remember what it is like to forget, and some will remember, while others are meant to be cast in a spell of amnesia." Turning their gaze from hers, they busied their hands with laying a ring of golden pebbles around her tree; and when the circle was completed. Beaudry stood up, poised and taller than before, dusting off their hands on their thighs.

"You are a special being, mistress, and I am sure in time, when you have settled into this place, you will regain memories lost. You must rest and nourish yourself. Should you need me, just think of me, or tell the wind; the wind always knows where to find me." With those words, Beaudry dissipated.

Indra was left alone, satisfied with her new name and its sound. She was amazed at what had just happened, with Beaudry and all of the Fae around her. She felt wonderment, and was ready to explore her surroundings and the endless potential that was her body. She did not have to travel far before she found a creek; its gurgles were sounds she had never heard before, as if chanting and laughter were pouring out of it all at once. Kneeling down near a stagnant place in the creek where still water pooled, she peered over to look upon herself.

The creek's reflection was crisp; Indra saw herself, with sharp details and glowing radiance. Her form was elegant and beautiful.

Relieved at the sight of herself, she happily examined her features. Her skin was translucent and supple; it had a golden sheen over a woody brown, the color of an acorn seed. Curving from bust to hips, she was satisfied by her womanly form. She wore no clothes or coverings. Indra sat happily naked by the creek-side, as the hypnotic chanting of the water lulled her into a dreamlike state.

When she leaned in a bit closer, she saw the mercurial color of her eyes, flowing like a moats around her small black pupils. It was then that gravity and memory crashed into her awareness all at once. *Nami, Malva, Eithar, the virus grid around Earth... the transfer, her soul's departure and arrival on Earth!* She now recalled her mission, her intention to investigate the darkness through the world's shrouded grid. Indra felt the tether reaching through herself, passing into Malva and then on to Celosia -- that's right, *Celosia* was her prior name. Despite the sudden memory, the tether's connection was not very strong; but she was relieved could feel it at all.

Indra was certain that in time, the tether would strengthen, and she could contact herself somehow. She was exhausted, yet relieved to have any memory of who she was before arriving in this new and strange land.

But what is beginning a life? To inhabit a body, to immerse yourself into a new world? She felt initially stunned by the task of integrating into a whole new world, and she felt the need to sleep or rest... to sink into a soft heather of wildflowers and process all that had just happened. So Indra laid back, dissolved into the flowers, and napped.

Later she woke, unsure of how long she had rested. She rose up and realized her body was moldable; she could shape-shift. She knew this because as she woke, she was part flower-covered moss and ground as malleable as clay. This was an exciting discovery. As she sat up, rousing her mind from slumber, she willed her body to change shape. Guided by thought, her body shifted. She spent a lot of time playing with the forms she could take. The moss and flowers receded at her will, and she slowly became clear as wind and swirled upwards into the trees, flowing with the sap. Like electricity running up a wire, she made it to the canopy and had a good look around at the lands and mountains. A beautiful pyramidal structure composed of flowing water shimmered in the distance.

The view was natural and alive, nothing dark to speak of; she didn't see any sign of the virus, only mist that hung like a fluffy wool rug over parts of the canopy. It was clear that there was no visible foul play at work here; there was no vibration that was out of the natural rhythm. Indra spotted a giant being swirling about in the wind, a formless wonderful energy that even from this distance felt wise and carefree. The formless being began gaining opacity and opalescence as it drew nearer to her. The glittering wind was taking on shape and density, like that of a giant swarm of birds. It felt as if the being carried messages; the wind appeared to weave through all living things, as it had when Beaudry was chanting.

Excited for connection with new beings, Indra whispered lightly into the wind, "Hello, You are magnificent." With that, the wind snapped as if to rear its head towards Indra. Indra continued, "My name is Indra, and I would be pleased to know you; Beaudry had informed that you can travel far and wide, learning many things."

The wind responded by flying above, creating a spiral around Indra, a giant magnificent bird woman flittering with particles. She finally settled onto the canopy top to join Indra. When seated, the wind was smaller, like a woman wearing a cape of sparkling fluid. She sat across from Indra and spoke:

"I am familiar with you and your landing here. I have awareness of most beings in this realm; my body is stretched across the globe, able to tune into any part of it at any time." The woman gestured with both arms sweeping upwards. "A friend of Beaudry's is a friend of mine."

Indra smiled widely.

The wind spoke again, "As for my name, I have many; but you may call me Aria. I fall in love with all the beings I twist around and through; in many ways, I have no boundaries. I am gifted in knowing the secrets that lie within a soul. I explore them to understand, listening for their whispers and their prayers." Aria gave Indra a knowing look, and slyly eyed her up and down, as if scanning her for any secrets. Indra felt an almost violating tingling sensation all over her body. Aria was eccentric perhaps even a trickster, and Indra was hoping her own secrets were not visible. Aria made an interesting facial expression and shook a thought from her head as she sat back casually.

"Indra, you have a lot to learn about this realm and its nuances. Most souls have been cycling around here for some time, and are familiar with how everything all 'works.' Despite knowing nothing about this realm, there is somehow knowledge inside you... so much random information, like an untapped well."

Indra half perked up at this, feeling once again her boundaries breached by Aria. Aria turned to look at the view, took a deep breath, and her face morphed into something serious.

"You should know, there are many complexities to this place, and I am neutrally invested; I am uninterested in the task of anything to do with sides or hierarchy in these lands. I do bidding for no one." This matter-of-fact statement took Indra by surprise, but she understood, at the very least, that she had a lot to learn. She hoped that despite Aria's aloof demeanor, that she could be an ally and help her learn about this place, as well as track down the virus and its darkness.

"I am not from here, true; I have only just arrived," Indra responded. "I must share with you my reason for coming to this realm, as I am here for a specific reason, one albeit that I can hardly recall." Indra shrugged, unsure of how to go about explaining her life story to a strange being. "I am here to find the darkness that encapsulates the planet. I have been summoned by those of the stars who live among your galaxy to come here and aid. It is not clear to me where I need to start looking. Something has landed here and upset the balance; I intend to discover why, and intervene if I can." Indra was surprised to see confusion on Aria's face. A long and solid silence prompted Indra to ask, "Do you know of what I speak?"

Aria slid side-to-side, dismantling her form and then snapping back into a more sharpened shape. "Nothing encapsulates this place; there is no great deal of strangeness or darkness here. Fengári, the Moon Deity, makes sure of that. But I did see something, a long time ago -- a meteorite fell from the stars. It fell fast, with great heat and force. I was glad to see it had chosen a course for the sea, so when it crashed it merely splashed and sank into the waters. It did create waves that disturbed a few coastlines, but nothing too unusual." Aria shrugged, and had certainty in her voice. "The only thing odd about it was the field around it; it was fuzzy and gray, unlike any energy on the planet." Aria looked down, and then spoke again.

"It was about as strange as your own unusual arrival here. Skipping all formalities and processes."

Indra nodded at this and murmured sighs of disappointment under her breath.

Indra sat and thought quietly for a while, considering the fall of Fengári, and the tangible darkness that the virus emitted. But Aria had mentioned the Moon Deity several times already; and then Indra looked upward and saw that the Moon was no longer ashen-gray, as it was before; instead it was heartbreakingly beautiful, shimmering with muted colors of teal, powder-blue, and greens. Indra was shocked; the concept of time travel hadn't occurred to her. But time was bendable throughout the cosmos -- and she had arrived early. Fengári had not gone dark yet.

It had not crossed her mind that she might have arrived on Earth before Fengári's light went dim. A possible advantage presented itself here, and perhaps there was time to tie the line off before it all unraveled. But *when* had she traveled to? How long did she have? Realizing she had been sitting quietly for some time, she smiled and put on her most casual face, full of charm as she leaned in closely to Aria.

"Well, hmm, if you see anything strange again will you let me know?"

Aria nodded at this. "I can do this for you, but I wonder what you can do for me in return?"

Indra looked up, unsure of what a favor from the wind would entail, but for now she was not concerned with what it might be.

"Of course; I would be honored to return the favor."

Aria became solid and condensed, with an air of seriousness. "I will not ask of anything from you now; I have no specific ideas just yet, but I feel that somehow a favor from you will be useful at some point." Indra smiled and agreed wondering what commitment she had just gotten herself into.

"Just call my name if you wish to know anything, and if I see something of great alarm, I shall find you." With that, the wind swirled, and Aria was gone. Well, as "gone" as wind could be.

Indra, now sitting alone, processed the encounter, relieved that she had arrived in a time when Fengári still shined brightly within the Moon. The incarnation process of Earth was still being orchestrated by a deity. It was surprising that Fengári hasn't made contact with her. *I wonder how many other beings incarnate here beyond her will?* Indra asked herself. From what she could guess, it wasn't many.

Swiftly, soaking back through the leaves and branches of the canopy, Indra melted herself into the forest floor. She lingered in the sparkling darkness of the underbelly of the tree. It was surprisingly spacious and glittering, with roots like stalactites dripping with luminous bead-lets. She was cozy and felt comfortable; this enclosure felt familiar to her, if she could only grasp what it was. She closed her eyes and traced back to her previous epiphany, that she was Celosia; and there was a tree spirit, Nami... then it got fuzzy. Indra stretched farther into herself, and saw a cave, a cave that was her home. *Of course. No wonder this earthen space feels familiar.* Then, something else, importuning from the attic of her mind. She thought of stars and the distant system where Malva lived, and wondered, *Has she found her way to Earth as well?* There could be no way of knowing for sure. Time was now a tangible factor. She would have to wait for more news on from Aria and wait for events to unfold. She would have to be ready to intervene.

Layer 10: Izar - Something Broken, Something Whole

Izar slept deeply on the forest floor that night. He had a blanket and a thin mat that merely provided a clean, dry surface to lay upon. He woke early with the dim light of sunrise, and breathed a deep gulp of fresh morning air. He felt as though all the creatures of the forest were staring at him, and laughing amongst themselves. He set to creating a small filter for water with a funnel, a cloth, clean gravel, and charcoal. He built a small fire and set to boiling the water he had filtered; then, pulling dried herbs from his bag, he brewed a warm drink from plants he and his mother had grown.

He sat for a long while and centered himself, to prepare for a journey, one of the sole reasons he had come to the Irati forest on this occasion. He had packed with him a small bag of dried mushrooms that Elenuta had harvested on the coast last fall: *Psilocybe azurescens*, a potent mushroom that opened the door to another world. Or at least, that was what she had told him. His body was tense with the morning air and nerves.

He had overheard Elenuta and his mother speaking about them, where to find them and how a journey was a serious endeavor, to be treated with respect. A ceremony. She had cautioned him on the potency, and he planned to take most of what she had given him. Seven small caps, and he would see how it unfolded. Izar had fasted before his journey, aside from the floral herbal brew; however, he did set aside some dried fruit in case he became hungry and needed it quickly without having to rummage about in an altered state.

Izar's palms were slightly clammy with nerves as he held his little friends in his hands. After a few deep breaths, he put them in his mouth and chewed. The taste did slightly turn his stomach, so he promptly drank his brew to wash it down. The brew had early blooming herbs in it -- lemon balm, a variety of mints, and astragalus root from last season. He also added some dried rose petals from last year's harvest, to lend a floral and loving aroma to ease his heart. These flavors quickly removed the fungal taste from his tongue.

While he waited for the mushrooms to take effect, he brewed another pot of herbal tea and put out his fire, just in case he lost himself too much to handle such matters. Then he waited, and breathed; he took in the morning light and listened to the birdsongs. When he noticed that the surrounding forest was breathing with him in woven patterns of symmetry, he realized the fungi were taking effect. He stood to walk around, with the strong urge to relieve himself, and made his way over to a more private area to tend to his bodily needs. After this, the warmth of the rising sun, felt like glory on his skin, and he rinsed his hands in the pond. He found that he was overwhelmed by the sensation of love and beauty for the living world, and the world unseen to most. His heart was pounding in his chest, and then seemed to melt like butter in a dish. The sensation of his body and its limbs was almost silly somehow, and the texture of his flesh felt spongey.

Izar laughed aloud and stretched, using his body like a finely-tuned instrument to create handstands and climb amongst the trees. Sounds became louder, like the sound of fabric brushing past his ear, or the sound of mulch beneath his feet. In time, the trip became much stronger, and the need to lie down was sudden. He chose to lie against an oak tree at the edge of the pool, where there was soft moss and small flowers like creeping thyme that made a perfect bed. A state of reverie and unity overcame him; was this what he was looking for?

Thoughts passed like flashes of light, and images along with them, of places and people he had never met; they flew by quickly, with no way to keep track of them or make sense of them. At the height of his trip, he wasn't sure if his eyes were closed or open. He felt as if the tree was holding him like a lover, a comfort he had never before known; he felt whole. It was in this dreamy state that he heard whispering in his ear, in a language he did not understand. This did not startle him; in fact, he almost didn't open his eyes.

When he slowly lifted his lids, he saw the light outline of a woman, lying next to him where the root of the oak tree had been. Her outline was faint, but her eyes were clear, as clear as any he had ever seen. He looked into the silvery lavender pools and sank; he saw beyond time and into the layers that composed her. His eyes welled with liquid, and he could not speak. Whether this was due to the mushrooms or the sight of her he did not know.

She blinked slowly and tilted her head at him; her question, beyond language, was clear in his mind. "Who are you?"

He responded, "I am Izar." When he spoke his name out loud in a horse, hushed voice, the sound felt foreign to his vocal cords in his current state of psychedelic limbo. She responded in the same strange way; in his mind he heard her say, "Indra." She looked at him, and again lay her head upon his shoulder.

They lay together like pieces of clay, sinking into one another atop the moss beneath them. He burned the image of her into his memory so he could never forget, fearing she would fade with waning trip. Her iridescent skin was dark slightly golden, as if she were the source of light itself. Her hair was twisted and long, with sporadic curls woven with leaves and vibrant blue flowers he recognized, star-shaped *Gentiana acaulis*. Her face was small and feminine, soft, sharp cheek bones and a small pointed chin, almost heart-shaped. Her eyes were slightly wide-set and level with her ears, which were so small and sharp that they barely peeked out from beneath her hair.

Even though she felt solid next to him, her form was slightly fluid in shape and density, morphing in each new moment. Izar did not want the moment to pass or for her to disappear. He let his mind flow with feelings of great appreciation and adoration, in the hope she would pick up on his thoughts, as she had done with her name. In the brevity of that moment, he knew that he would be hers for all of time... and perhaps somehow already had been. He drifted off.

Suddenly, he awoke in the twilight of dusk with a great hunger in his stomach and clarity in his mind. He sat up, immediately looking to his side for Indra. Despite his hope, he had somehow known that she would be gone. Where she had lain, the oak tree root lay now, large and curving. He breathed out and stood, only to quickly fall as his foot caught a twist of the root. Falling forward like crumpled canvas, he landed on his arms and chest, and overall he was undamaged and unharmed; but he heard a crunch in his coat pocket that set his hands scrambling to his talisman from the sea.

There were a few small crumbles of dried barnacles at the bottom of the pocket, and the object was split nearly in half. Sighing with slight disappointment, he pulled it out from its home. With the clean break across its middle, he saw that it was not a rock, but actually was a small box, beaten by time and water. On the inside lay faded satin, like spider webs, as well as a small ring.

It was tarnished silver, with three stones cut and facetted into different sizes: a sapphire the largest, a pale aquamarine, and the smallest, a peach-colored topaz. It was simple and beautiful. He smiled to himself upon learning that he had been carrying a ring around in his pocket all this while, and the day he found Indra was the day he discovered his talisman's true form. Was it a sign?

He held the ring in his palm, inspecting it, knowing that he must give this ring to Indra somehow, so she might know how he felt. As he kneeled to stand, his head went dizzy, and all the blood in his body seemed to thicken with the early summer chill. In need of a blood-sugar boost, he bit into some black figs he had left out for easy eating.

After this, he was wide awake and thirsty, so he drank and drank his now-cold herbal brew till he could feel his body rehydrate. With no light left to do much, it was the perfect time for star gazing. He rummaged through his pack with cold, numb fingers and produced a pair of gloves, a warm knitted hat, and a sweater. Sitting, he slowly assembled himself, the soft coverage giving him warmth and relief. Grateful for sweaters, he smiled with how cozy he was; he brought his mat and wool blanket over to the tree, and laid down beside the curving trunk. His head was positioned so he could just barely see the stars at the edge of the tree line. Watching them sparkle above him, they all still moved a little, as if the sky were breathing, as his mushrooms were still slightly in his system.

He spoke tiny pieces of poems to Indra, and rested his gloved hand along the tree as if it were her again. Izar hoped that she was real, not just a figment of the mushroom trip. He chewed on these thoughts as lights of blue and white zipped around the forest, and a gust of wind held the oak tree's canopy in a rustling for quite some time. It was the only tree rustling, and Izar took that as a sign that she was indeed real;

in the moments following, he focused to keep his mind clear. He had practiced thoughtlessness many times to the record Elenuta had given to him; he had found his inner stillness was a muscle to tone, just like any other in his body. During this stillness, a pair of owls hooted for a long while; he admired their sonnet, listening to them converse while the creek bubbled and frogs croaked. He was truly in a state of peace.

The wind whirled again, taking with it a torrent of old leaves and lichen. During the commotion, Izar heard a voice. "Eithar, is it you?"

Straining to hear it clearly, he was now sitting straight up and lifting the hat away from his good ear. "It's me, Izar. Indra, is it you? I wish to see you again..." Izar sat with his blanket at his lap, reaching into his pocket to find the ring that lay safely against the lint and crumbled barnacles. "I have a gift for you. The love and beauty you have shared with me is beyond anything I have ever known in this life; I know it was for but a short moment, but looking into your eyes has enlivened something within me. It feels ancient, like a memory almost forgotten."

Izar extended his hand with the ring and held it towards the tree. "This is a token of my appreciation, to have felt such beauty and depth. I will dedicate myself to being near you for all of time." Izar felt as if he were witnessing this promise and sentiment coming out of him, rather than thinking of the words to use. He was unsure from what well of passion this declaration was pouring. Nearly shaking with nerves, he remained as still as possible, holding out the ring with his eyes steadily focused on the oak tree in the dark.

Little lights like dust motes flew towards him, softly hovering and congregating around the tree. In just a few seconds, more came to surround the tree and Izar, like a thick shimmering membrane, providing a subtle glow. There was giggling and rustling coming from the darker parts of the forest, but that did not shake Izar's attention, although it did excite him to know that something was actually happening in his life. He knew with his whole soul that Indra's eyes are the eyes he had been seeking.

This was the beginning of the life he was destined for.

Izar felt thousands of eyes peering at him from all directions, and these witnesses fueled his confidence. He wanted the audience of Indra's kin to witness, to make it more meaningful. Thinking back to Elenuta and his mother Lila, he remembered them doing blood spells under the Moon; he would watch as he hid behind a tree, intently curious on the rituals order and presentation. And never had he had a moment to utilize such a ritual, as there was nothing he really desired to use such forces for -- until now.

With that, he drew his blade from the loop of his belt and cleared his mind of any clutter from the past or future. He let his body ground into the Earth like a tree, while concurrently extending his soul upwards, into the stars. Izar inhaled a long, slow breath to speak his heart. "Indra, for my whole life, I have sought a soul like yours, a beauty that is not only produced from the physical sight of you, but a measured weight that comes from your soul. A weighted gravity, like a star that I cannot help but orbit. I must know more. I want to spend hours just learning how you breathe. My heart is yours, whether you want it or not.

"With this ring, I promise dedication to your service, and with my blood I show my loyalty and will to protect you always."

At this Izar made a slice into his palm, and blood welled slowly. It definitely hurt a bit more than he expected, but that was no true concern of his in this moment. He pressed the ring and the blood onto the highest curve of the tree's root, and held his palm there, pressing with his eyes closed, focusing on the feelings that were coursing through him. Feelings and emotions drive the strength of magick; the emotions ride out on the electromagnetic waves that emit from the heart's field. If the magick has enough directed emotion, it is far more likely to echo through reality and manifest. He continued speaking with his eyes closed.

"Perhaps through feeling this blood, you will know me and my family's linage. Perhaps you will detect my passion and respect for life, or perhaps you will think of me as dramatic and over-the-top; but I feel I must make it known to you, Indra, lady of the forest, where my heart is anchored."

Indra, unbeknownst to Izar, stood invisibly behind him, observing his pledge. This was not the first time a human man had stumbled past her tree and vowed instant infatuation. Over time and observation, she had witnessed the broad spectrum of humanity's behavior. In fact, she knew men very well. The arrival of the virus changed had everything, including human behavior. She no longer fell foolishly for their passionate pleas and animalistic needs, for they became more violent and aggressive as the virus slowly infected the world. But this one, this man, she weighed, was different.

Over and over again, with great hope, Indra had awaited Eithar's arrival, searching each pair of eyes with determination; and until this day, no eyes had shown as much promise as this silver pair had. Was this Eithar's soul, lost in human form? Time on Earth had warped her perception, hardened it and encapsulated it with the cycles and linearity. It felt as if oceans of time lay between this moment and her last moment with him on her golden disc. Time was like a dull blade on her memories, whittling timber into toothpicks. This potential of having found him softened her posture; she stood behind Izar as he knelt. It *could* be him, with a new name and new face, as she herself had adopted long ago. And what luck: such a beautiful form knelt before her, perhaps one of the most handsome humans she had ever seen.

Izar was on his knees at this point, and as he removed his bleeding hand from the oak root, he left the ring sparkling in the sparse moonlight. Even though it was covered in Izar's blood, it still burned brightly. To his surprise, his blood was absorbed into the tree with great speed, vanishing before his eyes. With that, Indra, wispy and translucent, stepped slowly from the tree, her eyes locked onto Izar's. Without breaking eye contact, she walked toward him until they stood but inches apart. Indra lifted her hand and placed it gently on the back of his neck, while she placed her other hand onto his chest, just over his heart. Indra spoke, and he understood in his mind what she was saying; but his ears did not recognize the language. It was not Euskara or Spanish.

"You give me curiosity, and I accept your gift and your loyalty. Earlier you consumed the fruit body of our realm; it can make it easier for you to see my realm and the beings in it. It still courses through your system, and it is allowing me to touch you and speak to you without me bringing you into our realm. In the past, I have brought humans into my realm, only to see them relax into bliss and in time blossom into madness. When I bring them back, they are never the same, and have trouble integrating back into their world, as the veil separating these realms has been torn instead of slowly opened." She paused, as if looking back in time, shaking her head in regret and guilt.

"I can see that your veil is open already; your pulse is steady and calm. You are a seer of both worlds, and can see me and my realm at your will. The magick of the fruit body has enhanced the gift you already possess. Will you join me, where it is safer, within my realm? Time will pass much slower there; the math is not exact, but when you return to your world, months may have passed. This can cause problematic situations in your life if you stay too long; be aware of this."

Indra stopped speaking, and it almost appeared that she was listening to something while in a trance. A small bead of translucent silver slowly rolled from her eye, as if she had heard the world's greatest song. She blinked and now looked at Izar; her sharp eyes had softened and darted around slowly, as realization spread into her awareness. Whatever it was, she quickly regained her more guarded and clear demeanor and spoke again.

"Will you come into my realm, where it is safer for me?"

Izar nodded with calm certainty; he did not feel the need to speak at all. Indra nodded back. With her hands still fixed onto his neck and chest, a rush of wind blew towards them, and the small dust-mote lights were pulled towards them like a vacuum. Izar felt hot and cold rush from his feet to his face, like a cold sweat. He could tell they had arrived when the night around them melted into purple and peach twilight. The sky was filled to the brim with stars, so many more than he had ever seen, even out in the darkness of the forest with no lights for a hundred kilometers.

Here, everything was still placed as it had been, but it was altered. The tree root still held the ring, and Izar looked at Indra and reached past her to take the ring and present it to her. Her eyes followed his hands, and she tilted her head slightly at him. When they both faced each other again, Izar place the ring it into the palm of her hand.

Indra clasped it and bowed her head slightly. She found a finger for the ring and put it on, a wild grin spreading over her face. Izar looked down, and bent to remove his shoes and his socks, with a little wobble to his balance. When his bare feet felt the cashmere softness of the ground in the elemental kingdom, he felt pure magnetic electricity rush up through his body. His vision was sharpened, and he could see all the beings that truly existed; in a nearby flower shrub, each petal and leaf was its own dancing being. Each piece of the shrub moved independently of one another, and yet somehow the shrub moved as one. The color spectrum was miraculous, far beyond that of his realm. The integration was overwhelming, and it brought Izar to tears. He silently wept at the marvelous beauty around him, for it was actually there all along.

Indra watched him as he wept, and wiped a tear rolling down his nose. She whispered something into the drop of water and sent it to fly away with what looked like the swirling wind.

Indra took Izar by the crook of his elbow and guided him around the tree; then she squeezed his arm more tightly, and in a flash they moved across the landscape. They stopped abruptly at an overlook where there was a seating area completed by swirls of rock, wood, and moss. Beautiful cushions, fashioned from furs, were scattered about. Indra motioned for Izar to sit, and she made sounds he could not replicate if he tried.

Following those sounds, small creatures swirled into the area, bringing a large platter filled with colors and smells that instantly soothed Izar. Indra encouraged him to eat and become one with the realm, to regain some of his strength from making the transition. Each bite had gorgeous flavors that were delicate and rich all at once. There were fruits he had never experienced, assorted nuts, small sliced meats that were layered with herbs and wrapped in dark, leafy greens, small wooden cups with warm nectar, and clear, chewy biscuits that Indra called Jubees.

She immediately took one and ate it with a sigh of satisfaction. Izar picked up one as well, and savored its flavor, which was hard to pin down. He fancied them; they were delicious and filling. He hadn't realized how hungry he had become. When he felt sated and even a little buzzed from the food, Indra asked him to tell her the story of his life, and how it was that he had ended up here in her forest. She asked him to spare no details, so it took a great deal of time. It was not obvious to Izar how time passed in this new realm; he didn't feel tired, nor did he ever need to use the bathroom, which was a plus, seeing as there were so many creatures everywhere that he could not be sure what was private.

Indra listened with delight, curiosity, and extreme focus to his story. He even got her to laugh a few times, which startled them both, as her laughter was so radiant and piercing that it roused the nearby animals. She had a great curiosity for his stories at sea, and how it was the ring came into his possession.

As they sat quietly, reflecting on the story of his life, Izar asked if he could embrace her. When she replied with a nod, he moved over to sit behind her. Sitting taller than her, he put a leg on either side of her, and firmly and gently wrapped his arms around her, feeling her breasts lightly resting on his forearms. Slow and easy breaths rose and fell from her belly, where his arms rested. His chin he placed to the side of her head, and closed his eyes, knowing he would sit this way forever if he could.

This comforted them both so much they didn't dare to move for some time. Although Izar felt the desire to lay with her, he would rather be invited than interject his desires onto her. So instead he focused on her breath, and learned all of the secrets each exhale released. One would be surprised at the sort of secrets dispensed from the lungs. What Izar heard the clearest was loss and grief; for whom or what he was not certain, but it was tangible.

Layer 11: Paesh - Somewhere on Earth in 2019

Gray skies hung low at the tree line; the air was thick with quiet. My small, shiny black dress shoes felt too formal for this occasion. I continued slowly down the sidewalk, holding a balloon in one hand and a note in the other. The official plan was to attach the balloon string to the letter and send it on up. I knew that if God really sat up in his heavenly place, then he could certainly receive a simple latex balloon with a note in tow. The letter read:

God, if you really are real, I'll need some proof.

This was written in green crayon, and honestly I'm not sure if I even knew how to spell or form words; but he's God, after all, he'll know. I fumbled with that shiny, useless string they use for balloons. Once it was questionably secured, I sent that note up and walked away. While walking away, I smiled at a woman with flowers in her hair; she was beautiful and seemed out of place." Paesh rubbed the palms of her hands together as if they were cold, and continued speaking with a shrug. "The memory itself is foggy, and I'm sure that each time I think back on it, it shifts ever so slightly. So I likely floated on to the next moment of childhood. Being five, my brain hadn't fully developed into a conscious state, so I get why it's so dreamlike. I digress..." Paesh looked over the coffee table to find her glass of water, and took a sip. Her eyes met Genevieve's, who kindly smiled and nodded for her to continue.

"It was difficult, to say the least -- being young, I mean. Not one adult will take you seriously. There's a loneliness that comes with a cultureless society, where community is dispersed and made of cardboard. I was lied to, placated, my body wasn't my own, and nobody cared about my dreams that felt so real. It wasn't all doom and gloom, though; I have many fond memories glistening like pearls in my mind..." Peash sighed a long sigh and casually took another sip of water; and then, chuckling, she rolled her neck slowly, casually stretching as if exiting the memories.

The therapist shifted in her seat and had another sip from of her ceramic mug, which was boldly molded into the shape of a woman's torso, with small, perky breasts. Steam swirled up from the quirky but functional mug. Her therapist was very pro-women, supporting women through their personal injustices.

Genevieve's face was serene as she inhaled the steam; she blew into her tea, and looked over at Paesh with cool nonchalance. "How does that make you feel about trust, Paesh?"

Paesh nodded and understood what her question revealed, and sat with that discomfort. "The inevitable truth of this Earth. The media-based socialization and dogmatic brainwashing that most countries on this Earth utilize. Blind belief, built on a foundation of lies, only to gain control over the herd!" Heat boiling in her throat, Paesh sat taller in her seat while she spoke. "It makes me feel that trust is not something I easily give, and I can see how far back in time that goes. Probably back into my past lives, too," Paesh joked as she ran her fingers through her short lavender hair and looked out the window. A gust of wind played with the leaves of one sleek madrone tree. It was peculiar, as the gust only circled around that one tree, which stood among many. Paesh found herself staring, intrigued, as the other trees sat perfectly still. Both women fell into a comfortable silence, and they sat in that for some time.

"I can completely see where you're coming from; our culture doesn't exactly breed trust. It's hard to rebuild a cracked foundation. But I know that with small steps in your present life, you can make moves toward being more open and trusting, with men in particular. Even I struggle with trust; it's a daily practice to move through it," Genevieve said, while following Paesh's eyes out the window. When Paesh's gaze finally met hers, she was greeted with a smile and a look that showed that Genevieve also truly struggled with trust. Even therapists sometimes need therapists. They both fell quiet again, soaking in the words and energy in the room.

Genevieve's office was relaxed; her plant colony was strong, and the decor was simple, bright, and clean. There was a light scent of sage lingering, while a diffuser dispersed lemongrass vapors that danced above the small, purring machine. Peash loved being in her office, as it was such a safe space. Genevieve was such an open and classy woman, one who was well-traveled and wise, strong yet sweet as a button. She felt timeless, as if she were old and young all at once. Ultimately, though, the weight of her wisdom gave her away. Although well into her late forties, you would never guess it by looking at her face.

"Genevieve, before we dissect it further, let me remind you that I think our time is up. My insurance doesn't cover these sessions. Let's call it a day. I don't want to run over on time again."

Genevieve looked out the window and laughed, with a little discomfort in her tone.

"Ah yes, the dreaded money talk." Genevieve said before she took a sip out of her mug. Her jet-black hair curled into large, perfect ringlets, brushing her shoulders. "Paesh, you've been coming here for a year or so now, and I rather enjoy your mind and company. Pardon my lack of professionalism, but I find myself seeing you as a friend, and I enjoy the expanse of our conversation and admire your openness."

She sucked in a deep breath, and let it out as she spoke, "I don't think I can see you in a patient/client relationship dynamic, nor bill you anymore. I don't intend to cause you discomfort or make you feel unwanted; I'm happy to refer you to another therapist if you still wish continue with that support." Genevieve had hopeful eyes, and fidgeted with her pen while she waited for a response.

It was Paesh's turn to laugh awkwardly, feeling so relieved that Genevieve was opening the door for this conversation. "I certainly didn't expect you to say that, but I'm glad you did. Genevieve, that is perfectly fine. I don't think I'll be needing a referral; I only wanted to sort out my feelings those first couple months I saw you. My... incident was my only reason for my coming, although all the time spent here has proven beneficial for me. I see you as a friend; you're such an admirable woman, and I feel so inspired by you. Your presence has a calming weight to it. I don't often meet people like you."

Genevieve made an humble nod at flood of compliments, giving an approving gesture. "Phew. Well, that was hard for me to bring up, but I'm glad you're not offended." The two women stood, Genevieve much taller than Paesh. Genevieve opened up for a hug, and they shared a small sigh and a laugh.

Paesh stood back and was quick to busy herself, folding the blanket she had used on her lap.

"My next client is probably out there -- he's always early -- so I'm going to get ready for that session. Don't worry about paying for this one, okay? Oh, and by the way, there's this bonsai class next week I think you may really enjoy. I can email you the information, it will be our first outing as friends."

Setting the folded blanket down, Peash nodded with a slight bow. "Great! I would adore the class; please do send me the information. Thanks, Gen."

At that, Paesh was out the door and on her way past the reception area. Seated there anxiously was Gen's early client, a man who looked like his name was Todd. He was too large a man for the small chair; slumped and sitting, he fidgeted, making his windbreaker scream with swishing sounds. He was anxious, that much was clear; so, avoiding eye contact, Paesh gave him a wide berth to avoid close proximity. When she cleared the hallway, she was a free bird gliding down the staircase.

On her way across town, Paesh stopped to grab a new dream journal at a local shop that made them with recycled, handmade paper. It was a little more expensive than most, but what else was money for? After she procured the journal, she made her way to the post office. Her mother had shipped her a package, one that required pickup; perhaps there was something valuable inside. The post office was on the route home, so she didn't mind. She just hoped the box would fit on her bicycle.

The post office was fairly slow, and there was the most pleasant person helping her at the window. His name was Warren, he was all smiles and easy movements. He wasn't in a hurry, nor moving too slow; he was relaxed and clearly enjoying the day. He handed off the package and checked her ID.

"Got a big one for you Paesh," He said with a small laugh to himself.

"I'll bet you do," Paesh retorted with air of flirtation. It was a big package and with some proper tinkering, she would be able to strap it down to her bike; thank God she had extra bungee cords in her bike bag.

She strapped the box to her bike, put in her headphones, and thought she'd call her mom while she rode for a little, to let her know she'd received the package. The phone only rang twice, as if Mom were waiting by the phone, expecting a call. "Hello, Paesh!" her mother boomed from the other end.

"Hi Mom, I got your package today. What did you send me, anyways? It's pretty big," Paesh said, navigating traffic and heading down the street.

"What's that wind sound?" her mother asked, annoyed.

"I'm on my bike, Mom. Can you hear me?"

"Oo, okay, be careful! I sent it because I had a dream about my father, your grandfather, the one you never met. In the dream, he wanted me to send you some of his last effects. There's a journal in there, something that was very dear to him. I have read it many times now, and I'll admit, it is strange... and difficult, because it is mostly in Euskara. I had to translate it." She fell silent for a moment.

Paesh was navigating past a crew of surfers on cruiser bikes while he mom was talking, and admittedly wasn't really listening all that well. "Okay, well, that sounds interesting, Mom, thanks for thinking of me," Paesh said timidly, unsure if her mother was done speaking.

"Oh, he would want you to read it. I'm clearing out the house anyways, and that dream was just so damn vivid! I thought, why not send it, you can get to know him," her mother said, with an eccentric flare in her voice paired with a shred of heartbreak, as if she were on the cusp of tears.

"I would love to do that, Mom. I'll let you know what I think when I finish it," Paesh said, curious about what her mom was talking about. She had seen only one picture of him, and even now the sight of his face escaped her.

"All right, dear, your father and I are about to sit down for dinner. I'll talk to you soon. Love you."

"Enjoy dinner, love you too, bye," Paesh said, almost automatically. She took the headphones from her ears and biked homeward.

The weather was agreeable, and post-sunset colors draped the scene with soft pastels. Riding her bicycle across town, strategizing through the park, using its small, paved bike paths to avoid the city's vehicle-clogged streets, flying gracefully, the small lavender curls that framed her face lifted wildly. Her breathe was strained as she exerted her way up the hill, gearing down with the suicide shifters on her drop bars. Her tendons pulled on her shins in different directions, her thighs hot and numb from the climb. When at the top of the winding bike paths, her view faced west towards sundown.

The grand city of Santa Cruz hummed, and the ocean lapping in the distance, a juxtaposition of worlds: From its grid-lain lights and towers, creating an echoing cacophony of machinery and bustle, to the flowing colors of the natural sunset sky and silhouetted tree lines, framing the view of the wild ocean. Paesh enjoyed the duality, but preferred the natural world, the small, peaceful sounds culminating in a symphony orchestrated by the natural rhythms. It was as soothing world that created the opportunity for Paesh to breathe full breath, a dilated larynx filling the bottom chambers of her lungs. The kind of breaths that caused her spine to tingle, almost sensually.

Her face was damp with sweat, glistening as she surrendered to some rewarding deep breaths at the top of the hill. Wind was spiraling through the boughs of each tree, as many different birds made night-time calls from their territory. These sounds layered with the croaks of distant frogs and crickets sharing tales that only the squeaking bats could listen to and understand.

Paesh dismounted her bike, and walked it into a grove of trees. She listened to all of the sounds amongst the comforting company of scattered humans, animals, the Monterey cypress, madrone, magnolia, redwoods, and a eucalyptus grove, a uniquely Californian mélange. A hillside teaming with greenery and movement created a wondrous body of texture, rich with life, that Paesh meandered through on foot, her bike at her side.

Luckily it was a cloud-free evening, a clear night. Peachy colors melted into the muted pink of the belt of Venus, while the swell of navy blue expanded across the sky. There was a comfort in this palette of colors; it calmed her nervous system. Finding a place to sit, Paesh rested atop the hill until the stars arrived, watching them slowly appear, as if God herself were lighting them one by one. Paesh kept her face to the stars until her neck began to ache from the strain. She was refueled by the starlight shining on her skin; when she felt recharged, she knew it was time to go home.

While rolling off on her bike, Paesh spotted an owl that had landed nearby with its cyclical screeching. She stopped in her tracks; rarely did she get to see owls. She cupped her hands in a specific way and made an owl call. Long ago, she had learned from a young girl at a camp in which she was a counselor.

As the young girl had instructed, she cupped her hands and found the channel for breath. This produced a clear owlesque hoot rhythm that made the owl go quiet. Suddenly, with wings outstretched, the owl set to soar, circling just over her head and landing back at its perch. Bonding with wild animals who were so naturally reserved filled Paesh with a secret joy, and probably fueled her ego a little as well. Whether or not the owl's movement was due to territoriality, making the wrong call, or intimidation, she still internally relished the act of connection and recognition.

Giddy, with a huge smile, Paesh looked up to see a man staring at her with a shocked expression, the whites of his eyes bright in the dark. Slightly startled, she leapt onto her bike and rode past him with caution. The young woman of 31 had always been an alluring oddity in town; her beauty turned heads and churned curiosity when she was in public, like an icy comet. She avoided most strange men like the plague, as she never knew what to expect.

She was as much aloof as she was aware, a deep-feeler full of mystery. In her early twenties, she traveled from town to town, seeking knowledge from those she met on her travels. From time to time she was pulled aside by those who could read energy or palms. They would comment on her potential in magic, and her soul's origin. A palm reader once found her in a grocery store and recognized her psychic gifts, relaying what he thought were important messages. Although sometimes startling, these messages were nourishment for her soul, and recognition for parts of herself that she normally hid from others. These moments of recognition were rare enough to make them special memories that kept her going when life felt mundane, little encouragements giving the undertow of her life meaning, a pull towards a greater plan and purpose.

As she pedaled, she barely held onto the handles, maintaining a poised posture for the duration of her ride. Her eyes, the shade of silver and charcoal gray, were invitingly big and shaped like the center of a *vesica piscis*. They were vigilant in the night on the dark streets towards home.

Parking her bike in the shed out back and locking it, she was humming sultry blues to herself. Turning to face the Moon shining on her garden, she went to pick some herbs by moonlight, using her garden scissors hanging on the fence post. Marsh-mallow flowers, delicate and white, were illuminated by the Moon, as if Hecate herself were imbued in each twisted bloom. While gathering herbs, she sighed with great admiration for the growth of the amazing plants.

"Oh, *Althea officinalis*, may you bloom even more after I collect some of your sweet flowers, thank you!" She exclaimed, when her eyes met the ground she sighed and raised her eyebrows, "I really must catch up on my weeding, there so many little clovers and crabgrass coming up!" she said, getting distracted looking down around the marsh-mallow plants. Sighing, she drifted over towards the veggies. "Looking sturdy and promising for all my fermenting, canning, and drying." Paesh plucked a cucumber while speaking to herself pleasantly, enjoying her own company. She also harvested some Roman chamomile and yarrow for her nightly herbal infusion.

The Roman chamomile smelled so sweet it was intoxicating, the scent clinging to her hands well after she put the herbs down in her kitchen. Growing her own herbs was a continual experiment. Paesh was orderly and timely as much as she was fluid and forgetful. Her work schedule kept her very busy, and added structure to her months. She checked her emails and messages while the water boiled. The light-blue glow of her cell phone lit up her face, making her look rather zombified. After responding to the sparse messages, she turned the phone onto airplane mode and put it in a special box to block EMF emissions.

With her brew ready and in hand, she made her way upstairs, to engage in some relaxation and stretching. While lying upon her floor, sheepskin shamelessly beneath her, she worked into some yoga poses and stretched. A typical evening on a day off, where she felt unhurried and relaxed. Slow breaths through the throat and belly were mindful and moving with the poses. Despite Paesh's focus, aimless thoughts flew past her awareness. Some days were clearer than others, but today was particularly thick with abstract memories and emotional attachments. She breathed deeper and moved herself into the present moment, stilling the waters of her mind.

She often felt like her mind was a radio, tuning into different stations. People from throughout her life -- friends, family, co-workers and men she had slept with -- had their own stations. She never knew why people were tuning in, but it was obvious when they did.

As a child, Paesh would practice visualizing techniques, seeing that everyone was connected by way of small, thin threads. She would imagine herself sitting at the center of a light-blue web of threads. When someone thought about her, that thread vibrated and connected her to a vision of that person. To an untrained eye, these points of contact would seem like passing thoughts, but when trained, the difference became discernible. Like two-way radios, contact could flow in both directions, although most people had their volume down, so they rarely heard the calls. This practice and occurrence was something she didn't share with too many people, because when she did share, and they discovered that her abilities were not a charismatic embellishment, they would distance themselves in consternation.

Paesh sat up and took a sip of her herbal infusion, the essence from her moonlit garden moving past her tongue, feeling the alien sensation of the muscles in her throat moving to swallow the liquid. She cleared her mind of past and future.

Resuming her stretching, she moved into child's pose, rocking her hips lightly from side to side, as to iron out any thoughts that wrinkled her posture. She ended her stretching session by just lying flat on her back. Her body's outline could be seen in the amber warm glow of candles and a salt lamp. A small stick of sandalwood incense twisted around her altar and the plants that garnished it.

Faces passed along her field of vision; they were faces she didn't recognize from her life, but ones that she had seen before in her mind. Peeking open one eye, Paesh rubbed her sternum with calm nonchalance.

Rising to look out the east-facing window, Paesh felt level with the Moon, drawn into the spell of her white circular surface, flirtatious trickery beaming down from her mysterious sphere, only ever showing the world one side of herself.

A kindred and auspicious connection to the Moon traced back into Paesh's past.

Starting at the age of seven, she would sneak out of her parents' house, quietly, so as to not wake any of her sisters. Bundled in a blanket, she would sit on the ground with a candle and Moon-gaze. It was never clear how long she would sit out there staring -- that part of her memory was fuzzy -- but she felt almost hypnotized by the need to do so. A strange feeling was held in the Moon, or vacant from it rather, as if no one was home and it was just the empty shell. Like a hermit crab long gone and crawled on...

Laughing at her own peculiarity, Paesh cracked the window open for a stream of fresh air. She was ready for sleep, so she turned off the lights and blew out the candles, and crawled into her bed.

The carpentry of the house was obscure, built with creative nooks and spaces. Her bedding area was perfect egg-shaped nook that fit her bed and some modest shelving. A skylight free of debris met the cedar paneling that lined most of the walls. Below, in the pillow fluff of it all, lay Paesh in peach and purple bedding. Textures of variety swaddled her; silks, cottons, and fake cashmere velvets blended into the perfect nest. Crickets dutifully sang the proper buzzing for dreaming. She drifted off to sleep.

There were no busy roads nearby, nor power lines overhead; it was simply quiet. The property, being on the edge of town, was secluded. Only the big lot and the wild trees bore witness to the simple life of Paesh. Set back from the long driveway, the eccentrically built home was small and quaint. Autonomy was hers, and it was a rental of course, but it was roommate free. Maybe one day, a lease-to-own contract would become a reality; Paesh had always hoped, anyway.

A light blinked on in the middle of the darkness, the warm glow of a crystal lamp beaming from the skylight. Paesh, with one eye open, quickly uncapped a pen and began to scribble down a long-winded entry on the last page of her thick dream journal.

My dream, waking at 02:29 on 8/22/2019:

A simple dream, with a simple setting, a dark place, but it's comforting. I see a small circle of light in the distance to my left. The scene changes, and suddenly there is water everywhere, making insane patterns and fractals. I feel shocked, but proud. There is a naked man, super-hot, with silver eyes (he looked like an Italian model I cut from a magazine to glue onto a vision board I made years ago). I watch him go. I see an oak tree. Red eyes of an angry man. Then I see a fire, as I wake up.

Paesh put her dream journal down and shut off the light; the dark room was quiet, and she drifted back off to sleep.

Paesh awoke later that morning, later than she had hoped to on her second day off. Slowly, she assembled herself, pushing through the monotony of morning chores. Watching the water fill up the washing machine, adding some biodegradable soap in a little at a time. The sound of the water roaring and splashing into the metal machine washed out all the small sounds and filled the laundry room. Paesh was completely in the zone, enjoying that her senses were muffled by this one giant sound. Just existing. A helpful sensory technique to drown out her typically overstimulated nervous system.

Paesh, having synesthesia, rarely got to drown out the intensity of her experiences. Synesthesia is a "condition," or rather an alternative sensory structure. Sensory information from one cognitive pathway in the brain can lead to sensory activity in an unrelated separate cognitive pathway. It had finally seen acknowledgement in psychology in the last couple of years, which gave Paesh hope that she wasn't insane.

Slam went the lid of the washing machine, and she was off to the next task: cleaning up the kitchen, putting away clean dishes, and making a small snack.

After she was nourished, she went out to weed the garden and harvest any vegetables and herbs that were ready, while listening to a podcast. Halfway through the podcast, she ended up switching to music, preferring to add some dance to her gardening tasks.

Gardening came easily to Paesh; in fact, most seeds wanted to grow for her. Blessed with parents who took pride in their own garden, she was raised tilling and weeding. Watching her family's food grow gave her connection. Her father, a first-generation Lebanese immigrant, was keen on gardening but was never the main green thumb. He would share some of his Teta's traditions and hacks to utilize the resources properly, through: bed-building techniques, making filtered rain-catchment systems, and tricks to keep the gophers away. He was crafty and capable, but he was a little rough around the edges for delicate plant care.

"Yalla, habibi, yalla!" he would call, waving to Paesh, (the only interested daughter) to come and see that his peppers were flowering. "Ahsant," she would say, encouraging her father and also appeasing his pride, which was an important factor for the peace in the household, or so she thought before therapy.

Paesh's mother, second-generation French, the true green thumb and producer of the garden's bounty. She was hardworking and just as excited as her husband when plants produced. They did not always get along in a healthy way, but they made a great team, and at the very least a functioning one.

"Come on, you stubborn root, will you *please* come out of the ground? You yellow docks are all the same, stubbornly holding onto your dark comforts!" Paesh muttered, while her arm was nearly elbow deep in the soil, attempting to extract the root. Although its medicinal properties were amazing as a blood cleanser, it was also highly invasive in her garden, dropping seeds if left forgotten to flower. Perhaps the land was trying to tell her something; sometimes when plants are invasive, perhaps they are just trying to be helpful.

Paesh worked her way around the garden, flitting from one task to the next.

When the Sun was high, she was finished with her gardening tasks. She brought everything in to wash, hang, or store, speaking to her cat, Moth, while she organized all the day's harvest. Moth lingered in the door way, sitting stoically, perhaps even listening.

After she had set everything down, she recalled her thirst; she was parched! While drinking a glass of water, she was reminded of the podcast she had partially listened to; a Jude Currivan, a cosmologist, had pointed out that all the water within us and on the planet is older than the Sun. Blown away by the cosmic recycling idea, Paesh enjoyed the water with a sacred enthusiasm. She was avidly interested in esoteric knowledge, which in these times of scientific discovery seemed to run parallel to quantum magics of the universe, taking great reverence in the exact precision that had threaded this reality together. *What luck!* she thought, while she poured herself another glass.

The distance from the Earth to the Sun alone was a miracle for biological life on this planet. Often anthropomorphizing everything, Paesh would imagine celestial bodies governing the forces, calibrating the elements, and fine-tuning details that birthed life. They shimmered and were classically form-optional beings, free from the bounds of a body and yet burdened with the responsibility of life. Her glass of water nearly finished, Paesh's mind was soaring loftily in a tangent of gratitude and the esoteric when a sudden crash startled the shit out her -- not literally, though. It merely caused her to choke on the last gulp of water.

A bird had crashed into the window with such force it had rattled the old single-pane glass. Running outside to see if the bird had survived, she stopped short of a white bird that was strewn amongst the pink peonies and ferns. It was unlike any bird she had ever seen before, with iridescent wings that were sea-foam green in certain angles of light. But at a glance, the bird was solid white.

Stirring languidly, the beautiful creature looked too rare to be wild. Perhaps a neighbor's pet bird had gone rogue and escaped. Although similar in size, the bird was not a dove, a cockatiel, or an albino parrot. *Perhaps it's a wild bird*, Paesh wondered as she lightly cupped it in her hands. Cradling it softly, she felt for a pulse and signs of bleeding. All was normal as far as she could tell; she was neither bird specialist nor a vet, but had always had a knack for nurturing and healing the living. With one hand, she made a small nest of blankets and towels situated in a basket, and then she lay the bird into the nest, where it rested, lightly supported.

Should the bird need water, Paesh tucked in a cup of water closely to the nest for easy access. Unsure of the next step, she lay the tip of her finger on the skull, very gently, just above the eyes. She envisioned sending little beams into the bird, filling it up with warmth and love. Realizing she didn't want the bird to feel trapped in her home, she brought the basket into the garden and placed it a place where Moth was unlikely to bother it.

Paesh went inside to use the bathroom when she heard her ringtone, the one she had been meaning to change, as it was painfully generic and startling. Standing with reluctance to see who it was, she crossed the floor and stared at the number. She did not recognize anything, save for the area code, 831 -- Santa Cruz local. She hesitated, but then cleared her throat, and answered.

"Hello, this is Paesh."

"Hello, this is the Santa Cruz Public Library. You have eight books
two weeks overdue. Today your late fees will increase to one dollar a
day per book for each day it is late," said the automated voice
representing the library, doing its best to sound delightful.

Paesh sighed and pressed the red end-call button. "Time passes so
fast! How did I miss that?" she chided herself, and looked over at the
stack of library books by her door or sitting patiently on her desk. She
had borrowed books on metaphysics, lucid dreaming, dream
interpretation, and ceremonial traditions for magic from a few cultures.
Due to her strange experiences, she had many questions and was on
the lookout for knowledge. She scoured the internet and books for
morsels to chew on. She did find some helpful gems in one particular
metaphysics book, pertaining to the concept of time, and basically that
time is like a string of consecutive moments. There is only the moment
one resides in, the present-now. The human mind, clever and
thoughtfully speaking from its rational place of protest, would fight
this concept to the ground, because it sees time as a line, forwards and
backwards, our calendars and clocks calculating, counting, and
quantifying.

Paesh had felt this moment, and the only place she could truly
understand the concept was on the liminal edge of "herself" -- that
place of brevity, where her mind was quiet, experiencing the literal
moment without the incessant chatter of the inner dialogue. No names,
no stories, no before, no after. This realization restructured Paesh's
beliefs and altered concepts. Reincarnation, for example; instead of
being past lives, weren't lives all just happening at once? Like a
layered cake? Paesh played with this concept in her mind after reading
the book, trying to understand it, like a child learning a language.

Perhaps that was why her books were late... because she was letting time get away from her. She had even created a metaphor for timeless reincarnation so she could explain it to others in an easy way.

Envision a bohemian beaded door-way curtain, hanging in the breezy entrance to a patio overlooking the ocean. Each individual string of the curtain was a singular soul, and each spaced-out sparkling bead represented a lifetime. When the wind blew hard through the doorway, the string or soul would move in the moment of the wind. Each bead, every lifetime, experienced the wind at once, in that one moment; not every part of the string equally, but experiencing the wave of movement none the less. If the string fell, all the beads fell to the floor, experiencing the inevitable rush of gravity. And even further the concept stretched; all of the strings, though separate, were still connected in the oneness, as they were all made of string and beads, creating the collective bohemian door hanger.

Paesh digressed from her mental metaphorical tangent, thinking again about the future, tilting her head and wondering if door-hanging beads would look nice on her back porch. The mind was a funny thing, always reminding you about tomorrow or yesterday. She bit her lip, finding the irony of life comical.

"I should probably return these books before I float away with my lofty existentialism."

Paesh got grounded and filled a tote with her stack of books, then made for the kitchen and grabbed a muffin to go, locking the door behind her.

The library was cool, the AC blasting, a dull hum in harmony with the muffled coughing and sparse quiet whispers. She returned the books and paid the late fee, totaling to $28.00. Paying the late fee felt helpful, like a necessary tax every reader should pay once in a while.

Outside again, when she bent over her bike, unlocking it from the metal rack, she remembered how in that very spot a little over a year ago she'd had a rather odd interaction with a rather odd young man. Remembering it like it was yesterday, Paesh revisited the memory.

While bent over unlocking her bike, the odd young man was suddenly standing uncomfortably close to Paesh. He was young, no older than 21; his face had a youthful doughiness and a healthy glow, and he had a sparse, shy mustache on his upper lip. He wore a black trench coat despite the heat, with wildflowers tucked in his faded black baseball cap. They were beautifully wilted, and had seen the heat of the day; petals of pink and orange dangled around his temples. He had likely picked them hours ago. It was a sweet, unusual, and startling experience all at once. Paesh saw that he was kind in the eyes; they didn't harbor the familiar far-off stare that most of the local drug addicts and transients bore. Instead, his silver-bright eyes were clear, staring straight into her own.

"Don't worry about your bird. She can't hear us, and the people on the sidewalk can't see us; I'm freezing time," he said, nodding matter-of-factly.

Paesh did not know what he meant -- perhaps he was schizophrenic -- but still, Paesh felt intrigued enough to hear more. Her curiosity was a receptive, beautiful thing; she listened and nodded presently, not skipping a beat, and decided to exist in his strange reality with him.

"I am your soulmate from all of time," he told her. "We are dancing like the Moon and Sun, circling around one another; you are the Moon and I am the Sun, forever in this dance. You are an angel, a part of the eleven angels; your life here will be protected. I don't have much time, but I'm your soulmate from all of time," he repeated himself. "I need you to choose a body for me. I'll come back for you, but I have to go now. Please don't worry. You are protected, one of the eleven angels, you don't have to worry." His face was serious, as if he were relaying something very important. Although in repeating himself, he was starting to sound a little crazy, his eyes were clear and he didn't appear to be intoxicated.

Paesh smiled a big, confused smile. "How will I know it's you?" she asked sincerely.

"You will know," he said, nodding at her curtly, as if he were going to war and making a promise for his safe return. His floppy wildflowers moved with his motions, and he handed her an envelope with something small inside of it and turned to go. The tails of his black trench coat whipped behind him, and he was already rounding the corner. It all happened so fast that Paesh couldn't react. He was gone.

"Well, how will you know what I'm thinking... shit, and what if I change my mind!?" she yelled out loud in the direction he had made his exit.

Not far away in the other direction, two elderly women were tilting their heads at her. "You probably *will* change your mind, if life has taught me anything," the older woman said with a smile.

"Thanks for that. Uh, I'm curious, did you happen to see a young man in a black coat just now?" Paesh asked casually, trying not to sound even crazier.

The women looked at each other, and the older woman spoke for both of them. "The one with the floppy wildflowers in his hat?"

"Yes, okay, I'm *not* crazy, but he said the strangest thing to me..." Paesh trailed off, filled with relief that her life wasn't becoming a sci-fi novel.

"He didn't say a thing. He just walked past all of us quickly... or at least, I didn't hear anything. And frankly, with these new hearing aids, I often hear more than I want to!" The two women nodded politely as they walked around her in a wide arc.

Paesh was left standing there feeling a little horrified, and secretly excited, holding the envelope. She had always hoped someone would love her like that, *through all time*. She sighed. She wondered if the old women might have been playing a joke on her, or perhaps the boy was tripping on LSD or something. It wasn't uncommon in Santa Cruz, as it was a transient West Coast Mecca.

She carefully opened the envelope and out fell a ring, a silver-tarnished band with three gemstones in it: one clear, one blue, and the third pale peach. It was an antique, no doubt; the stones had been cut and faceted with care. Her heart dropped when she had realized that she had seen this ring before -- in a dream she had had just a month ago. Her mind was racing, and she began breathing slowly and deeply as she put the ring on. It happened to fit perfectly.

The rest of that day, she spent her time making laps around town looking for the kid, but she never found him.

When she got home and reread her dream journal, and saw that she had described the ring with three stones with the same coloring, she was blown away. That night, she fell asleep with it on.

Paesh, still stunned and standing at the bike rack at the library, pulled herself out of her memory, shaking her head at the strange coincidences of the past, and looked down at her bare hand, thinking about the ring. As she was staring at the smooth veins beneath her skin, she gasped; the young boy had mentioned a bird, and that "it wasn't listening to them."

On the bike ride home from the library, she wondered if the little bird had survived the crash, and if it could be the bird that the young boy mentioned a little over a year ago. Upon arriving to her house, she checked on the bird, but to her disappointment the bird was gone. She figured it must have healed and flown away; or worse, an animal had gotten to it. Paesh shook her head and looked over at Moth skeptically, who was watching her from her perch by her food bowl.

Sunset sealed the day, and Paesh watered her garden, caught up on some reading, and completed some mundane household chores. All the while, she wasn't able to shake herself from thinking about the bird.

Layer 12: Malva - Behind the Scenes

Whirl-winded and stunned, Malva opened her eyes to see the dark walls of her crystal cave, the ends of the crystals all flowing in one direction. Her body weakened from traveling through dimensions and time, she sat breathing heavily while she strained to maintain the memories and dialogue from her journey into Celosia's realm. She knew that soon she would have to activate a portal to Earth, making a channel through time and space, so they could incarnate to Earth. For now, she would sit and rest, regaining her strength for the journey ahead. This would likely be the last time she saw the inside of this cave, so she moved the stones back into place, and quieted the subtle wind that still spun loosely around her. All became still and quiet. Malva coveted the moment.

Back amongst the Avior, Malva set to her duties as a captain and member of the Eleven. Calling a meeting with the Eleven was the first step; she needed to make them aware that she would be going on a journey, one she might not be returning from.

The meeting space for the council was always in a different location. Malva sent a telepathic message to each member, calling for a meeting. She gave them a time and a location. Every council meeting took place among scenery that kept things interesting and fresh with new energy. Being skilled in all of the elements, working together they would create their own venue. On this occasion, they gathered in a field covered in small flowers, all different colors bobbing in the strong winds, their slender stems somehow fortified against the gusts.

All members of the group were dressed in different colors; their form-fitted bodysuits were made of different materials, but all in the logical, practical fitted design. Meeting in a windy place as they were, they all had on a secondary cover, like a shawl or a poncho, as the biting wind carried with it a chill this day.

One of the members, with fur the color of orange sand like the dunes on Mars, had piercing green eyes that resembled crafted blown glass. He was the oldest member of the group, and his eyes told that story. Beginning the process, he raised one hand and planted his feet with a slight pivot, bracing himself. A crack opened up in the ground, splitting around the group in a circle. When the crack ended at its starting point, the other members in the group took their stances, and they all moved in a flow together, slowly spinning and raising the small island of flowers into the air. Loose chunks of roots, rocks, and dirt crumbled and fell from the piece of land that was on its way upward. One council member pulled the greenery into life, creating a caged dome of vines and flowers over them, protecting them from the wind's harsh presence. Flowing with the certainty and measured movements of Thai Chi masters, they all made their contributions. A shorter woman, with black fur and a purple knit shawl, created the eleven stone seats and helped keep the elevation climbing. Her yellow eyes were kind, but fiercely focused. When they reached an appropriate height, they all found their seats and settled in for the meeting that Malva called into order.

"Greetings, and thank you all for gathering. I have called the meeting in regard to the dark virus that is holding Earth captive, and its potential threat to our galaxy," Malva said, standing and turning her head slowly, looking everyone in the eyes.

"We have created the technology necessary to open a channel down to Earth, or at least a prototype that we believe will work," she continued. "For many years, I have known of my connection with the higher dimensional being Celosia, the Keeper of the Web of Existence. Days ago, I finally made direct contact with her in her realm," Malva said, her chin pointed upwards. Some of the members seemed to gasp or hold their breath, shocked, absorbing the information. The green-eyed man kept his face calm and knowing, as if he had been aware of this connection; as old as he was, he was not surprised.

Malva let the information sink in before she continued. "I made contact," she repeated. "When I did, I expressed the concerns of the Avior. Celosia is willing to incarnate into Earth and investigate the virus. With our shared soul-connection and Avior technology, I can create a channel where, as one, she and I will descend to Earth. Indeed, I have already opened the channel," Malva said, closing her eyes and inhaling deeply, her mind drifting briefly to her Lieutenant, Vivet, his silver eyes steadily following her.

Avior are highly telepathic, and it was certain the Vivet was listening and protesting for her departure. She had deep desire to let herself love him, but it fell short under-expressed. The two of them knew it was there, in fact everyone did. No one spoke of it. Taking a deep breath, she blushed as the others in the council also likely felt her momentary distraction. Regaining her train of thought, she spoke again. "Any day now, my soul will fall with hers, and our hope is to return someday with more information, or a solution. I ask that my body be tended to in the chambers, while I will do my best with Celosia to mitigate the situation."

The Council of Eleven looked at each other, communicating lightly, like soft white noise growing into a gentle murmuring. Malva felt the overall energy, one of relief and also of loss. The green-eyed member sat staring directly into Malva. "Are you ready for such plummet?" asked he. "You may become stuck there for some time, or at least it will feel that way. I commend you for your sacrifice, but I do not know if this is the best choice, and I know it is not mine to make. Your loss will be tangible, and we will tend to your body; I will see to it personally. As a tribe, we will funnel you energetic support, and hopefully, that will bleed through into the new reality." The green-eyed Feline blinked slowly and smiled, although he looked distantly distressed. Malva's presence would be missed, and in some ways the tribe might feel betrayed.

"How can you just abandon your responsibilities?" a council member called out.

"She is trying to do something about a growing issue; I think it's necessary," another stated in rebuttal.

"It is decided, and the channel is open; this is not up for discussion. I am merely sharing what is happening and I am requesting support," Malva said firmly, fiercely grounding her feet and looking everyone sternly in the eyes. "It has been an honor to serve you all, and an honor to continue serving you and the greater good of our galaxy." Malva bowed. "I shall take my leave; meeting adjourned."

Malva slowly evaporated, unbothered to help the council disassemble there floating island. Teleporting herself to the Weaver one last time. She knew her fall would be soon, and time was running out.

Appearing gradually, molecules assimilated like pixels, and Malva appeared in the kitchen of the Weaver's dwelling. The structure was a tall dome, where the opaque ceiling slowly transitioned into transparent glass-like walls that exposed the surrounding greenhouse and garden. Plant-life and food was closely integrated in the meal preparation space. There was steam rising from a pot, and a spoon was slowly stirring the contents with the Weaver's controlled telekinesis.

"So your time is coming, is it?" the Weaver asked, her arms opening up to embrace Malva in a grandmotherly hug. Her arms provided comfort that would linger like a hand-knitted scarf through Malva's descent. The embrace imbued her with security, reminding her that she was loved and everything would be well. The Weaver possessed encompassing power like that, with her all-knowing wisdom. She was a humble and simple figure in the community, and Malva loved her very much.

"Did you see Vivet yet?" The Weaver asked, like a prying mother.

"I have not..." Malva said, clearing her throat and walking past the Weaver to see what was steaming in the pot.

"Perfect! I invited him over for dinner, so you two will have plenty of time to speak and say a temporary goodbye," the Weaver said, grinning and shrugging sassily. "You're welcome."

"Okay, well, good, that's great, thank you for that..." Malva trailed of nervously, as her emotional expression towards Vivet had always been so mechanical and awkward, despite the way she felt inside. Malva began to feel hot and dizzy with nerves.

"Distress all you want, but Vivet is even-keeled and understanding of your strange affection, sturdy as an unmoving boulder in a river. He certainly loves you, regardless of your oddity," the Weaver said, crumbling something up and adding it to the soup, like a magician, while she lightly laughed under her breath. The smell of what was simmering was calming; the aroma was of a savory soup, filled with herbs.

The two women drank a warm beverage while the food simmered. When they were mid-discussion about Earth's strange perception of time, they both sensed Vivet approaching the walkway. Malva held her breath and looked around the room for an escape; she had never had to face these feelings or such a situation before. It was so much more difficult than being a leader, or being on the Council of Eleven.

"Good evening, Weaver, Malva," Vivet said, nodding at each woman; as he spoke their names. he bowed slightly to each of them. "Smells delicious in here. Thank you for inviting me to join you."

The Weaver handed Vivet a drink and motioned everyone to move outside into the greenhouse, where the plants were happily bobbing in a wind, with small winged creatures dancing about in the air. He took it graciously, his long fingers grasping the cup. There were many lanterns that hung unlit. Vivet closed his silver eyes and brought them all to light; the softly glowing telekinetic energy-powered lamps buzzed as they blinked on. They were sustained by a surrounding sea of telekinesis, a small example of the technology their tribe had possessed for thousands and thousands of years.

Vivet wore a simple gray suit form-fitted to his tall, strong body. His fur was charcoal gray with black stripes that ran horizontally across the back of his head all the way down the back half of his body. His eyes were a gleaming silver, like Malva's, which might have been why she had noticed him in the first place; as far as either of them knew, no other members in their tribe had silver eyes. It was not a common eye color, and they both were aware of that.

"I'm going to go put the finishing touches on the meal," the Weaver said. "Please enjoy the greenhouse while you wait; I'm sure you have some catching up to do."

"Lovely, and yes. Thank you." Vivet chimed in, his low voice rolling through the air, past the little winged creatures, catching their attention as well.

When the Weaver disappeared around the corner, they were standing face-to-face, drinks in hand. Malva let courage and bravery wash over her as she held his gaze. "Vivet," she in a formal tone, "I— I am going to Earth, to put it simply. I am helping Celosia, the Web Keeper, incarnate on Earth. Our souls are connected, as I showed you before in the ship. I have set our prototype into motion, with my own modifications. I am not sure when she will go, but when she does, her soul will descend like a rock on a string falling from a great height. I am also tied to that string, and when that rock passes through time and space past my own point on the string, it will pull me down as well," Malva said matter-of-factly, not sugarcoating anything.

Vivet nodded and looked around briefly, searching for something to say; but all that came out was his warm breath. His mind looked busy with thought when he finally broke the silence. "When do you leave?"

"It could be any moment now, or it could be a while. The way time works for her, it would be tough knowing when, but the portal is open and all I can do is wait," Malva said gravely, but with a sense of pride.

"I am grateful for your bravery, and what it can do for the galaxy, but the mystery shrouding your return is like a dark pit in my stomach," Vivet said, his arm reaching out to trace Malva's shoulder. He used his gentle strength to pull her closer to him. "Malva, I am sure you know that I love you. I love your bravery and intelligence, not to mention your beauty. I cannot imagine your absence," Vivet said, his shoulders sinking and his voice strained.

Malva stepped closer, so they were almost touching, and then she leaned in, and he held her.

Whispering, Malva said, "I love you too, Vivet, I'm just not sure how to coordinate love; it's so illogical and impulsive. True, your soul speaks to mine, and that is all I can verify for certain. I will miss seeing your face, and your own intelligence and loveliness." She continued to rest in his arms, awkwardly, while his grip tightened and then loosened, as if surrendering to a hard truth.

"Is there a way for me to go as well?" Vivet asked, his hand sliding down her arm to hold her hand, his grip tightening when he felt Malva's energy shift. It felt cold and sinking as her response to his question formed in her mind.

"No; well, I do not know. Our prototype is not foolproof. Even though I am holding the gateway open, I will be riding the wave of her descent, as our souls are linked. I'm not even sure if it will work. I cannot risk this process on anyone other than myself," she said, sighing, the weight of this responsibility clear. Malva continued, "It is valiant of you offer to go, but you are needed here. You will be replacing me here in many ways when I leave. We will need a new Captain. Perhaps in time, there will be clarity or a new discovery in any data recovered from my body while I'm away. Keep my brain activity monitored; keep my body maintained, just in case. It is possible my body will die. It is unclear what will happen, or if there is any hope for return."

Malva sat as the room began to spin a little; warmth grew to heat quickly in her solar plexus, a vibrating sensation ending her dialogue. She was not afraid, but she was startled by the physical sensation.

"What is it?" Vivet asked, taking a knee at her side, "Are you unwell?"

A glass of water floated through the air, coming from the kitchen, and lingered near Malva's hands. She grabbed the water and drank it down quickly. Her breath steadied and she began to cool back down, the light breeze chilling the glistening sweat on her brow.

"I'm not sure what that was," Malva said with breathy words, her eyes closed, one hand holding the empty glass to her chest while her other hand lightly traced the curve of her eyebrows. The motion seemed to soothe her, the repetition of it.

"Maybe it is beginning..." the Weaver said, rounding the corner with a tray of food floating before her. "I think you should get some nourishment if your time to leave is soon." The Weaver sat at the low table, with cushions and chairs hovering around her.

Vivet and the Weaver took their places around the table, and Malva used her mind to float herself over to rest upon one of the floating chairs, its curvy shape cradling her. Vivet moved close to her, his eyes following her movements, calm concern forming the lines in his face. The Weaver served the soup along with small doughy rolls, little spheres that were white in color. They all began eating quietly, smiling silently with gratitude for the delicious meal. Malva put the spoon close to her mouth and inhaled the scent of the soup. It woke her up, and she remembered how hungry she was. Her appetite returning, she finished her serving as well as the rolls.

"This was so delicious and grounding. Thank you for having us here," Malva said as she stood up. "Excuse me one moment." Malva walked away towards a hallway that lead to a washroom to relieve herself. She was feeling hot again, the vibration in her stomach churning again, and this time it crawled up her center and felt as if it would burst out of her head. Taking a few more crooked steps, Malva fainted, and lay prone upon the stone floor.

When she fell, the vibration shook her soul from her body; she didn't feel the fall, and she no longer felt hot as her soul found its way into a flash of light and colors, dancing around her like a kaleidoscope tunnel. There was a loud roaring, like ship thrusters; it was deafening until the drowning sound faded, and all was still and dark. It was wet and it was enclosed; there was pressure and movement. A burst of light and a chill stupefied Malva.

A little girl was born, her first gasping breaths choked up in a cry. A bigger being cleaned her off; she was unable to open her eyes, and her mind was lost to where and what was happening. She remembered that she was Malva, but the details were slipping away like a fish caught with bare hands.

When she first opened her eyes, she gathered that she was now human, amongst humans. She was able to think and observe as she watched the world around her, a helpless animal requiring the nurturing of a mother. She couldn't stand, or speak; she could not even feed herself. It was a challenging first couple of weeks to keep hold of her memories, but every day she committed to reciting them to herself in her mind in a language vastly different from the one the humans around her were using.

"I am Malva, I come from far away, I was once tall, I was once Feline, I am Celosia. I am here to see, I am here to help. Find the virus, find myself, and one day I'll return to my people, the Avior."

This was a ritual that got her through the insanity of it all, for being human was difficult. It was cold and hot, hard and dirty, but most of all being caught in the young body felt like living inside a prison. She urged her muscles to move with great struggle, and studied the language of the people around her, both body and sounds. She was a sponge, and she wondered if this journey was a big mistake. She wondered when she would be able to do anything at all.

Years passed, and Malva grew into a creative young woman of her tribe, but she learned that being openly intelligent was not always useful. When the day came that she was the proper age, she was allowed to choose her own name. She chose Ala.

Retaining enough internal wisdom from her soul, she had an innate knowledge that eventually gained her respect amongst her people. She was a lovely woman, with a round face and kind silver eyes. Her people were in the process of carving out a new way of life from their nomadic linage. Malva felt herself immerse into the story line and density of the reality.

She fell in love with a man, older than her, named Jushur; he was a kind man, a leader and a thinker amongst their people. When they united forces, being human didn't feel so lost and hopeless; falling in love and having someone on your side led to strength and hope for a new age of living. Malva began the cultivation of grains and starches to make food that could be stored. She used knowledge from her previous lifetimes to guide herself and these people towards stability and prosperity.

She never did find the virus. The only time she ever witnessed anything out of the ordinary was the day when Jushur came home from a voyage, and he was different. His body was free of scarring and age, he no longer ached, and as the years went on it was clear he wasn't aging. He confided to her that he had gained this strange curse from the sea, and was unsure if it was good or bad.

Sometimes, Malva would follow him in the night, when he snuck away to carve images and paint his dreams onto rocks. He was disturbed, yet flourishing. The images were not comprehensible designs; they were abstract and unrecognizable. Malva felt as if some of the images were familiar, but she could not be sure with the crude techniques used to create them. Beyond these strange wakings in the night, Jushur was the same loving man she had always known, and she felt that there was no danger.

The day came when Malva was ready to die; her human body was giving out on her. Perhaps she was homesick and willed her body to move on, or perhaps it was just the way it happened. When she closed her eyes for the last time, her soul was set adrift in a foggy place, where her memory was harder to hold onto.

Drifting through the lights and fog, Malva felt herself pulled once more.

Her soul, like a fish on a line, was moving without her consent towards a tunnel of fractal colors. She squeezed through the walls of spacetime, taffy on a belt. When she came to, gasping with breath, she found herself within the body of a human infant again, wet with birth, her body fatigued and cold, her cry scratchy and repetitive. As before, she repeated what was left of her mantra that she could remember: "I am Malva. I am Celosia. I am here to see, I am here to help. Find the virus, find myself, and one day I'll return."

Layer 13: Paesh - Crash Landing

Paesh woke up rested and ready for work. She made her way through her house, preparing a lunch and feeding the cat. Later, pulling her bike from the shed, she rolled down the road shaded by trees, and let the breeze fill her lungs.

When arriving at work, her body was a little damp with sweat from the bike ride to the lab. Paesh had brought a change of clothes with her, some loose-fitting yoga pants and a loose T-shirt. The biology lab she worked in required the staff to wear a lab jumpsuit anyway, so she could wear comfortable clothing underneath. Sliding on her lab shoes, she made her way to the kitchen, where she grabbed a sterilized thermos and water container and prepared her drinks for the mid-morning. She walked down the hall, and to the right was the section of the building she was working in. Tea and water in the crook of her arm, she began settling in and preparing for her day.

Paesh didn't love being indoors in the lab all day, but most jobs required compromise. There was, however, a perk to the bleak sterility of the lab, as there was field research too.

Their lab was responsible for studying bacteria, and the effects different bacteria have on the human body. There were other departments that studied mycology and the use of their compounds for various applications. That department did a lot of observation of how the mycelium network interacts with itself. When an environmental shift occurs, oftentimes a new species will colonize in the damaged location and balance the situation, which was the link between bacteria and the mycology department. It was a very forward-thinking lab, with funding from government grants as well as one large private investor. Paesh had great interest in the mycology department, but she was also content with the fascinating and endless journey there was to be had with bacteria.

Her lab lead, Tiago, walked into the room as she arrived. "Ah, good morning, Paesh, glad to see you, always early, very good. Here is a list of the samples that I need you to synthesize in solution and prepare for today's project." Tiago was exuberant and enthusiastic, always excited and ready to discover. Paesh never recalled seeing that man frown. He practically lived at the lab, no partner or children, so the lab was his passion and focus. He was short and had come from Brazil when he was just eight years old, so his voice had a slight accent that charmed everyone he met.

"Good morning, Tiago, and thank you. When the clock strikes, I'll get to it." They both smiled and he left the room, his shoes clicking with confidence down the linoleum hall. Another pair of shoes made their way down the hall as well. It was her current co-worker and lab partner, Jeff. He was quite strange and condescending. Paesh didn't let it get to her, but some days she prayed for a new project partner. She had had many agreeable and talented ones in the past, but for now she was stuck with Jeff.

To avoid having more conversations than necessary with Jeff, she put in her headphones and busied herself in the lab. There were many machines with long names at her disposal, and right now she was preparing small bacterial samples and putting them in a constant host solution. First, she sent all the sample dishes through the sterilizing machine; then, when they were out and cooled, she applied 5 cc of the base solution with a neutral pH. After this, she carefully added each bacteria sample on Tiago's list, and labeled them accordingly. From there they would be covered and placed in an agitator, where the solutions would be vibrated until homogenized.

Next, they were placed in a neutral environment -- in other words, the sterile fridge kept at 20 degrees Celsius. Later in the day, those samples will be introduced to a bacteria sample that was considered "good" for the microbiome of the human body. They were working on finding bacteria that could eliminate or alter various species of harmful bacteria that led to many of the illnesses in modern humans.

Paesh, hypnotized with her work, was listening to Bach Cello Suites and was lost in thought while her body was on autopilot. She thought to herself, *Everything is bacteria; this whole form, my whole body is a sea of bacteria moving together... perhaps all the tiny microbes — all the bacteria that make up the body are the ones dreaming up my life.* She was gazing out a window that had a lovely view of a thickly forested area when she was abruptly startled out of her reverie by Jeff, His sharp nasal tone cutting right through her music. He was standing directly behind her at an uncomfortably close distance.

"Um, excuse me, Paesh, but it appears you have incorrectly sent the samples into agitation. You were supposed to wait a 30 second count before putting them in machine. I counted only 25 seconds."

Paesh had had enough of Jeff. This was it; this was the moment where she finally lost it. "Jeff, why are you counting my sample times?" Paesh snapped while removing her headphones and turning to face him. "I have the same degree as you, and was hired to fulfill my role as a lab tech. If Tiago thought I was incapable of the job, he wouldn't have hired me years ago. And for your information, the waiting time before agitation is irrelevant; that rule of thumb is outdated! I have been receiving nothing but condescending 'manspliaining' corrections from you since Day One, and I will not stand for this! Mind your own damn snivelly business, and let me do my fucking job!"

Paesh was incandescent with rage, her eyes glowing silver and bright. If someone else had been in the lab, they would have said her hair was blowing in the wind, despite no fans nor breeze present.

Jeff's eyes were huge, and he became very quiet; he looked like he'd just seen a ghost. He very slowly took steps backward, and Paesh noticed that he had peed himself. She immediately felt a little guilty, and worried about what the repercussions of this outburst would be.

Jeff did not return to the lab before lunch.

At lunch, she checked the parking lot and did not see his little blue Prius. She grew somewhat concerned, but not *too* concerned, as she had been working with the goon for six months, and she was finally free of him. It felt nice to speak her mind, although her approach lacked calm communication skills, and was by no means kind. But what was done was done; what could she do now?

Later, Tiago came into the lab to check her progress and asked where Jeff was. Paesh was shocked, as given the snarky sort of guy Jeff was, she was certain he would have gone to HR or Tiago to express his complaints.

She admitted, "I sort of blew up at him today, Tiago; he's been so condescending, and he questions every move I make. It must have startled him, because he left."

Tiago nodded, and raised his brows.

"I have heard this about his behavior. I shouldn't have hired him, but he is my sister's husband's nephew. You are not the first to blow up at him, actually..." He trailed off. "Normally he goes right to HR, or me, so perhaps you really served it to him, eh?"

"So you're not mad at me?"

"No, Paesh. In fact, I'm surprised you never mentioned your uncomfortableness or issues with him before."

Paesh was relieved that she wouldn't be fired just because she'd stood up for herself. "Phew! Honestly ,Tiago, I was a little worried I might get the boot."

Tiago chuckled and shook his head. "No, no, not at all. Looks like you may have to tie up Jeff's loose ends before you leave today, though."

Paesh rode home that day with a sense of satisfaction, feeling proud of herself. So proud that hunger and time had evaded her brain, and she was ready for a solid meal, so she decided to stop at her favorite Thai place. It was almost on the way home and was literally the most magical dining place that she knew. It was called DD's Thai Kitchen, and the food was gloriously delicious.

DD's was in the neighborhood near her work, on the end of the street. Its wooden sign hung on iron hooks and was moving to the wind's dance. Rolling her bike down the bumpy cobbled driveway, her face was brushed with many overgrown tree limbs, as if she were in a jungle, which didn't bother her. Parking her bike in front of the few cars that were parked in the modest gravel parking lot, Paesh ran her fingers through her hair, only adding to its wildness. She instinctively checked the smell of her armpits to be sure it wouldn't be too bad for anyone sitting near her, and alas, it was not too bad.

There were many large, square wooden lanterns with colored paneled glass on four sides; the wood was carved with precise design, looking as if it were hand-carved in Bali. Inside the lanterns were strung cafe lightbulbs, and they lit the way to the back garden, where the outdoor kitchen and seating was. The tropical plants bobbed in the wind while the sound of the water feature flirted with her ears. The collective sensation was as if she was walking into the past, as the owner, DD, put special care into her ambiance.

When rounding the stone path, Paesh could see the outdoor kitchen with a roof and ceiling fans, with seating that was scattered around the garden. Large imported wooden benches, also carved in Bali, were dressed with cushions that met live-edge wooden tables set with lit candles and fresh flowers. Paesh let out a huge sigh of relief, and that signaled DD to look her way.

"Paesh! Welcome, Welcome, you have been gone so long! Why have I not seen you?" Beloved DD was a petite Thai woman with a sassy and confident energy. She walked up and elbowed Paesh lightly, to emphasize her point before giving her a hug. The side of her head was shaved, and she wore a twist of dreads in a large bun atop her head. Her arms were lean and toned, with bracelets clinking and sparkling clear to her elbow. She was beautiful, and unafraid to speak her mind. She had a beer in one hand and a spliff in the other. This evening she was wearing a white button-down blouse, jean shorts, and sandals. It was a simple outfit, but she made it look like gold.

"Hey, DD, I know I've been away too long. I need a beer and some of your magic food tonight. Sorry I haven't been in lately -- they say distance makes the heart grow fonder." At this, DD let out a laugh that cut the night and made a few of her customers look up.

"Sit, sit, perhaps your usual table?" Paesh sat per suggestion; it was close to the water feature and the kitchen, as Paesh loved to watch DD cook and sit close enough to gossip while she did.

"What will you have tonight to eat?"

"Tom Sum and green curry, please, medium spice plus a little more, and iced tea," Paesh, said with her fingers making a small pinching motion. DD put a small Indonesian beer in front of her, a Bintang, which means "star" or "heavenly body" in Indonesian. Paesh easily cracked the beer open with her keychain, and squeezed some lime into it. Taking a long, slow drink, she watched the small droplets of condensation drip down the bottle. It was cold and refreshing, and a rare treat, as beer didn't normally sit well in her stomach, but this beer was light and easy to drink.

She watched DD work seamlessly, chopping and grating the green papaya; she used a giant mortar and pestle to mix the papaya with the spices and sauce. She worked quickly and calmly, as if she had many arms; she was truly a food witch. If she wanted to put love into the food, there was love; if she wanted to put laughter into the food, there was laughter, and so on. When Paesh was served her food, DD sat down to talk while waiting between customers.

"So, Paesh, how is the boyfriend?"

Paesh choked on her papaya, and the spice hit her throat in the most imperfect spot. Her eyes watered a bit, and she smiled while coughing, embarrassed. Grabbing for her beer, she drank large swallows to chase the spice demon from her throat and stop the coughing. When she could breath, she responded, "You know me, on to the next. I can't seem to get out of this rut of man after man after man. I think three months is the longest I've ever dated anyone."

DD laughed at this, but then made a serious face. "What was wrong with Meelad? He sounded dreamy."

Her heart dropped; had it really been that long since she had seen DD? She gulped the rest of her beer to emphasize, and feeling a little sassy from the spice high, she said, "Well, turns out he was a fool, a puppet. A damn rich fool. Same ole story, a man finds me and goes completely nuts with false infatuation. Flattered by the attention, I entertain them even though I know they're crazy, because the stable ones are boring..." Paesh trailed off, looking dejected. "But I'm a paradox, because I also want it to be at least *somewhat* stable. I feel like the right man is out there. I'm sure when it's meant to happen, it will. I'm okay with being single, too -- it's serving me well right now."

DD nodded and gave her a knowing look, taking a long drag of her spliff. "Something tells me a man is looking for you as well, a special one; but it's almost like these other ones carry a darkness that intrigues you. Exploring your own darkness through these crazy men, maybe? Or maybe it's just the Santa Maria speaking," she laughed, leaning in and slapping the table.

"Enough about me, DD. How are your kids and husband, anything new?" Paesh asked, taking a big bite of her Tom Sum.

"He is boring," she said with a grin, "He is back in Germany for work again, so I'm eating in bed like a queen with the AC blasting!"

Both women laughed at this, relating on the beauty in alone time. A shy family turned the corner on the path, looking mystified, as most newcomers did. DD gave Paesh a wink, and stood up to greet the family; they didn't speak much English, as Santa Cruz was a big tourist town. There were many people from all over coming to visit DD's Thai.

DD was busy with orders after that, and Paesh watched her cook. It mystified her while she enjoyed and finished her meal. The food left her pleasantly full of inspiration from the spice and magic. She walked towards DD, hugged her goodbye and paid her bill.

She rode her bike home with confidence. The wind on her mouth was nice, as it still held residual heat from the food. But as she was gliding along the asphalt, her mouth airing out, she swallowed a bug, which caused her to swerve, and subsequently crash into someone's trash cans and fall into their yard. It was loud, and trash was strewn everywhere. Luckily, Paesh flew off into the grass, and only part of her body hit the cement curbside. For the most part, she was unharmed, save for a few bruises that would arrive the following day. The porch light clicked on, and a man came out to see what had happened. Unfortunately, garbage had spilled everywhere, and Paesh was sitting dazed amongst the rubbish, still coughing the bug out. It must have been a fairly large bug, so she eventually made the decision to just swallow it.

Looking at the sprawl, the man's face was concealed by the darkness. "Whoa, shit, are you all right?" He ran over and got a good look at Paesh and froze slightly, seemingly startled by the look of her face. "Did you hit your head?" he asked.

Paesh shook her head and got out a, "No -- I, uhh, sorry about the mess." She looked around at the mess of garbage, and asked, "Do you have any gloves? I swallowed a bug, and that was enough for me to crash my bike..." she trailed off, feeling stupid.

"Gloves? For what?" he asked. Paesh looked for her bag and rummaged through it, as sometimes she took gloves home from the lab, and she found a pair. Triumphantly she produced them from her bag, and waved them in the air. "Never mind! I have a pair on me," she said and immediately got work, putting the can upright and filling it with the scattered trash. The man stood there, stunned by the strangeness of her. Paesh looked over at him, as he wasn't moving, and noted that he looked as if he had come from Spain. He had kind eyes and was tall and lean, with dark surfer's skin and lighter eyes. He couldn't be over 35, Paesh assessed.

Breaking the silence, she said, "My name is Paesh." The man looked in her direction and came back to reality. He cleared his throat.

"My name is Louis, but I go by Lu," he said with a forced causal tone. "Thanks for picking up the trash..." he paused, "You don't need to do tha --—" Paesh cut him off with hand motion and he continued, "Okay, well, I know this is weird, but do you want a beer or some water or anything? Thanks for picking up the trash." He repeated himself. "I'm not creepy, I promise. I can bring it out here if that makes you more comfortable," He said, clearly feeling awkward.

He rambled for a bit longer, and eventually Paesh just laughed, used to having this effect on men, and said, "Sure, a beer would be great, an unopened one with lime, in case you're a creep in disguise and try to roofie me." She laughed at her own joke while she bent over, picking up the last piece of garbage, her shirt sinking low to show her cleavage beneath. She snapped up with excitement, tossing the last piece in the can, peeling off her gloves, throwing them in, and placing the lid atop it.

"Let's have that beer, then," Paesh said in a guiding manner, as she didn't want to be out too late. This would be the most beer she had had in a month. Obediently, the man left and returned with two rather fancy IPA beers, a bottle opener, and a small dish filled with cut limes. When he approached Paesh, his eyes flashed silver for just a moment before returning to soft green, and this made Paesh wonder if she *had* hit her head. However, she was no stranger to strange things, so she grabbed the beer and opened it before squeezing two slices of lime into it.

Over the course of the next twenty-six minutes, Paesh found that she enjoyed Lu's company, but did not wish to invest in yet another man. She learned he was single, well-employed from what she could tell, and clearly interested in her. Turned out he had never been married, never had kids, and had spent 34 years on the planet. All she could think about was, *Oh, not again, not another man-rollercoaster, oh fuck, here we go,* feeling herself being sucked into his energy. Attempting to stay strong, she thought back to her conversation with DD. She didn't feel all that inspired to get engaged with yet another man, so she suddenly slammed down the rest of her beer, and bowed somewhat awkwardly.

"I need to go... tend to my cats -- cat, I mean, cat, I only have one. It was nice to meet you, Lu." And quick on her heels, she spun off towards her bike, praying the chain was intact. This technique was one she used frequently to catch men off guard. It was a simple. It required redirecting the conversation mid-sentence, standing, stating something brief with an awkward cadence, and turning to move as swiftly as possible. It ALWAYS worked, and then she would be on her bike, flying down the asphalt and home before he could even finish his thoughts or his beer. It might seem weird, and rude even, but when you are pursued often, you cannot engage with everyone; giving centimeters leads to meters, and she just didn't have the energy.

Even setting clear boundaries and polite refusal would not stop a man from his hunt. He would push and push until all of a sudden Paesh found that she had once again caved. She was in another unfamiliar bed, and there was a stranger magically pressing all the right buttons between her legs to dispense dopamine. She was disappointingly weak. After that, there was the morning, the dark and early kind of morning. While the man lay passed out, Paesh would quietly collect her clothing from the floor and slip out the door, with her head hung shamefully low. So now, Paesh could give a fuck about confusing a random man she'd just met; no longer worried about accommodating the male ego, she used her tactic as always.

And luckily, she was on the road, and free to go home alone with the biggest smile on her face. When she parked her bike in the shed, she filled the cat's water and food bowls that probably also sustained the local raccoons, amongst other creatures. When placing the food container away on the shelf, she looked up and recalled the bird from earlier. She sighed and wondered what had happened to it. She turned for the door to go inside to get ready for bed -- and to her surprise, the white bird was perched cheerfully on the twisted natural wood railing of her porch. It looked at her sideways with one eye.

As Paesh moved near the bird, it did not scuttle or scoot out of the way; it merely stood where it was. "Hello bird, glad to see you're feeling up to it then," Paesh said in a New Zealand accent. Paesh loved accents above all things, and she had a knack for them. When she opened the door, the bird came inside with her, quite to her alarm.

The bird landed on the counter inside, and Paesh was unsure whether she should motion the bird outside or close the door and see what happened. She chose the latter. It was sort of exciting that a bird was choosing her; she had never had a bird willingly come to her. So she gave a speech, for what it was worth:

"Bird, welcome to my home. I'm closing the door now. Please refrain from shitting anywhere hard to wash, or anywhere other than -- this," she peeled open a newspaper and laid it out on the counter. "Also, here is something to munch on if you're feeling a need for a late night snack." Paesh poured some seeds and cereal into a small dish and put a dish of water next to that. "Lastly, please refrain from hurting yourself if you freak out and need to leave. These are clear, but they are windows," Paesh knocked on the glass windows and doors, "and they will hurt, as you learned yesterday. So if you need to exit, I'll leave the window in my room open, for your free-range departure."

Paesh knew she was odd, but who was to say that the bird could not understand? It was worth a try, anyway, or at least it was the thought that counted. Paesh sort of gave the bird a half bow, and extended her arms as if to say *mi casa es su casa*, and turned to go upstairs and wash her face, give her teeth a scrub, and sleep.

While opening the window near her bed nook, she heard the wings of the bird flapping, and it entered her room and landed just on the windowsill. Paesh wondered if that was that, a total fluke, and the bird would be leaving now that it could. But it merely stood on the sill as if roosting. It fluffed up its feathers and nestled into itself. So Paesh turned out the light and drifted to sleep.

The familiar orange glow of her salt lamp clicked on; it was 03:47, and Paesh wearily cried for a few minutes, quietly but deeply sobbing into her pillow. Finished with her tears, she grabbed for her dream journal.

Dream journal 03:47, 8/23/2019:

There were cool tiles under my feet, and a warm, dry breeze blowing lucidly onto my face. The stars were alight. I felt like I knew the breeze, almost as if I could see it. I couldn't tell where I was; it was very dark, and the stars were very bright. There was no Moon. I was calling to a man; his head was shaved and he had a dark black braid starting from the lower part of the back of his head. He turned and smiled at me with ancient, knowing eyes. He stared at me hungrily and yet respectfully, like I was a queen. His eyes were honey-colored, swirling with red. He wore eyeliner, oddly enough. (Where am I, burning man?)

The scene changed annnd -- well, there was literally the most glorious sex I have ever experienced. I was not sure which way was up or down. It was more the feeling and flashes of experience than a linear lovemaking session. When it ended, the scene shifted drastically and the man was over me, crying, grasping at my shirt, which felt drenched with sweat. He was saying something through his choking tears: "I'm me." I felt so much sorrow, I actually woke up crying.

Layer 14: Iós- Growing to Know the Plan

It was early morning on the eastern coast of the Mediterranean Sea; the Sun was climbing high, the waves lapping at the sand. The voyagers' vessel was docked on wooden blocks, and the crew was unloading supplies. It comforted Jushur to know that his tribe was gathered, and that everyone had made it safely. It was such clockwork synergy, the way their community worked together to organize the goods that their voyagers had procured.

Many of the tribe's women and children would come with supplies to greet the voyagers and help them prep the goods and make them ready for transit. Their goods consisted of reed baskets, roughly-made tools, animal skins, seeds, chunks of ore, plant roots, and fish. All items would be tied to two poles with netting between them, travois structured like stretchers which could be dragged by humans and animals or carried above rougher terrain. The fish that they had caught just before arriving on land would be smoked and processed there on the beach, as it would spoil on the journey; even though it would only take two hours to get back to the central part of their village, the Sun would not be kind to the more perishable items. The whole tribe would work together to process all the fish and make them stable for travel. It would be an awful, wasted journey if these tasks were not completed.

Although Jushur was the leader of the boat, he was not the leader of the tribe; in fact, it was the women who made most of the decisions for the tribe. It was the women who were looked to for guidance and strategy, for the tribe's survival. Women have intuition; they are tapped into the forces of nature itself, and the men recognized that without jealousy. The women of the tribe felt that every voice should be heard, and there was equality and diplomacy in their guidance.

Women did not force their way into power, either; it was simply that they were revered and honored for their cosmic role as the bringers of life. Women were seen as figures of inspiration and adoration, as they had known and felt the spectrum of pain and nurturing, wildness and tenderness.

The woman Jushur loved, Ala, was almost of age to be a woman of council. Her round and loving face bore eyes that knew all too much all too well. Her health was strong, and the knowledge of creating foods was her strongest skill. She had invented new ways to process starches, grains, and roots that kept their tribe well-nourished and thriving. The respect she received reflected that.

After the long day of organizing, Jushur had trouble sleeping that night in the camp on the beach. With the reunion of Ala and their child, he should be exhausted with all of the reconnecting, especially after their child had finally fallen asleep. Instead, a boost of great energy surged within him, which at his old age of 34 was welcomed but unexpected. Perhaps the ground revived his spirit, or maybe it was the reality of seeing the woman he loved and his child once again.

He lay sweaty, very much awake, while to his side Ala, she of great beauty, slumbered tenderly with the small child cradled against her stomach. The child stirred a little, but didn't wake, to Jushur's relief. Jushur was unsure of how to soothe the child; in his current state, he couldn't even soothe himself. So wide-eyed and awake, unable to relax, he made moves to go run off his steam.

Jushur slowly untangled himself from Ala and crawled out of the temporary tent-like dwelling. He walked away from all of the tiny dwellings settled just off the shore, most of them shrouded by the quiet sound of dreaming. Like the hoots from nocturnal creatures, random expressions of pleasure echoed lightly out into the night.

Jushur was now far enough away from camp and felt he could really breathe. He needed the sea's cool damp air to level out his body's temperature, and the salt within the mist to bring clarity to his lungs. This did help him focus, but something was wrong inside his body. The muscles wrapping his skull were taut and tense with knots, his vision blurring with sparks in his peripheral vision. Jushur felt as though lightning was swimming up his veins and into his brain. These sensations rose into a cacophony that peaked and fell into stillness, like the drop of a well-placed crescendo.

Jushur was suddenly more aware of himself, his senses heightened and his vision clear; looking up to the clouds parting like curtains to the stars, he could see every tiny light. His sight was crisp, along with his hearing and sense of smell. His muscles shivered and then flexed into tension, like a dog shaking off water. Scars on his forearm slowly began to flatten and became smooth; eyes widening, Jushur knew that something was different, some strange magic afoot. Mildly panicked, he thought back to the shark, wondering if the goddess of the sea had blessed or cursed him. While exploring his heightened state he jumped and stretched about, he felt as if he were losing himself to something else within him, and sensed great power and strength there.

A voice within his mind whispered, stretching its preverbal arms into his neurons, testing out the fine equipment. Iós was inside, now awake and settling within the mind and body of Jushur, calibrating to the new system that the human brain provided, a new system of consciousness that operated from a place of love, with a drive for survival; all made possible by the use of a very large and complex electromagnetic brain.

All of these sensations were new and very different from his stay inside of the shark. There was much more whirling around inside this mind than in the mind of the shark; it was extraordinary! Iós observed the language, emotions, and concepts that melted his sense of loneliness away. It had been a lonely abyss that Iós had traveled while floating in the void of space, and then into the void of the ocean.

This inner dialogue was far more advanced than he was used to, and yet in its "newness," it felt familiar somehow. Testing his control over the body, he willed Jushur's arm to move, and the arm went up into the air and waved in front of Jushur's face. Jushur's heart began to pump with more speed, the ventricle chambers responding to the angst of fear. Cortisol made the blood bitter, sweeping in from the adrenal glands. Jushur began to panic, spewing wild streams of language, possibly regarding the movement of his rogue arm.

Iós did not yet know the language of Jushur, nor the complexities of this new animal. It was clear this existence was not as simple as the entrained programs of the shark. Iós decided it would be wise to lay low and observe from within before he started to utilize this body. He would watch how Jushur survived, immerse himself into the lifestyle, and learn the language. Watch how to eat and kill. Gain understanding of how to survive on land within such a dynamic being.

In his relatively short inhabitance of Jushur, Iós had experienced deep emotional ranges that were unexplainable, and witnessed thoughts that bounced around and held their own dialogue. This was no shark; the operational function of this Jushur was bafflingly complex. Still, there was something familiar, and Iós felt more of himself stimulated and awake, like updating the newest version of a computer program, or using an old, bulky ancient model of computer versus using a sleek new laptop with more data storage. Iós felt as if memories were just in reach; there might now be hope to find out anything about where he had been before he was set adrift in space.

So, happily, he decided he would not take control over the body's motor systems or thought forms for now; instead he would watch and wait till the time was right. He had absolutely no clue how to be a Jushur; he was just glad to have a powerful vessel. He was in no hurry, as death was not coming for him anytime soon, that was clear.

Layer 15: Indra - Reflecting and Storytelling

Indra began to find ritual and comfort in the life of an oak dryad. She became well-acquainted with the beings in her forest, and observed the many subsets of cultures and magics. Her canopy was teaming with life and magic; it was truly delightful and far from lonely. In fact, she was hard pressed to find privacy. Above all the new exciting elements of her life, she loved the food with the most reverence. There were many delicious flavors and sensations she hadn't experienced in her cave. There were the small jelly droplets shaped like giant dewdrops or translucent bubbles; they were called *Jubees*, sweet and chewy-delicious confections crafted by the flower and water sprites, who were masters of sensation. Each drop was filled with essences like laughter, serenity, or sensuality. Sometimes small flower petals were pressed just under the surface, and those were among her favorite varieties. It was a true obsession, and any Fae sprite soon knew how to gain favor with Indra.

When she ate, or anyone in the Fae ate for that matter, the energy from the food was directly transferred into the molecules that manifested the consumer's form. Consuming the food of the realm was a way to really become one with it. At first Indra did not consume any food, as she was not accustomed to such things, but in time she became lightheaded, and Beaudry came to quick realization and aid. They hurriedly gave her meat and fruits to bring her back to reality.

Beaudry was a true friend and ally in the realm; they were respected and a great influence there, governing all of the Pyrenees Mountains. They had been in the realm for so long, they undoubtedly had the most accurate historical information for the region. On a spectrum of governing, Indra was of lesser rank. She would always think of Beaudry as a teacher; it would take a great deal of time for her confidence in governing to truly flourish. That said, it did not take long before many forest dwellers treated Indra with respect, a lady of the forest. A lady who was responsible for knowing all that happened within her forest, and protecting all within it. For Beaudry, it was the same.

She did her best to get into character and do it well, as she did not know how long she would be there. Her tasks included protecting her creatures and maintaining healthy relationships with neighboring elements, boundaries, and nomadic beings that didn't belong to the territory. Unlike Aria, who did not have a permanent residency, Indra wasn't as free to roam; she was bound to the Irati Forest. The oak tree was her place of retreat, her home, and her safe space.

It took some time to learn even half of the creatures and beings who existed in the Fae Kingdom. Even now, she still did not know all of them, and was never surprised to encounter someone new. The most complex and confusing facet of the realm of the fae was that not all of the beings meant well; thus the need for protection. These malintent beings were varied on a spectrum, from tricksters and the foolish to the lesser few who thrived with the forces of destruction and chaos. This was not something to eliminate or fear, but was a force to be held in balance, as life on Earth was a place meant to experience this balance and feel both aspects. Fengári and Ílios worked in harmony to create this for others to experience.

As time passed, Indra grew concerned that Aria never had any information on the strange energy that crashed into the ocean. Indra grew restless with her initial mission in coming to Earth, and wondered when she would ever go home and see Eithar again. Despite this anxiety, she was grateful for the friends around her, especially Aria. Her spirit was lovely, and her friendship was of great importance to Indra. In time, Indra learned that Aria was an Earthly incarnate of Fengári. Her presence on Earth was one of the ways she kept consistent observation of the happenings in her realm. Everyone looked after something in this universe, it seemed.

Aria, despite loving all beings, did invest extra time into Indra; she truly enjoyed her company. They would meet often at the water temples, or any bodies of water. These were soothing places, where the sound of water drowned out their conversation, which was beneficial in case anyone had the mind to eavesdrop. Indra, beyond the memories of Nami, had not experienced a friend like this, in the flesh with day-to-day story lines in a life, sharing meals and experiences. It was real, and raw, which meant it was not always comfortable, as they did not always agree. They supported one another by listening. Aria listened especially well when it came to Eithar, because Aria understood love, as Ílios and her had been in union for eons.

The first time Indra remembered who Eithar was, shamefully, it was quite some time after taking her tree-nymph form. She not only missed him, but had forgotten him altogether. It happened while she was dozing with the foxes, curled up in a moss-covered knoll. A dream came as vividly as waking life, and a figure painted with the night sky walked towards her, one arm outstretched he spoke, "If you wish, I will always find you." The dream ended, and when Indra woke, she shot straight up from the mossy knoll, where the foxes, butterflies, rabbits, pixies, and leaves scattered at all once, all leaping away quickly from the sudden chaos, leaving Indra sitting alone, breathing heavily, with eyes as wide as Jubees.

She had to hand it to the small critters;'twas dutifully dramatic for the situation at hand. Indra screamed in anguish and after her wild sounds of anguish and proclamation, the forest was deeply silenced. Indra began to weep, as she had again forgotten him, not only before, but again!

It wasn't long before Aria arrived and settled down next to Indra. Aria moved the hair that was stuck to her cheeks with sweat and tears. It was then that Indra was able to share the small but meaningful story of Eithar. Aria listened patiently, as a friend. It helped Indra recall more about him when she shared her story, like pulling the thread on a cloth. It just kept coming, more details as the thread pulled further. Small flower sprites brought Jubees and thin slices of fish wrapped in leaves. Indra and Aria nodded in appreciation, and quickly devoured the spread.

"Aria, I must find him; he was supposed to be here with me, incarnating here on Earth. I am not sure where he went, or even what time." Indra knew that Aria was an echo of Fengári, undercover and observing. Aria had access to different timelines and incarnations on the planet. Aria would be her best bet to find Eithar.

Aria sat collecting all the information, and washed down her snacks with water she had brought from the temple well. After finishing a glass, she poured herself another cup.

"I can do my best to look for him, because I know that is what you would want. I am happy to do it, but I will say, it is not something easily accomplished." She drank the whole cup swiftly, and reached out to fill the glass again, apparently very thirsty. "Indra, I know this must be confusing and painful, the loss; we will see what we can see, but searching other timelines is like looking for a grain of rice on a beach. He did not incarnate through the Moon. It is possible he is in the human realm, which can make the perception of a soul veiled."

Aria gave Indra a serious look, one of understanding and apology. Indra's eye began to well with tears again. "What if he didn't make it at all, and I do not know the way home?" Indra began to sob, knowing that one day Fengári would go dark, and the souls here would be trapped, perhaps along with her, without Eithar. This was something she knew she had waited too long to share with Aria, but she was not certain how to present it now, as so much time has passed. The day would come, however, when she needed to share with Aria what she really knew.

"Indra, love will always find a way to grow, like the ivy or bamboo. You think it's gone and, no, no, it is never gone; it takes root and reforms again." Partially following what Aria was saying, Indra nodded and rose to stand directly in sunlight, and let it wash away all the emotion and loss she felt for Eithar.

Life went on in the Irati Forest of the Basque Country, until the day came when Aria finally saw something, the strange energy that had crashed on Earth long ago.

Aria came streaming in like the winds of a hurricane, causing all the limbs of the trees to creak and moan with the force; some even came loose and fell down to the ground. Leaves were set to life with a menacing flitter, pulled around in Aria's torrent vacuum. Indra knew right away the reasoning for her speed; she could feel the urgency. When they were met face to face, Aria spoke, rather loudly and out of breath.

"Indra, I have seen it! The energy has surfaced at last!" She choked a bit, gasping for air. Indra handed her a cup of water, as Aria was always thirsty, so Indra had become accustomed to providing things to drink.

After she finished drinking a couple of glasses, Aria spoke. "It swarmed like a mist of gray static around a human doctor, a handsome man. No more than 27 years old, I wonder how it is that it could be that way."

"Perhaps it is contagious, requiring a host body, and not its own?" Indra said, her eyes distant with the thought of how quickly such a thing could spread.

"The man lives in place called Egypt, a place covered in sand, temples, and jungles. Well, at least that is where I saw him. A well-known prominent man, he seemed, a good man from a good family helping his community. He may be the first of his kind, inclined to be a healer," Aria said, her eyes lofty and dreamy, her affinity with healers obvious. Indra looked confused.

Aria continued, "The world is slowly developing, villages that were small settlements are growing larger as the years pass." She shifted, to sit now that she had calmed down a bit and relaxed herself.

"I'll explain. Long ago, we created an advanced civilization here on Earth, complete with high technology and in harmony with nature. The humans and Kingdom of the Fae were more connected and aligned then. Many beings incarnated here to experience life in a body, as limiting as the human form was, but life was easier then. All harmony, no disease, no hunger, no struggle.

"Ílios and I grew complacent with the rhythm of that life. So together, we decided to start again, and try something different, something more challenging. So we wiped that civilization away, sank it beneath the seas -- after all the occupants were safely off-planet, of course. We were temporarily under construction, as it were. We wanted to see how evolution with our new incarnates would grow; would it be fast or slow? Would it even happen at all? So we grew humans again, simple and natural. Many brave and intelligent beings rose to the challenge to incarnate in the beginning, and they were very excited to try the more rustic and dynamic experience."

Aria looked over at Indra, whose eyes were wide with amusement, while she took small bites of a lavender Jubee, maintaining eye contact, she sat completely entranced, fascinated by the sheer power her friend possessed. Creator and destroyer of worlds. She marveled with anticipation and childlike wonder, waiting for Aria to continue her story.

"Anyway, the evolution of this new wave of Earth is still happening, and it is going well. There is peace and pain. There is feast and famine. Birth and death. So as you can imagine, it is interesting for a healer to arrive, finding plants to use and being truly in tune and in touch with the world. It is exciting and gives me a sense of pride; but what is surprising is that he has that strange energy around him."

Indra straightened, her Jubee consumed. "That is beyond extraordinary," she said. "This Egypt -- how far is it from here, and what can be done?"

"I think for now we watch and see, see if it becomes more than one, or if it stays in the man. There is no telling how to contain such a thing; killing the man may only make matters worse, and would perhaps be the greatest shame and loss. This man is bringing so much growth to the villages. Plus, even if we did waste a gift like the doctor, perhaps the virus would merely find another host." Aria sighed deeply and shrugged her shoulders. "What more can we do?"

"I suppose for now, not much but observe. I feel helpless, as I cannot go there and do the watching myself." Indra slumped and sighed loudly, feeling as if her existence on Earth was a big mistake, a task too large for her to handle. She couldn't even leave the damned forest.

"Indra, when you came here long ago, how was it you saw this place? I wonder, if you can connect with your other self, if you could utilize that to see as well? I'm not sure where you came from, but perhaps from that vantage point you could see this man. I know you come from great power, as even now I still feel the star's buzz coming off you like the perfume of a flower. Perhaps this advice is far too delayed."

"I am not sure why that idea had not occurred to me. I sense that my connection is rather veiled, but it would be worth a try. Thank you for providing the immediate news; I will not waste another moment without trying to connect to myself." Perhaps she could even find Eithar, Indra mused. Her whole soul, underutilized, lent some feelings of shame, and she didn't know whether to laugh or cry at the time wasted.

Indra's eyes sparkled, brimming with hope. A fire was stoked inside of her now. "Thank you for coming to find me, Aria. Keep me updated. I'm off to go internal." Indra said, as she stood, wasting no time. She moved and morphed, heading towards the quiet retreat of her tree.

She moved quickly, her body taking the form of a deer, wispy as a ghost, leaping through the forest with hopeful bounds. It did not take long before she arrived at her tree, which was by now twisted and tall, glowing with golden light. To get inside, she only had to walk through it and melt down into the root system, where she became very small and could enjoy the spacious wooden nook. She had the space outfitted simply and cozily.

Inside the den was one bowl-shaped chair of carved and polished oak. Thin veins of gold were sparsely intermingled with the design. On top of her smooth, shallow bowl were furs and rugs woven of silk from the butterfly colony. The space was perfectly fit for sitting and focusing, as well as recharging with the energy of her tree. The bowl acted as a conductor, projecting energy and holding it as well. Despite the enclosed wooden space, there was fresh air circulating, and that helped her focus in the small space.

Indra sat, and really settled into the furs and silks on the wooden seat. Taking slow, intentional breaths, inhaling into the cavernous depths of her belly, she settled in. She sat like this for a long while, as if turned into a breathing stone.

In her mind, saw a light-blue cord, anchoring her to the planet; she also saw that it rose upwards infinitely, as far as she could tell. So she climbed the cord in her mind, rising up with it until the Earth's realm no longer surrounded her. Instead, she was somewhere sleek, white, and shiny, where the cord was passing through what appeared to be a woman. This being was feline yet humanoid, wearing a royal blue bodysuit of velvet that hugged her lean curves. She did not seem to see Indra, but sensed her presence.

Malva turned to look towards Indra, eyes fixed and curious, sensing something. Indra attempted to speak, but she had no voice. So she went close to Malva and used her index finger to lightly touch the feline on the forehead, directly on the third eye. This made Malva step backwards, and everything went white. In this whiteness, Indra no longer saw the Feline; instead she was standing in front of a young girl, a human girl. The light-blue cord ran through the chest of the youngling. Her eyes were silver, filled with confusion and sorrow. She was holding something, a floating ball attached to string and flat white paper; she let it go, and they both watched it rise into the sky. Before the girl moved on, she looked right into Indra and smiled at her before walking away.

Then a whipping sound cracked, and everything went dark as

Indra found herself snapping back into her body, sitting within her bowl under the tree. She sat trying to keep the images of Malva and the child in her mind's eye, remembering how their energy felt, and what their faces looked like.

Indra spent more time practicing inducing these visions, but there was no way to communicate with the others, let alone convey the timeline on how to track the virus. She would just have to depend on Aria for the time being, but it didn't stop her from trying.

Layer 16: Iós - The Split

Jushur woke suddenly in the dark of night, his face beaded with sweat, panting and gasping for breath. Startled by his surroundings, he moved his head to look at his side, where he saw Ala next to him, still asleep. He had forgotten where he was, as he had been traveling earlier that month; it was strange to be home and on land again.

He slowly made his way from their sleeping mat and out of the adobe room. Their small dwelling was on the ground level, and unlike the other dwellings, he didn't need a ladder to climb down. Every night, Jushur's slumber was broken by the same jolt of energy, and every night he left his home to go outside to check the stars. This became a ritual of his. The stars, who twinkled to greet him, were always in the same locations in the night sky, indicating that he woke at nearly the same time every night. His body temperature would cool in the night's air, and the pores on his skin would contract.

The dreams that he had every night were all varied in theme, and they were unlike any he'd had before the return from his voyage all those years ago. There were no bad dreams and there was no pain, but there were strange characters he had never seen before, wearing strange clothing and speaking strange languages. His mind stretched taught like the skin on a drum to keep their images in his mind. In time, he took to recording what he saw in his dreams through various media. When he would wake in the night, he would go outside and view the stars, drink some water, and chisel pictures in clay, or use charcoal to draw on stone. He always did this for at least one hour, and then after he would go back to bed with Ala, who as far as Jushur knew was unaware of his nightly ritual.

His life had been like this ever since he was touched by the shark, as he liked to think. Jushur felt it was a blessing from the gods, as he was free of pain and aging, unlike the rest of his village. Some people in his village thought he was kissed by the gods, and some thought him to be cursed by them. His daughter was now the age of 15, putting him at the age of 49 years. He was one of the oldest people in his village, and hadn't aged more than couple of years since that voyage. Ala was now sick and dying slowly, and it was painful for Jushur to watch; she was still the most beautiful woman he had known. Every day he told her that, and every day she listened and smiled. His heart was slowly shattering to watch her fall away from him in time, which to him felt like it was standing still.

The day of her passing approached; he could almost smell it on the vapors flowing from her skin.

Their daughter, Anik, had already chosen a man in the village to make a child with. She had been living away from Jushur and her mother for many Moon cycles. She was as beautiful as her mother, strong, bright, and gifted in making bread for the village, a knowledge that her mother had passed on to her.

One day Jushur was at the village well, which was located at the heart of the village. He was filling himself a cup of water to drink, and some larger skins to bring back to Ala. He marveled at the advances that 15 years could bring a group of nomads. They had tools, water, irrigated gardens, and dwellings of clay. All of the hard work and memories brought tears to Jushur's eyes; he was overwhelmed with pride for his people.

As the tears fell down his face, something deep lay inside hidden, observing these emotions streaming past. Iós, after all these years, was still within Jushur. Iós, lying beneath, gained understanding of human survival and sustaining a body such as this. He felt love as Jushur felt it; he also felt the pain of loss that love brought. Iós became attached to the life of Jushur, and was happy to sit back and feel all that he felt. There was so much more here than in the life of a shark, for love and sex were truly something to savor. He feared that if he took over Jushur, Ala would recognize the difference, and the love and the sex would go away. So he stayed hidden and he enjoyed the love that humans were capable of.

The day came, though, as Jushur knew it would. Ala passed in the night, and he woke to her stiffened body beside him. He laid next to her for a long while, through the morning and until the Sun was near setting. He kept her on the sleeping mat, and dragged it closer to where the wind would blow on her face at the opening of their dwelling. He covered her with a cloth, and couldn't sleep; instead he watched the night sky, and sat near the opening of the dwelling with Ala, telling her of his strange dreams.

The following morning, he walked across town to tell his daughter and other villagers the news. Anik took the news solemnly, with quiet, small tears; she held her head high. Knowing that there was work ahead of them to help her soul travel home, they made an announcement in the village that Ala had passed; and many people cherished her, so the news spread quickly. Later that night, the people would come to the ceremony for her soul.

Together, Jushur and Anik walked to the jungle to collect big leaves and flowers of different colors. When they emerged from the jungle, Jushur handed the pile of leaves and flowers to Anik while he grabbed his knife from his waist and began cutting dry brush on the edge of the jungle. He also collected any small sticks that could be used to start a fire.

Jushur and his daughter split paths, and he brought the kindling to the edge of town, where a cliff overlooked the sea in the distance. The big orange Sun was starting to sag lower in the sky. They had to make haste before the night fell.

This cliff edge was the place where they burned the dead, a windy spot where fire burned well and the soul could catch on the breeze and leave the Earthly planes. It was tradition to burn the body at nightfall, so the soul might use the stars as a guide home. Jushur sat and began to build the base of the pyre, using wood stacked in a pile nearby. He focused and wept as the structure of wooden logs started to take shape. He filled the pyre with all the brush he had collected, and said a blessing for the fire to burn brightly and turn his wife's body back into the ash from which she came.

On the other end of town, Anik had walked back to her parent's home, arms full of leaves and flowers from the jungle. It was the woman's, or in this case, daughter's job to prepare the body for the burn, to clean, wrap, and give the body and soul a blessing.

She arrived at the opening of the house where her mother lay, surprisingly serene eyes and peace held in her frozen face. Ala's face was sprinkled with wrinkles of a life well-lived that bordered her eyes and mouth. Her daughter wept softly while she used a knife to remove her mother's clothes. Using water and cloth, she cleaned her mother's body. Even while removing the waste that was pooled beneath Ala, the daughter was unmoved by the smell and cleaned her carefully, with grace.

Once her mother was clean, she went to the shelves where a few spices and pigments were kept, mixed the yellow powder with some water, and brought it back to her mother. She murmured blessings while she created a design on her mother's forehead, nose, and chin. It was tradition to mark the dead with a blessing.

After this, she then wrapped the body in leaves from the jungle. They were long enough to wrap around and then tuck under the body. She worked methodically to wrap her mother safely in the jungle's arms. The flowers of many colors were placed around the whole body, tucked into the edges where Ala's body met the mat. The last touch to this preparation was to fix a water flower, more specifically a blue lotus flower, onto the forehead where the third eye hid beneath. This part required more of a stomach, and the daughter's forehead beaded with sweat as she prepared a needle made of fishbone, and thread made of plant fiber. The needle and thread would pass through the flower and then loop through the skin to secure it to the body. Anik's hand shook slightly as it pierced the flesh, but she quickly pulled it through, tied off the thread, and put away the supplies. She rinsed her hands in the dish of water, to cleanse them from death; and she bowed towards her mother and left for town to collect people for the ceremony.

Jushur and Anik reached the center of the village at nearly the same time, both solemn yet strong. The Sun was sinking halfway beneath the horizon, casting many colors onto the clouds in the sky. This beauty was a good omen for Ala's passing; it would be swift, without a struggle.

Many of the men in the village offered to help carry Ala to the edge of the cliff, and the procession began. Grandmothers brought plants to burn in the fire as an offering, and mothers brought balls of sap from jungle trees, to keep the fire happy. The whole village gathered to send her soul off to the sky.

The ceremony was simple; the fire was lit, and some sap was added to keep it happy while the wind blew. Jushur gave a blessing out loud for everyone to hear, and as the fire grew large, they placed the sleeping mat and Ala on top of the wooden stacks and flame. The people then all stood back, away from the smoke and smell of burning flesh. One villager brought a drum, and the drum was played in a constant rhythm until the body was completely burned. The night was clear, and the drum played until the stars had shifted in the sky. Everyone stood to leave, and return to their homes while only the family stayed behind. The two remained until the fire was completely burnt, which was just about when the Sun would rise again. The two eventually laid back and watched the stars dance. They marveled when the stars ran across the sky, wondering if that was Ala's soul dancing amongst them.

After this devastating blow, life moved forward; and Iós was also feeling this sense of loss from death. He had never known it to feel like this in the ocean. He missed the love, the companionship, and the sex. Now that Jushur's partner had died, Iós became restless and unsatisfied with the continual empty days. This was where things began to change, and Iós began to meddle with the life of Jushur. Iós would begin to take control when a beautiful woman would pass by; he would feel complete hunger and lust for their bodies. He would battle with Jushur's will, but never fully took control. He had come to respect Jushur and his position in the village.

Nearly ten years passed after Ala's death, so many moons that Jushur had lost count. His daughter had grown and had children of her own. He enjoyed the new life brought into the village. But in the evenings, Jushur indulged in drinking spirits. One particularly sideways evening, full of a fruit wine made from dates, Jushur was stumbling through the main part of the village. A young woman caught his eye, and Iós perked up at this. Her golden skin was supple and soft, and her curves were inviting and bouncing with each swaying step she took. Iós spied her and followed the woman to the well. She was collecting water and singing to herself. Iós took full control over Jushur, as Jushur was completely dizzy and dumb with drink.

He approached the woman at the well and smiled at her; he reached for her hand and asked her to put down the water and come with him. Jushur was an attractive man, and mostly respected in town, so at first the woman was flattered and followed him.

Iós guided them around the corner into a clearing, where soft sand bordered the jungle. He grabbed her face a little more forcefully than was necessary and began kissing at her. Like a hungry dog, he was aggressive, biting the sides of her neck. It was clear there was confusion and discomfort from the woman, and she tried to slow him down. She was somewhat willing and interested, but confused at what to make of his aggression.

But Iós was now in a trance of desire. Despite her pleas for him to slow down or stop, he began ripping up her dress and forced himself inside of her. He grabbed at her breasts till they bruised, thrusting into her without tenderness or regard. The woman wept; she was unable to stop him while he completed his carnal release inside of her. Iós was unaware and un-empathetic, as for him it was the most glorious thing he had felt in a long while. He was at the wheel, and relishing the power.

Afterwards, when he came to his senses, he saw beneath him a horrified woman, crying with fear and hatred. He saw that he caused her to bleed in more than one place. As much as he had enjoyed every moment of his act, he was deeply disturbed at what he had caused. Jushur's wife was never hurt, and she was always in a state of pleasure and moaning during the sex act. What had he done? He was ashamed; he tried to help assemble the woman, but she crawled back in fear that he would hurt her again. She gathered herself, slightly dizzied with pain, and ran off. Iós was confused at what had gone wrong; he did not know the fine tunings of love or tenderness as he thought he had. He did crave sex, and that was thrilling and powerful, but he was looking for more -- to feel love between two people with the sex. He was worried at what may happen in town with the woman and Jushur. So he quickly dissolved himself back into the recesses of Jushur's mind, and they laid passed out with drink's sleep, in the sand.

The next morning Jushur woke up to two men splashing him with a bucket of water. He was startled, but groggily so; he blocked his eye from the morning light with his hands. The two men began yelling at him and asking many questions, slapping his head and urging him to stand up. They got him roughly to his feet and dragged him into a nearby dwelling and threw him onto an adobe bench.

They explained what had happened last night, retold by the woman's perspective, that Jushur had raped her. The father of the girl and many villagers were enraged that he had done such a thing. They were also not sure how to act, as the conflicting nature of the situation. Jushur had always been a good man, an important figure in town, and a leader for voyages. He had never come close to doing harm to anyone, but there were some who suspected he was touched by a dark spirit or cursed, and this view did not help his case. If there were any villagers on the fence, they were now convinced he carried a dark spirit. This act would now push many people to believe he was dark, and perhaps he would be the first to be exiled from the village.

The two men were friends of Jushur's, and had been on voyages with him more than once. To them, he was normally their leader, someone to look up to; and now they were filled with doubt and concern for his soul.

Jushur was beside himself with confusion. Had he really been so drunk that he would do that to a young woman? He was ashamed and terrified that he could not remember it; the last thing he saw was the young woman walking by, and he remembered being quite tossed at that point, unable to even walk straight, let alone force himself on a woman. His lack of memory made him question himself.

Being the good man he was, Jushur asked to stand before the town and make an apology, and that the town could decide what his punishment was. He was escorted by the two men, as they walked and Jushur stumbled to the center of town. When they arrived, one of the men went to fetch the girl's father and other people from the village, to deal with the matter at hand.

Jushur waited in the Sun, disheveled, counting the grains of sand beneath him as the town slowly gathered at his expense. They would collectively decide his fate as a village. Jushur's palms were sweating, and his head was pounding, while deep within his mind Iós knew he had caused trouble and change for the both of them.

The father of the woman Iós had raped was angry, pacing back and forth, while fuming like steam trapped in a sealed pot. Jushur kept his head held as high as he could, even though he was ashamed, making brief eye contact with the angry man. The angry father wanted to castrate Jushur, making his idea known to the village. Most of the villagers disagreed, but there were a few that nodded with contemplation. This was a good sign; Jushur had enough respect from the village that he would not face such a punishment. Some yelled, "Exile him, his darkness is unleashed!" Jushur looked up at this, and he decided to speak.

"I will go willingly, and my dwelling can be used for a family that needs it more. I am ashamed; I was very drunk on the date wine, and do not remember doing anything of such dark nature to the young woman."

Cutting the commotion to a halt, a woman made a loud sound with her walking stick; its rain- sound rattling silenced the villagers. The old crone walked towards Jushur, passing through the crowd. She was the oldest woman in the village, her back slightly hunched, the skin on her face relaxed with many deep lines showing her age, like the rings of a tree. She came up close to Jushur, grabbed his chin, and looked directly into his soul.

She looked until it appeared that she had seen something, something interesting and telling. "Jushur's soul is of pure heart, he is not one to fear! But a dark spirit, the dark spirit of the sea, lives in him, waiting for the moment to attack. We cannot blame Jushur, but we cannot have him here." The woman let go of Jushur's face and gave him a sincere look of sorrow, patting his shoulder and turning to slowly walk back into the shade of the crowd. In this moment, the wind stirred with great force, swirling through the palm trees and the hair on people's head. The breeze was a relief from the growing heat, as Jushur was sitting in the Sun growing more dehydrated as the minutes brought the Sun ever higher in the sky.

The wind held its strong current around the village for some time, and this quieted the people. In time, the people understood that the wind was speaking to them, confirming what the old women had said. The town decided that at sunset, Jushur was to leave, and would be given a boat in trade for his dwelling. Jushur saw his daughter in the crowd, her face displaying mixed feelings -- surprised panic and also uncertainty. After it was decided as a tribe, Jushur nodded and made promise to leave at sunset, with a small boat that could be manned by one.

As Jushur walked back to his dwelling to gather his tools, his daughter followed him there, keeping her distance from him, but following him still. When they reached the dwelling, Jushur turned to her and apologized and began to weep; he was sorry he had to go, and of what the dark spirit within him had done. He did not know how to move the spirit from himself. Jushur went to embrace his daughter, who received his embrace, unafraid that his darkness was contagious. She had always known him to be this way, and never once was she afraid of him before.

"I am filled with regret, that I will not know your children or be here for you when you need me. I do not know where I will go, but it is time for my journey to move onward. I have always been a voyager," he said, forcing a fatherly smile of assurance. He grabbed her delicately on each shoulder and looked in her eyes. "Please do not think of me or remember as a monster. I will always think of you till I make my journey to the stars." It took everything within Jushur to not break into a full-on sob, but he managed to keep it at streaming tears. His daughter was visibly distraught, but she was brave like her mother.

"I will never think of you as a monster or the dark spirit of the sea; you are my father. always kind and strong." She gave him a quick nod to seal her statement, and looked around the small adobe dwelling, her eyes recording the memory of them there for the last time.

Jushur sent his daughter away so he could pack and rest before his journey. The Sun was at high noon, and he did not have long before he must embark on the journey to wherever it was. His head still ached with the sugar from the date wine, and he immediately drank water until he was filled to the brim. He slept, bloated and tired.

He woke as the Sun was making its way across the sky, sending shadows to grow long and thin. Jushur grabbed his bag for travel and collected everything he felt was necessary for his journey. He took his knife, a set of clothing, a metal tool used for carving and shaping wood, a few medicinal herbs tightly bound by leafs and fiber, an animal skin for water, a gourd cup, a ball of tree resin the size of his fist wrapped in leaves, dried meat, dates, and salt. His bag was brimming almost to the point of discomfort, but once aboard the small vessel, he would not have to carry it. He gave one last look at the place and made his way down to the water's edge, which would take just near an hour's time. He wore his hat woven with dried strips of palm fiber, as the sea was no forgiving place when the Sun was out.

Iós was in shock, blown away by how quickly dynamics can change in the nuisances of human society. He was in some way excited for the upcoming adventures, but the thoughts in Jushur's head worried him. He never experienced the inner dialogue of Jushur as dark and as sad as this. Such a strong man, broken so easily by the loss of his people. Iós felt something he had not felt before; he felt guilt, but the feeling was fleeting, like the attention span of a fly. Iós didn't linger in that mind frame for long.

When Jushur made it to the water's edge, he found that the beach was comprised of a beautiful white and fine sand. The sea sloshed onto a sand break instead of rock. Set further back, on the dry sand, was the fleet of wooden boats that had been built by the village. They were propped up by blocks far enough from the highest tide when the Moon was at its fullest.

A small boat shaped like a wide canoe was already dragged to the water; the small sail and mast were adjustable, with ropes tied off at the rear of the boat, where the main steering oars also were. The design was for a fisherman, so that one person could control the boat with greater ease. It was still laborious work, and after a week's stretch it would be exhausting. The boat was long enough that Jushur could lie down comfortably. It was a good boat, one he had helped design and make, so if there were a problem at sea, he could at the very least understand how to fix it.

He took a deep breath and crested the sand dune, and when he did, he saw a crowd of twenty people at the beach who had been blocked from his view before. None of them bore hostility or anger on their faces, but sorrow. Many of them were the men from his voyages, as well as the friends of his passed wife. As he walked up to the crowd, a few men clasped Jushur's forearms and placed their other hands on his back, gesture of brotherhood and friendship. He smiled with relief, as he did not know what to expect. A woman handed him a basket of food -- wrapped bread, dried meat, dates, citrus, salt, smoked fish in a ceramic pot, and dried cactus powder, which can normalize blood sugar if the food supply is low. There were other little wrapped packaged that were tucked underneath, but he could not tell what they were.

He accepted the gift with a big smile and tears. He bowed in gratitude, and packed the basket and his bag into the boat, under the seat. There were not many words shared; only the eyes carried the weight of communicating such complicated matters. There were no words for the situation at hand, as it was all new and confusing for everyone.

Jushur got in the boat, and all villagers placed a hand on the boat, a blessing tradition. After this, the strong men helped raise the small anchor rock and push him out to deeper waters. Jushur tightened the sail, and took the rear oar into his palms, and he directed the boat west towards the setting Sun. He planned to stick near the coastline to his north; that way he could anchor and make camp on a beach if he needed to.

He was off, the breeze at his face, drying his cheeks, leaving only trails of salt where tear tracks once raced.

Inside, Iós felt alive and ready for the adventure, ready to explore new places and new things he had never seen. Ready to find love again, and perhaps more sex that did not end with sourness. He learned how Jushur operated the small boat, how careful and at ease he was at the oars, using the stars above to direct him correctly; each constellation bore a name and a story for easy remembrance.

He sailed mostly at night and in the early mornings to avoid the day's heat. He would then set up a blanket tied to the mast, making a shade for sleeping. As soon as the Sun was low, it was cool enough to continue, and not far away was the darkening of the sky and its twinkling map. The boat was swift, and for some hours at a time, Jushur felt the rush and joy of the sea, forgetting his exile and cursed life. While on the boat, his rations kept him stable for some time. However, there was no way to cook or store any fresh-caught fish on his small boat, and he was soon low on water.

So one early morning, as the Sun was beginning to warm all it touched with the rising dawn, Jushur set a net in the water to see what fresh food he could catch, planning to anchor and head to shore to cook himself some fresh food and hunt for water. When he checked his net, there were a few bigger fish caught inside; he was happy and surprised at how easily fish came to him.

He sailed closer to a shore with sand instead of rock, and anchored his boat with the loop rock and rope, wedging it between some bigger rocks under the water's surface. Moving carefully to not lose the fish, he grabbed the net and walked them to shore, where he swiftly chopped off the heads and gutted the fish with his knife. Laying the fish fillets on some dried leaves he had brought, he placed them in the shade, while he dug a pit in the sand and collected something dry for a fire. When all was ready, awaiting the first spark of heat, Jushur reached into his pocket and removed a stone as clear as water. It was harder than any rock he had known, and beautiful as water frozen in time. This was the most special and useful tool he owned, as with proper sunlight, it could start fires. He had found it while digging for clay to make the adobe dwellings of his village; it was in a small pocket as deep as Jushur was tall. It was a secret he never showed anyone, as he was worried it would be taken from him. It was his special secret. Somehow, through the blessings from the Sun and the magic of the stone, it focused a small beam of light that burned smoke to flame! He considered it was a gift from the spirit of the Earth.

Jushur waited by his pit for the Sun to be high enough, and he used his stone to light the fire. Cooking his fish was easy and quick, a task Jushur had managed countless times. When it was done, he sprinkled spices and salt from his home and squeezed the citrus fruit on top to make the fish easier to eat.

It was divine! So glorious to eat fresh fish and feel the power of the fish inside of him; he could sense it bringing him back to life, and he was also ready for his daily sleep. Unsure of the island's safety, he went back to his boat with his net and tools, and slept on the boat until the cool air and low Sun woke him up. He was very thirsty; his water stores were very low.

So he climbed back into the sea and made his way to the beach to find drinkable water. Often times, as with Jushur's home, freshwater flowed to the sea. As Jushur had made many voyages, he was used to finding water, as his crew went through water fast. He was the best on his crew at finding it. He had observed that the place where he was now was far more lush than the land of his people; there were more bugs, more plants, and likely more animals. It followed that there must be more accessible water. When he crossed into the tree line, the air was cooler and damp; it tasted sweet and alive. Birds sounded alarm at his presence, and Jushur tasted the air as he walked. Different channels of air tasted different, and bore different weights. Often, air passing over fresh water had a particularly clean and cool taste; it tended to hang heavier. If you excelled at hunted for streams, you would know the difference; it's a gods-given instinct, and not many possess the skill.

Jushur took many steps deeper into the trees, until they opened up into a clearing where two giant rock walls started low on either side and grew tall as they spanned out, forming a canyon. Jushur found himself standing in the center of the canyon, where a stream of very cold fresh water flowed. He immediately went to rinse his face, hands, and arms. The water was ice blue, rushing with swift speed, making its way towards Mother Ocean. The whole of his soul was overjoyed with relief at how close the water was to the shore. In the past, it had sometimes taken nearly a day's hike to reach, not to mention transporting its weight for a large crew. This was effortless. It felt that despite all the bad things he had faced, something mystical and beyond him was on his side. He made his gratitude known for the ease at which the water of life had been found; he leapt and smiled before he settled down to fill his skins.

With his water stocked and nightfall upon him, he sailed off again, unsure of where it was he was headed. Despite his inevitable loneliness, he felt that he should spend time alone and away from people for a while. This brought Iós awake and made him angry; he internally protested this by taking control of Jushur's arms, stopping them from movement. Jushur became aware of the dark spirit then, and sat still, trying to calm himself. The being took over Jushur's voice so he might listen to him speak.

"Jushur, we will *not* be spending life in isolation; that is not in your best interest. It is to my regret that I got us exiled. I admit that I raped that woman, and I enjoyed every second of it. But I did not understand the pain and trouble it would cause. I miss the pleasure of your wife, and the feelings beyond the body. Jushur, I have been a part of you for long years now, and we will have to work as one."

Jushur's mind was racing like a rabbit hunted, his arms still frozen, his vocal cords occupied by the spirit. All he could do was think, and his mind was wild with feelings, anger at the mention of his wife and what he had thought was private, at the rape of the young woman, and at the loss of his village. He was amazed by the power of the spirit, how easily it took over his body and voice. He was confused; why had the spirit waited until now to make itself known?

Hearing all of these thoughts, Iós responded: "I enjoyed your life. It was something I had never before known. The love, the food, the community, and the sex; it was beauty, and worth keeping quiet for. Before you, I lived inside that shark for hundreds of years, and its life was not even close to the same. It was dark and dull, and there was no love. This is something special to humans that I am fond of. Don't bother asking where I am from, as I do not know. I found my way to this planet from the stars, and now I am here."

Jushur was stunned, completely wide-eyed to learn that ever since he'd touched that shark, a star-being had lived inside of him like a parasite, sitting back and enjoying the ride. He now understood why he did not age, and did not tire from his years and lifestyle. This was fully a gift and a curse.

"So, Jushur," continued Iós, "can we make an agreement, or shall I take over for now? You can rest while I sail. We can be friends, you know, working together to live long and travel widely."

Jushur agreed to the rest, as he was curious what would happen when the star-being took over completely. He asked in his mind, "Will I see, will I remember, or will it be like before with the young woman, when I remembered nothing?"

"It depends. Before you were drunk, and now you are not; we can see what happens. I will take over until the Sun comes up; and in the morning, we can see if you recall anything."

Jushur agreed, feeling he didn't have much of a choice; plus, with his life now beginning again, there was some intrigue and some power to this unusual situation.

Like Iós had promised, at dawn Jushur woke up, so to speak, remembering sailing through the night like a hazy dream. If he focused too hard on it, it would slip away; but he did recall some of the time when the star-being took over.

"So, Jushur, did you recall me sailing in the night?" asked the star-being.

Jushur answered in his mind, "Yes, a bit; it was fuzzy, like a dream."

"I do not know dreaming, only the mentioning of it from watching your life. I cannot see where you go when you dream; that is when you disappear. It was interesting to sail, alone, without your conscious mind awake. Do you see what I have made? So you can sail by day if you choose, as I imagine you don't wish to go to sleep now." Instead of a shade for sleeping, the being had made the blanket to cover the seat where the oars were, doubled over itself so the shade was dark and full.

Jushur was impressed, and actually happy to sail in the day; he was ready to be awake. This was the first time he'd felt that this situation might not be so bad after all. At the very least, he would not be alone. The star-being was not as dark as he had imagined.

"What can I call you, star-being?"

"You can call me Iós. It is a name I have given myself over the years, as I learned about the concept of naming."

"Very well then, Iós. I like your idea for the shade; you know to me too well. I would be restless if I tried to sleep again."

Jushur stood to stretch slowly, so as to keep the boat balanced. He loosened the sail, checked the surrounding water, and then dove into the sea, to stretch his body and to urinate. Jushur hadn't noticed it before, but he had greater sense within the water; small movements underneath caught his mind's attention. This startled him, but it was powerful. He tried to open his eyes underwater, and it did not burn as much as it had before. He could feel movements in the water through his flesh. He sensed sharks, small fish, dolphins, and whales in the surrounding mile-radius around his boat.

He quickly came up for air, and carefully got back into his boat, slumping over the edge so as to not tip it.

Iós and Jushur learned something that day, both coming to the same conclusion at once. Now that Iós was strong and fully awake side-by-side with Jushur, the powers and knowledge from the shark, skills that Iós had absorbed, were available to Jushur. He could now tap into those skills -- and the memories of the shark. Anything that Iós inhabited would likely lend to new knowledge and new gifts.

Layer 17: Izar - Choosing Realms

Intertwined and enjoying the landscape of the Fae, Indra and Izar sat musing about the human realm. Indra sat nestled with Izar seated behind her; they were basking in the ease of each other's company, savoring the brightness between them. Izar had just shared his entire life story to Indra, and he was growing more curious by the moment. He wanted to know more about her life, how old she was, and how it was she came to be.

Izar's voice softly broke out into the air. "Indra, will you tell me about yourself, as I have shared with you?"

Indra nodded solemnly and squinted into the distance, planning to be careful with her words. She then shared a great deal of her story; she shared how old she was, and why it was she came to Earth, but there were many things she left out, things that were too complex for the moment. After all, she couldn't yet be sure if Izar was to be trusted.

In that lack of trust, Indra stopped halfway through her story to stand and stretch; she looked like she had grown bored and tired of telling. Izar watched her glorious body curve and flex with every move she made. Her body was fluid as water, and he could not take his eyes from her beauty, wanting to drink her up or bathe himself in her.

"So, Izar, what do you think of my story so far? Does it amuse you?"

Izar brushed the hair from his eyes, and was unsure how to respond at first. Her age did make him feel slightly immature. Her story did amuse him; in fact, it fascinated him, and inspired many questions within him. What, exactly, or *who* rather, was this dark virus that had landed on Earth? Then Izar thought of the war and all the power struggles in his own mortal world, and his mind drifted like light snow swirling just above the ground. He forced himself to quiet his mind and focus on answering Indra, as she was waiting, her wry smile fading by the second.

"Indra, I am not sure amusement is the right word; but I am intrigued by your journey, and the grand adventure that one soul can take. It feels fanciful, as if I might suddenly wake from the mushroom trip I took in the woods. Although, despite its fanciful nature, it makes perfect sense, it does stretch my mind taut; it makes me question my own origin." He threw both his arms up, shrugged, and sighed a huge sigh.

"Magic and personal matters aside, the virus you spoke of, the one inside of the doctor from Egypt... I'm not sure I fully grasp the concept, but I want to understand. Because the reality is this: I have seen the cruelty that follows greed for power and territory. I am a simple man from a small town, and even still I know the world is infiltrated with it."

His eyes drifted off thoughtfully. "The knowledge alone that this thing is somehow a singular being, one with a potential face and name, unveils some of the looming mystery and helplessness that many humans face. We feel as if the perpetrators of greed and wars are faceless, nameless entities so entrenched in power that we won't even know where to look, or even who or how to fight. But this, this means something can be done!" Izar said with motivation in his voice.

He paused and walked up to Indra, and grabbed her hand. "From what you have told me so far, I imagine that there is more to tell, and I will not press you with knowing it all now; your life has been long. I can wait. But I can say this much: Earth is a dark and beautiful place, and I would love to see more love in it."

Indra's face displayed a small, thin smile, admiring his mind, but quickly it faded, becoming stoic once more; and she nodded. "There is more to share, but before I am willing to share, I must be sure I can. Also, remember this: time is flying by in your world, and I do not wish to ruin the course of your human life. What I need to see will not take too long."

Indra walked across the seating area, and ventured back onto the grass holding two cups. "Come with me; we will go now to the water temple."

Izar followed her easily, and he knew it would always be easy to; he knew right then and there that it would be near-impossible to leave her by choice. He kept quiet, admiring her walk through the scenery, a landscape lush and teeming with life, just as faery tales had described it. He did not want to speak out of turn, for fear he might say the wrong thing. There was still so much he didn't understand, and unwilling to chance it, he kept his mouth shut.

They walked for some time; as they advanced into the changing terrain, Indra gave explanations for the landscape and the beings within them, speaking about the history and temperament of certain creatures they encountered on the way. She stopped when they arrived at an enormous giant sphere. Upon looking closely Izar saw it was made of flowing water, cascading down in a spiral pattern. Indra placed the two cups under the water; they quickly filled, and she handed one to Izar, while drinking the contents of her cup slowly. Izar drank his, and did not expect the water to taste so cold and clear. It was by far the most hydrating and beautiful water he had ever tasted.

"It is tradition to drink from the water temple before entering. This is so the water spirit can get to know who is entering."

Izar tilted his head at that comment, and smirked at the pure strangeness of this realm. He finally felt like things made sense; how perfect this place was, compared to the human realm he was from! He finished his cup.

They left the cups on the ground, and Indra walked through the water; Izar followed not far behind her. He could see her silhouette break the water's flow, and she was surrounded by a rainbow mist. The view felt hauntingly familiar, like déjà vu from a dream; but then again, maybe it was the water he'd just consumed, as he could feel it seeping into his mind like a special kind of wine, loosening his tightness and shyness. Inhibitions aside, Izar made his way through the water wall, welcoming the cold water onto his face.

Inside it was surprisingly large -- larger than the volume of the outside of the sphere, if Izar had to guess. Most everything inside was made of water, except for a few natural stone structures. There was a lagoon in an earthen basin of light-colored stone that grew up into an arch over the top of the lagoon. Beyond that, all in sight was made of water, flowing in all sorts of directions and patterns.

Indra startled Izar from his wide=eyed wonderment by motioning for him to take his clothes off, lightly pulling at his shirt. Izar did as he was told, and was not in the least shy, as the water he drank gave him confidence and a sense of euphoria. His body was beautiful, too, and he was aware and proud of his well-carved form. He was strong, but not overly bulky, and his skin was like Indra's, dark and olive. His silvery eyes shone brightly, contrasting with his bronze skin amidst all the mist.

Indra, her eyes opening a little wider, was not sly about looking at Izar's manly endowment; indeed, her eyes were filled with interest. He was caught between motives, and then thought better of it. Shrugging the moment off, trying to contain that part of himself, he was hoping he could keep his impending erection at bay, as it was not an ideal moment for one. He wanted to show Indra he was in control of himself, unlike other men. Indra had already been naked the whole time, so he had become accustomed to her form.

They walked into the lagoon; the floor was smooth and it felt cool on his feet. They walked until the floor was suddenly no more. At first Izar dipped under a little, unaware of the drop. There was a giant cavern beneath them. Elegantly, Indra treaded water, and Izar matched her form as best he could. He was all lean muscle, and it took more work for his body to stay buoyant.

"We will go beneath, and do not fear; you will be able to breathe there," Indra said with an alluring softness.

Exhaling all of his air, Izar took one more giant breath out of habit, and let himself sink; which, given his muscle density, he did easily. Nervous to take a breath, he held it in. Indra noticed this and leaned in to kiss him, which he received graciously until he started to take in water; he didn't know whether to keep kissing her or drown. The feeling was unnatural, but she was right; when his lungs were full of water, he was not suffering nor drowning. He breathed freely.

Their faces still close, Izar leaned back in to kiss Indra again; but flirtatiously shy, she turned, and he kissed her cheek, feeling a little stupid. Moving forward, they continued to sink, deeper and deeper, the circle of light above getting smaller and dimmer as they went. They finally made it to a depth where there was no trace of light. It was there that Indra wanted the water to know Izar, and it was so quiet in that void of sensations that Indra could hear Izar's soul. She did not let go of his forearms, as she did not want him to panic or get lost in the darkness. He was calm with her touch, and felt not even close to panicking. He was merely awaiting whatever it was they were doing down there in the dark.

Indra closed her eyes, and remembered a time when Eithar and she sank submerged in her cavern waters, and she heard the song that their soul-frequencies made together. She did not want to get her hopes up, but she had to investigate. Indra leaned in slowly towards Izar, and she lightly touched her forehead to his, also pulling her hips snuggly into his. Their bodies were now completely touching. Indra sank into herself as she had begun to practice all those years ago. Completely centered, she focused on the man before her, surrendering to his touch.

Izar, slowly understanding what to do, also sank into his place of stillness. It was by no means as practiced nor as still as Indra's, but he could still sink into a place of focus and clarity.

Indra heard a quiet song, as if music were playing at the end of a long, carpeted hallway. It was muffled and distant, but Indra could still hear its melody. She was both shocked and elated to realize that it was the same symphony that had put her into bliss and peace long ago. The quiet, muffled symphony of their souls played while they floated, meshed as one, in the abyss.

She did not wish to move, as she now felt glued to the man, never wanting to let him go again. She had waited so long for him to find her. As he had promised, he *did* find her, deep within the forest she was unable to leave. It took him some time to do so, but that was of no importance now. Eithar was here, or at least she thought he was, and they were glued together so seamlessly in the moment that it was hard to differentiate whose body was whose. She did notice the difference when something hard pressed into her stomach. She was tempted take him there in the dark, but the water temple was not a place for that.

Eroticism aside, how could she relay this very important news to him? Would he remember, or would he run? Her head now spinning, she fell from her inner self, no longer focused, their symphony fading away. Wondering what Izar was thinking, she moved her forehead from his slightly.

Izar's focus was loosened by the movement; he could sense Indra's brain working, and it triggered his own. He had never felt so connected to or understood by someone so lovely and perfect. He knew that Indra was the one he had been searching for, but now what? Now that he'd found her, what happened next?

Izar was thinking all this when he felt her move her head away slightly, but he did not let her get far, and he leaned in for another kiss. This time, it was deliberately passionate, but soft and slow; he wasn't hurried or wild, only there in the moment with her. This kiss shattered his reality into a thousand tiny pieces, and it took everything in him to not want all of her. So he ended the kiss and moved one hand to hold the side of her head, just near her ear.

Indra realized that it was time to leave the deep waters, as things between them were getting heated. She said something, again in a strange language that he could not understand; this brought a small thread of light shining in from their left, which connected to Indra's throat. With swift, fluid movements, she brought them both towards the direction of the thread. They moved through the water quickly, and a circle of light appeared ahead and grew larger.

Crashing through the surface, Indra breathed the air easily, and Izar did not. First he had to cough up all the water that had filled his lungs. Indra waited, unconcerned, as she knew this would happen. Once Izar caught his breath, he let out a deep baritone laugh that made the water around him ripple. Indra cocked her head sideways at him and smiled, treading water easily, like a butterfly treads air. Izar looked up at the stone arch, to see that the water's shape had changed drastically; he pointed up so Indra would look.

Her jaw dropped, as Izar's did. There were thin spirals of water twisting around one another, like the double-helix of DNA. Those spirals were then twisting among bigger ones of the same shape, and so on, a glorious fractal of moving water displayed between the stone archway above their heads. Indra spoke again in the language of her people, and a low sound gurgled from the water, echoing all around. She responded to the gurgles with something else, but the water did not speak again.

Izar looked at her with questioning eyes. "What was that? Have you ever seen the shapes like that in the temple? By the look in your eyes, my guess would be no."

Indra took a deep sigh and swam to where they could stand on the floor of the lagoon. "The water spirit of this temple weighs the souls that go into its dark depths. When surfacing, it will display what it feels, like a mirror. And no, I have never seen such an intricate display, as it weighed both our souls together."

"Is it a bad display?" Izar asked.

"No -- it is neither good or bad, only telling. I just feel it, feel how the imagery moves in me, how my body reacts to it. It is a truthful telling to listen to your feelings."

Izar nodded, and began to walk closer to the shallows, where his clothes lay on the bank. He stood beautifully natural, looking as if he had been touched by the gods, and Indra watched him as he marveled at the full view of the shapes swirling around them. He took a deep breath and closed his eyes. Opening them again, refreshed, he took in the information, and appeared to be weighing how it made him feel. He shook his head, and smiled.

"Indra, did I pass your test?"

Indra quickly moved in the water until she was close to him. "I had to see before I told you more. Now I know whether or not I can trust you."

"Ah, I see," Izar said. "You still didn't answer my question, though. How about this one -- it's easier to answer, and less personal. How much time has passed in the mortal realm?"

Indra looked a bit disappointed; she really did want to tell him that she trusted him, that he had passed the test, but Izar had shifted the conversation. "So far, since you have been here, we have spent about two months of time in your realm; not enough to disrupt your life, but as you can see, it has not felt like much time has passed since you arrived, and if it continues, it may disrupt and confuse those who care about you," Indra said, forcing cool aloofness.

Izar's face was calculating, but not shocked. He had taken her word for it earlier when she mentioned the time change, and was prepared for the news. He noticed her shift in mood.

"Izar, earlier, you pledged loyalty and passion in the forest, a promise, and I will hold you to it. We have a deep connection that I now recognize, and I invite you to stay here with me, and live a life much longer if you choose. I also understand you may need to leave and settle your affairs in your other realm, perhaps with wife and children, or other family..." Indra said bravely, extending an invitation for Izar, and yet clearly jealous, her last sentence falling more quietly from her mouth, second-guessing everything. She spoke again before Izar had time to reject her or answer.

"As I told you before, I came here on a mission to this planet, to mediate the virus and alter its strength somehow. To free the souls that are trapped on Earth, and then return to where I came from. It is taxing to think of doing it alone, but I will if I must." She stepped out of the lagoon and twisted the water from her hair, leaning slightly to keep the water from running onto herself.

Izar, smiling at her icy and independent nature, clearly perceived that the walls protecting her heart were strong and unyielding. "First of all," he answered, "I have no wife; nor do I have any children, to answer your first question. In regards to leaving, I *do* have a mother and father, however, and by now I'm sure they have growing concerns about my absence, which I will need to tend to. As for your invitation, I know it's forward of me to say, but I have been looking for you my whole life. Now that I have found you and am formally invited, I wish to stay with you and help in any way I can. I am not sure the way to accomplish this task, but I am willing to stand beside you and do my best."

Indra's hopeful eyes filled with relief, and then impatience. She had a feeling he would have to say goodbye before he could really say hello, but she did her best to let the impatience melt away. Because truly, it was admirable for him to care so deeply for his family; as annoyed as she was that he would have to leave, she knew it spoke of his character and heart.

"I will leave as soon as possible," he told her gently, "so that I may return as soon as possible. I do not think I can go long without seeing you again. I fear that if I wait too long, my heart will fall out of my body and melt. I finally feel that there is a reason for my life; it has been ignited, and I want nothing more than to be at your side."

Izar walked up to Indra to kiss her gently and look down at the ring he had given her. "I meant what I said about loyalty, and I *will* be back. The whole journey should take me two weeks my time, and that's considering all factors of delay. For instance, if I cannot find a car to take me back towards my home, or if my mother has a hard time understanding." Indra perked up at this, as it would not be long at all in her world.

"My declaration of loyalty may feel overwhelmingly new. It is a lot of pressure, as equally as it is enticing. I cannot help it, though; you, are my priority, and I will not lose sight of that." He quickly dressed himself and bowed towards the arch to thank the water spirit. He looked back at Indra, nodding at her, as she knew the way out.

Before he knew it, they were back at her tree, and as Indra was no fan of goodbyes, she smiled and placed her hand on Izar's head and spoke wildly in her language. Taking his hand, she squeezed it closely to her chest, her touch warming his hand to where it was noticeable hot, but not painfully so. "This is so you can find my tree again," Indra said, her voice suspended in echoing whispers.

And snap, Like a rubber band, he was back in his realm, mid-morning with temperate weather. Still feeling the heat on his hand, he looked and saw that there was a wooden ring on his finger, one inscribed with what looked like gold. He could not read the words, but it made his heart sing like no song it had ever sung. His whole soul was completely alight with purpose and love, no longer playing hide and seek with itself; finally, he was found.

Strewn camp supplies displayed the weathering of time. Everything was windblown and rained on, covered in tumbled mulch, gnawed on my forest denizens. He quickly gathered his things, and while packing realized he had to urinate. He hadn't had to use the bathroom the entire time he was in the other realm, not once. Which was odd, but was actually a relief. Relieving himself in some nearby bushes, he felt the satisfaction of a welled-up damn breaking open. With his pack on his back, filled with his belongings, he then made his way from the forest. Nearly whistling the whole way to the road, he walked joyfully, basking in the Sun. He was following the road in the direction of home, waiting for a car to drive by and hopefully pick him up.

He looked down at the wooden ring on his finger and smiled. It was a keepsake that proved it was all truly real.

Layer 18: Paesh - Seeing the Same Face

Paesh awoke, late in the night, and clicked on the orange glowing salt lamp to write in her dream journal. *Waking at 3:47, 8/24/2019.*

It starts in the sky, and I can see many stars. There were two beings. My perspective was from one of those beings; it was me, but it wasn't me. I couldn't see myself, as I was the experiencer. I would have needed a mirror. I saw these outrageously entrancing silver eyes, always looking at me throughout the dream, sort of overlain like a filter over my sight, floating within my view. In the dream there was a metallic swirling ribbon that twisted as if caught in midflight across the landscape. I was watching a man sit on the ribbon. I had the awareness that I knew him, and even though he didn't look human, he was indeed a man. He was almost formless, and I could tell he knew me too, and was so relieved to see me. He was filled with sorrow. Then there was music of unspeakable beauty echoing around us. Then the setting and scene shifted. Violet light. Warmth. Love. It felt like a long life lived, condensed into a fuzzy haze. Then there was a massive sound like tearing paper and heat; I remember turning back to look before leaping into a violet flame. That's when I woke up.

After completing her entry, Paesh tucked the book and pen on the shelf, half asleep, and clicked off the light.

When she woke up in the morning to the music of her alarm, her eyes followed the wood-paneled walls to the window where the bird was perched, awake. Noticing Paesh's open eyes, the bird made a sweet, short whistle. Paesh was so excited by this new and wild friend that she was giddy. A huge smile was plastered on her face. "Good morning, bird, did you sleep well?"

Paesh scooted out of bed, and pulled back the sheets and blankets, making her bed so she wasn't tempted to crawl back into it. A moment later, adjusting her faucet for the shower, she took off what little she had on and hopped in. The essential oils in her soaps really lifted her energy and sent luxurious steam through her whole bathroom. When she was refreshed and exfoliated, she was ready for the day, popping out of the shower and drying off. She attended to all of her morning rituals, ranging from vitamins, makeup, and tinctures to stretching, and of course some tea.

While in the kitchen, Paesh noticed the sweet bird had taken one shit, as far as she could tell; there was only the one spot on the newspaper. Perhaps it was someone's pet bird, she thought as she made breakfast. When she sat down to eat, the bird came flying downstairs and back onto the counter, heading right for the bowl of little bird munchables. They ate in silence, enjoying the meal and taking in the energy needed for the day.

Paesh looked over at the bird and thought, *Hmm, maybe I should give it a name to address it more personally if it chooses to stick around.* She chewed some more as she thought, her crisp apple making a small apple-juice mist with every bite. "So, bird, I was thinking -- if you would like to come and go if you please, the window upstairs will always be open. Also, I was thinking we should do names. My name is Paesh." Paesh pointed to herself when. She then pointed to the bird and waited. The bird said nothing of significance. It was a bird, after all. But it did fly to the floor near the door and tap on the wood with its beak.

Paesh went over, feeling a little sad, and opened the door. "Well it was lovely to have you stay over, come back anytime." And the bird took off, just like that. Paesh left the door open for some fresh air, and sat back down to finish her braised greens and apple. When she was washing her dishes, the bird came back and landed on the counter. It had brought something in its beak, and dropped it on the counter.

It was a stem of light-purple holy tulsi flowers.

"Wow, what beautiful flowers I see you've found in the garden. Is this in response to the name question?" Paesh pointed to the bird again with her chopsticks and said, "Tulsi?"

Surprisingly, the bird made a small whistle at that name. Paesh was completely beside herself. This was by far the coolest and weirdest thing that had ever happened to her! Now she had a bird friend named Tulsi. How strange -- each day just kept getting more and more outlandish, but in the best way, literally surprising at every turn. Paesh laughed out loud.

Looking at the clock, she saw that she was still on track for making it to work on time if she left promptly. So, Paesh told Tulsi that she was leaving, and would return as the Sun was setting; and when Paesh walked out the door, the bird followed. So she shut the door and locked it, but let the bird know the window upstairs was open if she needed to go inside, as well as fair warning about her cat, Moth. Paesh felt like the bird was truly hearing the words she was saying; it was incredible.

When rolling away on her bike, she noticed she couldn't help but smile. To her surprise, the bird was following her, a good ten meters up and one behind her as she rode. Literally, a dream come true. It was like having a proper familiar or spirit animal. Paesh was glowing as if she were the Sun the whole way to work.

She waved to Tulsi as she went indoors to work, changed her clothing, and prepared for the lab work as usual. While sitting in the lab waiting for Tiago, she heard footsteps coming down the hall. It wasn't Tiago's sound, not his cheerful loafers' click. It was a little squeaky, sounding practical, like sneakers. She turned to look at the door, and she had to pick her jaw up off of the floor, as it was *Lu* walking through the door -- the man she had met yesterday, when she crashed her bike and ridden away before anything more could happen.

"Whoa, Paesh? From last night?" Lu said, also picking his jaw up off of the floor.

"Yes, hi, what are you doing here?" Paesh asked, worried that maybe he had followed her somehow.

"I've been working with the mycology department from another lab, but just got a transfer call yesterday to see if I wanted to work on a different project. Apparently the guy working this job quit."

Paesh laughed out loud, "Wow, that's an extreme coincidence! Glad to have you on the team -- it certainly beats Jeff. I didn't realize he quit, since he was here just yesterday." Paesh knew it probably had to do with her exploding at him, but to hell with it, good riddance. There was a small curiosity that pulled at the back of her mind as to why he'd peed himself; that was unusual. She brushed it aside, as Lu was staring at her while she was off in thought.

"Well, Lu, since you just arrived, I assume Tiago didn't show you around yet. Would you like a tour?" said Paesh with forced professionalism.

He gave a slight bow and nodded. "I would like to see what we're working with, certainly." So Paesh gave him the down-low, rules, rooms, projects in motion, and more specifically the details about the machines in her lab, as well as their functions and maintenance. It took about 30 minutes overall to walk him around. That was when Tiago came in.

"Sorry for my tardiness; I was on a phone call regarding the employee who left us, and you know how HR can be." He chuckled nervously, wringing his hands. Paesh noted his odd behavior; come to think of it, she had never seen Tiago act so strange. This got the hairs of concern to stand tall on the back of her neck.

"Paesh, may I have a word with you in the hall, a private matter? Oh, and is it Lu? We spoke on the phone. I am so happy for you to arrive so quickly. We appreciate you being a part of our team," Tiago said, sounding truly grateful and professional.

"Happy to be here. Paesh took the liberty of showing me around this morning, so I can get started on some smaller tasks until you both return to give me direction." Lu smiled at Paesh and his eyes flashed silver again, so briefly that Tiago didn't notice at all.

The two left the room, and Tiago walked down the hallway, motioning for Paesh to follow him. His shoes clicked, a familiar sound, but in the quiet hallway and given the mystery of the situation, every click echoed loudly, matching the pounding staccato beat of Paesh's heart. She had never been fired before, and she wondered if she would be, and what was wrong. Taking a deep breath as they turned the corner, they met at the surveillance room door. Tiago, still wringing his hands, looked at Paesh as if searching for someone else inside of her.

He knocked on the door, and a small, old leathery man opened the door, his face kind and weathered from a life in the Sun. Tiago began speaking in Portuguese to the old man, who nodded and gave Paesh a wide-eyed look as he exited the room.

"That is my uncle from Brazil. He does not have his green card, and I pay him under the table at the lab here to do maintenance and surveillance. Please don't mention that to anyone."

Paesh nodded with sincere seriousness and replied, "Of course; I would never think to say a word. I didn't know you had any family here, and now I know why you don't speak about it."

Tiago nodded solemnly and then gave a slight smile, "He is a good man, just doesn't know much English; he is a stubborn old bird when it comes to that sort of thing. Anyway, enough about that; this is about yesterday with Jeff." Tiago turned to look at the screen and prepare the footage. "Paesh, you have been working here for four years, and you are by far one of the best employees and people I have ever met. Never one complaint about you. But I want to show you something that gives me quite an alarm, and is the reason Jeff has been admitted to a mental hospital for a little while."

Paesh gasped and covered her mouth, completely unsure how what had happened would cause Jeff to need mental care, even as her stomach dropped into her shoes.

"Are you ready? Maybe you should sit down. Let's both sit down," Tiago said, sliding chairs away from the desk to sit in. Paesh looked down and sat, feeling completely puzzled about what she was about to see.

The file played, and the view showed see Paesh putting the covered samples in the fridge, the neutral environment. She had her headphones in and was clearly looking into the distance in quiet reverie and contemplative thought. Jeff, looking more snide than ever, stepped closely to Paesh and began pointing to his watch and speaking. Then something happened that Paesh wasn't prepared for: when it was clear she was getting heated, she suddenly grew taller by at least 15 centimeters. And that wasn't the strangest part: her face changed, her eyes growing larger and farther apart, as her skin took on the purple tinge of lilac flowers.

Paesh burst into laughter. "Okay, very funny, Tiago. This is hilarious, and the anxiety I felt up till now has been pretty good punishment for me yelling at Jeff. Nice work." When Paesh looked over to see that Tiago was not smiling, or even close to laughing, he caught her eyes and looked at her with the most nervous, serious, and confused facial expression she'd ever seen on him. He shook his head without a word, and ran back the footage. It played again, and they watched that footage repeatedly.

After about the fifth time, Paesh began to sweat, and to think at lighting speed. No way was she some kind of purple Hulk. This had to be some kind of fake. She hadn't noticed herself change, so how could this be? Or was it real? *What's happening to me, have I always been like this, is that the reason for my incident a year ago, is this why that bird is following me, am I a monster?!*

She told her boss, "Tiago, I have no idea what this is, or what's happening. This has to be a fake or a flaw in the film, or something. I normally don't get angry -- it's something I've suppressed since I was a child -- but yesterday I just let Jeff have it, and if this is for real, I get why he peed himself. I'm hot, are you hot?" Paesh said, standing up and fanning herself. "Can we go outside?"

Tiago was looking at Paesh kindly, but with mild caution, which made her feel like a monster. He saved the file to a folder and uploaded it to a USB stick, then deleted the original copy and handed the stick to Paesh. "Here, keep this. I don't think it should stay at the lab; it should stay with you." Paesh grabbed the stick and put it in her pocket. They both exited the room and took a back door to the outdoor break area that led into the shaded protection of the woods, where the air was cool and breezy.

Paesh sat directly on the ground and took a deep breath with her hands covering her face. She was startled when something with tiny clawed feet landed on her shoulder; it was Tulsi, the beautiful white bird, coming to her rescue. Tulsi was not afraid of Paesh, and this comforted her instantly. Tiago sat on a nearby log, scratching his head and looking at the bird curiously.

"Is that your pet bird?" Tiago asked in a cool voice, trying to change the subject.

"No... well, no, she's a bird that hit my window the other day, and I put her in a little comfy spot to heal and she's been sort of following me ever since. I call her Tulsi, like the basil," said Paesh with cool nonchalance, trying to change the subject. But unable to truly just move on from the subject, Paesh asked, "Tiago, are you going to fire me? Are you afraid too, like Jeff?"

He Paused, his mouth tight, "I'll admit, at first I didn't understand Jeff's crazy muttering on the phone last night, and I went to check the surveillance. It did startle me a great deal." Tiago paused, "But honestly, I am not afraid; if anything, I am curious, and of course, being the scientist I am, I want to run tests and panels." Tiago laughed nervously, hoping he wasn't speaking out of turn, and quickly corrected himself. "I don't mean to make you feel like a lab rat. I mean, just for curiosity's sake, just a pleasure project that we can investigate together, and maybe it'll give some answers." Tiago pulled at his collar nervously, hoping not to upset Paesh, but her laughter relaxed him immediately. Paesh was a kind woman, always pretty cool and agreeable for the four years he had known her.

After Paesh stopped laughing, she told Tiago, "Actually, that was one of my first thoughts, that we could do some tests on me at the lab! I'm not sure it'll lead to any findings, but it's worth a shot. I'll be honest, Tiago -- some strange stuff has been happening to me lately, and as scary as this is, I'm more intrigued than afraid."

Tiago nodded at this. "I understand. It's like something out of a cinema, or like a sci-fi book, sort of exciting, no?" Tiago quickly added, "Also, first and foremost, we can just keep this between us. I won't tell a soul, nor will my uncle. Your secret is safe with me, especially if Jeff comes and tries to poke around for footage or anything. I'll just play dumb." He winked at Paesh. This gave Paesh great relief; she hadn't even thought of Jeff doing that.

"I wonder if it's too much to ask if I could take the day off and sort of collect myself -- I'm feeling a little scattered in the mind. We can tell Lu I'm having a family emergency and they called the lab to get ahold of me." Paesh ended on a higher pitch, to indicate it was more of a suggestion than a question.

He nodded easily. "Of course, of course, take the day to relax or more; just let me know when you'll be back and we can get started on some tests."

"Thanks, Tiago, I'll be in touch on my timeline," Paesh said. While she stood up and dusted herself off, Tulsi took off for higher limbs. Luckily she had her keys and her phone in her lab coat pocket, so she removed those items and handed the coat to Tiago. They parted ways, and Paesh made for her bike to head home.

Unlocking it, she looked around to make sure Lu wasn't looking, but she did notice a new vehicle in the parking lot, probably Lu's. Of course it was a perfectly sexy motorcycle, go figure; Lu kept getting more attractive by the minute. Luckily, she had other things to think about beyond men, at least for a few days.

When Paesh made it home, Tulsi in tow, she eagerly rummaged through the fridge to see what she could whip up. She found some veggies, some bone broth, goat cheese, kimchi she had made herself, and some rice in the cupboard. She quickly got to work, starting a small portion of rice, while in a separate pot she set the broth to low heat with astragalus, kombu, and ashwaganda root mingling in it. She used a third pot to steam the random assortment of veggies and prepared them with a light lemon, lemongrass, shredded ginger, and oil dressing. All the while she was singing, singing a tune she always sang while doing creative or domestic projects. She had learned it in a dream she'd had years ago, and it had stuck with her ever since.

Tulsi watched her with one sideways eye from the counter, looking at her multitask, clanking around dishes and tasting small bites. When everything was ready, she added the miso to the broth and stirred it till it dissolved; then she put everything in its own separate small dish. She loved eating this way, with small portions of different foods; it made her feel well-rounded and light. Her spread complete, she felt ready to sit and eat. Chopsticks ready, she dug into her meal, and didn't look up till it was finished.

Paesh washed the dishes and showered off her day. While in the shower, she couldn't help but replay that video clip in her mind. The being she had turned into was familiar somehow, and beautiful in an otherworldly way. She was grateful she didn't look demonic or slimy. *It could be worse,* she thought. Forcing herself to stop wasting water, she turned the knob reluctantly and toweled off. She wasn't sure what else to do with herself. "Weed the garden?" she wondered aloud.

Then her cell phone pinged a few times in a row. Her service was patchy out here at the end of the road, and sometimes a flood of messages would display on her phone screen all at once.

A few of them were reminders for the bonsai course she had signed up, per her counselor's suggestion; she had completely forgotten all about it, and checked the time. "Phew, thank God for the calendar reminders, I still have two hours till it starts. Don't want to waste that $120," Paesh murmured to herself out loud. So she pillaged through her closet for a little bit to find the best attire for the task, something classy but plant-friendly. She found a seafoam-green button-down blouse with sleeves that were pinned up with buttons, and some loose black trousers with nice big pockets. She adorned herself with jewelry, natural perfume that was customized for her, and some light makeup, just enough to accent her eyes and cheekbones. Her hair was wavy with big curls, and would dry on the way there in the wind from her bike, so she left it wet.

Paesh went out to assess the garden; she'd neglected to water yesterday, and it showed. She unraveled her hose, attempting not to get dirty, and watered everything well. The cucumber leaves were looking a little stressed; they would be calling out for help if they could speak. After watering was done, she fed Moth and filled her water dish. She took a deep breath, and nibbled some of the herbs that were planted on the edge of her garden, letting them sit in her mouth and absorbing the energy and the flavor. "Nothing beats fresh-picked anything," she said out loud.

Paesh was alone a lot, and often spoke to herself out loud; she was unaware of how to turn it off. She'd shrugged off the attempt at changing that habit years ago, and enjoyed the fact that she could keep herself company.

She was not looking forward to socializing at this bonsai class. She'd just figured out today why she was so different -- boy, had she! -- but hadn't had the proper time to process it. But she pushed her anxiety down and got on her bike. The address for the bonsai place was on the west end of town, where the coastline followed the road. The driveway to the class was long and winding, uphill, which worked up a little sweat. At the top there were at least 15 cars parked. There was an open plateau of space to park in front of the house, which had a great view of sunset, which wouldn't be for a while. The house was well-manicured, as one would expect; after all, the bonsai master lived here. Paesh felt a little nervous, checking her outfit to see how dirty it had gotten on the journey; she quickly assessed that she looked 11% more disheveled than when she left her home. Not too bad; she was going for a relaxed look anyway.

She sighed, and walked up to the open front door. As she looked back to her bike, she saw Tulsi sitting on her handlebars, looking around at something moving -- perhaps some crickets on the ground, or another bird.

This gave Paesh an extra boost of confidence as she crossed the threshold into a social experiment. Given her day, she wasn't sure she was all that up for it, but she was never one to waste an investment.

In the doorway she was greeted by a young child, who was adorably enthusiastic and shy all at once. The boy must have been eight or maybe nine, and half-Japanese, she guessed. He was the kind of cute that made Paesh reconsider motherhood, so sweetly full of innocence and wonderment. He bowed, and pointed at her shoes. "Ill take those to the back door, so you can put them back on when you go outside," he said with a sheepish grin, and took her hand to guide her through the main hall. The house was clean with marble floors, a very classic Zen Japanese-style home, with a lot of wood paneling and open clear space.

The boy guided her further through to the kitchen, and left to put her shoes outside. Everyone was assembled in both the kitchen and the porch, casually drinking tea or sake, and eating small adorable hors d'oeuvres. Paesh spotted Genevieve right away; she had a knowing smile and greeted Paesh with a hug. "Hey you made it! Glad to see you; you're right on time, before all the good food and drink is gone," she winked.

"I think I'll start with some tea, and work my way to Sake. I don't think I have seen you with your hair up, I love it," Paesh complimented, exaggerating her shoulders to give an air of flirtation. Genevieve received the compliment with a big smile, and made a slow turn to display her whole look. Paesh applauded, and smiled. It was nice to see Genevieve; she had a way of making others comfortable. She guided Paesh towards the tea table, which wasn't far away. She gave her a hug, and mentioned she would be right back.

The tea set-up was lovely -- a few traditional pots with a different tea at each pot. Paesh gravitated towards the green tea; loose leaf Genmaicha, to be specific. She sprinkled some into the pot, and saw a tea kettle with hot water in it, so she poured that into her pot. She counted for 71 seconds until someone tapped her on the shoulder. "Is there enough for two in the pot?" a man's voice came from behind her.

Oh my god, she thought, *it* can't *be.* But when Paesh turned around, she saw her new friend Lu, standing there with an immense grin on his face.

"You can't make this stuff up," he laughed. "I promise I'm not following you. But I saw you walk into the kitchen a minute ago, and nearly lost it laughing. I thought it would be funnier to approach you more gently." Lu was looking rather chic in black dickie shorts with a silver button-down shirt, short-sleeved and unbuttoned on the top. He was very handsome.

"How did you hear about this place?" Paesh asked, while distracting herself by turning to pour tea for two.

"I came once before; Jon and Grace hold this event a couple times a year, and I know Jon from surfing. I finally came last year, and it was really fun. So I figured I'd come again, as I don't have much of a social life." He fidgeted with his bracelet, and looked up to see that Paesh was handing him a cup of hot tea. "Oh, thank you, what kind is it?"

Paesh cupped her tea with two hands and blew on it. "Genmaicha. It has toasted rice in it, which I'm a huge fan of." The little boy ran up and grabbed the pot, checking if it was empty first, and then bringing it with him to a glass bowl filled with wet spent tea leaves. He used wooden tongs to get the tea out it, then used water to rinse out the stragglers. He swiftly returned it to the tea station. Paesh and Lu both nodded at the boy. "Nice work, Bo!" Lu said with sincerity. Bo looked shy, but acknowledged Lu with a small wave. They both sipped their tea with a long, quiet pause.

"Three times in a row. Should be the last time, don't you think? They say coincidences come in a set of threes," Lu said with complete coolness.

Paesh laughed and sipped her tea, "Well, unless you count the lab. That'll be every day."

That apparently reminded Lu of something. His face changed and he said quickly, "Oh, I forgot, are you okay? Tiago said you had some sort of family emergency today. I know it's not my business, but if I can help, I will."

Paesh froze, but only for a half a second, not enough for him to notice. She hadn't created a story yet, as she'd thought she would have more time to conjure up a casual lie. "Oh yes, thank you for your offer. I think it'll be okay, but he did have quite a scare today. I'll know more tomorrow."

She chuckled in her mind; it was all true, so there was indeed very little to worry about. To her great relief, Genevieve was making her way over, and Paesh gestured for her to come join them. She walked like there was no ground beneath her, an absolutely stunning woman. She wore a long-pant jumper that was navy and made of silk; it looked tailored to her form.

"Lu, this is my friend Genevieve; she's the one who invited me to come. Gen, this is Lu. He's a new co-worker of mine who just happened to be here also," Paesh said, motioning with her hands. While they said their hellos, Paesh spied that the table nearby also had sake on it as well. Even though her tea was unfinished, she poured a fair amount into her cup, while Gen and Lu chatted. When Paesh turned around, they were both side-eyeing her. She shrugged and muttered, "I know it's bad luck to poor your own, but all things considered, I'm feeling pretty lucky today."

They both laughed at this; then Gen looked at Paesh and asked if she would come with her for a moment. Paesh agreed almost too easily; she didn't want Lu to feel completely ditched. So she gave him a tentative pat on the arm, winked at him, like an idiot, and went with Genevieve.

"I want you to see the back garden and have a walk around it, it's just marvelous! I know how much you love to garden." Genevieve said casually as she grabbed the crook of Paesh's arm, as they strolled out the door and both searched for their shoes. Feet protected and ready, they crossed the porch and around the corner, where the path to the garden began. Paesh gasped at the amazing collection of plants and statues. Everything was laid out in a spiral, and it was quite large for a couple to take care of alone.

An arched trellis stretched for a good five meters; growing on it were fully matured climbing vines of clematis, wisteria, and butterfly pea flowers. They twisted together beautifully, all cool shades of purple and blue. The scent was to die for! Genevieve leaned in and squeezed Paesh's arm. "Isn't it gorgeous?" Paesh was speechless. Genevieve unable to resist also murmued, "So is Lu, by the way, and he seemed to be quite interested in you. Have you worked with him a long time?"

"Not at all. Actually, it's quite a weird situation..." Paesh told Genevieve the whole story, from crashing into Lu's trash cans till just now.

"That's quite an interesting example of synchronicity. I'm not sure how I would feel about winning the lottery, myself," Genevieve joked. They continued to tour the garden, and the vegetable patch was just amazing, thriving and intermixed intentionally. There were plum, cherry, and pear trees on the edges of the garden, decorated with shining objects and wind chimes to keep the birds away.

Speaking of birds, a white one was headed Paesh's way without her knowledge. Tulsi delicately made her way to Paesh's shoulder and settled down, which gave both women an initial spook. "Wow, I can't believe a bird just flew up to your shoulder!" Genevieve exclaimed. "You *are* a little faerie, aren't you? What should we do --?"

Genevieve looked around as Paesh spoke up. "Don't worry, there's nothing to worry about. This is my new friend Tulsi. She crashed into my window a couple of mornings ago, and now she follows me around. She's a beautiful and intelligent bird, and is one of the stranger things that's ever happened to me. I quite like her." She looked at the bird and smiled. "She's like my sidekick. Now it won't sound like I'm talking to myself all the time anymore. This bird has listening ears."

"Okay, wow, that is *amazing*, and I'm a little jealous. What do you mean, she has listening ears?" Genevieve examined the bird and smiled at her, extending her hand. Paesh wondered if she could show Genevieve instead of explain, because she probably wouldn't believe her.

"Tulsi, I don't think you're a bird who does tricks, but I do wonder if you can show Genevieve that you understand what I'm saying. Can you bring us all cherries from the top of that tree? We would be super-grateful." Tulsi looked around and took off in flight.

Genevieve gasped, "No way, did she really just --" Genevieve fell quiet, watching the bird fly to the top of the cherry tree and pluck at a branch, causing the tree to shake a little. She swiftly returned with three ripe black cherries, landing on Paesh's shoulders once again.

Paesh opened her palm, and Tulsi dropped two cherries into her hand, keeping one for herself. "Thank you, Tulsi. Now Genevieve can understand; she's a good friend to me, and I won't ask you to do anymore party tricks, I promise." Tulsi made a small peep, and flew onto a nearby rock to eat her cherry.

Paesh held her hand out with the two cherries and turned to face to Genevieve, with raised eyebrows and a huge grin. Genevieve was shocked, her mouth wide open, "Holy shit, that is the coolest thing I have ever seen in my life! Extraordinary..." She trailed off and grabbed a cherry. They both broke into laughter and ate the cherries like five-year-olds celebrating the most innocent but perfect prank.

"It's official -- you *have* won a few lotteries!" Genevieve said as she wrapped the cherry pit in a napkin and put it in her pocket. "You're always opening my mind every time I see you; there's always something new to learn. Apparently magic is real, completely affirmed this evening."

Paesh nodded. "I agree, magic is definitely real. Tulsi sealed the deal."

Before Paesh could say anything more, a gong sounded, and Jon and Grace stood at the door's threshold, getting everyone's attention. "We're ready for the bonsai trimming and training now, if you all would join us in the main greenhouse," Jon announced. Everyone put their small plates away, kept their drinks, and migrated to the greenhouse.

The greenhouse stood nearly seven meters tall; the main frame was metal, but there was some wooden cedar paneling instead of glass on the ceilings and siding, probably to keep it from getting too hot. The long walls of the building were made of glass panels, and most were propped open for air flow. When entering, there were five steps down. "Watch your step," Grace called out, her sake cup sloshing slightly. "I live here, and even I forget." The lower floor produced a cooler atmosphere, a more self-regulating temperature and humidity with a gravel floor and flagstone slabs. The rush of cool, richly oxygenated air refreshed Paesh's senses, and swept past her in all the right places as she placed her feet onto the gravel.

The greenhouse was long, and felt much longer inside; it was a grand 50 meters, or at least felt like it. There were two stone ponds that lined the long walls; it appeared their foundation was set deeper than the level of the gravel. The top of the stone wall was lined with blue tiles in many shades, some pieces were more translucent than others. The water had blue lotus flowers growing on its surface, but they were not yet blooming. As the water bubbled via scattered pumps, one could see fish below coming up to eat something from the surface. It appeared there was a system at either end that pumped the water up a line, to recycle it for watering. It was gardener's heaven.

Along the windows that sat propped open were narrow shelves covered in tropical plants of many varieties, including ferns. Above those, there were other shelves that held only succulents, as they were the ones receiving more sunlight. Their peculiar defined bubbly shapes were pleasing the eyes, and their phi-ratio patterns of growth were plainly visible. It appeared that plants seldom fell ill in this greenhouse, and the couple took great care and pride in their exploration of the plant kingdom.

Down the center of the room, further down, there was a beautiful live-edge wooden table that was completely set for the bonsai experience. Many tiny trees sat awaiting the shaping of their destiny. There were a number of varieties; Jon and Grace would later inform everyone they were bodhi, *b*aobab, common beech, juniper, olive, Indian banyan, and Chinese elm. There were at least two of each kind. Each little tree sat in a low ceramic bowl about a foot in diameter.

Next to each bowl was a pair of clippers and thick wire. In the center of the table were watering cans, plant food, and bowls of gravel and moss. There were stools for sitting at each station, each with a pillow on top. This was truly a glorious sight, and the most exceptional greenhouse Paesh had ever had the pleasure of being inside of.

Altogether, it looked like there were about twenty people milling about, waiting for direction.

"Please, find a seat at a tree that speaks to you," Grace said with a knowing smile. Everyone looked around, examining the trees, and swirled around the table in a current of query. Paesh found herself next to Genevieve as a gust of wind came blowing through the propped open windows. Paesh thought it was sign to stop at the tree she was in front of, which was an Indian banyan; and Genevieve, to her right, sat before a juniper. She looked across the table and Lu sat there; meeting her gaze, he raised his glass to her, and Paesh returned the gesture. Lu had chosen a Chinese elm. It was confusing, but Paesh felt like she was falling for Lu, and it upset her a little; she couldn't surrender to the pull of another man's tide. Not again.

Grace and Jon stood at the opposite ends of the table longways, and Jon spoke. "My grandfather was a master of the art of bonsai. He grew up near Kyoto, in Japan, and served as a master gardener for the temple near the famous Sagano Bamboo Forest. He lived a quiet life by the river, and spent his days caring for the landscape around the temple. The story goes that my grandfather was fishing one day when he was in his early adulthood, and he watched my grandmother cross the bridge above him. His heart stopped then and there on the boat; he knew that one day, he would marry her. His job was simple, and he was not the richest man, but he was willing to do anything to impress her family. So he crafted a bonsai tree for her. He spent months tending and bending this little tree to be as beautiful as she was." Jon smiled at this thoughtfully.

Taking a sip of sake, Jon continued his story. "In seven months' time the tree was ready. It was a Deshojo maple, with vibrant red leaves and a pale white trunk. He worried that perhaps she would already be married by then, but with the little money he had, he needed to present something to her family. He found out where she lived, and told her she was the most beautiful woman in the whole village. My grandmother was shy, but accepted and cherished her tree, and it was that simple; she was in love. Her father, proud of the tree, asked my grandfather to make more for their yard, and so he did. Soon the whole village knew of his precision and connection with the trees, and everyone desired to have a tree he had designed in their home or yard. The traditional art of bonsai runs in my blood, and I'm happy to share what I know with you tonight."

Grace chimed in, "In Japan, the culture is richly entangled with spirituality and nature. Shintoism in ancient Japan was and still is a way of life more than a religion; it is a belief in *Kami*, spiritual energy."

Grace animated her hands as if they were riding waves. "The belief is that Kami exists as a force of nature, like a current of life within all things, living and sedentary. In Shinto belief, gods came down from a heavenly place to live in the oldest pine tree atop a mountain -- the Pine Tree Matsu, meaning *waiting for God's soul to come down from heaven.* Pine trees are often planted at the entrances of forest shrines to invite in the soul of a god. Which is what Jon's grandfather did; he tended to shrines in the forest, making space for gods to arrive.

"The Japanese language is poetic, and instead of a word defining a singular thing, it often shares a whole concept. Such thoughtfulness is what we want to cultivate in our space today. It is with great pleasure we are joined here to find inner awareness to properly hear the *Kodama*, which is the tree's soul and its echo." Grace raised her cup and motioned a cheering gesture, and everyone raised their cup as well.

The lesson was underway, and every tree species had its own technique. After the basic foundational principles were shared, Jon and Grace went around giving advice and guidance for each tree style. Turned out the banyan was a complex tree to pick, but it was still challenging and fun. Wires were used to twist limbs without breaking them. As it wasn't springtime, only minor pruning could be done to the tree, but next year, during spring time, there could be another round of deeper pruning and wiring. This would be an ongoing project that Paesh was more than excited to maintain.

Paesh peered over the top of her little tree to spy on Lu and watch his careful work. He had beautiful hands, strong with long fingers, twisting the wire with care. His design looked like DNA helixes, twisting upwards and away from one another. Seemed fitting for a biologist.

When everyone was about complete with their tree, Jon and Grace went around and handed out cards for at-home care for the trees by species. The trees were heavy, and everyone was soon carrying their new potted friends out of the greenhouse and into their cars. Paesh hadn't thought about how she would get hers home, as she had ridden her bike. When she carried her tree outside, it was nearly sunset, and it was shaping up to be a glorious one. What a spectacular view Jon and Grace had!

While Paesh was lingering in the drive, setting her tree by her bike, Lu didn't miss a beat, and offered to give her a ride home when the night was over.

"Thank you -- that would be great. I thought you drove a motorcycle. Will my bike fit in your car?" Paesh asked, with sake-charmed confidence.

"I do ride a bike, but I knew I would need to haul home a tree or two today, so I drove my Jeep. I have a bike rack on the back, so it's no trouble at all," Lu said as they walked over to his Jeep. It was a relief that it was an older and well-utilized vehicle. *Must be his surfing mobile,* Paesh thought to herself. They put the pots in the back on the flat floor, and rolled down the windows to cool the car down.

Back in the kitchen, everyone was eating again and enjoying the splendors of sunset in the most magical garden there was. Some people were even cheering as sunset took some wild turns in its color palette. By the time it was dark, everyone was saying their goodbyes and expressing gratitude for the exceptional evening. Everything was so perfectly curated and timed that it was money and time well spent. Paesh thanked Genevieve enthusiastically, and they made a date for lunch in the coming week before saying goodbyes. Genevieve winked at her, nudging her head in Lu's direction. Paesh blushed at this, because Genevieve knew all of Paesh's secrets, especially when it came to men.

Now it was time for the drive home, which she was both dreading and excited for. Unfortunately, this car ride would show Lu where Paesh lived, which was not an ideal circumstance by any means, but such is life; it happens.

Lu opened the door for Paesh, and as she went to sit down inside, Tulsi joined her on her shoulder again. Lu was startled by this, and amazed, as it made Paesh appear even stranger and more mysterious.

"Uh, uhm, yes. This is my friend Tulsi. She will be riding along," Paesh said confidently, hoping it would work.

"Cool. Very strange, but cool. Never a dull moment with you so far. I'll fix your bike to the back real quick and we'll head out." Lu spoke to Paesh like he'd known her forever, his initial awkwardness completely evaporated. When Lu got in the driver's seat, he assured her he had stopped drinking two hours ago. "It was funny, though, after only 10oz of sake, I looked up at you while you were twisting your bonsai, and your skin was subtly lavender, but shimmery. I'm not sure what brand of sake they had, but I think I was a little tossed for a second there."

Paesh laughed awkwardly and became a little nervous, feeling hot she rolled down the window, "What a lovely color; I wish my skin were lavender," she said wistfully while looking out the window.

"So, where am I headed, I have no clue where you live..." Lu trailed off, slowing down the car.

"Oh, shoot, of course. Take a right here, and keep on that street for about 3 miles until Tulpa Street, then you'll go left and follow that one for a while. When we get there, I'll share the last few directions. It should only take us about 15 minutes."

They drove in silence, watching the Moon start to rise over the ocean; it was waning from the recent full Moon. When they got to the end of Tulpa, she motioned for a left and another abrupt left, and then they followed that road all the way down. Her house was at the end of the street.

Tulsi sat in Paesh's lap, nestle in the crack where her thighs met. Tulsi was sleeping, or at least her eyes were closed; Paesh she wasn't very familiar with birds' tendencies. But then again, birds didn't normally listen or stay long enough to be observed.

Lu was a complete gentleman upon arrival. He grabbed her bike and brought her potted tree to the back porch. While setting it down, Moth, the black-and-white cat, twisted through his legs. "This must be the cat, then," Lu said, looking down at the creature, being careful not to step on it or trip.

"Sure is. Moth is her name. Thank you for the ride, and grabbing my things, I really appreciate it," Paesh said, avoiding eye contact. She finally met his eyes, making no movement towards the door, "See you at work in a few days?" she asked.

"I'm looking forward to it. I'll be a little lost without you in there, even Tiago too. So your return will be helpful. I hope your family is all right," Lu said as he went in for a simple hug. It was a hug that could calm a killer, and in the brevity of its duration, Paesh fell back in time and melted into the sea. When he let go, it was like peeling off a Band-Aid, or turning on the light in middle of slumber.

Lu walked towards his car, and Paesh waved, with likely the most hypnotized look on her face. She heard his Jeep make its way back down the road and disappear into the night. Knowing he was fully gone and far enough away, she broke out into a massive sob, one she could not control; nor did she know where these emotions were coming from.

"Lu saw me shift in the greenhouse... who else saw it?" she wondered aloud, sitting on the step of her porch. "It didn't even happen when I was angry; if anything I was the exact opposite of angry in the greenhouse, maybe slightly intoxicated, but hardly more than a little tipsy...why?!" she moaned.

All the confusion and lack of answers made her think back to a time she had buried, another time where there were no answers. This was the incident that she'd a little over a year ago, was the main reason she's started seeing Genevieve in the first place. It was normally locked in a place where she could live free from it, like it never happened at all, not having nor wanting to access the simmering well that was always waiting there for her... a source of deep pain. Tonight, it looked like it was coming out to play.

It was winter in Santa Cruz when it happened, which meant cold rain would be forecast, with some brief yet coveted sunny days. This one was not one of those days, but it was a day off from work at the lab, and Paesh had been invited to a rather fancy charity gala, not something she was typically invited to. She had met a wealthy man at a wine bar a month back, and he had asked her to come. He had even bought her a dress for the occasion. She felt flattered and fancy, truly adorned and cherished, and he was a genuinely sweet man.

He arrived to pick her up in his new Tesla. She still remembered the smell of his car; it was clean and safe, but the horrible smell of new cars would forever be burned in her brain. To this day, she could not sit in a new car. They arrived, and they looked like an amazing couple ready for the red carpet, her arm linked in the crook of his-his... his name. Paesh tore into her mind even further. "What was the man's name, it was something foreign -- Milad!"

Milad walked her up the brick-laid path to a rather daunting mansion. She wondered what such a home would cost, and who owned it? She had never been in the presence of people with so much money and affluence. It was unnerving, but Paesh loved acting the part. Of course she knew that anyone who was in the market for a second yacht didn't become that rich doing the right things. The people surrounding her were likely those who funded the corporate machine and the pharmaceutical industries.

Inside, everything was precisely as an outsider would expect: unbearable conversation, fantastic wine older than herself, and amazing food set up with the finest aesthetic. At one point, Paesh had to excuse herself from Milad's company and find the bathroom. She found a man in a suit, the same suit all the staff were wearing, a simple black tuxedo. He directed her to "Walk down the hall and make a right at the labeled door; from there it will be obvious," he said with a smile.

After finding it, Paesh managed to get the dress disassembled enough to pee. When she was done, she found she could not get the dress back *on*. The zipper had broken. "Damn," she thought, "The most expensive dress breaks on the first wear, of course." There were no women who came in the bathroom who may be of assistance. Twenty minutes passed, and Paesh grew impatient. "Perhaps the bidding had already begun," she thought, while gathering the dress on to the best of her ability, and emerged back into the hallway to find the staff at the end of the hall. But there was only an older gentleman standing in the hall. He had appeared to be looking at his watch, a smart one; Paesh laughed to herself in her mind, *Probably another tech industry billionaire checking on his stocks and his 18-year-old girlfriend.*"

The man looked up at Paesh, affronted, as if he had heard her joke. He cleaned the expression off his face swiftly, and nodded at her. He was handsome and fit, but older, maybe in his late fifties. "Are you all right? It would appear your dress is malfunctioning." the man said with a very helpful and kind way; he sounded truly concerned.

"It is. Do you know how to get ahold of the staff? Maybe they have a pin, or a spare dress..." she remarked, jokingly.

"This is my house; Allen is my name. I can certainly see that we get you into another dress. I have closets filled from my ex-wife, and she was nearly your size then," he said, looking her up and down as if appraising her like a dog at a show. "And you are?" Allen asked.

"Paesh, and I would be most grateful. My date has probably worried I've fallen in!" she said, still holding the top of her dress up and around herself like a towel.

"Follow me; we can get upstairs this way without crossing in front of the auction. With your attire in this state, I'm sure that would be quite embarrassing." Allen motioned, turning on his heels he headed down the marvelous wood flooring, artistic inlays guiding the way.

She followed him for what felt like five minutes, taking turns and stairwells she couldn't keep track of, nor did she think to, as this man was helping her. There was no need her to feel guarded or sense the impending situation. Looking back, Paesh felt so stupid. They entered a room and he pointed to the closet, showing her the many dresses. Allen chose a lavender one. "This one will look nice with your skin," he said, and handed it to her.

"That was odd, lavender," Paesh thought now, sitting on her own wooden stairs; she hadn't remembered that before. Then she sank back into the cold, sharp memory.

"That dress will do perfectly," Paesh said grabbing the dress.

"I'm a gentleman," Allen said with a bow, and he left her to change, closing the closet door, but there was another sound, the click of a lock. Unsure, if it was an unusual sound, Paesh changed into the dress, and it was a comfortable, breathable fit, unlike the tight one she had on before. It was actually quite to her taste, it even had a light golden sheen to it. But, alas, the distraction of the perfect dress could only go so far, and she dreaded that the door was locked intentionally. She took off her heels, wanting to feel more able to move like an animal ready to run. Touching the handle, it did not budge; she was locked in, and now she began to panic.

"Allen, the door is locked, are you there?" Paesh asked, forcing the calmest nonchalance, and even faking a little laughter into the question.

"I am here, and unfortunately, I'll be needing something from you, and it will seem... unusual." Allen said with shuddering coolness. He spoke in a casual tone, as if he were talking to his grandmother about the weather.

Paesh immediately thought of the two times she had been raped, and honestly, there was relief in knowing what to expect, give or take some dark details.

"Don't worry, I get plenty of that; that is not what I'll be wanting from you, that is too easy. I could have convinced you to give me that without locking you in a closet, of that I am certain. If you want this to be painless, I suggest you drink the cup on your right; it is an opium tea that will numb the senses; it will make your blood cool and steady."

Allen is so matter of fact, Paesh thought, *So slimy... how did he know I was thinking of rape? Could have been a lucky guess. I suppose he will do as he will; men with money like this can do whatever they want. What about Milad, will he worry? Maybe he's my chance at a rescue.*

Allen chimed in again, "Milad won't be finding you; it only took a few sentences to tell him you were seen leaving with another man. Milad is gullible, which is why I chose him to get wine with me, and that's why I encouraged him to ask you out on a date. Too bad, he is a good man; he was quite fond of your eccentric ways."

This was a nightmare. Paesh wanted to make it stop, so she grabbed the cup, smelled it. It *was* opium; it had the distinct bitter scent that the sap produced. Paesh was no stranger to that flower's resin; she grew her own small crop every year, just to have a small supply for an emergency. She liked to be in control of her medicine supply.

Tasting a small drop, she tasted nothing other than chamomile, mint, ginger, and opium. *Odd*, she thought, *Such a mindful blend for opium. Who the fuck is this guy?* she screamed in her mind. Before she changed her mind, she gulped the lukewarm herbal tea. She may as well let it all happen; at the best she would go home tonight or die painlessly, and the worst... well, she didn't let her mind go there.

"Don't worry, my aim is not to kill you, it's merely to see," Allen said. "Fabulous, bottoms up, I'll be around in fifteen minutes to fetch you."

Paesh knew this would be the longest fifteen minutes of her life. to occupy her mind, she took every dress off the wall and stacked them in the corner of the rather large walk-in closet. She would make a bed of dresses to sit upon while she waited. When gathering the last armfull of dresses she spied a door, a menacing skinny doorway, that gave her a horrible feeling. She wondered, looking for a way to open it, *Perhaps it's what he meant when he said he would be around.*

She threw herself on the dresses, and tried to think about something else... and she did not accomplish that attempt. The pit in her stomach only grew. As the minutes passed, the familiar buzz of opium sank in, and her anxiety levels reduced greatly. She thought, *Fuck it, it will be over soon. Maybe he wants my kidneys. I do have rare blood. A/B-negative. Either way I'm here, and this is my destiny. I need to be calm if nothing else.*

At last, finally, the door opened, and Allen stood wearing a startling white coat. He motioned for her to follow. She felt surprisingly calm and light on her feet, deciding to stay barefoot.

"I see you made a mess in the closet," Allen remarked with amusement in his voice.

"It was the least I could do in return for your warm hospitality." Paesh slurred thoughtfully, truly not caring anymore.

As Paesh guessed, there was a medical table with supplies and two chairs, a completely stainless sterile environment. The tools on the tray did not include any knives or an anesthetic, this gave Paesh huge relief, as she would be keeping her kidneys.

"Have a seat, this won't take long," Allen said, putting on gloves.

She followed his command, and sat. He tied a stretch band at just above her elbow, and sterilized the spot on her skin where people usually insert a needle. She saw empty tubes that were awaiting blood. He asked her to make a fist and he found the best vein.

"Easy does it," he said as he sent the needle into her skin. She took in a long breath and closed her eyes. He filled five tubes of blood, and she became hot and dizzy from the loss. She hated giving blood. When he finished up, he removed the elastic band, "That's all I'll be needing from you for now. When you can see straight, we will go."

Paesh was relieved and untrusting. But he was true to his word. When she was clear enough, she walked with him out another door, and through a hall that eventually led to a back garden.

"I have arranged a car to take you anywhere you would like to go. I also have a gift for you, for your participation. Any further investigation on your part would not be in your best interests, but you already know that people with this much money can do whatever they want." Allen said, straightening his shirt.

Paesh, dazed, wondering what the fuck had just happened to her, walked towards the black car sitting idle. A man in a suit opened the door for her, and she got in. Inside, there was a pair of sandals and a designer-brand duffel bag.

Paesh did not have the driver take her to her home; instead, she had him drop her off at Health Food Market, where a male friend of hers worked.

"Paesh, hey, nice dress," Will greeted as she approached his register. "Hey, are you all right?" he asked with growing concern.

"No," she said flatly. "Can you take me home? I had a strange night... I can tell you about it later." When she said this, Paesh was still a little dazed, slurred, and overly calm. The calm that shock brings in its wake. Will got her home with swift heroism, no questions asked. Like a gentleman, Will waited to see that she got inside before backing down the road, and he was gone.

Once inside, Paesh opened the bag to find that stacks of $100 bills filled the duffel bag up to the brim. She immediately went to the bathroom, vomited, and climbed into the shower.

She had stayed there till her water heater gave out, and the water had grown cold.

Later, putting the dress into the top of the duffle and zipping it closed, she moved the damned bag into the back of her closet. She had only checked it once in the past year, to remind herself it had been real.

That aberrant experience was her biggest reason for seeking therapy from a female-focused therapist. It was why she trusted no one, especially anyone who had a lot of money.

Tulsi chirped, as if she had been a quiet listener of the whole story. Flapping her white wings noisily, the bird moved to sit beside Paesh on the steps, and they both sat there silently, listening to the crickets. The only thing that moved were the tears that continued to fall down Paesh's face.

Layer 19: Iós - The Tipping Point

Iós and Jushur sailed by day and night, in search of a new village to become a part of. It would be difficult, not having a common language; but they figured they would manage easily enough, with their skills, to gain favor in a new tribe. If Jushur had learned anything from his voyages, it was that few tribes were skilled with crafting boats, for example. That was a valuable knowledge.

Jushur also knew he needed to find a new woman to appease Iós, to find someone to engage in regular sex with, accompanied by an emotional bond. This was a daunting task, though he knew in time that he would move on from the loss of Ala, and find interest in a new connection. But the need for Iós was pressing; he could feel the tension in his own body swelling with hunger.

As Jushur learned more about Iós, he found that the star-being had access to his thoughts, but not all of them. He began attempting to keep himself conscious when Iós took over his body. He had to fight for awareness, as if within a dream, and he did not always succeed. Usually, he was able to see what Iós was doing. It was blurry, as if viewing a scene through a thin cloth, but he could get a feel for what was happening to his body. For instance, Iós masturbated a lot, at least five times while he sailed; this was how he could tell Iós was hungry for a woman. His sexual needs felt animalistic. Beyond spying on Iós, Jushur also had a safe space to think for himself without Iós listening.

As much as Jushur enjoyed the new mysterious power that came with Iós, he also had no choice, and he did not trust Iós fully. He had to be careful of his own thoughts. So Jushur's new hobby was exercising the strength of his mind while asleep and awake. It kept him busy as they sailed, but it was not always easy; in fact, it was far from easy. He never truly got through a day mastered in his mindfulness, but every day he tried.

Neither Jushur nor Iós knew what would happen when Iós left his body. The only time Iós had left a being was when the body of the shark was already spent. They had no way of knowing if it would kill Jushur or not. For now, Iós depended on Jushur, and that kept him alive. Jushur did have a sinking feeling that when they found a tribe, Iós would find a more useable host, extracting more skills, but these were only thoughts he could think when Iós was unaware and at the helm of his body.

They traveled this way in isolation for the greater part of a year, creating small camps for months and moving with the weather; it was back to the nomadic life. But in time Iós grew restless, and was no longer content with the maddening isolation that he had brought upon

Jushur and himself. "We must find a village soon," he told Jushur. "I do not wish to hide as exiles any longer; we are powerful, and should be welcomed in any tribe!" Iós was fierce with his words and his movements, and Jushur complied and agreed that it was time to seek out people, and a place to cultivate a home.

They took to the sea again, and began their search for signs of habitation along the coast. Finally, when they passed a promising alcove and stretch of beaches, Jushur saw smoke. They anchored the boat and walked with ease through the sandy shallows; there were rocks, but the water was so clear that it was easy to avoid unsavory steps onto urchins or any hiding rockfish. The landscape wasn't as lush and tropical as in other places they had made camp, but Jushur was certain that smoke meant people. Within the first fifteen minutes, he came across signs of a village. He became nervous and excited, as all villages were not created equal. Some were very hostile, and Jushur made sure he had his knife handy. Iós chimed in, "Between us, we have wits and strength."

Jushur chuckled. "Who is the one with wit?"

Iós replied, "You, of course; I am still learning, but I bring power and strength, and I keep your body regenerating."

Jushur walked with careful steps, following the tracks of others, smelling smoke from a fire accompanied by the scent of meat cooking. He slowed as the thicker trees and plants opened up into a clearing. He stood with his legs bent low, surveying the scene. The farthest point in the clearing was towards the east, where the fire was coming from. To the west there was a deep-flowing creek. The area had been cleared of brush and smaller foliage, but there were trees that provided shade in this apparent gathering area.

Jushur decided to walk into the area, certain that the people were already aware of his presence. They were. To his right, a small child ran out in front of Jushur; he was close, but far enough away to keep him from harm. Jushur opened his hands, raising them up, palms flat, as if pressing against glass between him and the boy. He squatted and nodded at the boy, pointing to his water container, then his mouth, and then the creek. The boy continued to stare -- he couldn't be older than five -- just staring at him with blank curiosity. Then a young girl of about twelve, wearing nothing more than a cloth around her waist, stood next to the little boy and aimed the same blankly curious stare at Jushur. Jushur could feel Iòs become tense at the sight of a female, and this worried him. He could feel the hunger welling up inside of him, but Jushur was intentional with his thoughts. "Iós, she is too young, and you will be patient; do not let your strength bury us both. They are watching us."

Jushur could feel Iós relax a bit, but the feeling did not fully dissipate. The next person to walk out of hiding was an old woman, her skin like leather and her eyes like knowing gems. She took a seat next to the boy and girl, giving Jushur the same testing stare of curiosity and silence. Again, Jushur slowly pointed to his water container, his mouth, and then the creek, but remained as cool and as steady as the three strangers. The next to join was pregnant woman, of age maybe twenty; she was full with life, every part of her glowing and plump like ripe fruit.

This made Iós tense again, and this time it was stronger; perhaps it was the smell of a pregnant woman, her hormones making their way into Jushur's nose. Jushur could feel a swelling between his legs. If he Jushur became fully erect and aroused, it would be tough to control

Iós, that much he knew for certain. So what could he do? He thought, and had to think quickly, as all was going a little fuzzy.

He grabbed his knife, which caused sounds to rise from behind him in the brush, but he took the knife and stabbed it into the ground. Luckily the ground was soft, and largely clay. He then moved onto his knees and bowed forward, hands flat on the ground, in a child's pose. While he moved into that position, he kicked up the dryer dirt with his hands and purposefully inhaled it and got it in his eyes; hopefully it looked more casual than crazy.

This disturbance was enough to break Iós out of his hunger trance; his swelling instantly began to wane, and Jushur took a deep breath. "Iós, for now if you can, will you sleep in there, or close your awareness before you get us killed? I will get you a woman, but it will only come with patience, not strength." Iós said nothing; Jushur only felt a stillness that he hadn't in weeks. Perhaps Iós had listened to him, and for that he was relieved.

In time, the tribe came out one-by-one, waiting and watching him. Eventually he sat back up, onto his knees, and again pointed to his water skin, his mouth, and the creek to the west. This time, a man with a knife came closest to him and reached out for the water skin; he grabbed it and handed it to a woman for her to go fill, motioning to the creek, muttering in some language Jushur did not know. The woman returned and handed the full skin to the man with the knife, who then handed it back to Jushur. Jushur smiled, nodded his head in a bow, and took the skin. He drank, happy to get the dust from his mouth and face; when he had had enough, he put the strap back over himself and continued to sit.

This was not an unusual process, for some tribes to observe a newcomer thus; Jushur had done something similar when trading on a previous voyage. It was his hope that they would share food with him next; that was typically the next gesture. But there was a sudden sound, a man from the village running up to the group, smiling and repeating a certain word. That word murmured through the village, and all eyes set onto him.

The man with the knife used a stick to draw something that looked like his boat, and then he pointed to Jushur and back to his drawing of the boat. Jushur nodded, and put his palm on his heart, as if to gesture it was his. He spoke, repeating their word for boat, and then saying his word for boat and pointed back to the picture. This made the man smile. From there, the tension moved away, and most of the village got up and went back to what they had been doing before. Except for the men of the village; they remained and ushered him to walk back towards the sea.

Arriving at the boat, it was clear they were familiar with the sea, but were not the best at swimming or navigating the water. Jushur boarded his boat and moved ropes and oars to display the way it worked, and then took some dried dates from his storage and made his way back to the shallow water, keeping the dates just above the sloshing waves.

He showed them the dates, and ate one in front of them, and held some out for them to try. Two of the men happily did, and their eyes grew big; they do not have date palms here, perhaps. He held his hand out with the remaining dates, and the others sampled them after witnessing the approving smiles. They were all wide-eyed with the flavor.

The curiosity toward building boats and learning to use them was a big factor in the tribe's extension of hospitality toward Jushur, he knew. There was so much to the art of traveling by boat: navigation, dealing with storms, tides, food and water storage, and directing the boat itself manually, to begin with. It would ensure his stay in the village for some time, and that was enough time for him to find someone for Iós to bond with. The star-being was still laying low, almost as dormant as before; he had listened to Jushur, which was worth something. It was an insight that Iós would not find a new host and leave Jushur behind so easily. It would not be soon, at the very least.

A month rolled on with slow progress; the language barrier was exceptionally difficult. There were many drawings in the sand and hands-on instructions. The culture of his new friends was not all that different than Jushur's, except that the climate and surrounding plants made for different food, different dwellings, and different materials for boat-making.

Neenah, a younger woman who lived on the outer edges of the community, was known as a healer, a woman who spoke with plants and spirits. She took a special interest in Jushur. When she first spied upon him from a distance, her eyes were measuring his oddities, calculating his mannerisms. She watched him every so often, and her elusiveness did not stem from fear, but from a place of knowing. As her dwelling was farther away from the main village, Jushur had never seen her before; he had only heard her name from the other villagers.

One evening, under a black Moon, when the stars were the most visible, Jushur was with a group of villagers showing the way he used the stars as a map for boat travel. They all sat on the beach huddled around a small fire. He taught them with the language from his village.

Each constellation and major star had a story to go with it, and for the stories, he drew pictures in the sand. The stories helped lock in the memory for easier absorption of the mind. After Jushur had enough with teaching for the night, he sat alone on the beach, drawing in the sand with a stick, wishing he had some date wine or something familiar from his past.

Neenah approached him and sat next to him. He motioned and used the word for child as if to say, "Where is your child?" She smiled at this and laughed, shaking her head in such a way as to express, "I have none." She carried something with her in a ceramic cup; it was liquid, and smelled a little like wine. She offered it to him, and he gladly took a sip. The familiar taste made him relax, and his wish for drink was answered. They drank the alcohol together, unable to really say much except through pictures in the sand and facial expressions.

Neenah had a long face, with a strong brow-line and high cheekbones; she had the gaze of a warrior and the features to match. There was beauty in her hard lines and edges, but her silver eyes were all too knowing. Her skin was dark, dewy, and she looked only around the age of seventeen. She was tall and lean, with strongly defined muscles. She wore little clothing, only covering her lower half and around her shoulders. Jushur was entranced by her striking features, watching as they morphed while attempting to communicate.

When the cup was finished, she came closely to Jushur, and touched his forehead, and in his language she said, "Shark spirit." She then removed her clothing and urged Jushur to do the same, and he was more than happy to comply. She was wild and strange, unlike Ala. He felt a powerfully ancient arousal taking place between them. In the height of their rhythmic dance, she slowed her movements almost to a full stop. It was then that Iós emerged from almost a full month of dormancy, and immediately took control.

Jushur watched to be sure what was happening, and Neenah noticed and welcomed the change; again she said, "Shark spirit." Iós was not violent, but he was a stronger force with a greater hunger, and it amused Neenah. Jushur was grateful for this accomplishment, and he took himself to bed in his mind, still mildly enjoying the sensation of his body's release as he faded away.

Time passed, and the season became a wet one as the months passed. Luckily, there were caves to be inside of and structures to keep them covered from the rain. But the cold that came later was difficult, and it wore on the boat even though it was docked on the beach. Animal skins were coveted and helpful, given how cold it was. While inside a cave, Jushur showed the people small examples of adobe construction. It took longer to dry in the weather despite the cave's coverage, but he had built an oven, crafted from water clay and plant fiber from dried reeds. It was a design his village used, inside their adobe structures as well as outside. He showed them where the fire should go, and how to build one properly to create less smoke. When constructing the oven, he chose a spot near the cave entrance so the little smoke there was would move outside rather than stay inside the cave.

The excitement it brought the tribe was substantial. No longer did anyone have to watch the fire in the rain or wind, or struggle in the smoke to cook food. This created more free time to make more improvements. More ovens were made in the course of a month, one in every cave and a few outdoors under sturdy structures. This made hot water and hot food easier to prepare, as well as heating the caves themselves. Wet wood could also be dried next to the oven faster than before.

It wasn't long before Jushur's standing in the village climbed. His small improvements added up in shorter time than one might think. The village also held Neenah in high regard, though they also feared her otherworldly connection. Before Jushur arrived, Neenah had never chosen to stand by a man. When Jushur and Neenah stood together, the village as a whole was skeptically receptive. They were respected and feared.

When good weather came, Jushur could repair his boat and begin teaching the others to build more. He would modify the design, but it used the same technique, notches, and joggles. Planks with notches would fit into the recesses of another board, sealed tight and waterproof. Tamu, Jushur's most dedicated and intelligent student, was a great help on the first boat made. He had a knack for the art of boat-making, and it gave Jushur pride to pass on such a skill.

The village was flourishing; they were irrigating a garden with hollow wooden pipes from the creek, and cultivating food plants. Jushur showed the people bread making as his wife had discovered it years ago. Everything was going well; Jushur and Iós lived in complete balance. The sexual beast was fed, and they both enjoyed Neenah and this new life.

But time passed quickly; years flew by, it seemed, and the village grew into something like the one Jushur had left long ago. The villagers, especially Neenah and Tamu, were starting to notice that Jushur was not aging by much; not a scar nor signs of weathering marked his skin. As their own bodies aged and weathered, things began to change again. Jushur had come to love Neenah, and Iós even more so, but her body was aging, and soon death would come for her.

The day would come where they would have to burn her body after her death.

That day did come, and Iós was filled with inconsolable rage in the beginning, unable to cope with the loss and love he was a part of creating. Without sex, he was tense and more carnally charged to do unspeakable things.

At first it started with hunting animals, the thrill of kill and feeding the village; but then there came the day of disagreement, and Iós killed a man who opposed his views. He killed him quickly in cold blood, for everyone to see. None of the villagers knew what to think; they were shocked and angry, especially Tamu. He knew this was not the kind and wise Jushur; it was something different, something different in his eyes.

Iós changed after that killing; it made him feel powerful, somehow truly alive. The monster within him was awake and hungry for dominance and territory gain. Jushur hardly saw the light of day, and was biding his time while lying beneath the conscious surface. He began planning his own demise before full control was lost. He no longer wished to host something so uncontrollable, so evil. Jushur did not want his face and soul to be tied with the destiny of Iós; he knew he had to do something.

While Jushur was watching from within his dreamlike state, he saw villagers approaching Iós with weapons for fighting. They sought revenge, and now that the village was equipped with knowledge, they would kill him. Jushur prayed for their spirits, because he knew they would lose; Iós was almost unkillable, able to heal from small wounds with rapid speed. What was more was that he was strong, and aggressive like an animal. One by one, he easily broke their necks or made fatal blows to their skulls. He didn't even need a weapon. All seven men were dead within minutes.

There is truth to the saying "having a taste for blood," as every kill Iós committed made him hungry for more. The origins of a monster dawned with his growing taste for blood.

The only time Jushur could take over was when Iós had finished enjoying a woman; there was a small window of time where he was able to act, but he had to move fast and not let his thoughts give away his plan. He had had a lot of time to prepare himself, fueled by his disgust and need for justice, for all this to end.

There was a berry he knew of that was extremely poisonous; the villagers had made it clear in his first month with them that it was a fatal poison. They had lost a child to the berries only five years ago; he was young and the berries were bright and inviting. Jushur made his way into the jungle and collected as many of the berries as he could find, and stashed them in a bag around his shoulders. There was not enough time to eat them without Iós becoming wise and aware to the plan, and the star-being could make himself sick to be rid the poison. So, instead, he stashed the bag with the berries and went back into dormancy, just as Iós was beginning to wake.

Iós woke with hunger, a desire for sex and for blood, and this time he would do both at once: he would kill the poor woman after he was finished with her. He carried out unspeakable acts upon her. Jushur was so sick inside that he did everything he could to be strong and ready himself to eat the berries, just after this dark scene was at its end.

When Iós was drunk with power and blood, he sank into a sleep, which was when Jushur, like a sleepwalking hero, retrieved the bag and ate every berry with great speed. He lay down and put himself to sleep as well. In just ten minutes, they both woke clawing in pain and shivering with a nervous system malfunction; they lost control of their bowels, and their lungs slowed into suffocation. Death was coming for them both.

It wasn't easy, but Jushur was at peace, knowing he was no longer part of such cruelty and violence. It was not him; it was Iós. And above all, it was time for them to die.

The next day Jushur lay cold and dead, the morning light climbing in the sky. His body without pulse; his silver eyes stared into the distance, death's glaze beginning to cloud the color. Jushur had accomplished his goal. However, Iós lay inside the body unharmed, in dormancy. He would wait inside the flesh, soon set to rot, for he could not die.

Above, vultures and crows circled, sensing the dead. Jushur's body would make a meal, and perhaps through the inviting touch of a bird, Iós would take to the sky.

Layer 20: Indra - A Life Before the Virus, Memories Through Aria's Eyes

Time passed, without any further information on the strange energy surrounding the Egyptian doctor, that Aria had spied long ago. Life in the Irati Forest slipped back into normalcy and routine. There was ongoing order in the forest, that Indra helped maintain. Her presence and name had grown respected and cherished.

Despite the overall copacetic society, Indra was pulled into the conflict between the Light Singers and Saprophytie. Saprophytie was a being of multiplicity, an important yet unpleasant being. He thrived in the environment of decay and transformation, bringing the bacteria and fungi to feed on the dead. His life was focused on the decomposition and rebirth of all things. He could multiply himself to be anywhere upon the globe, but one of his main dwellings was in the Irati.

The Light Singers, individual beings of a more numerous species, were a clan in charge of influencing the blooming flowers and sprouting seedlings, breathing life into the humbly awaiting plants. In some ways, you could say their role was the same as Saprophytie's, but on the opposing end of the cycle and spectrum. They fought tirelessly with the death-bringer, bickering about territory and aroma. Wherever Saprophytie went, the musty stench of fungus and rot followed him. He could not help the state of his odor, but it stunk nonetheless. He was mostly a humble creature, keeping to himself and sharing in friendship with the mushroom beings. However, sometimes he would delight in eating the Light Singers; they were much smaller and full of life's breath. This was where the true contention lay between the Singers and Saprophytie.

The Light Singers were dainty little wisps, looking very similar to the bloom of an onion flower, and if you're not familiar with its spherical shape, then perhaps the dandelion seed puff that comes after the yellow flower has passed. Light Singers moved about bringing life and beauty. The sheer number of Light Singers surpassed those of the other species; they were abundant, as their job was vast, far, and wide. When Saprophytie realized his taste for the Light Singers, he began to consume them more and more often.

In the Fae Realm, there is an overall balance to maintain, albeit painful. Creatures eat creatures. Life eats life, as Indra herself consumed meat and living flowers, and yet she still maintained a relationship and fondness with all the woodland creatures. Planet Earth was based around consumption, and one could justify that; however, there was a fine balance to the dance, and Saprophytie was taking more than what was balanced. The queen of the Light Singers visited Indra when the problem became too much for just her species, because Saprophytie's main home was within Indra's domain. Indra was empathetic and motivated to help, although she found it ironic and troubling that the bringer of decomposition hungered for the light.

Indra ventured out into the forest to find Saprophytie and confront him regarding his behavior. The area where his dwelling lay was known, and she swiftly approached through the terrain. Autumn, in full swing, covered the forest floor in mist and fallen leaves. The scents of rich soil and fungi filled the air; it was sweet and earthy, blooming with mushrooms. When she made her way to the known area of his dwelling, she used her nose to take her the rest of the way, until it was clear Saprophytie was near. When she came across a rotting log, the scent grew in potency.

Saprophytie was sitting there working his magic on a golden-horned fawn that had died, likely in an incident from the elven hunt, as Indra could see the fletching of an arrow protruding from the animal's chest. The fawn was struck but not immediately killed, and must have wandered off to find a place to die. She moved closer to Saprophytie, observing the beauty in his magic. His was a necessary magic, one seldom acknowledged. It felt like an ancient magic, too, that entertained no audience nor received any applause. 'Twas a reverence for the unseen miracle of death, and its cycle into rebirth, to begin again. This magic was alchemical and dark; it was the thankless underbelly of life that would one day come to intimately know every living being. In a way, Saprophytie was the reaper, but not for souls; he was the tender of all things physical and ready to rot.

"Hello, Indra, hold steady a minute; I'm almost done here," Saprophytie said, as he concentrated, moving his arms in circular motions. He was moving small swarms of particles and bringing them through the body. From the wound where the fletching sat, small white mushrooms grew and opened, like tiny umbrellas guided by the swift orchestration of Saprophytie's arms. In a way, Saprophytie was bending time, or speeding it up rather. In the mortal world, time moved slowly, and the fawn would appear there too; alas, no mortal would perceive its majestic golden horns, pure white fur, nor the fletching now covered in small mushrooms. Most elements transpose into the mortal realm, they just appear more average, less dimensional, as most mortals cannot see beyond the veil.

Saprophytie squatted low, still finishing up his work, and Indra assessed the sight of him. His body was varied shades of gray, and yet light hues of familiar colors painted him, like a statue of stone watercolored at random, an abstract collage of muted color. Pale-green brushstrokes crossed his pearl-white eyes like a mask. His eyes were starkly bright against the muted tones of his flesh, and they beamed with the all-knowing eyes of a man older than dust. He was a sight to see, startling at first, but also eccentric and beautiful in his own right. He had no hair; his head was smooth and perfectly rounded. He stood at a high altitude, with a slender frame; his long, thin fingers and nose were exaggerated and knobby. His most startling feature was his mouth; lips as thin as blades of grass parted to show teeth that were electrically blue gemstones, each faceted to a point like skinny pyramids crowded together. His smile was alluring and hypnotizing, drawing in his prey, no doubt. At least the last view his meal had would be of marvelous gems. The stones seemed to facilitate clear diction and exaggerated the magical tambour of Saprophytie's voice, Leaving his words to echo in her brain like a melody from a dream.

Saprophytie, appearing to finish his motions turned to face Indra; his movements were slow but precise. "How may I be of service, Lady of the Forest?" he asked, giving a slight bow of his head.

"Hello, Saprophytie. What a beautiful magic you can conjure; I have never seen your work in action." Indra looked at the fawn, which was pleasantly overtaken by delicate mushrooms.

"I appreciate that, but I imagine you didn't come all the way to find me just to compliment my magic," Saprophytie said with raised brows and a smirk.

"I did not; I am actually here to speak on the behalf of the Light Singers, and wish to hear your side of the story and restore some compromising balance. Cutting straight to the matter, I have been in communication with the queen of the Singers, and she has relayed to me that you have been consuming triple the number of Light Singers that you normally do."

Indra paused to pull her hair back and twist it into a beautiful tangle of curls and leaves. She continued casually, "As you well know, the Light Singers are not often born; it can only happen during a lunar eclipse when the Moon is fully covered. The brevity of this window leads to less creation than your consumption. So, firstly, I ask you why. Why is it that now you take more than ever?"

"Hmm, interesting question, but I only have a simple answer, and that is this: as of late I am hungrier, as if a stretching void lies inside of me that is hard to fill. I do feel for the little creatures, they create such beauty that I admire, but I cannot help but eat them. Something in their breath of life fills me like a drug." Saprophytie said this with his eyes shining brightly, his arms emphasizing the rush of eating a Light Singer.

"I see, then. The natural balance is shifting inside of you? You are aware that you are eating more?" Indra said, tilting her head and morphing her body towards him as if to get a closer look.

"Yes, I suppose so; I do not consume more in gluttony or greed, nor in spite of violence, though it is death. We all consume something that was once alive, moving that energy along. But lately, it seems that my job has doubled or more, and more of me spreads thinner. There is more for me to decompose as of late, more work to be done, more of me splitting myself across the whole planet, and more energy calls for more energy, do you follow me?" Saprophytie said, looking down at himself and back up to Indra, his pearly eyes displaying truthfulness as well as a soft weariness.

Indra's voice became more serious, more to the point. "I see, and your magic and skill does not go unthanked; I am truly grateful for the cycles you complete. The shift I have been expecting must be beginning, but from where and why I do not know. It makes sense that you are the first to feel the direct effect of this shift. There is a dark energy that arrived on this planet long ago, you see, and now perhaps it is gaining traction." Indra thought of the virus, and the killing to come, the beginning of his takeover plainly obvious. She feared that this was just the beginning of the changes that would ensue. Saprophytie nodded at this, his eyes blinking in mutual understanding and contemplation.

"I cannot ask you to starve so others can live, but perhaps there is compromise; have you ever eaten a Jubee? They too carry an essence of light, and there is an affect like a rush when you eat them. I eat them consistently and they do not cause depletion; they are made by the flower and water sprites, and I'm sure they would be happy to make them for you." Indra stated this hoping he would give it a chance. "In fact, I have brought some with me, as I always have them with me; would you like to try one?" Indra took two lavender Jubees from her shawl's pocket, and presented them to him; they were clear and glowing with invitation.

"I have never had a Jubee, as one could imagine the sprites do not take the scent of me well, and I rarely get to speak with the creatures," he said, as he accepted a Jubee with his long fingers. Watching him eat the Jubee was horrifyingly marvelous, as with every bite, the light from the food moved into his gemlike teeth, making them shine an electric blue. After consuming the Jubee, his thin mouth curled into what Indra thought to be a smile.

"Did you like it?" Indra asked, with hopeful tones and forced coolness.

Saprophytie nodded his head in delight, and laughed, "I almost like them more than the Light Singers. I have never known such a delight; there is laughter in the light that comprises it. How have I walked on this planet so long without ever coming across such a confection?" he asked, almost concerned at his lack of awareness for such things, looking distant, wondering what else he may have missed out on.

Indra gave him a maddening grin, and laughed delightedly. "I can arrange for them to be put somewhere for you, so you can always have access to them. Would this please you, and reduce your dependence on the Light Singers?"

Saprophytie looked at Indra like a carefully-poised dog waiting for a treat. "If I am supplemented with these, then I will have no need to over hunt the Light Singers. I have a cave in the area where they could be left; perhaps Beaudry could craft me a box of stone where they could be placed for safekeeping."

Indra tilted her head, suddenly realizing that Saprophytie and Beaudry were two of the more ancient beings in the realm, and of course they would know one another. "Perfect. Beaudry is the finest stone craftsman I know. Will you show me the cave, so I can relay the location to the sprites?"

Saprophytie stood tall and nodded at Indra curtly, as if to alert her he was ready to move. He moved like a flitting shadow, but Indra was able to keep up relatively easily. They looked like light and dark playing tag across the forest. When he stopped at cave, he extended one arm in presentation as if to say, "Ta da, this is it." Saprophytie spoke: "I'll have Beaudry build me a small stone temple here, across from the opening of the cave, as I fear the sprites will be leery to come close to the opening of my home. I know what many creatures think of me, but such is the life of a hermit." Saprophytie sighed and smiled at this, but his eye displayed clear sorrow at the thought. "If only they truly knew me, perhaps they wouldn't be so afraid."

Indra sighed along with him at this. "It is their loss, I suppose; but from now on, I would be glad to know you as a friend."

They met gazes, and bowed at one another. "Thank you for your friendship and solution, my lady. The last thing I need is more darkness shrouding my already bleak reputation. I must be off, there is much to do," Saprophytie said, woefully sarcastic. He smiled and then was off like a black jaguar in the twilight.

Indra memorized the location of this cave and went looking for the sprites and for Beaudry. She shared her perspective and wishes to the sprites, that their Jubees would save and preserve the lives of the Light Singers. Water and flower sprites depended on the Light Singers the most, and they were proud to help, as well as terrified to serve a being they normally feared. Along with some heavy bribery, they agreed that Indra would have to escort them for the delivery, to show them the way and serve as a protector for the first couple of trips.

Indra requested that he be delivered seven Jubees every day, to ensure that he was well stocked. A being working so tirelessly deserved an offering every day, to show gratitude and respect for his service. One day, the sprites would not fear Saprophytie, despite his odor and reputation.

To make the gesture more ceremonial and well-rounded, Indra decided that water from the water temple would be brought, along with seven Jubees and a small offering of any kind: a leaf, a flower, seeds, or a stone. They would leave the Jubees and offering on a plate carved of magnificent oak wood, wood that Indra herself carved from the underbelly of her own tree. That plate would make it known to the forest that Saprophytie was an ally and friend to Indra; he would have something tangible to mark her appreciation.

Now, for the temple, Indra called for Beaudry, the way they had taught her long ago, with a sound that was unique to them. Beaudry arrived not more than ten minutes later, as always well dressed in light colors, their silver hair frozen in a perfect style. Tastefully adorned with jewels and gold, Beaudry looked like a ruler of a mountain, keeper of precious metals and gems.

"Beaudry, thank you for coming so soon; oh, how I have missed your well-dressed form and beautiful face!" Indra said as she moved to hug Beaudry, who returned the embrace with a long and patient squeeze, like one you would receive from a patient being of the mountains.

"I take it you are curious about Saprophytie; he mentioned to me that you came to see him," Beaudry said casually, sitting on a nearby stone that shifted to fit their body more comfortably.

Indra nodded and took a seat atop the moss on the ground. "I am, and also I was hoping to discuss a little temple that you might build for him," Indra said as she smiled, swaying her oak- colored body in flirtatious favor. "I am curious how long you have known him, and what your overall sense of him is? I myself feel trust for him, and respect his magic. However, I tend to find love for all beings, and will be sending sprites, hopefully on their own one day, to bring him offerings. Should the sprites have anything to fear from him?"

Beaudry looked sideways at Indra, their eyes squinting sheepishly. "I have known Saprophytie the whole time I have existed here. He lived here well before myself; indeed, he is the undervalued hero of the planet. Although he does hunt beings for food, I don't find it different from eating an animal or a flower. His heart has always been pure of intent. He is always buried in his work of recycling life. You could say I'm an admirer and a close friend. I have always had an eye for him," Beaudry said, blushing a little, the rose color climbing up their cheekbones. "I would not concern yourself with the safety of the sprites. If he promised no harm, he will respect his word till the day he perishes."

Indra was filled with relief, this information reinforcing her intuition. Indra found Beaudry's secret admiration romantically wistful.

"Well then, my heart is at ease, so let us discuss this temple. I'm sure he humbly asked for a stone box, but I wish for it to be something magnificent, something that can close so the Jubees stay fresh inside," Indra said with eyes gleaming, images of ornate carved crystal and golden embellishments flashing past them.

Beaudry smiled and spoke. "I would love nothing more than to create only the most beautiful shrine for him. It would bring me great pleasure."

So they sat, planning its architecture like giddy children. Abruptly, Aria swept in and sat herself down next to Indra. "Hello. What are you two so giddy about?" asked Aria, with breathy, huffed words.

"We are designing a shrine, an offering stand for Saprophytie to honor all his hard work. Saprophytie is complex, albeit at first the sight of him is perhaps startling; but he is truly dedicated to his work." Indra said, while twisting all of her hair into one giant swirl affixed onto the top of her head.

Aria had a serious look on her face, and nodded at Indra. "Indra, would you mind taking a walk with me?" Aria asked, reaching for her hand. Beaudry was busy in thought, wanting to create the perfect temple for Saprophytie, knowing full well who he truly was. Aria and Indra glided away as smoothly as snakes to sit down by the grandest river in all of the forest.   Exhausted, Aria slumped with speed and force onto the ground. This force blew back the small curls framing her face. Indra could sense there was heaviness in the air. By the look of Aria's form, they would not be discussing small things. Her body was a gray-blue, and she was denser and smaller than normal, her silken tendrils barely billowing in the wind. Despite this change in her appearance, she was still magnificent and beautiful with her bright-blue eyes staring blankly into the river's currents.

Indra decided to open the conversation, as Aria looked lost for words. "Saprophytie has been hunting more Light Singers than usual, which I first I misjudged. When I went to see him; his reasoning was not from a place of malaise, but from a place of hunger and being overworked. He is finding more dead, and sometimes he finds the bodies in horrible states. There is something more at play and out of balance. I feel that you have similar news, pertaining to this virus, and his expansion."

Aria made small rhythmic nods, taking in the information. "I see; that is troubling. I too have seen and spoken with Saprophytie, as there is even more to that story. But I'll tell you from the beginning." She took water in cupped hands and splashed it onto her face. "Indra, I have far too much to tell you; I would rather you saw it instead, from within my memory." Aria lifted her left hand and waited for Indra to respond. When Indra nodded with consent, she leaned in to emphasize that she was willing.

At that, Aria put her hand onto Indra's hand and they both fell back slowly into a dream of a memory, with Aria's consciousness leading the way.

When they landed, soft-footed as fish, in the memory, all was glossy and clear. The memory was experienced in the first person, as if from Aria's eyes. Indra had not seen Aria in a very long while; this whole time she must have been following the virus.

Whoosh: the scenery whirred, and they were at the beginning. Her watchful eyes first spied the dark energy surrounding a tall, slender man, the doctor who was known as Amenhotep, a prominent and powerful person allied with the Egyptian Pharaoh. He was not hard to look at; actually he was quite stunning, as if forged from gold. His head was shaved, save for the back where he wore a long black braid; his facial hair was similar, all shaved save for a short beard on his chin and mustache on his upper lip. His eyes were honey amber with swaths of red, captivating and unlike any human eyes Aria had ever seen. If the wind could gasp, she surely did then. The most confusing part of his appearance was that despite the dark cloud around him, he did not look or feel like a monster, at least not to Aria.

As the memory relayed, Aria was intent on learning; she did not let the virus out her sight, and followed him around as closely as his own shadow. He was a physician for those royal and poor alike. He was dark and also light, as he tended carefully and diligently to those who were sick, young or old, rich or poor. His heart was clearly warm and big somehow, despite the simultaneous torrent inside of him.

Through the first couple of days, Aria saw that his aura of "gnats" would shift from large to small from one day to the next. On some days it would be dark and cloudy, and on other days it would be just a slight buzz of speckled gray. When it was speckled gray, Aria spied that the swaths of red in his eyes were subdued, were instead mostly the golden-honey color. There was something confusing at play here, a shift like oceanic tides.

One evening, when the Moon was black, Amenhotep stood on a tiled deck outside of his dwelling pavilion. He was observing the stars, with his honey-golden eyes that were swirled with swaths of red. His cloud was thick, although it was harder to see in the dark. Curiously, she herself blew closer to him, blowing though his hair which fell at his back unbraided; she blew through the very beard on his face, and she blew through the reeds that were his eyelashes. She became the air that filled him, and within his breath, inside his body, she could feel his heart beating. Like tasting flavors, she read the energies and secrets inside of him. They swarmed around her like fruit flies to souring melon. There were many beings within him, and that startled Aria. How could all this fit into one small human form?

Beneath his flesh flowed a shark, a raven, a vulture, a tiger, a falcon, a whale, a scorpion, a snake, a monkey, a wild dog, a horse, and many men and women. It felt like there were more, but she could not read them all by the time she was exhaled. Haunted, she did not dare go back inside. She had seen enough. He contained the spirits, power, and intelligence of all the creatures he had harbored inside. This was where the dawning realization struck Aria like a drum, resounding shock at the speed at which this all transpired.

It was during her shock that a woman called out from the pavilion; she was as delicious as a carefully designed dessert. She walked closer to stand next to Amenhotep; they were well paired, even royal, two beautiful forms about to be tangled into heap of sweat and pleasure, that much was predictable. But there was more than sensual desire hanging between them. The female smiled at Amenhotep, with seasoned secrets and stories. Sparks flew between them like a million fireflies, each one alight with a memory of how their love came to grow and mature.

Amenhotep walked towards her as if hypnotized, hunger and love pouring from his eyes into hers. It was erotic to watch their passion unfold, like the blossoming of a nocturnal flower. Aria could not help but watch; indeed, she even learned some new things. Nothing, save for some shimmers of ravaging darkness in his movements, was amiss; he was truly among one of the loveliest things she had ever seen. If Indra were not inside a memory, her eyes too would be wide with wonder.

In the weeks to come, there was another characteristic that Amenhotep displayed. He never showed signs of aging or scarring from wounds; he was as supple and shiny as an elemental being. In the heat of the Sun, Amenhotep was out in the surrounding jungle, foraging for certain plants with a curved knife, like a small scythe. When he over-assumed the density of a trees bark, the knife came down faster than expected and he cut the palm of his hand open. His hand was dripping with blood, and he observed it in curiosity, with not a hint of pain or concern. The cut slowly began to close itself and heal with no sign of the wound, save for the drying blood on his hand. He continued his harvesting and found an oasis pond, with many blue lotuses blooming on top of the water. Picking a few of those flowers, he folded them gently between leaves, and he made his way home by sunset, back to his pavilion, where the same woman waited for him there.

Amenhotep was the Pharaoh Iry-Hor's chief advisor, and from day to day he was in and out of the Pharaoh's quarters. His pavilion was nearby, so at any moment he was available to assist with anything medical or advisory. One day, Aria saw that Iry-Hor was ill with dysentery; perhaps he had eaten something contaminated or perhaps had contracted a parasite, but he was white and sweaty with dehydration and pain. This pain had lasted for days, without any ability to keep food or water down. It was looking bleak for Iry-Hor.

Of course, Amenhotep was there by his side in no time, and the dark cloud around him was thick like a rolling storm cloud about to burst with rain. When he laid his hands upon the Pharaoh, Aria watched how he changed bodies; it was as simple as one long, electric touch. Iry-Hor was stunned and stared at his ceiling; the cloud grew around him and began healing his form. His sunken, dehydrated skin swelled with health and life once again; any scarring along his arms and feet miraculously healed with only a couple hours. Inside him, the virus was imparting its coding and amending all of the body's ailments.

To Aria's surprise, after a few hours of Amenhotep watching Iry-Hor's health improve, he again placed his hand on his king's forehead. Instead of staying inside the Pharaoh and having complete dominion over the land, the dark cloud again swirled and whooshed out of Iry-Hor and back into Amenhotep.

Aria was startled, as it appeared that sometimes, the virus used its power to help others, "But perhaps it was due to power and gaining favor," she mused. In the following weeks, she witnessed Amenhotep again using his dark cloud, to heal a young girl from the village surrounding the royal territory. She was on the edge of death, and he brought her back to healthy vitality, with no favor to gain but bags of grain and cups full of joyful tears. He left empty handed, giving a few slow, humble nods with the dark cloud surrounding him, walking away through the rice fields as the Sun was rising.

In the early morning light, he crawled into bed with his beloved after a long and lavish bath. He simply held onto her, and breathed into the back of her neck, taking in the smell of her. At this he fell to sleep, happy and peacefully, like child.

Days rolled on and Aria watched, and nothing too dark seemed to be happening. There were killings, and there were small wars between neighboring villages, but there was not severe cruelty. There was, however, dividing poverty and imbalance in the wealth distribution. But beyond that, Amenhotep did not present as anything as dark or as evil as she had thought.

That is, not until the day when the woman he loved became ill. Her name was Imi. Her once full and supple form waned with the attack of a parasite that Amenhotep could not cure. Weeks passed, and he could not heal her with any plant or concoction. So he attempted to go inside of her, his cloud swirling with veracity. He placed his hand on her forehead, but nothing happened; like a sponge already too saturated with life, her body would not accept the virus. Amenhotep was beside himself with rage and confusion, and most of all, fear for her loss. He sat with her day and night, doing everything he could to stop whatever it was that was killing her.

The fateful day came Imi breathed her last, her beautiful silver eyes closing forever. Aria noticed that her last breath was sweet and floral, like the flowers of the Fae. With that last breath outwards, her soul was off, leaving her body. This was when everything became clear to Aria; that his darkness came in cycles, and that there was bloodshed to come.

Amenhotep's loss fueled a rage that could have tilted the Earth on its axis. The days to come were filled with many random killings, and he planted seeds of war and the need for territorial gain in the leaders of Upper Egypt. The divide between village and Pharaohs became even more drastic. Poverty grew, and worship culture budded and grew.

Amenhotep began flitting from being to being, playing games with the world of politics and the monarchy around him. His energy traveled from living creature to living creature by way of touch and will, gaining knowledge and power by circulating around the planet. The virus was hungry for blood and carnal acts, terrorizing and feeding off that power. The monster was in complete control of whichever being he wanted to be. She learned that he had a name by which he called himself one night when he declared it to one of his victims.

"I am Iós, and there is nowhere you can run that I will not find you and rip the beating heart from your chest!" He screamed this with a dark delight that resounded into the surrounding trees, causing all the nearby birds to take flight. In the scuttle of birds, he slit the throat of the man who stood helplessly awaiting his death.

Whoosh! This was the end of the memory, and all became blurry, like being underwater. Indra and Aria opened their eyes, facing the twilight sky of their realm, lying there quietly for some time, letting the horrific information sink in.

Alongside them, the great river flowed, lightly brushing their toes. The curling curves of its currents were soothing on the soles of their feet, as if pulling away the vibrations of hatred that they had just witnessed.

Indra and Aria eventually sat up, sighing, confusion on their faces, the emotional caprice of what they'd seen draining them of all their words. In time, Aria stated, "His energy grows stronger, and his power to evade my watchful eye is keen. He is starting wars, creating opposing religions, implementing killings, and encouraging violence for fun. He travels worldwide by animal, using each animal like a suit..." Hers was the most hopeless of voices. They both sat and watched the water flow.

"Saprophytie has also mentioned that there are many more dead animals, perhaps ones that housed Iós. These dead animals seem to retain a... residue, as if contaminated by his presence inside them," Aria continued, eyes gleaming with disgust. "It appears the animals died of natural causes, but it is tough to know what it all means. We will be monitoring their offspring, and any other animals that have made contact with him."

Indra chimed in, her voice glacial, "Aria, there is something I must say, and I fear that you will not forgive me." Avoiding eye contact, she continued, "I... I knew this day would come; it is why I came here, in an attempt to restore balance. I was summoned by representatives of a race of beings who share your galaxy, and had growing concerns about Iós spreading beyond the planet. I came from a place in the upper planes, where my higher soul dwells."

Aria sat very still, waiting to hear more; she was as unreadable and calm as a poker player. Dragonflies skipped past their feet on the surface of the water, leaving trails of light behind them.

Indra went on, her conscience pouring out like a dam overfull, "My true name is Celosia, and I hail from a dimension where I see and monitor the web of all things in the multiverse. I do not create and I do not destroy, but I can adjust. When summoned, I came to adjust the imbalance here on Earth, but found that it was no use from a distance. I was unable to do anything from afar, so I incarnated here to learn and hopefully help." Indra reached to the river, took some water in cupped hands, and drank; ready to continue speaking, she turned to Aria, making full wild-eyed contact with her.

"There was a time when I gazed upon your Moon; it was gray and dormant. Its ashen surface adjacent to an Earth encapsulated in darkness. There was suffering and hate, and it was known that one day, you just... went dark. You sacrificed yourself somehow, shut down the incarnation process, and did something to protect the souls you had helped incarnate here, as many of them became trapped. The virus needed food, a source of power to draw from, and it was from the suffering of souls; at least, that is what I gathered. It was bleak, and I am sorry I did not tell you before; I did not know what was best. I have been slowly recovering the details of my memories, upon meditating and sitting in vision."

Indra's eyes began to well with tears, and she continued, "When I arrived here, everything was normal. I could not control when or where I landed. It was a gamble. At that time, I didn't remember as much as I would have hoped. Beyond that, there was no problem existing that I could attend to. I was uncertain when, how, or if it would happen. Please forgive my secrecy and lack of transparency. But now that I see how quickly this will all unravel, I worry that we are too late."

Aria was silent, waiting to see that Indra was completely done speaking. She sighed and drew another deep breath. "You know, it's funny; I thought I would have more time to figure it out too. It's funny when you know where your end is. Well... it's not really the end; in fact, I like to think of it as a transformation. All the same, it is an uncomfortable waiting game."

Aria gave Indra a knowing look. Indra's face was wet with tears. "Indra, the day I met you, I knew your secrets; you were merely the messenger, and I cannot blame these atrocities unfolding on your secrecy. I built this place with Ílios, and it is my responsibility to bear; I invited souls here. This is not a situation where you are to blame. In fact, no one really is..." trailing off, Aria brought a strong wind to the surrounding trees, rolling the branches nearest to the water; her face was filled with enjoyment, as if seeing it all for the first time.

The twilight skies cast mystery onto everything. Color and lights swelled with buzzing and scintillation. There was love in the movements all around them.

"I really will miss life as it is now, with love flowing through everything. It is a source of great pride and gratitude for me. But alas, it will shift."

"So you knew all along that this day would come?" Indra looked down at her toes, bending them into a curled shape. She continued, not waiting for a response from Aria. "I suppose that makes more sense, that you would know. A foreigner incarnates to your planet and asks you to keep an eye on a mysterious darkness..." Indra laughed out loud at how extremely thickheaded with assumption she was. "How could I hold such a secret from you?"

Aria smiled at this and nodded, with a little pleasure in Indra's embarrassment. Her face lit up with a sudden memory, her face twisting into a grin. "Indra, if you recall all those years ago, you agreed to fulfill a favor for me."

Indra nodded and smiled at this. "Of course, and I am still good for that promise."

"Marvelous. When I go, and that day will come, I need you to stay here. Despite you thinking you can do nothing from here, that is untrue. Your energy is like an exotic herb infusing into the web of this plane, like tea in hot water. You will be able to bring balance to this darkness, despite the lack of clarity. What is clear is that you have a tolerance for darkness, and that will make you invaluable for the balancing act." Aria sucked in a big breath and bit her lip slightly, holding back tears.

"Even though I know it is what must be done, I am a little afraid. I cannot liberate all the souls, only those that have bodies; and even then, that is a tall order to accomplish. As we speak, I am within the Moon doing just that." Aria looked up at herself, the big bright Moon gleaming with cool jade colors. "Right now there many formless souls scattered around the planet, and I cannot extract them. I feel like I have led them all into this unknown trap."

Aria moved herself swiftly into a standing position, and looked at Indra with a forced, brave smile. "I am afraid that with all the evacuation processes in the Moon, I must go; I cannot afford to have any part of myself not dedicated to that. I must save whoever I can. In order for me to protect the galaxy to the best of my ability, I will need to shut down the portal inside the moon. It is a tough choice to make, but I fear that leaving it open could cause affects farther-reaching than just on this planet alone. I have to make tough choices, and I'll have to do it soon. Time passes faster in the mortal realm, and each day brings more darkness."

Indra swallowed the hard lump in her throat; it felt like she had swallowed a Jubee whole. Her eyes were frantically seeking, and moving around quickly, her head tilted up towards the sky, as if following the trail of a bat. She was looking for a way out, a reason, some small detail that could fix everything. But there was no magic solution.

"The wisest thing to do is not always the easiest thing to do. Aria, you have a big heart; you are making a choice you feel is the safest. Very understandable. It may be one of the most difficult choices you will ever make. If it were me, I would also shut down the portal, for it is better than something more devastating, like destroying the planet or infecting the galaxy. With this choice, there is hope for the souls to one day be free, and polished to perfection by all that they are learning here, myself included. I will rest easier knowing that no one will be able to truly die here; they'll just be stuck." Indra phrased the end of her encouragement speech in the tone of a question, because in truth, she really wasn't sure if they could die or not.

"Theoretically, they should be safe, but anything is possible, and I am not sure what Iós is capable of. There are no guarantees, but when he casts his viral grid around the planet, like I saw in your memories, all souls will reincarnate and recycle again and again." Aria looked down, truly disappointed with how this all was unfolding. "Also, there is no telling when he will do this, so I must go evacuate all the beings while there is still time."

Indra opened her arms and nearly tackled Aria to the ground with a hug; she held her firmly for a while, hoping to give Aria some of her own strength. While embracing, Aria spoke.

"I am not sure if I will see you again in this form; perhaps I'll still be here somehow, or perhaps not. I have never done this. Also, I forgot to mention... Ílios only knows I am evacuating the souls and that there is a big issue, but he is inclined to destroy this place with souls in it or not. If he knows I'm somewhere on the Earth discorporated, he will not destroy the planet. So if you ever see him, let him know I'm sorry. Promise me that you will do what you can, and I will do what I can."

Quickly, she peeled herself away from Indra, and turned without a goodbye. Aria swept herself upwards to the Moon, as if sucking up all of the wind from the Earth with her. She was gone, and Indra sat alone, processing all the information.

Layer 21: Fengári- Disintegrating

Once Fengári arrived in the Moon, no longer on the Earth as the wind, all parts of her were busy at work, tending to the layers upon layers of beings who lay inside, asleep in dreams.

There were millions of bodies, all stored and dreaming their Earthly experience, each one carefully wrapped in woven white blankets made of spun Moonlight. Fengári was able to split herself into many selves, tending to these beings. She would produce her silver scissors from within her flowing form and cut around the beings; to anyone looking, it would appear she was cutting nothing in mid-air above the person, but if looking through her perspective, it would all come into focus.

She saw lights streaming from each person, all representing a part of their consciousness and perception, like wires hooking up audio, video, and sensation. These small light cords she cut and adjusted to disconnect the body. It did not take long, but it was a complex process. She used her intellect to work smarter, not harder. Getting as many souls off planet as soon as possible was the goal.

For example, she could unplug someone who protected a tribe from lions; she could unplug the lion's food, and that way at some point a few people would die by the lion's hunger. Although death by lion was not glamorous, at least they would be free in their deaths to return to the Moon portal. There was a strategy so she could remove as many beings as possible without having to individually cut each person out at once.

Many beings woke up confused and jostled, as they were ripped from their experiences mid-action. This was jarring for the souls, and they often woke up with protest and a desire to return. Fengári had to explain to everyone that this was a necessary evacuation for their own protection. They were told that if they were left inside, they would be stuck there indefinitely.

A few veterans asked to be put back in, regardless of the risks involved; Fengári put them back just to get them stop talking. It was an exhausting process that she thought would never end. Many souls had arranged transport for the time of their souls' planned return dates, and now they had been marooned early; so many strange beings were left waiting on the shores of the Moon.

Fengári came across one of her favorite souls, the Weaver, a Feline originating from within her own galaxy. Upon waking her suddenly from her slumber, she was disoriented, but calm. Fengári explained the situation, and the Weaver offered to help with transportation; she had a vessel tethered and waiting for her, so she zipped back to her planet and returned with a larger ship and a team of Felines to help get everyone back to their systems, or at least somewhere close.

The Avior loved galaxtarian work, helping others; being of service was the lifeblood that fueled their existence. Their aid was truly a blessing for Fengári, as she needed the help; there would be thousands of beings who had no way to leave the Moon. The Weaver was calm and clearly concerned about Fengári's stamina and the well-being of all those left on Earth.

As time passed, Fengári and the Avior continued to worked together to get everyone off of the Moon. The Avior sent out a distress signal to alert any neighboring star systems to come to their aid in response to the chaos. Several different races came to assist with large transport ships. As Fengári worked tirelessly, the ships came and went, ferrying the stranded souls to safety.

Fengári, although endlessly grateful, was too busy tending to all of the incarnating beings to extend more than a general thanks to those who helped. It was while she was in the middle of cutting light lines in multiple places at once that the end began. The threads were no longer cutting. Fengári knew that she had retrieved everyone that she could at this point, and now she would have to shut it all down. She briefly appeared on the surface, to motion for the ships to leave the Moon. The ships headed out and anchored nearby, watching to see what was happening.

Inside her world, Fengári took many deep breaths to calm herself. In one corner of her mind, she could hear Ílios asking questions, needing updates, wondering if he should shut down his systems.

Fengári responded to him with a brief exiting statement: "My love, I cannot bare to let souls go to waste in our creation. I need you to keep all these systems live. I'll be down there on Earth to do what I must; I will love you eternally, and hope to see you down there somewhere."

She didn't even let him respond; she breathed deeply and shattered every portal at once, their liquid reflections melting and cracking with great force. The light in every portal room shut off, one by one, eventually turning the hollow of the Moon into a dark, empty place. All that was left was Fengári, staring out onto Earth, her eyes blazing with the calm fury that fueled her last act. She saw that the Earth was slowly becoming gridded with strange triangular patterns. Dark lines were making their way across the planet, crossing and weaving a strange geometric shape.

The progression felt slow and fast all at once, and Fengári knew she would have to be swift.

In her last act, Fengári magnetized all the love and harmony she had ever witnessed on Earth. She breathed in the beauty of all things ever created, expanding with each breath, becoming larger than she ever knew she could be. Before the last lines were linked, setting the dark cage to light, Fengári propelled herself with such speed and such loving fury that she shattered herself into tiny shimmering particles of seafoam green. They moved and swarmed through the small gap in the grid, and she spread herself far and wide across the globe. She infused her love and protection into the very fabric of the plane. All things living and inanimate received the shimmer from Fengári's soul, her consciousness permeating all things.

This shimmer was like a secondary grid, one of opposing force, one that reminded potential host victims of the grandeur to be found in this creation. All of Earth was quarantined with Fengári's affection... and above that, a cage of darkness.

Her consciousness would be the hope for redemption; although sometimes a small thing, she would serve as the silver lining in the world, the needle found in the haystack. Her shimmer would be the day off, the birth of a healthy baby, the fall of heavy rain in a drought, the sight of buffalo stampeding across the open plains, the perfectly played song on a guitar, the excitement of a first kiss, the freedom from a cruel marriage, or the long-awaited breeze on a hot day. Her small signs of hope would occur and recur forever, if need be, until the day balance could be restored.

Layer 22: Paesh - Test Results

Paesh found it hard to sleep after the memories of her abduction came rushing back in full force. To keep it from replaying in her mind, she strove to feel normal and tune out, like the rest of the world often did. So she stayed up watching two of her favorite movies; without fail, they always brought her ease. Setting the proper movie-watching scene, Paesh lit some beeswax candles and Japanese incense, her little laptop whirring to life, lighting her face while she searched her movie library.

The first movie she played she had seen so many times she could quote the dialog. Often, it served as background company for her lonely nights, even though some would say it was a man's man's movie. It represented something that had always been lacking in her life, and the movie never failed to produce tears -- like a prayer for hope that there was a good man left in the world somewhere, a hero. A noble man who was willing to do what whatever it took to serve justice and protect those he loved. Although there was darkness in the main character, Paesh felt it was an honorable darkness -- a darkness that still had a moral compass, that led the protagonist on his journey for true justice, defending the honor of his mother and other innocents. Of course, Jason Mamoa, representing that hero in Paesh's mind, was certainly overly-idealistic, but she would rather have a fantasy than face the truth of the men she really knew.

Paesh hadn't known many heroic men; perhaps her father counted, but fatherly heroism has another time and place. "Maybe men don't learn how to be good men until they become fathers," she mused.

Being a woman, Paesh had experienced cruelty from all of the genders... though not all guys were cruel, she amended, feeling bad for entertaining such black-and-white generalizations. She thought about Lu for a moment, not wanting to pigeonhole all men; however, math was math, and numbers never lied.

All her thinking had stirred up too many thoughts, and she needed something to calm down, so in between her movie sagas she took a tea and food break.

Upon the ritual of checking her cupboards, ones that she already knew would be void of easy snacks, she stared hopelessly at sardines, grain-free flour, rice, and dried garden vegetables in jars. As usual, she had to whip something up. Multitasking, she boiled the hot water for her warm bevi while she preheated the oven. Grain-free zucchini muffins with little chocolate chunks would do the trick; she had all the ingredients. Hands effortlessly began measuring and stirring, the recipe embedded in her memory. The process took her all of eight minutes, from start to finish, to get them in the oven -- the same amount of time it took for her water to boil. She scanned shelves lined with jars full of herbs and medicinal mushroom powders, some home grown and some imported.

"Cardamom pods, butterfly pea flower, lion's mane, turkey tail, skullcap, chamomile, padnam leaf... and hmmmmmm, what else...?" she muttered to herself while gathering jars and tapping the counter. "Ah, blue lotus!" Taking a varied pinch from each of the selected jars, she added them to the French press along with the hot water. Her muffins baking and her herbs soaking, she figured there was time for a quick shower. Pleased with her efficient timing, every step up the stairs pressed pride into the wood.

Despite her strange night, everything was flowing well; her shower was divine and her body meticulously oiled. Her muffins had baked to perfection and went well with the soothing and softening herbal blend. For a moment, life felt good and normal. Crème de la crème. She hardly even thought of her shapeshifting in the lab, pushing that aside for tomorrow's concerns; it was too late to beat her mind into a pulp.

Ready for her next movie, she chose Fantastic Fungi, a newer film directed by Louis Schwartzberg. It was an incredible documentary that featured many of her heroes, particularly Paul Stamets. She had seen it many times over, as the imagery was so beautifully done, with many scenes of nature, which lowered her cortisol. She passed out while watching it, and drifted into a comfortable sleep. The warm bevi and movie had done their jobs.

An orange light clicked on and filled the sleeping nook; tired arms reached out for a dream journal, the one in its usual place. Hands slowly patting the shelf, turning animated in dismay when there was no journal. Hands more lucidly scrambled around the wooden shelf, reaching farther than before. Sudden relief turned strained hands limp as they found the familiar smooth texture of the handmade journal, its cover crafted from woven ribbons of silk attached to its backboards. The journal had just been tucked little farther out of reach than she had remembered in her dreamy state. Book in hand, she cracked the journal open, the spine stiff with newness, the pages slightly stubborn and crisp. With the cap of her pen in her mouth, Paesh began to write.

My dream, 04:02 8/25/2019:

I was in a cave; my skin and form were not my own human form. There was the distinct smell of jasmine and dirt. There was a hallway and a stream, which I followed till the dim light became bright. I was in a green place, and then upon a golden disc. Standing at the center, I noticed that now surrounding me was a 360-degree mirror. Suddenly, next to me there was a tall feline being. There was another woman, a being who had golden-brown skin and plants for hair; there were ancient-looking female humans, and there was me as well, human Paesh standing among them. Lingering over my shoulder was a cloud of dust.

The cloud-like being spoke, her voice surprisingly clear. She said, "Nagda 3147 consumed us all, and also showed us the way. A black hole is like a vacuum. It pulled us in; like a blender it stretched us and mixed us around, scattering us through space and time, the highest form of death and birth perhaps... Now I am within you, and you and you... learning, adjusting, balancing..." the cloud-being said, while her faint arms pointed at everyone in the mirror. Suddenly, everyone vanished, and I was left alone in the mirror, and I spoke something into the mirror before it shattered and I woke up. I think I said, "We should return. The reason we came, the reason we left." The words came out so matter-of-factly. If we came from somewhere, why were we here? And where was here?

The orange light clicked off, and Paesh fell back to sleep, completely exhausted from the day before. When she woke, the light outside revealed it was beyond later than normal -- it was nearly noon! Initially scrambling for work, she stopped, recalling she did not have to go in. Sighing a deep breath of relief, she settled back into her bed, lying flat, staring out the skylight, watching the day brighten. She laid there, unmotivated and untired. Later, she managed to take a long and relaxing shower; the smells of pine and lavender essential oil were lifted up by the steam, and it soothed her senses. She just wanted to forget about all of it.

After drying off, she rummaged the kitchen for a snack, and then milled through her garden and played with her cat till the Sun was low. Relieved the day was over, she was shamelessly ready for more sleep -- as if dreams to come were pulling her back to bed.

An orange light clicked on, and pen to paper, Paesh wrote with one eye open:

Dream Journal at 02:22 8/26/2019: There was a warehouse. I was wondering through it, the floors that were made of rivers and objects I cannot recall were sailing past me. Suddenly, I was at a ceremonial burial on a cliff's edge; a woman lay on a stack of wood, her face pale and stiff with death, a blue lotus flower sewn onto her third eye.

I jumped off the cliff and found myself underwater, which then became the galaxy. When I turned to see Earth, I saw that it was covered in an electrical netting. It looked like the geometric shell of a virus, actually... my scientific brain in the dream posed the question, "Is that a virus?" When suddenly, to my left there was a being, light green and blue silks covering her form. "They are all trapped in there. Do not forget your promise, Indra." I looked down at my feet, and wondered to myself what promise I had made. Then I woke up.

The next morning, Paesh woke early, with the urge to be busy and back in the lab. The dream from the night before lingered in her head, especially the imagery of Earth with a giant geometric web imposed on it. She wondered if maybe everyone on Earth was actually trapped here somehow, her thoughts digressing as she stretched a little bit to start her day. She had more pressing things to think about; today she was deeply excited to do self-testing with Tiago after work. All this strangeness in her life was tipping the scale, and questions were piling up onto it; on top of that, her dreams were even stranger, and somehow they seemed to be stringing it all together.

While staring at herself in the mirror, all dressed and ready, she looked closely, on the odd chance she might find something hiding there. Unblinking, she stared into her own eyes until the details of her face softened and then melted away; she was left looking into her eyes, as if they were just floating disconnected from her body; but there was nothing unusual. No shape shifting, nor purple skin. Disappointment broke her trance, as she could not summon her shapeshifting in this way.

A sound startled Paesh fully into focus. Tulsi was pecking at the tall and skinny bathroom window with adamant repetition. The bubbly-styled stained glass skewed the details of the bird, but her head was craned curiously, tapping at the window. One familiar eye staring through the blur of glass made Paesh laugh out loud at her life.

Paesh was relieved her little friend was back; she wasn't certain if Tulsi was another fluke comet passing through her life, like a pit stop, or a potential friend who was here to stay. She felt comforted by the presence of her little friend, felt familiar and comforted by a wind-rider like this bird.

Paesh moved to unlatch the window, but remembering it swung outwards, she let the latch be and switched off the light making her way downstairs, hoping Tulsi would come down to the door. She wasn't super-hungry, but knew better than to go to work thinking she was above food. Opening the door, she entered the garden, quickly harvesting vegetables and herbs to make a colorful garden salad, adding some figs and goat cheese in a separate container to her lunch box. She then filled a water bottle and made a thermos of tea to go, and with that, she was outside, putting her bike saddlebag onto the frame. Tulsi parked herself on top of the bag with grace, and stared at Paesh.

"I guess you'll be headed to work with me? I'm glad to see you haven't gone and disappeared on me," Paesh said, while throwing her leg over the seat and making her way down the drive.

Upon arriving at work, she saw Tiago's car as well as Lu's Jeep in the lot. There was a slight giddiness in the bottom of her stomach; despite her fear and disdain, she was actually looking forward to working with Lu. Bracing herself, taking a deep you got this breath, she opened the lab doors to find the familiar sterile smell and a whoosh from the AC greeting her. Everything felt normal, at least for that moment.

When she was suited up, she found a chipper Tiago enthusiastically discussing the test results from the project they had been working on for weeks. His hair was methodically gelled and combed to immobile perfection, glossy and fashionable. Lu looked like a wreck, tired and pale, but he was following along in the conversation with the appropriate smiles and verbal interjections. His eyes had bags underneath them, and his face had a thicker beard than five o'clock shadow, along with some light scratches; maybe he'd had a long night out, Paesh concluded, trying not to think of him on dates with other women. Her internal possessiveness shocked her.

"Good morning, Paesh! I hope that you're doing well, and that everything is all right with your family," Tiago said, as if he had practiced it in the mirror before work. He winked at Paesh, which made her laugh inside, as Lu would certainly fail to pick up on the practiced nature of Tiago's concern. In fact, Lu wasn't listening at all.

"Everything turned out fine -- thanks, Tiago," Paesh said, stowing her drinks on the designated shelf of the break-room fridge. "So, what did I miss?" she asked, trying not to sound overly excited in front of Lu.

Lu turned to look at Paesh, and he seemed to inflate a bit; he smiled a soft and comfortable smile, like he had known her his whole life. In that moment, his color improved just slightly. Despite his weary demeanor, she clearly brought life back into him, and she tried not to blush. She did everything in her power to not walk over to him and melt on the floor at his feet; she wanted to sink into him like lying on memory foam, she wanted to hide her face in his neck. But no, now it was work, and there were rules. Paesh was a sane and professional person, and she was able to work with this man despite her unavoidable attraction to him.

The day was long. It dragged on, like swimming while wearing all denim. They were mainly documenting results, and deriving new hypotheses from those results, creating new and more refined tests to execute in the coming weeks. The foundational information was laid down; they just had to run with it.

Tiago left the room shortly after they discussed the game plan, and Paesh was left alone with Lu for most of the day. When lunch came, he asked her if he could join her. The answer was obvious, and he slowly followed her out to the cool air of the nearby forest where, in the protective shade, there sat an old wooden picnic table. It took Lu longer to walk, and Paesh hadn't noticed he didn't keep up with her pace until she made it to that picnic table. He was limping. Tulsi sat in a nearby tree, eyeing them both from her perch, and Paesh waved up at her but didn't say anything.

This was a choice spot for lunch, a chance to get out from under the fluorescent lights of the lab. Lu was trying not to wince, to cover his pain with a smile. He brought with him a lunch and some water. It appeared to be left over dim-sum or dumplings. Adorable buns pinched up into a twist sat in a glass container; they made her mouth water. Paesh was obsessed with adorable little pockets of food; mess-free sensible food for sensible people, she mused while she unpacked her salad.

She was growing concerned and curious about Lu's physical state.

"Lu, what happened to you? Are you okay?"

Lu didn't move to eat; instead, he laid flat on his back down on the ground. He clearly didn't care about the dirt, or the bugs; he was so exhausted that he just rested his eyes and smiled. "I'm actually beginning to think I'm not okay," he said from his spot on the ground. Paesh looked at him, questioning his comment with her eyes while she opened her packed lunch. She was hungry, craving the tang of her bright citrus salad dressing.

"Can I do anything to help you? Do you want to talk about it?" Paesh asked, taking a bite of her lunch.

Lu, responded strangely, "Paesh, since I met you, I have been having these incredibly strange dreams. They're all different, but they all have you in them... or at least, I think it's you. I haven't been sleeping that well," Lu said, his eyes still closed, his arms stretched out in a T shape.

"Is that so?" Paesh asked with a mouthful of fig. "Is that the reason for your limping and wincing today? It looks like you've been hit by a bus."

"Hah," Lu projected a short laugh. "Last night was sleepless for a whole other reason. I got run off the road by a car while on my motorcycle. I feel lucky to be alive, but I probably should have stayed home today," Lu said, wincing as he moved to sit up and look at Paesh. "But I wanted to see you in case you came back today..." Lu shook his head, bashful as he ran his hands over his face, as if rubbing it would wake him up.

"What!?" Paesh asked, completely horrified, "Oh my God, LU!" Rushing over to him, nearly choking on her salad, she blurted, "What happened? Are you sure you're not seriously hurt?"

He turned his whole torso towards her, showing that his neck was unable to move, "I can't turn my neck, but I think it is because I cracked some ribs," Lu said, eyes wide and thoughtful. "Maybe I should go get checked; the pain has gotten worse in the last couple of hours." He blushed and looked at Paesh. "I think I need your help getting me there. Would you drive me to the ER in my car? Luckily it's not across town in this traffic," he said with casual thoughtfulness.

"If it was in another city, I would still take you," Paesh said with nurturing eyes. "Do you need help up?" She stood, her arms extended. Lu smiled graciously, grabbing hold of her strong yet delicate wrists, and hoisted himself upwards with involuntary groaning sounds. Paesh gathered Lu's untouched food, and her own lunch that was nearly half finished.

"Let's get you in the car with the AC running, and I'll check in with Tiago," Paesh said as they broke the shaded protective threshold of the forest. Sun blinded both of them, and they walked slowly, squinting towards the old Jeep.

Paesh ran inside the lab, looking for Tiago; she found him in his office reading over some paperwork. Breaking his silent concentration with a small knock, Paesh tilted her head and asked if she could come in.

"Of course, sit down," Tiago said, while marking a stopping point in his reading.

"Actually, I don't think there's time to sit down. Lu crashed his motorcycle last night, and I think the pain and potential damage is kicking in. He had asked if I could drive him to the ER, and then once he's settled, I'll head straight back," Paesh said, her words spilling out in an effort not to keep Lu waiting.

"Oh. Oh my, shit. Really? Why did he come in today, or rather, how did he manage to? Please take him there, you still have about a half an hour on your lunch anyway, so no rush," Tiago said with his face wincing, looking as concerned as he was confused.

"Great, thanks, I'll be back soon! When I get back, maybe we can get started on some testing," Paesh said, with a quick smile as she darted back down the hall and out the door to Lu's Jeep.

Upon entering the car, she saw that Lu had reclined the passenger seat, and he had his eyes closed. His eyebrows moved in Paesh's direction, acknowledging her presence in the car, appearing to relax; the muscles in his jaw loosened, and he breathed a calm exhalation, letting out what could have been a sigh of relief.

Paesh rolled down her side window just a smidge as soon as the car was in motion, figuring that along with AC, fresh air was also helpful.

"Lu, you didn't touch your food. Do you want to manage getting something down before you get to the ER? No telling when the next time you'll be able to eat." Paesh said this while handing Lu his lunch. A small sound came out of him, and he cracked one eye open.

"I suppose I should... who knows what medications they may give me. I can't handle those on an empty stomach. Thanks for reminding me," Lu said, pain plain in his voice; his eyes were wide open now, and he was staring down at his lunch. He began eating, at first small bites that looked very forced, but after a few, his appetite seemed to increase and he managed to eat most of his lunch while they sat, driving in silence.

"It's strange... you got in an accident, and still remembered to pack a lunch." Paesh said, smiling, while her eyes were focused on the road, as they were boarding a highway ramp. She continued, "What happened, anyway? Were you going too fast?"

Clicking the container lid shut, Lu was still working on his last bite, contemplating, as if recalling a distant memory. Paesh remembered she had refilled his water in the lab, and reached behind her seat to grab it. She handed it to him, in case he needed it. He looked down, surprised, and immediately drank the water, swishing it in his mouth and swallowing. He looked repaired by this sustenance and water, if only slightly.

"It was strange," he said at last. "It wasn't quite dark, and there weren't too many cars on the road. I was completely sober and headed home from the grocery store; I just needed a few things to make dinner." Lu paused, and took another drink of water.

"On my way home, out of nowhere, a shiny black vehicle came at me head-on from the opposing lane. It had no lights on and was all blacked out -- the rims, glass, and paint. It looked fancy, like a Tesla, but it was a different make. It was extremely hard to see. I couldn't hear it coming over the roar of my motorcycle; it must have been an energy-efficient car, it was so quiet. Like a ghost riding the night. It certainly caught me by surprise." Lu trailed off and closed his eyes to finish his story.

"The road was curvy, and there was a small sloped ravine on my side of the road. When I saw him headed towards me full speed ahead, my reflexes steered me off of the edge and down the ravine. I sort of jumped off of my bike, but still hit a few trees and landed on some rocky ground. My bike lay wrecked ten meters away. Its lights were still on and pointed back at me, illuminating the surroundings. It wasn't that far of a drop, maybe five meters, but it was enough that the climb back up after the crash felt difficult... disorienting, really."

Lu stopped to swallow his spit. "When I reached the top, the car was gone. Maybe they hadn't even known they ran someone off the road." He lifted his hands in a modified shrug. "It was terrifying overall, but I managed, as I've seen and have been through worse things. So I called for an Uber, and went to my friend's house who was a med school dropout. He checked me out, but there was only so much he could do from his condo, which was mostly just checking for a concussion... and luckily, I was wearing my helmet." Lu stopped there, as if his story was complete, and closed his eyes again.

Paesh nodded at this, but inside she was outraged that someone would drive on after running someone off the road. "Oh, Lu, that is extremely intense, and terrifying! I'm glad you're alive and mostly well, but what a long night for you. I imagine your bike has seen better days, and that I'm truly sorry to hear," Paesh said with honest condolences.

While they drove in silence, she imagined the shiny black car, some rich idiot checking emails and using automated driving. But wait; automated driving had sensors, and the car wouldn't be allowed to drive without its lights on. It would be an automatic function, or an incessant beeping would force you click them on. Paesh mulled over these thoughts, leading her to conclusions that were more paranoid and strange. Having lights off, in that style of car, would make turning them off intentional. If it were a new energy-efficient car, it would be hard to drive without them on, given all the safety programs and what not. Also, many of the new cars had sensors along the vehicle for lane changing, so an object in the road would trigger the brakes and beeping. This car was clearly in some sort of manual mode, and inside was either a drunk man on a rampage with no worries about recklessness -- or someone intent on running someone off the road. But why Lu?

This made Paesh think of the night at the charity gala, where she had ridden in a Tesla with Milad, and in another technologically advanced vehicle on her return home. The second one was even fancier than a Tesla, although she didn't see the brand.

Her thoughts jolted to a stop when she nearly passed the turn for the ER. Slowing the car quickly, it lurched while she turned into the drive, giving them both a jolt. This caused her precious cargo's face to wince at the bumps and strain of the turn.

"Sorry," Paesh said, "I nearly missed it; I was sort of lost in thought about the black car. It's complete insanity that this happened. I'm so glad you're all right. Let's get you checked out," she continued, while slowing the car and turning the wheel to park.

"I can manage from here. If you wouldn't mind driving my Jeep back to work, I can take an Uber back," Lu said, unstrapping himself from the car and slowly sliding out. "I'm sure they'll just give me pain meds and some X-rays to make sure I'm not bleeding out. That said, maybe you can accompany me to dinner tonight, or I'll order takeout and you can swing by. You know, make sure I'm alive," he said, smiling his most charming smile.

"I'll consider it. I suppose it would allow me to bring your car back to you as well. Just give me a call when you're home," Paesh said.

"But I don't have your number; we haven't done that yet," Lu said matter-of-factly, as it was likely on the forefront of his mind since he's met her.

"Oh, right, of course. Here is it," Paesh said, taking her card from her purse pocket. Lu accepted it and tucked it lovingly in his shirt pocket, giving it a pat for safe keeping. His eyes glimmered a silver hue that caught the light, mercurial pools circulating around black pupils. This time it wasn't a flash; the silver lasted until he was out of sight. Paesh was filled with curiosity, hypnotized, and felt butterflies all the way back to work.

When she arrived, Tiago displayed concern for Lu out of formality, but it was clear he was chomping at the bit to get some testing underway. They brushed aside reviews of their current project, and started creating a space to test Paesh. They first set to labeling and sterilizing sample dishes and tubes. When everything was prepared, it came time to sample Paesh; they took hair, saliva, urine, and skin samples (which was slightly painful), and lastly there was blood. Her palms began to sweat, and her body felt overcome with heat. The last time her blood was taken, it had been against her will.

She noticed, looking down at herself while Tiago was washing his hands across the lab, that her skin seemed to be shimmering and changing hue. Her anxiety, or maybe extreme emotion, must trigger the slip in shape. Closing her eyes, she took some leveling breaths and reminded herself that this was a choice, one that she had willingly consented to. When she calmed, she opened her eyes, the room was still, and her skin was back to its olive color.

"Tiago, did you see that?" Paesh asked with muted excitement.

"I didn't. What happened?" Tiago said, annoyed that he had missed something.

"I am anxious about giving blood, and my skin began changing hue slightly. I felt hot and overwhelmed, but then after some deep breaths, it subsided. Maybe we can check the security footage after?" Paesh said.

"Hmmm, anxiety and anger triggering shifting; I marvel at the bodily process that must be happening under those circumstances! Perhaps we can do cortisol injections if we are really feeling curious," he mused, testing the waters of Paesh's willingness. Her face showed opposition, and then contemplation. Tiago laughed. "Of course, only if you wish to. Darn, I'm bothered I missed it; we can check surveillance after we draw the blood," Tiago said, while approaching her with his supplies.

"Are you ready for the blood draw? Do you have a problem with needles? I assure you I am a trained phlebotomist, and am quite efficient and quick. If you tend toward lightheadedness, let's grab a pillow." Tiago said, his professional dialogue ringing out with practiced use; no doubt he had spoken those words many times before.

"Yes to the pillow, and about how many tubes shall we fill?" Paesh asked, wishing she had eaten more of her lunch. "Do we have any candies or something, in case I start to have a sugar drop?" she asked with a sheepish grin.

Tiago rushed out of the room and then returned shortly with a pillow, a bottle of water, and a small pack of fruit chews. He was triumphant, and when Paesh was situated and set, he prepared her arm. He was as quick and swift as he had promised, filling all six tubes with care. Paesh became hot and sweaty around the fourth tube, and began to use the pillow to prop up her fading consciousness. When there was pressure and the removal of the tourniquet, Paesh stirred from her sweaty daze, and immediately ate the fruit chews, which she barely chewed; she just swallowed them. After that, she rested her head back on the pillow and waited for herself to feel right again.

Tiago took the remaining blood from the stationary butterfly needle, and used it to type her blood on a small paper card, filling each circle with water and blood. When he finished that, he concluded she was AB RH negative. This was just so he didn't have to waste a tube on typing her blood, as the typing only actually required a few drops.

When Paesh stirred, she drank the bottled water, and her body felt better; her damp neck was now cool with the AC blowing onto it, and her vision was clear and lucid.

The two scientists worked quietly with a whiteboard. They sent two samples to a part of the lab that did genetic mapping. They would track the proteins, changes in chromosomes, and the genes themselves. Her blood was already pretty rare, but Tiago pulled some strings with the blood bank and ordered a few samples of AB-negative, to cross reference for any abnormalities. Those samples wouldn't arrive for a day or two, though. They sat for hours, proposing other testing methods on whiteboard, postulating the best ways to examine the blood and various DNA samples. Ultimately, though, the next steps would be determined by the genetic mapping test. So her samples would sit in a cold and sterile environment until it was time.

On the drawing board, they expanded their thoughts beyond blood testing, and wondered if there were any neurological scans that she could undergo; and potentially some tests with cortisol injections and stress-response activities. Tiago, being the social scientist he was, had many connections at the university in many branches of medical science. They decided perhaps they could do some scanning while they were awaiting the blood sampling results. So tomorrow, after work, they would both go to the local university so Paesh could undergo more testing in another field of science.

The Sun was nearly under the horizon by then, and they both decided that they would check the surveillance, and then it was time to call it a day. When they played back the footage, it was clear Paesh's skin had briefly gone lavender and iridescent, although her body didn't shift shape at all, and her eyes remained the same. As soon as Paesh closed her eyes and calmed down, her skin returned to normal. Tiago was puzzled and blown away, as if seeing it again for the first time. He had that look on his face, like he was planning new ideas for experiments. They walked quietly down the hall and secured the lab with lock and key, then waved good bye in the parking lot.

Tulsi was waiting on the basket of Paesh's bike, and was quick to follow her when Paesh headed towards the Jeep. Paesh and Tulsi got into Lu's Jeep, and while she let the car warm up, she checked her phone to see if he had contacted her for dinner. Of course, he had left her several messages.

The first reported that he indeed had cracked ribs; not too severe, but he would need to take it easy. In the second one, he reported that he had no internal bleeding. The third was a photo of his arm with his ER bracelet, holding a beer with a lime in the top. Vibrant colors served as the backdrop, a marvelous warm sunset with small blurry outlines of a patio. The photo had a tag line attached, "Still want to meet me for takeout, at my house?"

Paesh responded to the text with a picture of his Jeep, and a tag line that read, "I think I'll keep the Jeep." She headed towards his house, as she remembered the way there from crashing her bike in his lawn. Sending another text while at a stop light, she asked, "What sort of takeout shall we order?" with a winking face.

When she arrived in his driveway, she felt some anxiety; she barely knew the man, and yet she was drawn to him like a magnet to steel. The door was open, with a note that said, "In the back," so Paesh removed her shoes and made her way through the house. The decor was sexy; the man was simple, yet he clearly had a love for plants, as his house was filled with bright greenery and colors of tropical foliage and flowers. It was impossible for her to not smile at the well-managed plant life. A deep breath sounded from her mouth and nose, taking in the dedicated energy.

"Hello," Paesh called, her voice carrying soft question and flirtation through the empty tiled hallway towards the patio.

"I'm here," Lu said, his voice harsh but chipper.

Paesh cleared the doorway leading outside to see the pale tail-end of sunset colors still illuminating the sparse clouds. Lu sat with a pillow behind his back, his legs stretched out in a long lounge chair. He looked a little more rested, and he seemed to glow when Paesh sat next to him, his fondness for her blatant.

"So, what are you hungry for?" Lu said, looking up at her. "Wow, I'm surprised at how my stomach feels every time I see you," he continued without shyness, looking at her with dreamy eyes. It was in that moment that Paesh realized he was probably on painkillers, and feeling a little more than confident with his words. Deciding not to encourage that conversation just yet, she moved the topic to food.

"What shall we order for takeout? I personally could do sushi or Thai food. I think I'm better off with something light; I'm not too hungry." Paesh relayed. "Speaking of light, do you have a light beer for me as well?"

"How rude of me... I got a little distracted. Please help yourself to anything in my fridge." Lu gestured with his arm waving high, his hand sort of making a flapping gesture. "Also, that's perfect, I think we should order Thai food. I know this really cool spot named DD's that has amazing food, and I think Uber will deliver," Lu said, taking a sip of beer and thoughtfully reaching for his phone to make an order.

Paesh moved slowly through his kitchen, in no hurry to return to the porch; she had a feeling she might be staying quite late. His fridge was surprisingly well-stocked for a single man, with plenty of healthy and fresh foods. There were a few light beers on the top shelf, with a bowl of limes right next to them. Paesh set herself up with a beer and a lime, as well as a glass of lime water for Lu. Her consecutive days of consuming alcohol in the past week was starting to surprise her. Such an abnormal ritual for her, it was; normally, to relax she made herbal teas or used micro-doses of mushrooms here and there to shift her consciousness. But she was finding alcohol to her liking, beyond the damage it was doing to her liver.

Joining Lu, she passed him the glass of water, which he gladly accepted and drank easily.

"I ordered us some Thai food -- green curry, Tom Kah, and some Tom Sum, with medium spice; what do you think?" Lu asked.

"Perfect. DD is a great cook, and I prefer her Thai food to anyone's," Paesh said, sipping on the beer. "So, tell me, Lu, before you mentioned your accident today at lunch, you were saying that you were having these dreams," Paesh prodded, side-eying him.

"Ah." He nodded. "Yes, they've been so vivid I may as well be watching a movie. Every night is different, and they're not necessarily good dreams or bad dreams. Sometimes they're startling. The reason I mentioned it to you is because you're in some of them," Lu said pointedly, tipping his glass to her. "But you aren't as you are now; instead, in the dream I just know it's you, and sometimes in the dreams... I, uh, well..." Lu drank more water, biding his time.

"Go on," Paesh said with slight kicking encouragement, but truly she knew what he would say, and wanted him to say it.

"Well, in the dreams I'm always looking for you, and sometimes when I find you, there's incredible sex... well, not even sex," he looked up, grasping for words. "It's honestly more like lovemaking, because in the dreams, my heart nearly bleeds for you. I wake with an aching heart, reaching for someone who isn't there. I know it sounds insane, but I'm mad for you, Paesh, at least in my dreams... and maybe now in my real life, too. I honestly can't tell the difference between the feelings." Lu said this as if trying to do a math calculation in the air in front of himself.

"I realize this is a lot to just throw at you, but I'm feeling a little more than confident with the pain pills I'm on. If you feel uncomfortable, please feel free to go." Lu shook his head, embarrassed by what he'd just said. "I mean, obviously you're an independent woman, you can do what you want, but just know that I get if you think I'm crazy, but I'm hoping that you don't."

He finally got all of his words out, smiling and looking at Paesh. Bewildering silver eyes stared at her, nearly glowing in the encroaching darkness. Hopeful pools of silver found her eyes even in the dark, searching for something within them, searching for some sort of response from Paesh, who was sitting quietly sipping her beer, wondering how to respond.

Paesh was not startled at all; in fact, she was surprised by how pleased she was with this information. It made her body relax, because even though she had resisted her growing feelings for him, she knew it wouldn't be long before she would crash like a wave on the sand, or a bike into trash cans.

"What did I look like in the dreams where we had these beautiful acts of sensuality?" Paesh said curiously. "And also for the record, I like insane; its far more entertaining, as I myself am a bit crazy," she said a little more quietly, as if confiding a secret.

"Phew. Well, that settles that, then. Hmmm, you looked interesting. Like a human, but different. You were shimmery, with golden-brown skin underneath, as if your skin was breathing this moving, powdered gold. Your hair was moving as well, woven with flowers and moss. You were wild yet stern, almost chastising me sometimes, in jest but also seriously. Your eyes were bigger and more wide-set, but relatively the same, still silver as they are now." Lu went to drink more of his beer, only to find it was gone.

"As for me, I was a man, normal and human, but not myself. My skin was darker; I was someone else, someone younger with long, dark, curly hair. My perspective was from the first person; I was in the body, so I couldn't see much. I remember that I was wearing a wooden ring with gold writing on it." Musing, lost in the memories of his dream, Lu sighed deeply.

"Although, beyond the beauty from the dreams, I experienced extreme chaos and loss; there was fire and grief. I was on a boat at sea. There are many fragmented story lines and feelings. I've been waking up with strong emotional charges inside of me, like I have something unfinished that's important, but I don't know what it is." Lu rubbed his forehead, "The only certainty is that you are a part of it. The first night I met you, when you crashed into my trash, was when this all started happening; I barely dreamt before that night."

A great chime sounded -- Lu's doorbell. The Thai food had arrived. Lu had already paid on his card, so Paesh went to grab the food from the delivery person. On the porch was a teenager staring blankly with stoned eyes, his arm held out with the bag of food. Paesh grabbed it and closed the door carefully, so as not to startle the stoner from his haze.

"Paesh, before we move on from this conversation and eat, I want you to know that I realize we're working together, and I realize we met just four days ago... but I can't ignore what the universe seems to be telling me. I'm fond of you, and the word fond is actually a disservice to how I feel. When you're near, it feels as though the quiet of dawn is a blanket around us, the liminal place in time before birds begin their morning calls. All I want to do is sink into you and know you more. Every day, I wish to learn more about who you are." Lu said this all while becoming animated and passionately heartfelt, his words clear and deep, with strains of sorrow peeking through. When he finished his statement, the sky was dark, and Paesh could hear him breathing. He seemed to be trembling with emotion.

Paesh was frozen, receiving the proclamation of love and desire with silence. It was like seeing fireflies in the dark, it was like jumping off of a cliff, it was like viewing something strange in the night sky, it was like staring into the eyes of an approaching wildcat.

Paesh finally found her words. "Lu, thank you for sharing your feelings. It's actually refreshing to hear an expression of raw emotions coming from someone. I've never been so caught off guard, but I don't mind it." Paesh set down the bag of Thai food on the small table.

"When you look at me," she continued, "I feel so comfortable. Your eyes are something I've seen in my dreams. Strangely enough, since we've met, I've seen your eyes change color. Sometimes your eyes are blue and sometimes silver, did you know this?" Paesh said, tilting her head.

"Yes, they've been doing that ever since I woke up from a coma a year ago. I had a surfing accident on a reef break. The doctors have nothing to say about it, mostly because they probably have no idea what's going on," Lu said nonchalantly. "So you feel it too? I'm not the only one with these intense feelings?"

"No, you're not. And sheesh, Lu, you're quite the adventurer, like a cat with many lives -- please be more careful! But honestly, your eyes... they feel like a lighthouse in a storm to me. There's something between us, and you aren't crazy for expressing it. Although I'm not sure how to go about all this..." Paesh sighed. "Feelings and whatnot aren't my strong suit, I'm sort of a mess..." She shut up and drank the rest of her beer, then went to the kitchen and got them both another beer with a slice of lime; she also brought plates, bowls, and cutlery out to the patio table.

"It's like you can read my mind; since we met, you're a step ahead of my thoughts, as if responding before I need to say anything... it's amazing and strange. But enough of my declaration of feelings, maybe we should eat," Lu said, his face likely red with a blush, his voice cracking at the tail-end of his sentence.

Paesh made a short nodding motion and started to serve the food onto the plates and bowls, while Lu quietly watched her in the dark.

Her arms were graceful, and each motion she made was effortlessly precise; even if she were to drop a plate, she would do it so perfectly. Disappearing for a short moment, Paesh went inside and grabbed the candles from his kitchen table. Placing them strategically, she lit them, giving their food the proper visibility that it deserved.

"I have a porch light, but I think I prefer this ambiance," Lu said with a mouthful of green papaya salad, his chopsticks perfectly directed under the fine dexterity of his fingers.

They truly were a handsome pair, eating in the dark, busy with their food, sharing shy eye contact in the flickering candlelight. When they were finished, Paesh brought the plates into the kitchen and washed them quickly and efficiently; she didn't want them to sit, as Thai food never smells good in the morning.

When she went back out onto the porch, she saw Lu moving to stand; he probably had to pee. He nearly lost his balance. This made his face strain with a little discomfort, and he sucked in air through his teeth. "Hah, that hurt. I'll be right back, just going to use to the bathroom," he said while he moved slowly down a long hallway opposite the kitchen. His house was one level, long and low to the ground; there were many windows and doors, which made it feel open and alive.

Paesh waited on the patio, and wondered what the hell was happening; she was having a small pep talk with herself out loud, a quiet whispering, as she often did. "What the hell? Is this a good idea? Is he a good guy? What if he's connected with Allen, what if he's lying and he says this to all women?" Her mind was relentless and went on and on, and she was startled when she saw something move out of the corner of her eye. She hoped to God it wasn't Lu, hearing her insane muttering of doubt. To her relief, it was Tulsi, flapping her wings loudly in contrast to the quiet of the night. Landing on the back of the lounge chair where Lu was sitting, Tulsi made some screeching calls, unusually loud ones.

"Hello. I haven't seen you since we arrived here. Hopefully you got something to eat as well," Paesh said, feeling guilty somehow for not being able to provide food. "What do you think of Lu?" Paesh asked.

The bird responded subtly, and it was unclear what she was trying to communicate; but she opened her wings and puffed up big, her feathers ruffled, and she stepped from one side to the other. Paesh wasn't sure what to make of it, but when Lu made his way through the door, Tulsi took off and landed somewhere in the nearby tree, her whistles soft and melodic in the distance.

"Is that the bird from the other night?" Lu asked with wild amusement. "You really are a different kind of woman! You can speak with animals."

"I'm not sure if talking to myself out loud in the presence of an animal counts as speaking with animals, but I'll take it. And yes, it sure is; she's an incredibly smart little bird that sort of fell into my life a couple days ago. I can't speak with animals per se, and I myself am not sure what to make of it." Paesh sighed and leaned back in the lounge chair next to the one Lu had been sitting in earlier.

"Can I tell you something else that's strange?" Lu asked, the spice from the food reactivating his loopy demeanor.

"Sure, go for it. I'm pretty sure we're beyond any normalcy here," Paesh said, with her head tilted back, enjoying the beer as it washed away the spice and fish sauce that lingered in her mouth.

"When we were in Grace and Jon's greenhouse, working on our bonsai trees, I remember looking over at you, and your skin had changed color! It was lavender and gold somehow; it was the most beautiful hallucination I've had ever had." Lu said this while looking upwards at the stars, laying back in his lounger.

"Hmmm, is that so? Interesting... I wonder why you saw that," Paesh said with subtly mockery, to evade any conversation about what was really happening with her.

"It almost looked like one of my dream versions of you. It lasted for about a minute while you were thick with focus, wire in hand," Lu said, nearly whispering, his head setting back onto the pillow and his eyes shutting.

Paesh went inside and grabbed two blankets she saw on the living room couch. She covered Lu, and the corners of his mouth curled upwards. He made a small "mmm" sound and kept his eyes closed. She sat next to him on her lounge chair, draping her body with the second blanket. She was comfortable and pleasantly full, and soon closed her eyes too. They both slept on the patio, their hands nearly touching.

Around 3:06 in the morning, Paesh woke, reaching for her light and dream journal to find she didn't know where she was. This shock brought her into full lucidity, and she woke up completely. To her right she saw Lu, who also just barely had his eyes open.

"Looks like we fell asleep out here." Lu said with the scratchiest of whispers, shifting in his lounge chair and pulling the blanket up closer to his chin.

"I forgot where I was for a second. I wanted to write my dream down, and then I realized I wasn't at home. It's a little chillier tonight," Paesh said willing her blanket to be thicker.

"We can sleep inside... I have two bedrooms, and there are thicker blankets on those beds," Lu croaked as he slowly started to sit up. "You can also take my car to leave, or I can call you a car."

"I wouldn't mind staying here; one of those bedrooms sounds lovely," Paesh said with sleepy joy, yawn forming. As much as she wanted to sleep in the same bed with him, she knew it was wise to separate; plus, he was injured, so there wouldn't be much snuggling happening anyways. Paesh stood with her blanket wrapped around herself, slightly annoyed she would be farther away from Lu, but grateful she would be warmer.

They walked slowly, feet dragging, towards his hallway. There was a master suite with a connected bathroom, a spare bedroom, and a bathroom. Lu showed her into the spare bedroom; "Here it is, make yourself comfortable," he said with half-open eyes. He moved forward to hold Paesh, and lightly pressed himself against her and wrapped his arms around her. It felt so sweet and delicate, probably due to his rib injury. Paesh enjoyed the embrace; it was nice and warm, and she wished she had poor boundaries and that his body wasn't injured, because she would rather lie next to him. She sighed and said thank you, pulling away. Then she climbed into bed, and fell asleep feeling safe.

In the morning, Paesh woke to the soft colors of sunrise, casting in from the many windows in the room. She could hear Lu stirring in the kitchen, slow morning footsteps, bare feet on tile floor, each step sticking ever so slightly. Paesh was unsure how to interact after all that was said the night before; she wasn't good with emotional navigations. As excited as she was to know how Lu felt, it was simultaneously overwhelming; she had enough on her plate to deal with. Honestly, she just wanted to slip out of there and get to the lab, so she and Tiago could get to work on her testing.

Since they projected Lu would not be coming in, and they were a week ahead on their project, they had decided to dedicate their lab time for Paesh. Today they were supposed to get an appointment with one of Tiago's neurologist friends at the University. Apparently they had all the latest equipment, as their division was one of the leading labs in the nation. They carried the torch for some leading research in the field.

Paesh saw herself in the mirror on the wall and gasped; she was less then bright-eyed. She wanted to crawl out the window; in the daylight, she felt like a coward compared to her confidence last night in the veiled darkness. She sighed, and straightened herself as best she could in the mirror, slipped out the door into the bathroom, and took a small rinse in his shower.

Emerging clean and more confident, she entered the kitchen to find Lu drinking coffee, while there was hot water and a tea assortment in front of the seat across from him. "Good morning, Paesh. Glad to see you didn't sneak out the window after all I told you last night," he laughed as he rolled his neck around slowly.

"Ha, funny you mention that. Is this tea for me?" She sat down and started loading a pot with a Puerh Tuo Cha, a small pressed button of dark, earthy tea. It was one of her favorites, and she was surprised Lu had it amongst his selection on the table.

"I've never tried that kind; I wasn't sure what to do with those little buttons," Lu admitted as he watched her prepare the tea. "Jon is really into tea, and is always giving me samples to try, and I don't get around to trying them all. Glad to see it's finally being used." Lu sipped on his coffee, still looking a little inebriated. It was likely he had taken more medication.

"It's just fermented tea leaves pressed into these Tuo Cha, for easier keeping and storage. There are giant ones, too; Puerh is like wine, and it's more expensive with age. The tea elitists can tell the difference; I myself cannot," Paesh said, pouring the tea into the empty cup.

She continued, "We'll miss you at the lab today, but Tiago didn't seem concerned, since we're so far ahead on the project." She said this with a cool, relaxed tone; she didn't want him to come into work, as he was clearly the type who pushed himself.

"You're probably right; I should stay in and heal. It will be hard for me to stay put, but I'm sure I can catch up on some reading. There was this book I really loved, uhm..." Lu said, standing up slowly and trailing off, wandering around his house, "It's an incredible book so far, and I have been meaning to catch up on it," Lu said triumphantly, holding up the book and setting it down by his coffee.

They sat silently drinking their warm beverages with the cool morning breeze flowing in through the back patio doorway. Paesh smoothed her hair behind one ear, combing it back neurotically with her fingers, rhythmically soothed by the repetition of the movements. It was coming up on time to leave, and Paesh looked over at Lu, whose eyes were a dull blue today.

"I'll call you after work to see how you're feeling. Thanks for last night -- it was really nice to hear something so honest," Paesh she after taking the last sip from her cup. She held the cup, tilting it from side to side, watching the last drops trace the bottom of the mug. Pulling her phone from her pocket, she ordered a car to pick her up, the phone alerting Paesh that she had four minutes until its arrival.

Lu sipped his drink calmly, and smiled shyly, brushing the back of his neck upwards. "I look forward to it. I would be honored if you would return tonight for another dinner. We can start earlier, too, in case you need to get home and feed your cat." Lu stood to walk Paesh to the door; his movements were intentional and slow due to his injury.

"This day off will be helpful. I need to find my bike and get it out of that ditch. Call a tow company and my insurance." Lu said as if speaking out loud to himself, the mundane reality sinking back into his awareness. "Thanks for coming over last night to check on me and bring my Jeep back," he said, extending his arms for a hug.

They embraced snuggly and warmly, as comfortable as kittens in a basket. They held on until the car pulled up.

Today was going to be long and hopefully helpful. Paesh would visit the neurologist, and although it was exciting, it felt strange including a third party in the experiments. She wondered what their cover story would be for needing the scans.

Paesh made it to the lab in the same clothing from the previous day, and Tiago hardly noticed when she walked in. "Good morning, Paesh -- you're a little late today. No matter; it has given me time to check some of the results and put them into the database. Today, I think it's best we focus on your testing while Lu is still away. Come, come, see what results are popping up!" Tiago said, his face warm and his eyes a little tired around the edges, as if he had been up all night thinking of how to approach her case. Paesh could picture him in his loungewear with tea, and his favorite tool, his whiteboard, staying up till late in the night.

"Sounds good, Tiago. I would agree with that; I'm not so sure I could focus on work with all this stuff waiting in the background," Paesh said, while changing into her lab clothing.

They went to the computer, to analyze blood and DNA sample results. There was nothing unusual that they could see initially. The genetic protein data was cross-referenced in the database; Tiago also entered that information into a genetic database they had paid access to. The company that owned the database compiled DNA worldwide by way of selling ancestry reports to curious donors. Tiago was soon scrolling through looking for genetic matches.

The data showed in percentages; her ancestry displayed equal parts French and Lebanese/Mediterranean, which she knew from her mother and father, but there was also 8% Moroccan and 10% was showing as indeterminate. The database did not have a sample of anything that matched with it, so there was no category for her specific genome.

Tiago and Paesh stared at the screen, puzzled, for a long while. They searched other AB Rh-negative samples in the database, and found that there was also a small percentage of something unidentified in those. Tiago brought the program into its backdoor-format analytics page, so he could see the percentages and data on those carrying the undetermined genetic variant. To their surprise, it was only present in those with the Rh-negative blood factor; not only AB-negative , but also A, B, and O as well. The percentage ranged in size, even down to .01%. They also found that those with AB Rh-negative blood all had a percentage of French ancestry. This was puzzling, but then again, they weren't all that familiar with the database and the way it built its categories for origin.

That was all the data could provide, so they went back to the whiteboard, and Tiago left Paesh with the marker as he went down the hall answer a bell call for delivery -- likely supplies for the lab, or the blood shipment. With the marker in hand, Paesh drew a circle and wrote French in it, and then another circle slightly overlapping in a Venn diagram shape, which she labeled Lebanese. She then drew another smaller circle with a question mark in it, only overlapping the French circle. Off of that small circle, she made another circle and labeled that Moroccan. So on her mother's side, there was an indeterminate factor; somewhere down the line, there was a run-in with an indeterminate ethnicity. She stared at the board. She drew another circle with an A in it on the other side of the board as she thought of Mr. Allen, and his role in all of this.

When Tiago came in, a package nestled under his arm, he looked at the board, then looked at Paesh and sighed.

This was not groundbreaking, but they didn't let themselves be discouraged. Perhaps they could isolate the indeterminate genetic code and study that sequence. It felt like they had a direction to move in, and they prepped and put the blood samples into the machine, and let them sit.

They soon decided to lock up the lab and head off to the University, to meet with the neurologists that Tiago was friends with. Paesh was excited and nervous the whole drive. Tiago tapped his finger along to the music that was quietly playing in the background. "What's our cover story for our investigation?" Paesh asked as they drew near the university lab.

"We should keep it simple, and say we're studying the effects of neuroplasticity after implementing a new orally administered probiotic for the brain. My colleague, Dr. Jess Lambert, knows we work in bacteria and with the micro-biome." Tiago paused while looking for a good parking space; when he located one, he pulled in with one swift motion.

"To be honest, Jess doesn't know much about the microbiome and its correlation with mental wellbeing, so our details are better left on the muted side; we can prod him and have him explain what he knows, keep him distracted from our story." Tiago said, shrugging, "At the very least, I explained it was a side project, a small hypothesis investigation."

"Okay, that's easy enough, I can't wait," Paesh said, opening the car door and following quickly behind Tiago, who happened to walk very fast when excited or nervous... or angry. He might just walk fast in general.

Dr. Lambert was an exceptionally passive person, easygoing, contemplative. His long face was fairly free of wrinkles despite his age, and his eyes were a warm chocolate-brown. He was excited to get Paesh into a machine and set up with electrodes. While he connected her, he calmly explained how the machine recorded data and could pick up the brain's electromagnetic waves. He was enthusiastic about all the technical details that Paesh was pretending to comprehend. What was most important was that Paesh felt calm and safe around Dr. Lambert; that way, she would display anything unusual amidst her anxiety.

The process was all very sterile. Dr. Lambert really lit up when explaining the process and applications for the equipment. He sat behind the machine's computer while Paesh was hooked up. The machine ran for ten minutes, and Paesh was directed to think about positive memories. Silence hit the room when the machine stopped whirring and the data showed on the screen. Dr. Lambert's eyes were locked onto the blue glow of the computer, and he was quiet, as if the words had been stolen from his throat. He began typing and reformatting the image, perhaps looking at the data from another angle.

Paesh sat curious, with all the small electrodes connected to her head, feeling like a cyborg Medusa. "Is there something wrong with the machine?" she asked whilst fidgeting with the rings on her fingers.

"No -- uh, hmmm, I'm just going to check your connections again," Dr. Lambert said distractedly, before checking all of the cables and working connections. He hummed chaotically while he checked each facet of the machine. When he completed his check, he ran the machine again, for a new scan altogether. Tiago's eyes were huge, and his arms were folded across his chest; he watched the process intently without saying a word.

After the machine ran again for a good ten minutes, Dr. Lambert spoke. "I have never seen results present this way before... it's not alarming, and nothing is wrong with her scans. It's just that her hemispheres are both functioning at once. Her brain's neurological connection is magnified drastically, compared to..."

Dr. Lambert printed a copy of something on his computer, and then shuffled through some other papers before presenting two sheets to Tiago to look at. "See this one here? This is a perfectly healthy brain; in fact, this is my brain scan from a few weeks ago. As you can see, it presents differently; I know you aren't familiar with reading these graphs, but look at this line here compared to the line's fluctuation on her results." Dr. Lambert's eyebrows raised, and he handed the paper to Tiago.

"What sort of microbiome magic is this? This could be some sort of a major finding," Dr. Lambert started to say when Tiago cut him off.

"These tests were intended to be our baseline constant, to see improvement for when we start the experiment. We haven't induced anything yet. It would seem that Paesh's brain operates this way in general. We ask that you keep anything about Paesh confidential, of course," Tiago said as he handed the paper back to Dr. Lambert.

"Of course. I see... well, how strange, would you mind if we run a few more scans on another machine? Now I'm just curious if we can get a magnified read. I want to see how far her brain waves extend beyond her skull," Dr. Lambert said, tilting his head while he methodically disassembled the machinery from her head.

"I'm willing to try another machine. I didn't realize that brain waves extended beyond the skull... how interesting," Paesh said with a relaxed and casual expression.

"Isn't it, though?" Dr. Lambert piped up as he stood to lead them to a different machine on the other side of the building. As he led the way, he spoke back over his shoulder, like a tour guide. "This machine is so new, only myself and one of the private investors is allowed access to it." His face was smug, and he raised an eyebrow while he used his ID badge to open the door.

Paesh tried her best to remain calm, as the word investor sent shivers up her spine. Anyone with money interested in science made her start to sweat. Tiago must have noticed her stiffen, as he grabbed her hand and took an audible deep breath. It relaxed her.

"Paesh, do you need to use the bathroom before you sit in this machine?" Tiago asked, giving Paesh a hinting eye.

"Uhm, yes I do," she said slowly, and before she had time to think, Tiago lead her back out the door and walked with her down the hall, to the bathrooms.

"Your skin is changing colors, Paesh... maybe we should go, say that you have gotten sick or something," suggested said in a muffled whisper.

"Shit, really? Did Dr. Lambert see?" Paesh replied, equally quietly.

"Not that I can tell. Luckily it was dark in there, with the fluorescents warming up and all... but if it were to happen again while under his observation, it will not be something he would easily forget," Tiago said, with concerned fatherly tones.

"Yes, I suppose we should just go, tell him another time would be great... I am feeling dizzy, Paesh said. "I'll meet you out by your car."

Tiago nodded, handed her his keys, and marched off for his performance with Dr. Lambert. He was a true, dear friend to Paesh, and she admired their friendship and his thoughtfully protective attitude. When she exited the building, the blinding Sun sent her arm up in reflex to block the light from her eyes with her hand. And as she walked through the parking lot she saw a car -- a familiar black car, blacked out from windows to rims, plugged into a charging station.

Paesh's heart dropped; it was the car from the night she was held against her will. That car belonged to Dr. Allen. He was here now, and with the dark tint, he could even be in the vehicle at that very moment. She panicked, but had enough presence of mind to grab her phone and take a picture of the car. Then she ran to Tiago's car, unlocking it with the click of button. She popped into the front seat, relieved. She turned on the car and locked the doors, exhaling with panic. Although she was slightly comforted that Tiago's car was parked out of view, her heart was racing.

It took a long ten minutes for Tiago to arrive at the car; when he knocked on the window, Paesh jumped in her seat and screamed. She let him in, and then asked with a flustered voice, "What took you so long in there?"

Tiago, looked startled, and then slightly confused, said, "I ran into one of the lab's investors in the lobby of the building, Dr. Allen. He is quite famous in town, you know, but he always makes me a little nervous. He was asking a lot of questions as to what brought me in to see Dr. Lambert. It is such a small community; everyone knows everyone else's business. Anyway, it was a hard conversation to navigate," Tiago said, shaking his head. "Let's head back to the lab."

He turned to look at Paesh, "You know, ever since you started with the lab, he has always taken an inappropriate interest in you, and I always try to brush him off. I wonder if he knows something."

Paesh's stomach shrank to the size of a marble. How could she not have known that he was involved with the lab she worked at for years?! All along he had been there, lingering in the background. Following her. She shut her eyes and said softly, "Tiago, I have something I need to tell you. I have only shared this with, well -- no one, actually."

Paesh didn't even wait for Tiago to respond. She recounted the story of the night of the gala, with her eyes closed the whole time; during the end of it, tears were streaming down her face. Tiago was silent, save for some sounds of disgust and gasps of disbelief.

"Paesh, that would be an extremely hard-to-believe incident, had I not seen your shapeshifting for myself. It must be part of his motive and interest with you. This is all beginning to feel like we're living in a sci-fi novel. The insane bastard! I knew there was something off about him, something dark you could smell on him. He's so damned rich... what could be done, especially now?" Tiago's knuckles were white gripping the wheel, he was so angry and wild at this reality-shattering news.

"Paesh, I don't think you should come back to work today. This has gotten out of control, and it is clear something is different about you. I'm not sure our findings in the lab will bring any further clarity. I will work on what we have, and be sure the evidence and labels are concealed. It took me some time to convince Dr. Lambert; he was adamant about running tests on you again. He was so eager, so baffled. Oh, also, I grabbed the paper copy of your scans off of his desk, just in case."

Tiago was chewing on a toothpick and speaking rapidly, his Brazilian accent becoming more pronounced with each short breath. There were pauses between his thoughts, until he was suddenly quiet.

"Can you take me to Lu's house?" Paesh asked. "It's not far from here. I want to see if he's all right after his accident." Her voice was shaky, but she was hopeful with the thought of being near Lu.

"If you direct me, most certainly; he has quite the thing for you, you know. I have only seen him around you once, but it was so obvious I had to leave the room," Tiago said, smiling, glad to have something normal to think about.

"This is it, right here on the left," Paesh said, "Tiago, be in touch about what you find. Thank you for letting me take the time off. I'm sorry you're involved in this -- if it becomes dangerous, just abandon the research. I really appreciate your support; it's hard to find good people in this world, and you are among the finest." Paesh bowed and then shut the car door.

Layer 23: Iós - Finding The Forest

As the crow flies. Wings allow for a course that runs straight from Point A to Point B, unbound by terrain, trees, and bodies of water. With wings, there is little that can stand in the way. From the bird's-eye view, there are no lines in the sand, no territorial walls, only thermal pockets to surf and soar through, seeking the next prey or perch, to rest and recoup.

Iós flew away from Jushur's body. He held animosity towards him, as Jushur had taught him a way of life; he had shown him how to be a noble man. Jushur, a fine craftsman and a calm leader, was always skilled in communicating with others, creating cohesiveness in any group of humans. Iós recalled their memories as he flew; he missed Jushur.

Iós was surprised and grateful to find that when he was within this bird, he retained the conscious awareness that he had gained from being within Jushur. He was able to think, recall the past, and feel. Perhaps his hosts' bodies lent their own gifts and new strengths to draw from.

Iós pondered his relationship with Jushur for a long time while flying through the world as a crow. He wondered why Jushur had attempted to kill them both? Was it because he was unhappy with the long life? Or was it the difficult but dark measures Iós took to protect their tribe and territory? Was Jushur afraid to assert his dominance in a time of growth and fragility? Was it the loss of their love Neenah, slicing a rift into his soul? Or maybe he still missed Ala, from his life before, and when Neenah passed, it woke the sleeping wound Jushur was carrying. Perhaps they viewed power differently. Iós knew that Jushur was never capable of the darker tasks; he was not hungry for power and growth, expansion and dominion.

In time, Iós stopped wondering, and accepted the loss of his first friend, his first brother and teacher. He flew around, aloof to his own madness for power, blood, and territory.

As a crow, he became aware of the cycles of life and death, as he fed off the rotten and dead. This awareness also fed his delusion that death had no consequences. It was merely part of the greater plan for decomposition and the grand cycle. Experiencing this as a Greenland shark and learning it more so as a crow, the power of his new mind gave him the ability to observe his function within the world, and the circle of life. He soared for some time, learning the land below and watching the different tribes of humans gathering and traveling across the terrain with the seasonal changes.

Iós was in no hurry, and although there was loneliness that came with his contemplative time within the crow, he was learning a great deal.

Years passed, and he went from crow to crow, procreating for his new form, until the days of wandering had ended and his learning began. He spotted a tribe south of Jushur's initial home. They were gathering on the coastline of a large stretch of land. This landmass had taken Iós many lifetimes to explore its expanse. While exploring those lands, he had seen glorious animals and many human tribes, but in that gloriousness there was wildness, pure viciousness: the ruthless hunt of the lion and the honey badger, the endless pursuit of the antelope by the high-speed cheetah. These wild sights inspired Iós.

Initially, Iós was afraid to lose his wings. He didn't want to change forms, only to find that he could be trapped somehow. However, that fear waned, especially on the giant land mass, where there were always creatures arriving to clean up the dead. Iós learned to trust this cycle, and experienced many ways of life -- running with great speed, smelling with great skill, seeing with exceptional vision, and hunting with great stealth. There were vultures, crocodiles, water buffalo, cheetahs, lions, and ground birds to occupy. Iós got to know the wildlife and the different tactics that predator and prey utilized -- a long-term training project for someone who craved power and control, learning weakness and strength, and how sometimes a strength for one species was a weakness for another. As soon as he grew satiated with the knowledge, he traveled northeast, towards the Mediterranean Sea, landing himself in the body of a falcon.

Within his falcon form, he lingered around the tribe forming there. Jungle and harsh desert created a dynamic hunting atmosphere for those humans. Iós lingered in hopes to observe them, as these humans used falcons to hunt, utilizing the falcon's eyesight and location skills to find small prey. When the falcon struck, the humans would track the raptor's kill.

When they arrived to the scene of falcon and prey, they came to collect and split the bounty. It was not the fairest way to hunt, but there was a relationship built between the species, an understanding and gratitude. Iós enjoyed having a close eye on the humans. He watched, looking for the most beneficial human to invade, as jumping carelessly from human to human was not advantageous for a seamless integration. There was no rush, as Iós came to learn; he had all the time in the world.

Amenhotep was a healer, a master of plants, and appeared to have clean hardware that was well-utilized and functioning. Amenhotep was Iós' target host; Iós watched him for a year before he decided to invade. It was like hunting -- observing his stature in the community and the respect he had garnered in his lifetime.

Amenhotep rarely hunted with the falconers, as it was ritualistic and required knowledge, patience, and endurance. The next time he joined the hunt was when Iós made his move, and he hoped he'd chosen wisely.

Years passed as Iós waited within, watching the community work together to create a centrally located stone pyramid. The structure served as a gathering center for healing the sick. Its construction was aligned to the stars, and its walls were sturdy. The pyramid was not huge, but it was spacious enough to shelter those who needed healing. The temple took six full Moon cycles to create, and its completion was celebrated by many.

Being the community healer, Amenhotep was in a leadership role with in the temple. He worked day and night when there were people in need. Amenhotep not only healed the sick, but educated healed visitors on preventative medicine so that it was seldom that they returned with the same issue.

During this phase, Iós watched and came to feel comfort inside Amenhotep, enjoying the emotional rush of helping others and tending to their needs. He also felt the frustration and sorrow when the sick couldn't mend. He learned from within Amenhotep like a quiet disciple, an apprentice training under a master. Iós became aware of the subtle healing properties that came along with the geometric shape and resonance that occurred inside the pyramid, hypothesizing his own conclusions and ideas about the body and its potential; sometimes he was right and sometimes he was wrong. He felt little desire for blood and power when he was swept up with the rush of helping people. But when the job was done well, the people were well; and when the people were well, there was idle time, and this was when Iós grew restless.

When Amenhotep was idle, without patients, Iós craved mental and physical activity; he craved sex and power. The sporadic rush of saving people no longer provided enough adrenaline to keep him engaged. It was not long before Iós took over fully for the first time. This kept Amenhotep prisoner in his own meditative sleep. He did it differently than he had with Jushur. He took over quickly and fully, so Amenhotep would not know what was happening. His conscious mind was pushed into dormancy, a dreamlike winter. Iós started with small increments for these takeovers. Each time was an experiment, little by little seeing how much he could take.

It took a while before Iós could take charge of the body for long spells. When he worked his way up to the long-term takeovers, he used that time to gain favor with the village leader, planting seeds for more hierarchical structures and separation between the leaders and the commoners. He had blueprints for boats, ideas for cultivating crops, and irrigating with water. His knowledge was wealth, and the ruler, Iry-Hor, took Amenhotep in as his advisor and physician.

Iós had seen much in his travels as an animal; he bore a wealth of knowledge. He knew of other tribes and what their resources were, information and wisdom that his leader coveted and even feared. However, it was far better for Iry-Hor to keep Amenhotep in his loyalty than in the loyalty and alliance of another kingdom. Iós planted small seeds of fear and hinted at the need for structure and a kingdom with a strong fortress to create safety for him and his people. Iós left whispers of war like a trail of crumbs for Iry-Hor to find on his own, drawing his own picture of paranoid conclusion.

All these moves put Amenhotep in higher standing with the whole village, and every time Iós went dormant, Amenhotep awoke from his blackouts with shock and fear inside him, as days of time had disappeared. The shock never lasted long, and Amenhotep went about his day. When he realized that in his absence he had become more and more powerful and respected by the King, he did not fear the blackouts. This newfound luxury and support led him to believe that he was possessed by the gods themselves. They blessed him with knowledge, so he could better serve his king and the people.

Iós worked himself into the system. Amenhotep was now the advisor for the first proclaimed Lord of the Land, or King, Iry-Hor. By his design, strong structures were built with stone and clay. Iós created agricultural fertility, and an abundance of food that could be preserved, guiding the people on how to find seeds and where to grow them using irrigation. He picked a fertile location near the banks of the Nile, where the annual flooding brought abundance. The muck and silt deposited by the floods was mineral-rich and soaked into the dirt, creating a soil worth more than gold. These strides in their community were monumental and essential for the kingdom to become strong and stable.

Iós, using the knowledge from Jushur and his own worldly observations, infiltrated the minds of those in power. He didn't always drop the ideas when he was in charge of Amenhotep's body; sometimes he would leave clues for Amenhotep to do it himself, providing visual guidance in their quarters using diagrams and pictures. Iós used various forms to display them on, from leaves and clay to animal hides. Whatever he could use to deliver messages to

Amenhotep, he crafted it. In some instances, Iós would craft messages and clues in a such a way that Amenhotep thought the ideas and advice came from himself, or the gods. Iós primed him for this new lifestyle of blackouts, making them feel godly and holy, as if he were chosen and channeling messages from a higher source. And in a way, he was; it just wasn't happening as he imagined. Amenhotep started inducing his own rituals to have his dreaming time of visions, rituals that made it easy for Iós to shut him down and take over.

The surrounding villages started migrating to live under Iry-Hor's rule in Upper Egypt, and the unification under one law was slowly being implemented, resulting in many new families coming to the join in the bounty of the kingdom. Amenhotep, still the village's physician, had plenty of work to do in the healing temple as new people arrived, as many of them arrived in poor health. This was due to poor water quality and being malnourished from the strain from travel.

When Iós was in control, he had to maintain that reputation and lifestyle, and was surprised how fond he was of healing others. It gave him a sense of power that satiated some of his burning desires. The power to give and take life felt familiar, and fulfilled that same drive that had brought him to kill so many times before.

One day, Iós was leaving his healing temple to collect some supplies. There was a group of sick people who had become infected by bad water on their migration to Upper Egypt, and it had depleted his stocks. In his distracted haste, he nearly collided with a woman who was walking outside. She was young and blossoming, like a flower, her face sweet and dewy with vitality. Long thick hair veiled her.

"Excuse my haste—-" Iós said before his words dropped into oblivion. His mouth hung ajar when he saw the woman's silver eyes peeking from behind her hair. He was immediately alerted as well as frozen in thought. He thought of Ala and Neenah, knowing that there was something about that shade of silver... This young woman emanated something rare, and Iós felt it easily. He could almost hear a familiar song playing ever so lightly, as if muffled underwater.

The young woman, unstartled and calm, nodded. "Narrowly missed, no harm done, Amenhotep," she said, as the hair that veiled her face caught the wind and exposed the beauty beneath. Iós held his breath while he enjoyed the proper view of her. She gave a shy, knowing smile and began walking again, brushing the side of Iós' arm as she did so. The small hairs on his neck stood tall as her smooth skin brushed past, leaving him dazed and aroused. She was innocent and seductive; she was holy somehow, and it stopped Iós in his tracks.

Just as the woman was nearly out of sight, the wind blew, and brought with it the light scent of lilies from her bare neck. The scent, mixed with her pheromones, rode through the air into Iós' nose. He couldn't see, but the corners of her mouth turned upwards into a smile as she faded into the crowd. It changed something in Iós. He would not stop until she was his.

Iós immediately became thirsty for her; he wanted to know the sound of her breathing, the marks on her skin, and the sound of her laughter. Even though he had access to lay with as many women as he wanted, being an advisor, he was no longer content. He could choose any Priestess from the temple, and although they were skilled and practiced in the art of sensual and sexual magic, they were not this woman. Everything was beginning to turn upside down.

After that day, Iós never let Amenhotep surface again; he did not struggle as Jushur did, as Jushur had time and understanding to strengthen his mind. Amenhotep was willing, and was unaware of who

Iós was. Amenhotep was now locked into his own dreamy wintered mind, submerged and preserved like a glacial mass underwater. Iós shut that door and threw away the key. He could not risk Amenhotep ruining his chances with this woman. He knew enough now about healing that he could carry forward in his Master Physician's footsteps. He did not mourn the loss of his teacher, because in a way, Amenhotep was still alive within him, as alive as the shark, Jushur, the crow, and all the other creatures Iós had collected.

It was not long before he found her again; her name was Imi, and she had little resistance to Amenhotep's advances. When she truly sat with he, who looked like the town's physician, Amenhotep, she was fascinated to find that there was someone else within him. She did not know his name, and she did not ask, but she knew. Somehow, she had found what she was looking for; someone as ancient as she felt she was. She felt seen by him, and able to see the being beneath Amenhotep. She knew there was something more, something mysterious and dark, pulling her into his orbit.

For Imi's whole life, she had held onto bits of a mantra she had recited since she was a young girl in a language, no one else knew. "I am here to see, I am here to help. Find the virus, find myself, and one day I'll return." She knew that somehow, Amenhotep was the part of her mantra, and that it was her destiny to find him. Although now found, all she knew to do was to love and to help.

So Imi loved, and Iós adored her. Indeed, he worshiped the ground she walked on. She encouraged him to heal more and to love more, to breathe and control himself. Imi was the best thing that could happen to Iós, and quite possibly Iós was the best thing that had happened to Imi. The deep well of their connection could split the Earth in two.

Iós finally felt the warmth of love again; he felt soothed and whole. The once-empty place that was resting inside of him like a hallow egg was now filled. However, fate can be cruel, and Earth was fickle and temporary by nature.

After many years together in union, the rug was pulled from Iós, and Imi became ill, laid low very rapidly by a mysterious parasite of some kind. Her body became dehydrated and continuously purged all that attempted to hydrate it. Her skin was flushed and her body was weak; pain languished in her abdomen. Iós was beside himself with fear of losing her again. In the past, he had used his ability to invade others, to cure them from their ailments. He would immerse himself in the patient just long enough for them to self-repair. When they were healed, he would move back into his host body before the host would wake.

When Imi became ill, he made attempts to enter her body and heal her, so they could live and love forever. But she was immune to his immersion; her body rejected his electrical impulses, and thus he was blocked from healing her in the last way that he knew how. Her illness and its symptoms escaped him; it was like nothing he had seen before in the temple.

He laid next to her while she took the last breaths of her life. She died next to him, and her soul, although invisible, drifted up towards the stars.

That was the day it all became dark again for Iós; a shell like polished steel covered his heart. Out on his tiled balcony, in the darkness of the night, he screamed in anguish. All the crickets and frogs ceased chirping. He wept for hours on his knees, checking on her body and then back out onto the balcony. He was mad with rage and sadness.

The loss of Imi sparked Iós to carry reckless, cruel ideas out into the world, sharing his poisonous pain for all those on Earth to drink. Unknowingly, humans one by one would join his cult. He used Amenhotep's body for a long while, but he also traveled from village to village as an animal, to spy and instigate territorial battles. It was as if Iós were playing dark chess with the humans. He built empires just to burn them down. The world had footprints of blood and gold that could be traced back to him, as their source. Ages passed, and the Roman Empire was a special creation that Iós was quite fond of. It was his largest work of art yet. He was amused by the loyalty of men and the lengths they would go to in following their king and his religion. They killed so easily for territory, for gold, for honor; it fueled a power that Iós did not know he possessed.

Iós had channeled so much dark energy and power, like a sponge, from the murder and the religious devotion of his followers. His pain, stemming back to his love, led Iós to wall women away from power. He held a chip on his shoulder that instilled a woman's stature in his people that he ruled. Women were not to be trusted; they were capable of bewitching hearts. Iós created a time where men ruled and dictated the way in which the social world was shaped. This bitterness ensured he would never feel the loss and sorrow of love again.

However, magic has its own way of working around fussy tyrants.

As the human population grew in size, and colonization was evolving and expanding, Iós grew more powerful. His electromagnetic field, the essence he was made of, was now able to expand from an energy source he was only just beginning to understand. When he felt surges of energy moving through him, he cast the energy outwards, with the mind to enclose the planet with his signature, marking his territory. The whole planet slowly became covered with his energetic field, like pouring tar onto an apple. Geometric lines pulsed in the atmosphere, creating an impenetrable net. He wanted all the souls on the Earth to be contained, for his pleasure and his power. Most of all, he wanted to be sure that no soul could leave the planet.

Although he carried bitterness like a weight on his throat, he still mourned Imi, Neenah, and Ala. Even though outwardly he treated all women with little regard, he still wondered where she was. He wanted to have control of her ability to leave the planet, because one day, he would likely be ready to find her.

Iós recalled the vastness of space, and did not want her to transcend into such a vast place, where she might never be found. So at this point, no souls could leave the planet, and none could arrive. Iós noticed that when he did this, the Moon itself, until then icy blue and dazzling, went dark in his honor. This left the night sky darker, allowing more room for mischief as only the pale white light hung dimly in the sky.

Religion and wars kept Iós busy in the meantime. it was his favorite game, utilizing the spiritual element within each soul. This element proved to be an interesting tool to fuel war. By forcing religious beliefs onto his people, he convinced them to find spirituality through his lens, worshipping his god, which in turn funneled energy to Iós. The souls were powerful when unified in belief, and it sent waves of power into him.

Iós created a few religions, so he could pit the souls against themselves. Every time they committed an act of hate and murder in the name of their god, their souls would fracture, creating more souls to incarnate with amnesia and confusion. This grew his population, amassing more players to play with. When the souls returned to be reborn again and again, there came a point in time where they had all forgotten their origin.

Many beings were well-intentioned and found peace in the communal belief of belonging to a collective spiritual plan. These beings were benign, and often upheld some of the moral codes that came with the religion, picking and choosing good morals for their own lives. When a man named Jesus incarnated, his soul still somehow solid and awake, he spread messages of love and compassion. He urged those around him to remember that they were all the sons and daughters of God. But when Iós caught wind of it, he put a stop to his teachings, and used his destruction to lure in more followers to Jesus's religion, utilizing the good morals that Jesus had been encouraging to his benefit. Although at the time the people knew Jesus was crucified for opposing the Roman Empire, Iós would in time twist his words and explain the importance of his sacrifice for the washing away of Man's sin. It was easy for Iós to edit history, with his long life and control of the written word, including controlling who could and could not write or read.

There were not many options to opposing the monarchies and their forced religious wars, so many people found their own peace within the system, as many felt they had no choice but to join in.

Pagans also survived the rule of mandated religion; they were secretive and mysterious, continuing to live connected with the Earth and its ancient magic. Traditions were kept alive in the rural communities, who gathered to share stories that kept their rituals alive. There were pockets of souls that Iós could not dominate. Earth was not all war and hate, and many bright souls still gleamed, holding their own light, living responsibly by sharing love and kindness. There were still flowers, laughter, children born, the beauty of nature, and philosophy. People still had small farms and milked goats, swam in rivers, died of old age surrounded by family, and viewed beautiful sunsets.

Iós was powerful, but there was only one of him, along with the small circle of rulers he influenced. He was outnumbered, but he had advantages that no other humans had, and this made him feel like he was a god himself. And in truth, it would not be much of a game if there was no light to challenge the dark.

He continued to influence rule, and his Roman Empire began to fall, while his Germanic Empire began to rise. He took over animals and traveled all over the planet to create and possess bloodline rulers and monarchs, instilling their beliefs of superiority while planting seeds of paranoia. He controlled the books and libraries, burning spiritual and occult texts and keeping that knowledge for himself and his kings. This kept the commoners from revolting; he had to keep them uneducated, malnourished, and superstitious. He kept his commoners busy with taxes, making it difficult for them to buy land, provide good food for their families, and earn a living. He left them enough to keep them alive and happy, but not enough to be free. They were trapped under his systematic control.

They mined for metals, and began building more incredible tools and infrastructures, simple technologies propelling society forward... and sometimes backwards. He had it all running chaotically and smoothly, enjoying the company of kings and consorts. He enjoyed fine food and bathhouses, he accrued enough gold and riches to fill castles upon castles, but there was still something missing, and it nagged at him. Deep down, he was still searching for her, for Imi. He searched through the countryside and through village streets. He traveled from country to country by way of birds, but he found nothing.

Until one day, crossing from France to Spain, he took refuge in a forest from a heavy summer rainstorm. It was faint, the outline of her, but he swore he saw her. He blinked, his bird eyes wet with rain. He saw a nymph, a fairy woman, a Lady of the Forest that only the philosophers of kings spoke of.

In all his time on the planet, he never once saw a Faerie nor a mermaid. But he was certain that he saw her, shifting shape and moving with inhuman speed. When she made her way closer, unaware of his presence, she looked off in his direction, her silver eyes sparkling from the contrast of her acorn-colored skin. Her hair, long and twisted, was tangled with flowers and moss, draping over a body rich with curves. It appeared as though she had heard something, so she walked up to a tree, laid upon it -- and disappeared.

Iós was still, and he sat unmoving in the tree for days, waiting to see if she would return. He flew to the tree she had disappeared into, and examined it for some hope, some shred of detail that she existed at all. Eventually he fled the tree to forage, his body weak from his stagnant stakeout. He remembered the woods, and knew where he could return to look again, and he would return, as often as he could until he was able to prove what he thought he saw.

Layer 24: Indra -
Loving Monsters When the Moon Was Dark

After Fengári went dark, tides turned and all balance shifted. The dark became darker, and trust between the races in Indra's forest was weakened. Many beings, the elves for example, kept to their own kind; they were more cold and aloof than before. There were more creatures killed, and the forest no longer felt as safe as it once had. There was still beauty and brightness, beings who despite the darkness and change did not express sorrow or worry. Flowers still bloomed and birds still sang their songs, but there were places that were no longer safe to go.

Beaudry and Indra mourned the loss of Fengári for some time, as nothing felt the same now. Despite this, they had each other. They often visited Saprophytie at his cave to hear about the happenings around the planet.

"Hello, Saprophytie!" Beaudry bellowed at the opening of the cave's doorway. An earthy smell began creeping into their senses, and they knew Saprophytie was coming. When he breached the cave's door, it was plain to see that his face was tired, his energy spread thin. He looked brokenhearted somehow, staring far into the distance, as if he were peering through time at a memory long gone. His skin was still glowing, but it was his eyes that gave away his depletion. What were once bright white pearls were now flat and gray, sometimes flashing green as he was staring off into the distance.

"How are you faring, Saprophytie? It's good to see you, like the warmth of an approaching sunrise," Beaudry said with concerned fondness, reaching out to clasp Saprophytie's hand in a soft grip while holding his opposite shoulder. It was a common greeting that told a story of kinship, of brotherhood, and of respect. Beaudry was a deep soul, and they stared fondly into the eyes of Saprophytie.

"I am well, Beaudry; it is nice to see a familiar face in such a big world. To my surprise, there has been less killing of late, despite this darkness. Of course, everything still feels upside-down, but it also feels like it has paused, as if we were in the eye of a storm. I do not take this break for granted, and have been resting," Saprophytie said, his chest rising with a deep breath, and falling with a large sigh. Indra moved forward to hug Saprophytie, holding him for some time.

"I have brought you treats of all kinds, and a big water skin of temple water!" Indra said, grinning, and turning to show a bulging bag on her back.

"I am grateful; as you well know, since the fall of Fengári, the forests have become less safe. The sprites, sweet little wisps, do not always come to bring me my beloved Jubees," Saprophytie said wistfully, clutching a fistful of air. Although he was serious in demeanor, there was slight theatrical jest in his words and animations. Jubees were that good. Indra laughed and unpacked the bag she had brought, first handing him the water, as temple water was nutritious for the fae folk. Just as humans need minerals and vitamins to function, the Fae need the lifeblood of their realm.

Saprophytie was quick to pour the water into a rather large wooden cup. He drank as if he were inhaling it. Streams of water tracked down the sides of his mouth. He heaved a breath of relief when he finished the contents of the cup, eyes flickering brighter, like slow florescent lights. He stared at the spread Indra was laying out, then sat next to her in the downy comfort of the leaves and moss of the forest floor. Indra had brought so many Jubees, along with other confectionary treats! There were green-wrapped meats, nuts, and fruit. She halved the fruit with her hands, the skin of the fruit serving as bowls.

Beaudry kneeled down at last, sitting across from Saprophytie. Beaudry wore pastel pink, like blooming peonies, with their hair cascading down into loose braids. The calm and hopeful feeling their ensemble relayed was intentional. Beaudry handed a Jubee to Saprophytie, their eyes kind and intent. When Saprophytie ate it, his color-washed skin brightened. He sat, sighing with a smile, basking in the nourishing company of his friends, his mood clearly lifting. Saprophytie was the most misunderstood being in the Fae realm, and Beaudry was his biggest fan. Beaudry truly loved the underdogs, and undervalued gems in the rough. Perhaps it is because they had domain over mountains and minerals, gems and gold hiding concealed within the rock.

Eventually, after they were satiated, the group took to washing in the nearby river, swimming and stretching themselves. Even the Sun shined in the sky above them, despite its typical twilight backdrop. It was as if the Sun had appeared just for them, leaving them all feeling warm and limber as dough.

While lying about afterward, Saprophytie started sharing stories of what he had been seeing lately. "It was sudden; for many hundreds of mortal years, the Romans had risen and conquered so many territories; the killing was endless. The virus, whom we have now come to know as Iós, has been creating these wars, fueling them with religions that he has created. He has been destroying the innate magic of the souls. He convinces his people, with his charm, to follow him into battle and into death. He will just go from leader to leader and use them as puppets, like playing chess with himself, but using human bodies --" Saprophytie paused, as he was interrupted.

"Wait, sorry, what is chess?" Indra said tilting her head.

Saprophytie laughed. "Right. It is a strategic game, something mortals play on a piece of wood to exercise the mind. Anyway, I thought his killings would never end; and then recently, in maybe the last ten mortal years, there have been no wars," he said with raised eyebrows. "Only the momentum of hatreds that Iós's games have started are still playing out. I haven't spied his human appearance too often, which leads me to believe he has taken animal form as of late." Saprophytie moved a bead of water down his leg with his mind; it zipped and zagged, like a lizard not wanting to be caught. He became quiet and stared off into thought, sighing.

"The strangest part of it all," Beaudry interjected, opening up the conversation again, "Is that when these souls are persuaded to carry out these acts of violence and righteous hate, they seem to be shattering, fragmenting, and this is creating more and more people. More pawns for Iós' game, though I'm not sure what is in it for him." Beaudry's hands crumbled a fistful of dried leaves and spread it around in the water, as if spicing a soup.

"How many times can a soul be fragmented, I wonder?" Indra asked, contemplatively, staring upwards. "My hope is that there is a limit, and that it is repairable." Her eyes looked trenched in guilt; after that comment, she kept quiet for the rest of the time they all sat together, save for a few nervous laughs. Indra had a cryptic expression on her face, and luckily Beaudry and Saprophytie were distracted in conversation and swimming, so they did not notice.

When Indra was ready to go, she excused herself casually, with a big smile and a wave. Flashing into the distance like silk in the wind, small tears fell from her face. The tears lingered in mid-air, suspended in her vacuum of velocity. While moving through the trees, Indra's soul was screaming with conflict, for she knew why Iós was no longer killing, no longer propelling the wars and hate. She knew, because she had fallen in love with a monster. It didn't feel like much time had passed since Iós had wondered into her forest by way of animal; in fact, it felt like yesterday. The memory ate at Indra, and yet it filled her up. Indra had told no one, and as far as she knew, her secret remained one.

It was winter in the mortal realm, and snow covered the forest; all was quiet save for the sound of snow falling from low-hanging clouds plump as downy pillows. Indra found herself wondering through her forests on the mortal side, as snow was always something she looked forward to. It was a strange sort of death, a short-term burial that reset the clocks of nature. It was then that she spotted a red fox trotting along; when it looked up and saw her, the fox locked eyes with Indra. This was when she noticed that something was different about the fox. It wasn't from her Irati Forest; she knew most creatures that lived in her lands. Indeed, something was very different about this fox. It had a strange aura, one resembling a swarm of millions of gray gnats. Her heart flickered and sank; it was Iós, and Indra froze. She did not turn or blink; she held the fox's gaze.

Indra had been waiting a very long time to be able to encounter him; what were the chances? Every step the fox took towards her, there was a thick energy that rippled out. Lowering her stance, her strong legs lunged like a martial artist awaiting their opponent. Her blue cloak, the color of a robin's egg, was lined with fur, and concealed her form. The red fox came easily to her, stopping just shy of touching her, its fur dark against the snow. Iós sat and stared at her, tilting his head, his red-and-yellow eyes unblinking.

Indra had a longwinded speech committed to memory for a day like today, but the words got lost somewhere between her mind and her mouth.

"You have made a mess, Iós," was all Indra managed to say, her icy-cold heart and fiery rage neutralizing each other. Iós looked down and away, as if ashamed, acknowledging her words. He stood on all fours again and moved to put the side of his face against her ankle. He lingered there as if listening or waiting for something to happen. When the moment passed, Indra whipped her ankle, throwing him a few feet away. He slid unharmed across the snow, looking pleased with himself. If foxes could grin, he was grinning madly, staring up at her.

Iós looked her up and then down, and turned to run at full speed, the thick gray cloud following behind him like a cape. Indra did not know what had just happened; had he tried to invade her, but somehow failed? Had he become afraid? She did not know if she would see him again... until spring came the following year.

Indra was once again in the mortal realm, walking amongst refreshing normalcy of the forest; the flowers were simply beautiful, and bees made their way from nectar point to nectar point. Hearing footsteps coming from the east, she morphed into a tree, assuming the curves and height of a typical oak. When the footsteps came closer, Indra saw the cloud again; and she saw that Iós had taken a human form. He was inside a stunningly appealing Spanish man. His form was built for war, holding a posture that demanded authority. He had short wavy hair that was thick and hugged his head. Indra would have eaten him up in one bite if she could have, but his eyes told the truth: green marbled with red. He was not just a delicious man, he was also Iós.

"I know you are near; I can hear you. Do you like what you see? Does my form please you?" Iós said aloud, looking directly at Indra. She melted back into her natural form and stood before him. "I have been looking for you; do you recognize me?" Iós asked, his demeanor changing slightly, his eyes showing the smallest glimpse of despair and longing. When those windows into his heart quickly shut, he resumed his authoritative stare.

"Last time you were here, when the ground was covered in snow, did you try to take my body?" Indra said with icy accusation.

"I did, but likely not for the reasons you think. As you now know, I cannot enter you; somehow, you're immune to me," Iós said thoughtfully. Something in his breath and demeanor changed; he now appeared kind and gentle somehow.

Indra felt herself being sucked into feelings she did not wish to have; they were bubbling up inside of her, building like steam in a pot with a tight lid. She held her breath and closed her eyes briefly to steady herself. This man of all men, this darkness, how could she even dare not strangle him, encapsulate his host in ice, and sink him to bottom of the sea? There had been so much built-up rage inside of her. He was the reason she was here in the first place!

Opening her eyes again, she leveled herself, closing off the feelings pushing to the surface. "Iós, I do not know from whence you came, but what is it you want from this world, and the souls that you keep trapped here?" Indra's voice hung in sound waves that were beyond anger and hate, but flatly in a place of pure, shocked pain.

"I often wonder where I came from, as I do not know. As for the souls, they are a cathartic source of energy for me; there is no grand scheme. What I truly want from this world is standing right before me," Iós said, evading the question and removing the lid from Indra's pot. Her knees buckled ever so slightly as he moved closer and closer to her, reaching out to hold one of her hands.

He grabbed ahold while Indra stood frozen; his grip was soft and certain, and it sent butterflies throughout her entire being, small vibrations of pleasure tangible from such a simple gesture. Indra could not believe what was happening; how could she feel this way for such a hideous being? How could she bear to even be touched by a monster?

They stood there silently. Iós held her hand and stared into her eyes till the Sun set. Although no words were spoken, his hunger was tangible. Whether the hunger was for power, sex, or blood, she could not tell. As they stood there together, her mind was clear and steady.

"May I return to you... I do not even know your name. May I know your name? I will not accept no easily, as I'm used to making flexible adjustments to get what I want." Iós said this while releasing Indra's hand. "I will come back again and again, until you see," he said, furrowing his brows, emphasizing his certainty and seriousness.

Indra felt nauseated by his arrogant comment. "What will I see?" she asked, raising one eyebrow and maintaining a level expression.

"If I have to explain it, I think it spoils the magic," Iós said, turning to go. "I look forward to seeing you again."

Indra did not respond. She did not say yes; nor did she say no. She did not know whether to run after him and kill him, or let him return another day. There was caution there, as acting too swiftly or too impulsively with such a powerful being was not wise. Despite her desire to destroy him, she also wanted him; she was curious to know more about his power and allure. Surprise and shame were swirled together like patterns on marble, and Indra was left alone with her complex dilemma.

Indra kept it to herself; she did not share the encounter with anyone. Meeting Iós was her dark secret. On a particularly lethargic afternoon, as Indra was laying around with thoughts unending, something big occurred to her. When Iós was Amenhotep in Aria's memory, he'd had a lover; she had been unable to absorb the virus, and had died. Why? Who was this woman, and why did Iós imply that he knew Indra? Was she living other lives she wasn't aware of? Perhaps a version of herself -- "Malva!" She sat up with the rigid epiphany. Malva must have fallen too when she opened the line to come to Earth;

she must have been pulled down as well, or willingly came. The eyes of that woman, Imi; they were silver, now that she thought back to the hazy memory within the memory.

"If it is Malva, or actually me, then where is she now?" Indra wondered, feeling relieved that she was not the first one to ponder love for Iós. It somehow felt familiar and comfortable; and perhaps Malva felt that too, if she really was Imi. They were here together somehow, just with a different perceiving consciousnesses. Indra felt so foolish for not seeing it clearly before. "How could I forget about Malva? Wherever she is in this crazy world, I hope she's doing well; the short life of a human must be so tiring. Growing and trying, glowing and dying."

She hung her head low, feeling how hard it must be for Malva, so she hummed a high-pitched note to call in creatures with wings. Along came moths, butterflies, birds, and bats; and she sent them to search the world and send a love and blessing to Malva. A colorful cloud of magnificent winged beings made their way into the air like a thousand whispers and disappeared. Hopefully they would find and follow Malva, and that would brighten her day. This was a blessing of love and protection, to help with the confusion of consecutive reincarnation.

Months passed, and as promised Iós returned, again and again. Indra shamelessly let her guard down, time after time, charmed by his unsuspecting heart, which was deeper than the ocean itself. Iós was irresistible, but despite Indra's secret desires, she did not bend to the lust and hunger that was plain in his eyes. She felt in control of herself, convinced that she was somehow orchestrating an investigation. She was learning about her enemy.

Years passed. In time, all things decay and crumble, including the tall walls surrounding her heart. She let go. She jumped off her proverbial internal cliff, and stretched herself openly to him.

The only way that Indra agreed to meet Iós was if it were in the mortal realm. That was the best way to see him without anyone from her world witnessing her secret, because in the mortal realm, she could use Fae magic to create a container of privacy. It was not foolproof magic, but it was strong enough to keep out any potential onlookers. When they met in the woods, Indra would create a small cabin, a fort, a magical, comfortable cove of vines, wood, blankets, and moss. There was a place for a fire and small openings to let the light in. It blended in with the scenery, and served as a private meeting place. With her magic, she could easily will natural, living fiber to work with her; that way, she could build a new bower in different locations every time they met.

Despite these close quarters and intimate moments shared, Indra did not let her guard down or succumb to his lusty advances. For a monster, Iós was patient; he seemed grateful for the moments they shared, regardless of her openness. Like a smart man playing chess, he was waiting for the game to shift in his favor.

The inevitable day came during Autumn, when the air was crisp and the leaves were bright. The bucks in the forest were tense with sexual aggression and competition; they walked through the forest slowly and territorially. Indra noticed how the aggressive energy from the animals was also affecting Iós. Territorial energy coursed through his body like a current, and he was filled with desire to dominate and procreate. She had felt so strong and able to resist his seduction before, but now it was clear that her body was as eager and driven as his was to entangle in the comfort of their hidden place.

Colorful leaves covered the ground, making all the sounds from the forest more animated and loud, which helped to cover any sounds that were coming from their cabin. The vibrancy of fall was majestic, the trees' closing act before dormancy, declaring a proclamation of their uniqueness. The night was clear and cold with stars; and in the morning, the beams of sunlight slid in through the trees, highlighting the tiny jagged frost that lined the edges of all living things.

During this encounter, Indra and Iós stayed in their fort for three days and three nights. They would both leave and return as needed; Indra brought back things to eat and drink, as it was easy for her to provide all things while in her forest. But their outings were seldom and brief; they mostly stayed indoors. During those days, the dam blew open; Indra had never been so lost in lovemaking as she was atop the blankets made from fox furs, an ironic gift that Iós had presented to her. She was seeing stars as he first held her low waist close to his, as he moved ever so subtly against her. Breathing in the smell from her neck, he was wild. He was close and far away, equally. Her body moved with his, and his with hers, a shared control in the rhythm and flow. With Indra's magic, her body was permeable, like quicksand, and Iós was sinking into her, getting lost until they were both fully submerged.

Iós was well trained; he was not overly selfish. Although he was dominant and guiding, surprisingly, he did not only think of his own pleasure. They were covered in one sweet layer of sweat that helped them to slide and stick to one another. Indra was alive, for the first time in a long time. She felt filled up by Iós; his body was strong and thick. There was no escaping him now that he had ahold of her, and that only made Indra lose herself more. Just like that, she was wandering through a maze she hadn't known existed.

Each time she met with Iós, she learned more about the lives he had lived. He openly shared stories about his journeys, although he never spoke of love or his lovers. He rarely spoke about his life as Amenhotep; Indra guessed it was a triggering lifetime. This was evident, as every time the subject was grazed, all the hairs on his arms stood up, and his stomach tightened. His mannerisms changed and his energy became more anxious and agitated, his eyes glowed a deeper red, and he turned the conversation abruptly away. Indra did not push him, although sometimes seeing him this way pulled her from his trance, and she could see more of the monster in him, how hurt and angered he was about the world.

When Iós discovered how long Indra's life had been, his face displayed extreme confusion, and yet he was intrigued. Indra wondered if it had to do with Imi; perhaps he knew they were the same soul, but couldn't understand the timeline. After chewing on the information for a while, it was as if he internally shrugged, unwilling to solve the mystery in Indra's company. Despite this pause, Iós bloomed like a morning glory, and he opened himself up to her again. Indra's immortality was reassuring for a being who had lost his loved ones to death; he relaxed, as if he was no longer in a hurry, secure and stable, knowing that she could not die of illness or age. However, she withheld the most important information about her immortality, especially from a man capable of so much darkness, a man with the emotional caprice of a gymnast. Her mortality was a choice. Though she had lived for so many eras, Indra was able to perish if she were caught in the mortal realm while her home tree was destroyed. It would be a quick end to her life.

If her tree was destroyed while she was in the Fae, she would survive, but would no longer be able to travel between realms, as the tree stood as a portal extending its roots and branches into each world. The seed that she had ridden in on was her source of strength, as well as most of her magic. If her tree perished, she would become faint, like a whisper. At least that was what the Fae lore said; she had never met a tree dryad who had lost her tree and lived to share her story.

There was no way Iós could learn of her weakness, no matter how much she thought she loved him; it was something she knew she needed to hold back. Souls were stuck on Earth, and if she perished, she did not want to be cast out again and launched into another body and another life; she wasn't sure what would happen to her memory. She had had so much time to perfect and remember herself, but even with all that time, her connection to her other lives was far from clear. Indra could only imagine what would happen if she started from scratch with less memory. Especially if she were human! Each time she died, would it get worse? Would she fall further from the truth and become lost in it all, like everyone else?

She had become comfortable with her life in the Fae realm, and she had to remain aware of why she had come to Earth. Now that Iós was so close as her lover, maybe if she could love him, fix him, he wouldn't stay a monster. In a way, she felt that she was failing herself, lost to the draw of his charm, ashamed, on a runaway train going full speed ahead. Indra had rarely had to practice any form of self-control in her world; nothing else existed that was so enticing and yet so evil.

Then, on a full Moon in June, the unexpected happened. They met in a meadow, under an open sky, the evening warm and clear. Indra laid down the fox-fur blankets and layered protection magic around them, so they could not be seen. She also brought a basket of treats. What was a full Moon view without treats, after all? When they lay back, eyes staring up at the big full Moon, Indra was reminded of Aria and Fengári. She had a pit in her stomach that felt sour and rotten; Aria had sacrificed herself to stop this virus, and here Indra was, having a picnic underneath her hollow remains! It was a new low that dawned on Indra, one that half-shook her from her rose-colored view.

Sensing that Indra was pulling back, Iós threw himself into her, lacing her with firm caresses and whispering poetry. He spoke in many languages and nibbled at her ear, blowing lightly into it. Like a mother blowing on a child's wound, it was soft and slow, just enough to deafen the senses and get lost. Soon enough, Iós was making love to Indra sweetly, with strong movements. His face was nudging and pressed against the side of hers, and he whispered something into her ear: "I bind myself to you."

Indra, lost in the moment, said nothing, but his words momentarily pulled her out of reverie. They were alarming, somehow. But drowned by the sensations of the body, Indra let the statement pass over her like water. She only swooned and sighed with each movement.

Climbing upwards like mountain goats, they clung to slender ledges and then rose higher into the proverbial clouds. There was a quiet moment, at the top, where they both held their breath... until Indra fell with a shivering shatter, as if a frozen river had met the weight and force of a moving train, plowing through the icy walls, obliterating its solid form. With her eyes still closed, she could see small, shimmering specks of ice drifting through the air, trails of light tracing their path.

Iós held her still, and stared at her until her eyes opened. Her body, already iridescent, was covered in fine drops of sweat that reflected the light of the Moon, making her whole body look like a bejeweled flower petal. When Indra finally caught her breath, the drops of sweat had long evaporated, like her pleasure, and her eyes slowly opened to meet the red pair staring at her.

Something was different; she tilted her head. Iós mimicked her motion on the opposite side. Her body felt open, relaxed, and strange. All she could feel was the strange ocean that Iós had left inside of her, moving through her, defying gravity.

Iós shifted to lie boldly next to Indra, his palm on her hip and stroking past the lower fullness of her belly. This affection would normally cause Indra to swoon and snuggle, but this time she felt internally frantic, like a rabbit running from a fox. Iós did not notice her dismay as he continued staring at her in the same way.

Indra looked away from his eyes, which was difficult. It was like trying to escape the suction of two small black holes, pulling everything in proximity into their void. Not wanting to startle him, she swiftly unfurled herself and smiled flirtatiously; playing shy, she crossed the grass near the blanket and grabbed onto a low-hanging branch of a tree. Her body hung loosely while her arms did the work. She stretched and began to sing an old lullaby melody, one from her Fae people, in a language he would never know. It was a good defense against his charm, to use her own; and it did diffuse the strange tightness in the air, and soothed him as he watched her body stretch and dance around the tree.

Eventually, Iós made moves to stand, and assembled himself into some loose clothing. He bowed and reached for her hand. "Indra, I must tend to some matters in a land far away from here. I shall not return for a while, but I will be back. Do not take my absence as an exit. I will always return to these woods. I love you more than all the stars in the galaxy, more than all the power in the world. I am yours."

Iós said this while kissing her hand slowly and inhaling the smell of her, so he wouldn't forget it.

"I will be here; this is my forest, after all. Iós, I cannot make any promises of love. I will watch and wait till I can see action, and see you change the way you live your life. I know what you do, and what you have done, and I don't see love in it, not even hardly. I have eyes all over the world, and I am kept up to date on the messes and chaos you have created. Do not be confused by our rendezvous in the woods. Although we share love, I belong to no one." Indra spoke with poised posture and eyes as clear as glass, her words almost threatening. She wondered if he was capable of ending his wars and killings; would she be enough to quench his thirst?

Iós nodded and lowered his gaze to the ground, ashamed of the truthful reproach that followed his declaration of love. "I have not had the desire for power or blood in some time; I am trying to correct some of the messes I have made. It takes time to move the minds of humans. I will show you, and that is why I must leave," Iós said. With a quick nod, he gave a slight bow, one that felt truly humble. It was then that she was reminded of the man she'd seen in Aria's memory, a man healing the sick in the villages of Egypt. She knew somewhere in there was a reason she loved him, even though she would never admit it to him.

Indra smiled very faintly, longingly, with sorrow in her eyes; and like smoke into thin air, she dissolved, leaving Iós staring into the darkness alone.

It was not long before Indra found that she had become impregnated by Iós that night. She was ashamed, mystified, and happy all at once. How could she have a child with a monster from the mortal realm? *His* child. There was no way to have the half-mortal baby in the

Fae realm. It would not survive. The gestation of mixed beings was complex, and there were few success stories in Fae history. It was said the only way to deliver a half-mortal baby was for the mother to stay in the mortal realm for most of the pregnancy. Even though it was a risk, she knew she loved the child already, and could not let it die. Staying in her realm would snuff out the brilliant, small flame of life.

While Iós was away, before she moved into the mortal realm to bear his child, Indra visited Saprophytie. She wanted to see if he could give her any information. She wanted to see if Iós had kept to his word, if he was acting in accordance to his love for Indra.

Saprophytie was far less bright than the last time she had seen him, that day with Beaudry, when they swam and spoke of brighter days. No, this was the shell of a being, one who looked as if he had seen the darkest corner of the Earth and returned with haunted memories. He appeared less tall and slender than he normally was, his outfit hanging loosely on his form.

"Saprophytie, what's happened to you?" Indra asked, slowly folding him up in her mothering arms. She held him there silently, and they did not speak for some time. He was light and frail in her arms, his body using hers to stand.

"It was dark out there, and even I cannot bear the memories of the awful sight." His voice was flat and devoid of emotion. He took a deep breath and spoke with more energy: "For the last decade, everything was manageable; there was far less distress and darkness amongst the humans. A potential turning point, or at least many of us thought. It was like a breath of fresh air, a break from the chaos." Saprophytie's voice cracked, and his tone was hollow and bewildered as he continued.

"Then it changed. Villages were terrorized and burned to ground, women and children slaughtered and left to rot. Soldiers, like demons, defiled the dead and continued on their warpath from village to village. It was like a trail of blood crossing all of the continent. I could not even stand to see it," Saprophytie said, covering his eyes with his hands. He peeled himself from Indra. "I could not manage it all, so I called the fire, and its all-consuming flame. Together we burned it all, swallowing the mess whole; we could not leave it the way it was."

Unblinking eyes stared off towards the river, and then Saprophytie actually began to weep. She had not known that he could. He wept facing away from her for some time, until his body was limp. Indra wanted to comfort him, give him somewhere to lay. So, using her magic, she summoned vines and wood to twist into a nested resting pad. She used moss, cottonwood fluff, and flowers to make a soft place for him to rest. Guiding Saprophytie to lay down, she sang to him gently,

"Rest now, and let your memories wash away. Lay among these flowers, let their scent remind you of the beauty, the brightness still shining in this world."

She did this while covering Saprophytie with a blanket made from velvet-soft mullein leaves.

When Saprophytie relaxed into the comforting nest, Indra unpacked the bag she had brought. She always brought food for him, and she laid it on the edge of the nest, along with a water skin. Indra sat and watched him sleep for a long while, concerned about this new weight on his soul. What could have happened out there? Iós had left claiming he would be gone to mend the messes he had made, not create more.

While Saprophytie slept, a maddening flurry of thoughts invaded Indra's mind. She was furious with herself for her foolish belief in Iós. For loving him, for letting him touch her; the memories made her sick. Inside herself, she harbored a scream that would doubtless break all the glass in the world. Iós had lied to her; not only that, but he had committed such atrocities that Saprophytie was now crippled by their memory.   Iós had a monstrous hunger for blood and power, and it seemed everything he had said to her was a lie. Her mind tore him apart, shredding every beautiful moment they had shared together, painting it all black, erasing him from her heart.

Indra had to leave Saprophytie, so she summoned some nearby owls to perch on his nest, and watch over him. They were masters at watching. Landing swiftly, their feathers were stark against the canopy-shadowed forest. The white owls blinked their eyes and settled. If anything were to go awry with Saprophytie, they were to find Beaudry. When she knew it was safe to go, Indra left quickly, moving through her forest with a torrent of thoughts in her head.

Upon landing at her tree, she climbed inside, safe within its walls, to cry like she never had before. Uncontrollable waves rushed up from the bottom of her soul, continually crashing onto the shore. She thought about the father of her child, and felt inside of herself, searching to see if the child she carried was anything like Iós; but all she could feel was warmth and love. This was a relief that allowed her tears to slow. She knew her child was good, despite its origins. Indra wanted to give it a chance for life, even though having the baby would come with eye-widening complexities and challenges.

There was little time before she would have to cross into the mortal realm, to keep the child alive. The child was a miracle, and she could not extinguish this gift. But how could she raise a child without Iós knowing? Did he even have to know? Why did she ever have to love such a monster? She wondered this while she packed herself some supplies. "What will I do after the child is here?" she murmured.

She would not be able to keep his child in her realm; too many of the beings who dwelt there would sense the child's half-mortal origin. They would soon figure out who the father was, too, especially as Iós would return to the forest looking for her. If he could not find her, he would return again and again; he would not let her go so easily. It was all a recipe for disaster.

The baby was her dark and beautiful secret, and she needed a plan.

Indra wondered if she could live in the mortal world with her child, and somehow blend in. However, that option came with its challenges, as her Fae features and magic surely would not go unnoticed. Though she could use charms and glamours to mask herself, she was not sure if she could do it for her *and* her child, being so far away from her tree. That feat took a lot of strength, and would be risky in the newly religious, God-fearing mortal world. It would only take a few of the wrong people to see her before Iós would catch wind of her whereabouts.

Fae were easily recognized and feared by mortals. Times had changed, and where there was once harmony between the realms, now there was a rift. The thought of uneducated, malnourished, superstitious villagers hurting her child sickened Indra.

This all felt like some fated trap of destiny. It was such a strange situation. She did not know what to do, except prepare for the child that was coming soon. Indra would have to go into the mortal realm to grow and have the child. There was no choice.

When she was packed and ready, she shifted into the mortal realm, set to search for an answer. Knowing that she normally met Iós on the Spanish border, she spent all of her time on the French side of her forest. She created a magnificent treehouse high in a sturdy beech tree, perfect to keep them safe from peering eyes. No mortal being could easily reach its height.

A daily ritual was to observe the sparse villagers who passed through the forest. For the most part, they were mortal men, transporting goods and hunting. To Indra's interest, there was a particularly wise-looking woman who came to the forest on occasion: a radiant French woman, with modest and neutral clothing, no doubt to keep a low profile while she traveled alone. She came to gather herbs, roots, wood, and seeds.

During late summer, she sat beneath an oak tree to eat a meal she'd packed. Her long, oval face was beautiful, and her hair was jet-black and long, worn in a braid. Stunning green eyes peered from under the hood of her cloak, which were full of admiration for the simple beauty in nature. It was easy for Indra to observe the care she had taken in preparing herself a meal, which she ate with gratitude and enjoyment. The woman's heart was pure, and she was unafraid of traveling alone in the Irati . She traveled in the company of a horse, which meant she was not without means. Her clothing was simple, but when looking closely, Indra saw it was spun of fine and strong-woven materials.

Indra observed this woman curiously and closely, knowing this woman might be her chance. Months passed, and winter had nearly come to an end. Indra's belly grew to full term, but her plan for the child was still unclear. Yet, on a clear winter's day, there came the same French woman, and Indra decided to do something that took courage. Time was running out.

Wishing to appear before this woman, Indra positioned and timed herself so they would meet face-to-face on the path. The French woman was fast approaching on foot, the slight crunch of gravel alerting to her position. Indra was wearing her blue cloak that came down to her ankles, keeping her body warm, but in no way did it conceal the large swell of her belly. Birth would be upon her soon. Under her cloak, she wore knitted clothing she had taken from the passing carts of merchants; she had to do something to keep herself entertained and warm.

When Indra knew the woman was in earshot, she began singing songs from the realm of the Fae. She wanted to initially use the charm of allure to keep the woman calm; however, it could also backfire, as mortal ears could sometimes discern the tangible magic in the sound waves. Indra hoped it would set the mood with charm and persuasion so the woman didn't run.

The French woman's head turned at the sound; initially her face was alert, her eyes searching and scanning the trees. When her moss-green eyes locked onto Indra, they softened, and then focused lower, onto the bulge of Indra's belly. Her legs did not brace to run; the woman merely nodded with her chin held high, and she spoke.

"I am not afraid of the magic of the Fae, as know that I too have my own magic, if you wish to cross me." She was bold and strong, unflinchingly calm where most humans would have begun praying or running for their lives.

"I do not wish to cross you," Indra said, mimicking the language of the woman. "I actually need your help." Indra walked closer, pained by the sudden kicks from the infant inside her, her knees weak with the weight of the child. She walked close enough to touch the woman, and slowly kneeled at the her feet. "My name is Indra. Please, I need your help," she said with humility.

"I am Adalinde. And what could a Fae need my help for? I am goodhearted, but not so easily trusting," Adalinde said with cool honesty, clearly very guarded due to the harsh realities of a mortal life.

"I am carrying a child half-mortal and half-Fae. The child cannot exist in my realm, and I cannot blend in with yours." Indra paused, gritting her teeth with the weight of the baby's head pushing into her pelvic bowl. "I must shroud the child's whereabouts from the father, who is a dark man; and if I stay in the mortal realm, he will surely kill us both."

Adalinde weighed this information and took time to speak. "What will my village think if I come back with a child who sparkles with the eyes of the Fae? The risk would be great for me, with little reward for my assistance. I am without a husband; he died a few years ago." Adalinde was clear, with a calculated honesty. Women were not so easily granted freedom and autonomy in these times. She would likely be seen as a witch, or as an adulteress with a child and no husband. These charges carried the penalty of death in most villages.

Indra realized that she had to make it worth the mortal's risks. "I can offer you magic from my realm in exchange, and perhaps valuable minerals..." Indra looked desperate with the realization that the mortal realm also had its own set of complexities and boundaries she did not understand.

"What sort of magic can you offer?" Adalinde asked with inquisitive eyes, as if bargaining at the market. Despite this woman's cold, logical approach, Indra could feel her pure heart; she would make a strong and kind mother. This was also her only option. It was all happening so fast, and Iós would be returning to the forest soon.

"I can give you wood from my tree; it will protect your home, and be useful for spellcasting on the full Moon, the day when the veil between realms is thinnest. I can grant you magic to grow any plant that you wish, beyond the time of your realm. You can will a plant to grow within moments. And lastly, I can give you a drink from the water temple of my realm, in a chalice carved from stone. The water and the cup will infuse you with the energy of the Fae, adding to your charm and persuasion, in case anyone were to give you trouble. In trade for these items, I will require your help in my labor, and the protection and care of my child." Indra said this with grave eyes, welling with tears.

Adalinde nodded with seriousness. "This is not how I saw my day ending, but life is always full of surprise. I accept your offer, if all you say is true." Adalinde paused with caution in her eyes, "The father, this man of considerable darkness. If someone as powerful as you must hide from him, what would he do if he found me?"

"I will place magic on the child, and conceal her from being seen. I have enough for her, but I cannot conceal her and myself," Indra said, nodding seriously, hoping that this would all make sense despite the haste of the situation.

"Mmm; all right, let us hope she stays concealed, then. To be truthful, I have always wanted a child; and somehow this is a prayer answered. Even though it does come along with risks, I am willing." Adalinde looked down at Indra's feet, which were now wet. Water fell from between her legs, a flowing gush of primordial fluid. "It would appear that your water has broken, and there is not much time before the baby arrives," Adalinde said with wide eyes. "We need water and a safe place for you to feel comfortable and able to move the baby out." She grabbed the crook of Indra's arm, to guide her.

Indra nodded with something close to fear in her eyes; she had never known pain like this. It was something that she never felt in her realm. It was deafening and came in waves. Adalinde, however, did not look afraid; she looked informed and familiar with this process.

"Indra, we must walk to the nearby creek. Water will help. I have helped with a few births in my village; God must be smiling upon you to run into me on such a day," Adalinde said with a smirk and a knowing smile.

Indra nodded, and felt that destiny had in fact brought Adalinde to her, and that this was an omen that the baby would live a long and happy life. She was overwhelmed with the feeling of relief and gratitude.

They walked till they reached the creek, and it masked the sounds of Indra's cries and moans as the contractions struck her like lightning. She felt alive, more alive than she had ever felt before, as the pain brought her to such a dense place of sensation. Adalinde was easy and calm, supportive and yet firm, prompting her along with breathing and pushing. *Oh, the relief of the push,* Indra thought.

Indra splashed creek water on her face in the middle of contractions; she knew that in the next few pushes the baby would arrive. The pain was hot like fire, and then it was over, and Adalinde was holding onto a child, a baby girl, wet with birth. They cut the umbilical with a knife Adalinde carried with her in her satchel. She worked smoothly to wash away the blood and messiness in the cool water from the creek. When the baby began to cry, Adalinde handed her to Indra, a small, shiny little creature. Indra felt relieved to hold and meet her girl. She had not yet opened her squinting little eyes.

Indra's mind and body were able to recover lucidly, with her Fae blood, and she sat with her back against a tree, holding her child. Meanwhile, animals and moths gathered to surround the two women and baby.

Late day turned to night. In the buzz of the starlight, Indra called all the elements to join her, while still holding her baby. Swirling colors of fine-grained mist enveloped Indra and her child while she sang. The song moved the rock and water; it brought fireflies and lightning, it brought wind to blow, it was guttural, it was bewitching.

Adalinde watched in shocked admiration, as she sat quietly and held space for what she perceived as a protection spell around the child. All of the fine grains flew up into a plume and then down into the child's body, infusing her with the protective magic of the Fae. After that, the forest was still and quiet, so hushed that the only audible sound was that of the moths' collective fluttering, like brushstrokes in the air, painting a secret story.

"I must leave you, child, but know there is love from me to you always. Do not fear the mortal world; Adalinde will protect and love you. You are of Fae and mortal blood, so perhaps one day you will know both worlds," Indra said in a quiet voice, her face close to the face of her child.

Small, tired eyes opened softly, blinking, taking in the forest, in the dark. It was hard to see in the blackness of the night, but upon looking closely, the child's eyes were silver, and gleaming with love. Indra could hardly bear what would come next, but she knew the time was coming.

"Adalinde, here, take her. I will go back to my realm to retrieve what I owe you; I will be fast, but it will feel long to you, perhaps hours. Our times are different, but I promise on my life that I shall return." Adalinde nodded, and took the baby, wrapping her up with the cloak Indra handed her.

Indra was gone in a flash; she melted into the forest floor like butter in a pan. She had never moved with such speed through her forest, to her tree, where she would go inside and slice the inner bark. From inside her tree she also took one of three crystal chalices she owned. She chose the ruby one, carved with ornate details of flowers on its outer edges. It was a gift from Beaudry.

While heading towards Adalinde, she passed the water temple, filling the chalice, before phasing back into the mortal world. Indra's body had fully recovered from her birth while briefly prancing around the Fae realm, and she was relieved that the pain was behind her.

When she appeared again, Adalinde and her child were sitting against the same tree. Indra could hear Adalinde's quiet lullaby, and Indra sat next to them, reaching out to hold her child. "She is hungry, you must feed her," Adalinde said, pointing to Indra's breasts. Indra had seen the animals do this in her forest before; she felt stupid for not knowing that the child would be hungry, especially if she were anything like her mother. Before she attempted to feed her child, she dipped one finger into the chalice and dripped a few drops of temple water into the baby's mouth. After, looking pleased, Indra smiled and handed the cup to Adalinde, urging her to drink the water.

When Adalinde finished drinking the water, her skin glowed brighter and became supple. Her green eyes were alight in the dark of the night. Indra watched Adalinde while she breastfed the child, who latched on eagerly.

"The cup is for you. Made of ruby, it is worth more than gold, but it carries a strong magic that is priceless; for anything you drink from it will bring you closer to the Fae. Both of you should drink from this cup on the full Moon. And here..." Indra produced a slender and smooth piece of oak wood that was polished and twisted with splintery gold filaments running up its length. It looked like a small snake, frozen in mid-spiral.

"It will bring your home protection, and bring strength to any spells you may already know. Please use it with caution, as all magic has its price," Indra said clearly, while her eyes flickered with a wildness, small windows revealing the depth of Fae magic and its potential. "Do not become greedy, or mad with power, as the magic will surely turn on you. Madness awaits anyone who uses magic foolishly." Indra knew that she must drive this point home.

Calming the wild in her eyes, she continued, "The wood comes from my tree, and if ever you need to find me, this will be how. Perhaps one day you can bring her back, when it is safer here. We must be wise, and let the dust settle before then." Indra's eyes were hopeful, but she knew the truth, which was that she would never see her daughter again. Handing the wooden wand to Adalinde, tears fell from the edges of her eyes, the drops flying as if with their own mind to land on the child's head. Dancing tears traced the shape of a symbol, and then evaporated into the child's skin.

Adalinde took in the whole scene. The whole course of her life had shifted in a mere evening, but her heart told her it was all fated, as each moment locked into place. Nodding with deep appreciation, she finally spoke. "I will take care of her, I promise." Indra breathed an approving sigh, as she was not ready for the coming separation.

"For the last magic I will impart into you, a union with plants; and forever they will work with you and for you. As long as you have respect and love in your heart, they will always grow. It is, of course, best if no one ever sees you do this magic, but I'm sure you are well aware of those consequences," Indra said, while reaching for Adalinde's hand. She used one of her sharp claws to cut Adalinde's palm. Indra then cut her own palm, and she place them together, mixing their blood. Indra's voice became low and wild once more; it was startling, and the baby opened her eyes, still lazily drinking from the breast.

Vines, moss, and flowers grew all around them, bursting from the ground, slowly rising. The plants grew clockwise in a small circle that surrounded the women, upwards and then overhead, encapsulating them in a cocoon of greenery. In the hushed fort of the flowers and plants, Indra spoke. "Adalinde, can you focus and breathe deeply, concentrating on the magic that now runs within you?" She used one finger to trace up Adalinde's arm and to her heart. "When you are ready, you will remove the plants that shroud us from the night."

Adalinde closed her eyes and breathed deeply, as Indra had asked. When she became seated within herself and her energy was tangibly grounded, likely from the practice of her own magic, she slowly closed the blooms of the flowers, and the vines swirled backwards in time, recessing slowly. Her control was slower than Indra's magic, but it was still strong. Adalinde's eyes opened slowly, and sparkled with delighted amusement. Small lines of joy deepened at the corners of her mouth as she watched the plants recede.

When all the plants had disappeared, Indra and Adalinde sat quietly watching the small child, feeding until her small mouth fell tiredly from Indra's nipple, her eyes closed in a boob-drunken slumber.

She was mortal, but also bore a sparkle that would never fade. There were not many half-breed children in the world, and her blood would forever be marked with the magic of the Fae, one day passing it down to her own children.

It was not common for Fae-mortal babies to survive; sometimes the Fae women did not cross into the mortal realm in time. Most often, this happened with the Elves, as they also appear quite human when walking among the mortal realm, attracting human lovers and sometimes even falling in love. Unexpected pregnancies were rare, but they did happen.

Indra and Adalinde sat for some time, watching the baby sleep. Indra's eyes welled with tears again, her emotions heavy, as the time to separate drew near. It would be best if they all moved along, because Iós would surely be arriving soon; he had been gone for so long, she knew it was only a matter of time before he returned. Indra knew they were already spending time they didn't have. Passing her small bundled child away, Indra wept silently, and thanked Adalinde.

"I will send a wolf as an escort, to protect you both from the dark things in the night; and it will come back to me, informing me of your safe arrival to your home, as well as where your home is. Should you need anything, use the wood from my tree; I will hear you." Indra said this quickly, getting to her feet and making a call like a wolf into the sky.

They waited until they heard a set of paws trotting towards them, its footsteps were nearly muffled by the creek's bubbling. The wolf stepped forward and moved to stand beside Indra, its height astonishing; its head was at the level of Indra's breast. She whispered in the wolf's ear, and pointed to Adalinde. The wolf was pure white, its coat young and fresh, its eyes frosted blue. They were eyes that had seen the world grow old. Though she was informed the wolf was for their protection, it startled Adalinde, and she craned her neck, tilting her head, unsure of its safety.

The wolf came close to Adalinde, sniffing her and rubbing its face on her thigh. After a deep, surrendering breath and exhalation, Adalinde was calm, and turned her face upwards to the cloudless sky. Her face told that she was reading the stars, and knew where to go. One last acknowledgment; she embraced Indra, with the child between them, kissing both sides of Indra's face. Her eyes were steady and looked unwavering at Indra, showing that she was truly going to stick to her words and love the child. It was a look that mothers give one another, a deep and clean understanding that only women share. It was a look that sealed the whole evening.

With the child resting in her arms, and the wolf following by her side, Adalinde made her way through the darkness of the forest, fading from view. Her practiced footsteps were measured and quiet, despite the underbrush and its potential to stir up sound. She didn't look back.

Indra's soul became quiet, small, and still. Even though she knew fate had brought Adalinde to her, she was filled with sorrow.

She sank back into her realm, and went to hide within her tree. She hid there resting from the world for a long time, unwilling to leave its safety. She knew that she would have to face Iós sooner or later. Eventually, she would have to end her connection with him. After she heard from Saprophytie of the killings and burnings of villages in the name of a god, she was unable stand by him. His actions would have consequences. Leaving him would not be easy; his grip and his rage would be fierce, and she was not ready for such a confrontation, but she had to. She was fortunate he did not know about the child, and hopefully he never would.

But beyond Indra's knowledge, in the shadows of the night, there was a witness, a being who observed the birth of a child by a creek.

Layer 25: Eithar - Last Days with Althea

After Althea had shared her news of Nagda 3147's fate, and Eithar's nerves had settled slightly, he sat with himself, admiring the galaxy they had constructed. This abrupt change was still not something he desired, but he would not dare to watch Althea go alone; she was far too important to him. They were crafted of the same spark, the same soul, imprinted with the same harmonic sound.

Eithar moved himself through their galaxy, floating through it like wind until he reached Nagda 3147. He waited, watching that sun, like a father watching his offspring perform a splendorous act of creative art. The star was wildly beautiful, its arms of light and plasma whipping out and lashing back into itself. Nagda gave off a subtle rumbling vibration that could be felt even through the void of space. There was no stopping this predestined transformation; it was beautifully and formidably alive. Eithar himself had created the very fire that would transform his world; this was all his doing, and the beginning of the end was drawing near.

While Eithar floated, orbiting the soft pull of Nagda, it was clear its implosion was coming. The suction of high gravity was already noticeable. Althea arrived to his left, and observed quietly beside him. Although she didn't say anything, her soul was buzzing with curiosity and excitement. They watched together, and slowly their cosmic etheric forms began to merge as they were pulled into orbit, like a small ship on the outer edge of a whirlpool, its impending doom visible at the vertex of the swirl.

Nagda began to glow brighter, its center undergoing an enormous pressure and force that was compacting its core. This created flashes of light in a spectrum of color that was new to the both of them. Althea and Eithar were almost one as they orbited intertwined, moving closer and closer to the dying star, their velocity increasing with each orbital rotation.

"Eithar, we will always be connected, and wherever we go, I know that we will always find one another. Do not fear the loss of me, for we cannot break what is whole." Althea's words were melodic, smooth and loving. Eithar embodied her words, and still felt fear about their impending transformation. He was not content, but his love for Althea was so strong it kept him as brave as he could be.

Then the moment came when they were nearly face-to-face with the surface of the star. There was a quiet, bright light as an immense force pulled all of itself and the surrounding galaxy inward. A prolonged stillness fell over Althea and Eithar, as they were yanked into the darkness at the center, like oxygen gasped by mortal lungs.

It was quiet -- until all of the impact caught up with itself, producing light, matter, and sound at deafening magnitudes. Their entire galaxy had been sucked in and expelled elsewhere, like a vacuum-blender. Fractured molecules and force propelled and inverted, Althea and Eithar were split and merged with the matter of their own galaxy.

Aspects merged with basic sympathy; like paired with like. Magnetizing energies melted together in the push and pull of gravity. New elements were created and blasted through tears in time and space created in the implosion. A seam ripped open. A horn torus within a horn torus surrounded a center pinhole of excited ionized plasma.

Eithar felt his consciousness stretch away from Althea, but small parts of her remained with him, and him with her. Eithar felt pieces of his creations link onto him, like the red metallic scales of the Kitsune. Their particles merged with his own matter. This was an unexpected outcome.

Only small pieces of Althea remained with him; she was not lost, but she did not feel near. The sensations of merging with new particles climaxed until all became quiet and still, and Eithar was surrounded by the senseless darkness of space. He was soaring through darkness with a velocity from the blast, and his memory was hazy and fragmented. All was quiet, and in the quiet void, the memory of his life as Eithar recessed into dormancy.

Layer 26: Izar - Remembering Eithar

zar had to walk for quite a while to get picked up by a vehicle. A truck headed in his direction finally slowed and scooped him up. The driver was a young man, dashingly handsome; even Izar noticed that. He introduced himself as James; he was enthusiastic and spoke decent Spanish. He was clearly French, his accent thick in his throat. His hair was perfectly cut and styled, his face clean-shaven. Izar, was not aware of how quickly he had become unaccustomed to speaking to another human about simple matters, involving simple things. James was upbeat and curious, so it would be a rather long ride.

"Where are you headed?" James asked.

"I just came off of a long mountain-hiking expedition. I'm returning home towards Guernica," Izar replied, his voice rough. He cleared his throat as politely as possible; luckily the roaring of the truck broke the uncomfortable intimacy of the cab.

"Ah, you are far from home, a long journey. You are an adventurer? Now that the war is far enough behind us, it feels safe again, somehow," James said, with interested eyes searching far out on the road ahead of them, one hand gripping the wheel while the other held a cigarette. His window was cracked to pull the smoke out like a vacuum. He was lost in reverie; thinking, perhaps, about adventure.

"Where are you headed, James?" Izar asked politely.

"I am making a shipment delivery to a port in Santander, so lucky for you, your town is on my route!" James piped up proudly while he sucked down cigarette smoke.

Time passed, and the men didn't speak much. Izar stared out the window, and wondered how he would tell his family that he would be leaving. He would miss his mother's face, and worry that she wouldn't understand, thinking her only son was abandoning her. He shook his mind from it, and decided to think of Indra instead. He imagined her face, and her touch. He wondered about the rest of her untold story when the truck lurched slightly, distracting him from his thoughts.

"Whew, nasty potholes in these roads; lost a tire before on these heavy trucks!" James said, rolling his shoulders back as if he were prepping for a sport. "So, did you find anything interesting out there in the woods?" James asked, prodding for a story, adding, "I hear strange things happen in those woods, dark things that'll turn your blood cold and twist the mind. At least, that is what my Nanna believes, but she is a superstitious old woman."

"Not particularly..." Izar trailed off, wondering what to say, "I was looking for a few species of herbs for my family's herb nursery. I didn't find the bulbs, but I came across some seeds. I am glad the journey wasn't a loss; on the bright side, I did rather enjoy the stars and Moon." Izar hoped that his story felt convincing enough, and that James wouldn't pry further.

James tilted his head, nodded to himself; he turned and looked down at the ring on Izar's finger, just out of the corner of his eye. The sight of it made him freeze; his neck stiffened, and his eyes zipped back to the road.

"That's a mighty fancy ring you have there, from an oak tree no doubt, strong wood. Wherever did you get that?" James said through his teeth, his eyes straight forward, looking at the road.

Izar's mouth became dry, and he swallowed, imagining Indra's face and relaxing. In a calm collected voice, he responded, "It belonged to my mother's friend. She travels all over Europe, trading and selling strange objects. It fits me now that I'm older; when I was a boy I had to wear it around my neck on a chain..." Izar trailed off, looking out his passenger window, which was half rolled down. He decided to move the conversation along, move it towards something else. Something felt weird about this man all of a sudden.

"What is it you are delivering? Do you enjoy what you do?" Izar asked, hoping the question didn't come out too fast.

James turned and spat out the window, and sat straight again; he made one short menacing glance at Izar and turned his head back towards the road. "I am delivering supplies to a group of people. The details are not relevant, but it is important I make my delivery on time. I am never late for a job," James said, pulling at his collar with one finger, loosening it from his neck. Then he pulled out another cigarette from his shirt pocket and lit it.

"I see," Izar said, a little unnerved by the vague answer. What were the odds he had gotten picked up by a criminal? Maybe this man was involved with the warlords. Izar tried to calm himself down, and focused on getting home. He imagined the smell of it; he imagined the texture of the blankets on his bed, and the warmth of the Sun in the greenhouse. These memories calmed him down, and he tried not to notice that ever since the man saw his wooden ring, he had been acting strange. His movements were abrupt and erratic, shifting in his seat; his energy was anxious as he smoked one cigarette after the other.

Nearly three hours had passed, and Guernica was coming up when he recognized a street that was close enough. He offered that this would be a good stop; he needed to stretch his legs and walk a bit.

James slowed the truck down and put it in park. He turned to Izar, his red-amber eyes searching for something in him. James removed one glove and reached out his hand to shake Izar's. Izar took a deep breath and shook it, looking him directly in the eye, wary of the grip and eye contact.

"Thanks for the ride, James."

James held his hand a little longer than normal, and then released it slowly, as if disappointed. "Yah, sure..." James said, his eyes distant and baffled. His face looked as if he had been told terrible news. A look of vacancy and dread drained the color from his skin, as he put his glove back on.

Izar leapt out the car and shut the door, grateful he had escaped that nightmare of a ride. As soon as the truck was out of sight, he began running, running fast towards home. Something inside of him told him to run, and get as far away from that truck as he possibly could. Luckily it wasn't far, and knew a way through a few farmlands that met up with a meadow. He ran the whole way home, boosted by the strange feeling that the man had left him with, like a bad taste in his mouth he couldn't wash out. There was something familiar about it, like deja vu, but not in the good way.

When he spotted his home, he was relieved and slowed to catch his breath. As he walked up the pathway, he wondered who that strange man was, and what he was delivering? He was withholding secrets, the kind of secrets that could sink a ship. His amber eyes were nearly red in hue, the sight of them burned into Izar's brain. There was something dark and twisted beneath his fidgeting demeanor. It was almost like the man had changed along the three-hour ride. He was such a cheery man when he had picked Izar up.

But at last he was home, and the sheer relief of getting away nearly brought him to tears. He would see his mother and father, and then be off again to be with Indra.

As he approached the door, he saw that his mother was in the greenhouse. He wasn't sure what he would say to her yet, but he knew he had to start somewhere, so he dropped his bag and made for the greenhouse. Lila turned at the sound of footsteps on gravel, and her face was wet with tears. The look of surprise in her eyes was telling. When he was standing before her, she gave him a small smile and began to cry.

She moved forward to hug Izar, and he held his mother for a long time. His shirt grew wet with her tears. Her body felt limp and frail, as if she hadn't been eating much.

"I'm here, Mother. I'm so sorry I left you for so long on your own," Izar hushed in a soothing whisper, his baritone cracking at the end. Lila sobbed even louder, her cries turning to hyperventilation. "Mother, what is going on? Where is father?" Izar asked, pulling back and staring at her, gripping her delicate shoulders.

Lila was quiet, and looked down; she sucked in air and held it, until she couldn't keep it in. "He died at sea two weeks ago... a storm hit, and he went overboard..." Lila sobbed a few more tears. "In the chaos, the crew couldn't find him, the swells were forty feet... they lost Thomas as well," Lila said, solemnly sniffling, her face a wet mess.

"And you, you were nowhere to be found, off for a trip in the woods, only never to return! Both of my men were lost, and I have been here alone," Lila said, with the icy coldness and hurt of a woman abandoned.

Izar did not have the words to explain or to soothe her; but he held his mother again, and this time he was crying as well. The loss of his father, and the thought of his mother here alone with no one... What a selfish fool he was! Izar held his mother until they were both thirsty from all the tears shed.

They moved into the house and Izar opened all the windows, and decided to start a fire inside in the woodstove. Even though it wasn't all that cold out, he felt he needed something to do now that the Sun was going down. He knew he needed the element of fire to surround him.

He chopped some wood and brought it inside. Lila sat on the sofa, staring off into the distance. Izar, without thinking, grabbed two candles, one white and one black; a glass of water; an agate stone; and a single stick of incense, and then he organized an altar for his father Bolivar. He walked through the house until he found a photo of his father. This picture was a portrait shot, his sharply trimmed beard and bright eyes frozen in time. His face was traditionally stoic, but the edges of a smile turned the corners of his mouth. The story went that it was taken of him just after he had met Lila; apparently nobody could get him to stop smiling, except for this one photo, and even then, it was borderline passing.

Izar was quiet and stood there with his grief, staring at the photo now nestled in the altar along with the other items; the great bear of a man, honest and hard-working, stared back at him. There would be no more stories of fishing around this hearth. Lighting the candles and incense with a burning stick from the stove, Izar said a few words out loud for his father.

"Father, Bolivar, one of the best men I ever knew," He paused swallowing the hard knot in his throat. "..Who raised me to be a man. To be strong, but to be humble, to be proud, but not arrogant. May the ocean carry your soul to the next beautiful sunrise; may you know that I feel so proud to be your son." Tears rolled down to his beard, and his voice cracked with the sentiment. "...The way you loved Mom gave me courage, a strength to walk through this world armed with the knowledge that love, pure love, exists. I am forever grateful for that teaching. I honor your life, and all you have done for everyone around you. I love you, Bolivar, and I will miss you." Izar sat in front of the fire on the floor and stared into it, losing himself to the trance of the flames. He left the room in his mind, and he left his body; all was momentarily dark.

A great source of light and warmth started growing from the center of his consciousness, and suddenly he was in a sunny place, a place of fire and sunlight. Golden light surrounded him, and in the distance, someone walked towards him. A shadowy figure, tall and regal, came closer and closer until the blur of a man became clear. A bright smile and green eyes greeted him; it was Bolivar, his father. He didn't look exactly the same, but he knew it to be his father. He would recognize those green eyes anywhere. They were saturated to the purest version of green Izar had ever seen.

"Izar, how is your mother?" Bolivar asked, his voice low and clear, his face serious and curious.

"She is not well; she is in a great deal of pain," Izar said gravely. "I'm not sure what to do, Father."

Bolivar nodded, acknowledging the news of Lila. "Lila has been my only love, for all of time that I have known. Sometimes when we choose a life, we cannot always steer the ship; the waves were high, and they pulled me in. She and I will have to try again. Finding her on this Earth has never been easy, but I never give up." Bolivar looked upwards at the source of the bright light, and then back to Izar. "You know, you and I have more in common than you think, and I hope that you accomplish what you came here to do... or undo." He chuckled to himself and smiled, his teeth showing with great amusement.

Izar didn't speak, but instead tried to savor the words, and digest them in his mind.

"You should be getting back. Comfort her, but also know that you must go back to the Irati, as painful as that choice is," Bolivar advised, as he reached out and grabbed Izar in a long bear-hug. The warm, fatherly hug gave Izar strength, courage even, to face his challenges ahead.

When Izar opened his eyes, he was back in the warm living room of his home, staring into the flaming woodstove. He held onto Bolivar's words as if clutching a diamond in a room full of thieves, not wanting to lose a single letter. He immediately stood up and grabbed a pen and paper, writing down what he remembered.

Lila stared at Izar, and asked if everything was all right. Izar nodded as he scribbled, half-responding to her. When he set the pen down, he stood and handed her the paper, as he was not sure what else to do.

"I saw him, Mom, in a place surrounded by suns." Izar said shrugging, "This is what he said to me, and maybe it will bring you comfort somehow."

Of course, the words brought welling tears to her face, like a faucet leaking. Her hands were shaking when she set down the paper, and she closed her eyes.

"What is in the Irati Forest, Izar? Where the hell have you been? You have never vanished for so long without a warning!" Lila scolded, her tone sharp and motherly; the anger beneath her grief was plain, and rightfully so.

Izar kneeled, sitting before her on the ground. He held her hand, and cleared his throat, but the words were still caught there. How could he just tell her about all the incredible things he'd seen, and have her actually believe him? It was an incredibly hard thing to swallow when you were not there seeing for yourself.

"Mother, Lila, for my whole life, you and Elenuta have encouraged a magic within me. You passed on ceremonies and information of a world beyond this one. Out in the woods, nearly two months ago, I found it out there in the Irati Forest. I passed into the Fae realm." Izar paused, and looking down from side to side, collecting himself, said, "I never meant to leave you in the dark for so long. Time doesn't exactly work in the same way there..." he trailed off, hoping Lila would understand and not chastise him.

Lila looked at Izar's hand holding hers, her eyes fixated on the wooden ring and the gold symbols slicing through it, thin and ancient filaments catching the light. She noticed on which finger he wore the ring; it was the traditional marriage ring finger. She took a deep breath that was quivering with the echo of tears shed in the long weeks, her throat tight with the strain of sorrow.

"Izar, this ring, the symbols, the oak... my mother had an artifact resembling this ring. They were family heirlooms, rather, that were to be passed on to any first-born daughters. My mother had shared that these artifacts came from our ancestral grandmother Adalinde, who lived in the 1300s. My elder sister, Emma, bore the birth order to receive the gifts. Emma has also been blessed with a daughter, so the relics will pass on to her daughter when the time is right. Having a son or daughter didn't seem to make a difference in my mind, but so the family tradition goes." She paused, running a cool finger lightly over the surface of the ring.

"I remember the artifacts so clearly. There was a twisted piece of oak; it had these same golden symbols, thin slices like thread. I would hold it and hope one day it would be passed onto me, knowing full well it would go to Emma. My mother taught me the ceremonies and alluded to the Fae kingdom, the natural world. It was a very important and secret tradition in our family. The other heirloom was a ruby chalice, and when the Moon was right, we were to drink from it and honor our ancestors." Lila looked thoughtful, cherishing her memories. "Izar, the ring you are wearing looks like it could have been part of that twisted wooden wand; it's uncanny. Who gave this to you?" Lila asked, eyes imploring.

Izar's eyes were wide with confusion, as his mother had never shared any information about these heirlooms before. Perhaps it was a tender memory, as she was not the eldest and never bore a daughter. Izar exhaled a big breath. "Mother, I have met the Lady of the Forest, and I am deeply in love with her. She is part of my purpose; she has the eyes I have been searching for my whole life. Part of myself has lit up, a part of myself I didn't know existed. I have promised to return; I have pledged myself to her. She has given me this ring, and is awaiting my return... but I cannot abandon you in this place and time, not with Father gone," Izar said, choking up with tears; he lowered his head and began to weep quietly, weeping tears that exposed his soul, which was being torn in two.

"This is all very difficult to swallow, but I should understand more than anyone. I will not be the one to stop you. As it stands, my sister Emma is moving to America with her children and husband. In light of my recent loss, as I assumed the worst, that you too were dead, Emma suggested that I leave this country and start over. She offered housing with her family till I found my way. Their children are grown, but they all wish to travel as a family and start a new life," Lila said. wiping the tears from her face and straightening her skirt.

"I have agreed to move with them. They have already arranged for the transport and housing. I have already started my paperwork for my visa. There is nothing left for me here." Lila stood and walked across the room, up to the altar that Izar had assembled. She traced her finger on the glass over the photograph of her beloved.

Izar remained kneeling with the news. *What will become of the house, the garden, the greenhouse?* he wondered. This was what it felt like to commit and surrender to a newly-forming path. The fall of the tower was well underway, and bricks that he had laid so carefully were now loose and giving way to greater calls from destiny.

Izar stayed with Lila for a week, helping her pack and prepare for her journey across the ocean. She coveted some of Bolivar's sweaters and belongings, smelling each item with deep breaths as she packed

them into her suitcase. There wasn't much she could take, and luckily
Lila was a simple woman who never required many things.

Izar spent time helping his mother with the financial paperwork,
squaring up taxes and preparing the house deed to be transferred to his
name. She made him promise that he would not sell the home under
any circumstances, in case she wanted to return. He would have to
figure out how to maintain the home while time passed rapidly in the
other realm, but he promised he would never sell it. There was time
spent cleaning up the greenhouse, and cleaning out the kitchen. The
house started to feel less and less like home as the days moved along.

Lila would be leaving in a few more days, and Izar would take her
to the port himself and see her off. It did not lighten the load of his
loss, but it certainly altered the tone, as he wouldn't be abandoning his
mother again.

The day was bright, and the weather was promising. Despite the
recent storm that took her husband overboard, Lila did not show fear
or anxiety of the sea. Rather, she looked as if she were joining him. In
the salted air, the sea was his true grave, and he would be guiding her
to a new home. Izar hugged his mother for a long time, and they didn't
say much to one another, although Lila looked at Izar as if she had
many things to say, but no energy to convey all her words.

She turned and he watched her walk away. Despite her age, his
mother was youthful and gorgeous; heads turned as she made her way
onto the boat. Izar fought his desire to defend her from the looming
eyes of gawking men nearby, as her beauty would always turn heads;
so Izar contained his urges to punch the sailors who were standing
with their jaws slightly ajar, their eyes following Lila as she gracefully
walked up wooden ramp. Lila's sister Emma greeted her at the top, two

beautiful women off to a new world. They both turned and waved down at Izar; he returned the wave, bowed slightly, and turned to go.

That felt like the last time he would see his mother. She would write, but her letters would likely pile up at the house that he now owned.

From the port, Izar himself was packed for the forest, his father's knife at his belt and his mother's necklace on his chest. He found a ride back towards the Irati. He was hoping that he would not see James again, and his wish came true. He rode along with a quiet man, and it was a silent and pleasant ride. Before he knew it, it was only an hour's hike into the forest before he could hold Indra again. His anticipation was like water rolling at a boil.

The weather stayed pleasant, but the skies became overcast, and perhaps rain was on its way. Before long, Izar was back at Indra's home tree, where he had last seen her. He sat down and sank into a state of silence; he slowed his breath and cleared his mind. The birds were making strange calls in the background of his awareness, and rain started to drip, drop, down onto the leaves of the trees. Izar focused on the wood of the ring and called out to Indra in his mind. Faintly and translucently, she appeared before him, and kneeled down beside him, grabbing his hand and pulling him back into her world. He didn't have time to blink. The rain around them ceased, and Izar was finally back. He was stunned by the sight of her, as she had somehow become more beautiful in their short time apart.

Not many words were exchanged initially. Izar and Indra stood together and sank into an embrace that lasted an immeasurable amount of time. Something happened to Izar when they stood physically connected; beyond feeling utterly and completely at home he was filled with visions. He had visions of another time, and another life.

Izar let go of Indra and leaned back enough to kiss her slowly and softly on both sides of her face. He felt so comfortable being close to her, breathing her in. He did not rush anything; he was controlled and steady in her presence, ready to go anywhere and do anything for her.

Indra led them to a place to sit; she wanted to hear what had happened when he returned, and learn how his family had reacted to his departure. She wanted to know how it all made him feel. She was prodding to see if he would be staying for long, still uncertain of his ability to stay true to his word. She was well aware that life happens, and it didn't always stick to the brain's plan.

They walked into a clearing, where there was a warm breeze and tall flowers effusing a scent like hyacinths. They sat on soft moss that formed to their comfort. When they settled in, Indra turned to Izar. "How was your journey? How is your heart?"

Izar began to speak. "It was actually quite an emotional journey, as it all started with a strange ride home. The man who drove me to town was peculiar. He gave me the weirdest feeling in the pit of my stomach, like a man with two personalities. When he saw this ring his mood shifted dramatically; his manners became curt and rigid," Izar said, shaking his head upon recalling how bizarre the interaction was.

Indra sat tall, and turned her head to Izar with an immediate question: "What color were his eyes?"

Taken aback by the quick question, Izar thought backwards, straining in his memory, "Um, they were a red-amber I believe, not a very typical eye color; I remember that. He was curious about the strange things that happened in the forest too, as he had asked what I was doing out on the edge of it."

Indra closed her eyes and exhaled; she looked concerned. "Mm, tell me more, what else happened?" Indra asked. This made Izar confused; why would she be concerned with a truck driver, and let alone his eye color? But he let it go.

"I eventually made it home," Izar said, finishing his story, while Indra stared off vacantly, appearing to listen. "I found my mother in our greenhouse, hollow with grief. My father had died at sea two months after I had disappeared. With no word from me, she was left alone with the grief, mourning the loss of two. I entered into quite an emotional storm. I felt so hurt, my heart shattered, knowing that I had let her down and abandoned her to be left alone." Izar spoke quietly, small tears welling in his eyes. He cleared his throat, and continued. "My mother had plans, though, to leave; and she left for North America, with her sister and her family. So I helped her tend to her affairs and saw her off," Izar said simply; but if you looked closely, it was clear he missed his mother and his father. Indra hoped that time would mend these wounds.

Indra moved towards him on the moss and stretched open her arms, hugging Izar and kissing his temples lightly. "I'm sorry about your father; it is a great sadness. Your mother will rest well knowing that you are alive and well; perhaps there will be a time to see her again." Indra said in a soothing tone.

His eyes lit up, though, upon remembering that he wanted to mention his grandmother's heirlooms, and how his mother had recognized the ring's pattern and symbols. "Indra, there was something specific I wanted to tell you about my mother. She recognized the ring you made for me, the wood and its golden symbols. It was identical, she said, to an heirloom that has been passed down to the women who bore daughters in her family. She recalled from her childhood a twisted

426

wand of oak with the same markings. They were taught about this realm and used it for ceremonies, like a family tradition. There was another artifact as well: a carved ruby chalice that she remembers drinking from when she was a child. Isn't that strange?" Izar asked, tilting his head.

Indra's eyes went wide, and she nearly leapt to her feet. She stepped back and her face twisted into a strange expression. She was clearly thinking, calculating, and then looking up to closely analyze Izar's face.

"Izar, there is more to my story, that you must know, but it will take some time to straighten out. Instead of using words, let me share the memories with you, so you can see for yourself. There is something you must know," Indra stated, her shoulders and sternum dropping with an emptying sigh.

Izar was truthfully exhausted; he had just made it through an emotional spiral of loss. He did not understand what Indra meant, but he nodded. "I will gladly share your memories," he said, clearing a terribly parched throat. Before they lay down, Indra passed Izar some water from a vessel she was wearing. In it was the most delicious water of the water temple; it was purifying, and put Izar at ease when it touched his lips. It felt like coming home.

Lying down, Indra touched Izar's forehead, and off they went into her memories. She shared the fall of Fengári, the rise of the virus, and her eventual involvement with Iós. She avoided sharing the erotic and sexual memories, but she shared the birth, and the exchange with Adalinde. Izar watched, as if within a dream, the woman leave with the curling wooden wand, a ruby chalice, a child, and a white wolf. These were the artifacts his mother had described.

When the memories were complete, the two laid there on the moss with wide eyes, hands lightly touching. Izar was calculating in his mind the generations between him and Adalinde. His mind was fuzzy with the news of his ancestral lineage. He was, in fact, distantly related to the virus and Indra. They laid there, slowly moving towards one another without a word. They lay cuddled up without speaking, nor moving much. Their minds were both busy with thoughts and feelings. Wires crossed that had never crossed before.

If Izar was honest with himself, he did not really care if they were distantly related. If anything, it made more sense that he was drawn to her in the first place. He had just lost his father and mother, and he knew, even with this strange twist of fate, that he still loved her. His love went past the genetic combinations; he knew he was destined to be with her... although her love for the virus was a detail he could not ignore, as it made his stomach turn. Within his lineage he connected with Iós, and that was hard to understand.

"Indra, that must have been a huge secret, and so hard to hold in for so long. I'm sorry for the loss of your child; that must have been the most difficult choice." Izar whispered as he ran his palm through her hair. "You are a part of the reason I stand here before you today; you have brought me here in more ways than one. I do not know the customs of your land, but in human culture, it is considered unethical to be in romantic union with a family member... Unless you are royalty. I, for one, do not care for the rules, and these circumstances have a great deal of time between them. Forgive my forward assumption in you sharing your memory, but know it doesn't change how I feel," Izar told her, readjusting his arms underneath Indra and pulling her closer.

Indra had small, quiet tears running down her face. They were not accompanied by anguish nor contortion; the tears merely slipped down her expression-less cheeks.

Izar continued, filling the silence, "I also must mention a strange detail your memory has ignited. The eyes of the truck driver, James, were strikingly similar to those of Iós in your memories. Is it possible he still looks for you in the woods after all these years, waiting? Perhaps he is causing the conflicts in the countries that surround your Forest, to smoke your kind out. In the car, he grabbed my hand and held it for a long while, and when nothing happened, he looked disappointed."

Izar sucked in the air and made more conclusions internally in his mind. If Indra was immune to the virus's infiltration, then perhaps so was he. It was destined. But what could Iós possibly be doing lingering around the woods? Izar thought of the man that gave him the ride out only hours ago; was that Iós as well? Could he have followed him out here, to Indra's tree?

Izar shot up, his thoughts catching up to him. Indra was startled, but seemed to feel the conclusions that formed in his mind. "I do not think he can harm us here; he has no way of entering." She tried to sound reassuring, but her voice gave away her uncertainty. She moved slowly like a cat to sit up. "It is not unnatural to love within a distant family lineage here in the Fae, if you were curious. And as for my personal thoughts on the matter, I feel confused and astonished to know that you are the descendant of my child, the chain of events from my giving birth all those centuries ago. It was long ago, and my feelings for you have not changed. Within reason, the soul is what is important, despite the vessel. The genetics that created you have their purpose and influence, but they are not the only element at play here."

At that Izar leaned in and kissed Indra lightly on her flower-petal soft lips. It was a gentle kiss. It was full of understanding. His body felt no different in light of the recent news. Electric currents of passion zipped up his spine, and he knew that everything he felt for Indra still remained strong and true. He didn't care about Iós or his lineage, although he was grateful for the role it had played in getting him to her.

When he pulled away, he saw the corners of Indra's mouth curl up, and she looked relieved that, despite all her darkest secrets, she was still worthy of love. Izar did not judge her. He was too unconditionally available to support and love her. She felt oddly proud and relieved. Her long lost Eithar had made it to her, at last.

They sat and enjoyed the sweet comfort of their reunion. They lay, glued together, with no space between them. Izar found it easier to control himself; in light of all the information, this was not the time for anything complex.

Out of nowhere, Indra lurched forward in pain, squirming and moaning to cope, her sounds of agony breaking their shared silence. Moving onto her knees, she bent at the hips into a fetal position, slightly rocking. She gasped and swayed from side to side, flinching with patterns of sharp pain. Izar's face was a combination of worry and surprise.

"Indra, what can I do?" Izar said moving to comfort her, checking her body for the cause of pain.

"Something is wrong; we need to go to my tree." Indra said through her teeth, "Will you go with me there, carry me? I'll call Beaudry to help," Indra said, making an otherworldly sound to call for Beaudry.

Izar had Indra wrapped in his sweater and was carrying her when Beaudry arrived. Their face startled and their eyes calculated the scene. "Something is wrong with her tree. We must go to it; can you lead the way?" Izar said with urgent clarity. He was calm, but he felt wild with concern on the inside; he would not lose her, too!

Beaudry, quick to assemble, helped Izar, and they swiftly moved through the tall grass and back to the tree. They saw that her tree had sections in it that were gray and lifeless, like spots of disease infecting the trunk. The two laid Indra down in the twist of her roots, and she sank into the tree like water. Beaudry looked at Izar and was confused, but knew now was not the time for questions. In a flash, Beaudry was gone, and returned, just as fast, their face startled with horror.

"A man is cutting the tree! He has an axe and a saw, and he is wild with madness! He was calling out wildly, saying he would keep doing this until she showed herself." Beaudry was shocked in disbelief. "I knew this day would come; it was only a matter of time before Iós found her tree." It was clear Beaudry knew of their connection.

"Beaudry, I know we haven't met, but can you move me back into the mortal realm? I must see what I can do to stop him from causing her pain!" Izar ordered, urgently.

Beaudry nodded, and grabbed Izar by the hand. *Snap,* and he was back in the mortal realm. It was sunset, and he was face-to-face with James, the truck-driver. Izar had his father's knife and little experience with fighting, especially with an ageless man bearing the strength of many creatures. James, or Iós rather, looked disappointed; he shrugged and laughed at Izar.

"Well, I suppose this would be better bait; you were easy enough to follow here, like a dumb lamb leading the wolf to the flock. You are no threat to me, not with your father's knife; you will be easy to kill," James said with a voice so dark he could hide shadows in it.

Izar was admittedly startled by the sudden situation he was in; he knew it would be a stroke of luck if he survived. But he was loyal to Indra, and could not see her destroyed by this monster. He would do whatever he could to stop him from destroying the tree. Izar could feel Iós pervading his mind, seeping into it. It was as if his abilities to perceive went far beyond the average human capability. So Izar closed his mind and emptied it of thought, as he had done so many times before. It was then he felt a great power well up inside of him, along with a gust of great wind.

"Why would she pick you when she could have me?" Iós spat through gritted teeth, taking slow steps toward Izar. Iós held a large weighted axe in his hands, swinging it with measured motions. Iós moved like a natural predator, slowly advancing.

Izar moved to grab his father's knife; it was warm to the touch, as if it had been sitting near a fire. He moved closer to Iós, and quickly slid past him using his legs to slide low to the ground on the wet leaves. Using the sharp curved blade as he slid past, he managed to cut the back of Iós' Achilles tendon on one leg. Iós made a grunting sound, irritated; he used his other leg to support him, throwing him off balance. Without much momentum, Izar was low to the ground, just past Iós. When he tried to roll away, Iós clocked him in the head with the butt of his axe, knocking him out cold.

This was when Indra made her appearance in the mortal realm, just as Iós was making moves to finish Izar.

"Stop! Iós, what madness are you bringing to my forest? How dare you!" Indra screamed, her voice loud and protective. She moved roots from the Earth to hold down the legs of Iós, binding him where he stood. Izar was carried up out of reach, being cradled by vines that protected his limp body.

"You found yourself a new lover, I see. He is brave, but he is weak. He is no match for me, Indra. Why have you hidden from me, never a word, nor a goodbye?" Iós spat, his voice hot with anger. "I came back year after year, and you were nowhere to be found."

Indra's eye narrowed when she replied, "Iós, there was no erasing the monster in you; you did not change the wars, the death toll, the enslavement of the souls, who cycle lifetime after lifetime just to fulfill your conquest!" Indra said, her body growing taller and her voice more ominous.

Iós didn't flinch, not even a little.

"I gave you a chance to show me who you really were, and I saw that you did nothing to change it." The words fell from Indra's mouth like icicles.

Iós maintained a blank face, calculating, looking for a way to manipulate the situation, as he knew full well he could not repaired the mess he had made. Eyes lighting up, he changed the subject, his face hurt and angry.

"I heard rumors you bore a child... and gave it away to a human. Is that true?"

Indra blinked, her eyes darting to Izar, and then back to Iós. "There was a child. I would have died rather than see you anywhere near her. You are no influence for innocent life," Indra spat again, like a bear protecting its cub.

"Very well, then, if that is how it must be between us. I'm sorry, Indra, truly. You give me no choice; I will find you in another form, where you cannot hide from me," Iós said as he pulled a grenade from his pocket. When he pulled the pin, he grinned madly and then tossed the small metal egg onto the tangle of roots at the base of her tree. Before Indra had time to blink, her tree was obliterated; smoke and fire filled the sky.

A deafening blow struck Izar's ears from what felt like the inside out; he was startled awake to the chaos. His blurry eyes saw fire and smoke; he saw Indra look up at him, and her body collapsed to the ground, dissolving into ash and embers. He had failed her. He couldn't believe his eyes; his whole journey and plan had been obliterated. The rumors about explosions were true: all he could hear was ringing. while particles of Indra's tree and the Earth were falling around him, light pieces of ash floating to the ground. Izar was still weak from the blow to his head, and he lost consciousness again.

Within the dreamy darkness of his mind, his heart echoed with pain and loss for his family and for his beloved. He drifted through what felt like space, a void of blackness with beacons of light, gems suspended in the distance. Like a fish on a line, he was being pulled somewhere. The force of gravity was pulling his soul from its center, like a sail with a force of wind behind it.

He was pulled through blackness, with small jewels of light surrounding him in the darkness. Eventually, the pulling ceased and he was on the other end of that blackness. His soul integrated into a celestial body of familiar light. Aware of himself as bodiless, he could feel that he was a collection of small particles and elements. After some time spent floating, being pulled in what felt like a circular orbit, memories poured into him. An epiphany of where and who he was hit him like a flash of light. He was a cosmic deity; his name was Eithar, and he was entangled with another cosmic deity, his counterpart, Althea.

Memories like waves of information entered his mind, in which he was able to perceive beyond the small scale of his human self. But in that moment, he understood it all; everything made sense and it all came to him so easily. Memories of their small worlds and all of the creatures that existed on them. Images moved through him, like a quick tour. They were wonderful and unlike the creatures he knew from Earth. There was a newfound comfort in understanding of where he was from. He wasn't worried about his mother, or Indra; he didn't fear the loss of his human self or human death.

The two of them were orbiting the ledge of the black hole from Nagda 3147, ready to see what journey their creation would take them on. He was aware that this action was the catalyst for his experiences beyond this place. He observed Althea, and noticed bravery and anticipation emanating from her. It was palpable that she was ready for transformation, which he observed was different from his own internal feelings. He was not ready to die, nor to change. There were too many variables. He did not want to lose her; what if this was the last time he would stand beside her? These feelings hinted at the direction in which their journeys might take them.

The last thing he saw as his soul was stretched back through the blackness was Althea in her otherworldly form: a true goddess, magnanimous and wise, with beauty beyond beauty. Izar knew, as he tumbled back through the blackness, with absolute certainty, that Althea was also Indra, just as he was Eithar. That this was them before Earth. It all made so much sense to him there in that liminal place in space. Their universe was pulled inside out and sprinkled through spacetime; small bits and pieces of their world found their way into

Earth's galaxy. Their souls, their consciousnesses, fell like scattered seeds, only to mature into self-realization.

When Izar woke, he was on the ground under a blanket of moss, no doubt from Beaudry. They must have tended to his wounds, as his head wound was wrapped and cleaned with a foreign silken fabric. He laid there for a while and let his body relax while he recounted his vision and fortified it into his memory. It pained him to know that Indra was gone, but he also knew he would be able to find her again. Iós was nowhere to be found; he had disappeared after the chaos. Izar feared he would return for him in his weakened state, but perhaps he thought that Izar was dead, and had left him to bleed out.

Iós never came; and every time Izar slept, he woke with water and Jubees at his side. When he regained his strength, Izar left the woods, being sure to thank the forest spirits every step of the way.

His life after the fallout was lonely, and Izar kept to himself and his garden. He stayed in the Basque countryside for a couple of years. He used his solitude to write a memoir of sorts, from all that he experienced in his life until when he lost consciousness in the woods. He wrote about Indra, the realm of the Fae; and he wrote about Iós and the tale of the virus. Writing it down was the only way he could make sense of everything. He even took the time to translate some of it into English, as he knew he would be headed to the United States soon to be with his mother. He would never forget who he was, who he was from the beginning of it all, and perhaps someday someone else would be able to understand it too. He was Eithar, and one day he would reunite with Althea.

Izar wrote to his mother, telling her what had happened and that he wanted to come live with her. He found a caretaker for the family home and took a boat across the ocean to see his mother in North

America. All he brought with him was his leather-bound diary, a small duffle bag of clothes, and his wooden ring. He was wistful, sorrow lightly aging his face, but his beard was cut cleanly and his silver eyes were still bright. The cool, salted air kissed his cheeks and forehead, like sprites in a meadow. He felt comforted by his father's soul, which protected him as the boat bobbed onward to new beginnings.

Layer 27: Iós - Burning Bridges

After the grenade blew, Iós' eyes were cold and hardened, and still tears fell from them. Despite the monster he had become, he still loved Indra, a pain that had driven him mad with power and destruction. He walked from the woods till he reached the truck he had left on the forest's edge.

He strained at the truck's heavy door, which screeched with disdain, one long, hollow sound. He then drove himself an hour to a small cottage. It was private, quaint, built by James' father. When he made it inside, he took a clean vial from a cabinet in the mud room. He dropped in a utensil he had used to collect samples of blood. When Izar was incapacitated, he had used that opportunity to climb up and collect samples from his bleeding head. He had to figure out why yet another person was immune to his power of invasion. He labeled the vial, and then went back outside and around to the back of the cottage. Amongst the trees, there was a barn where large cages held many different birds of prey. Iós gravitated towards a barn owl, and opened the cage. He slowly fixed the vial onto its talon with a leather strap and buckle.

Whispering gently to the bird, he said, "Nothing to fear, little one." When James was done with the strap, he removed his gloves, and reached his hand out to take over the owl's body.

Iós took to the sky, and with the swift stealth of the owl, over many days he made his way towards Germany.

He was headed to Germany because Iós had been involved with instigating and leading the dark genealogical experiments during

WWII in the internment camps. Iós was eager to return, for when the war was over, his team had dissembled and gone into hiding. Some of them remained in Germany, including Joseph Mengele, who was his scientist of choice to embody. He would lead whoever was left to start over in America, under new names and under his command.

It was not safe for anyone involved in the Nazi Regime, but with his power to invade anyone, he could pull strings in any country at any time. He already had his claws infiltrated in the United States, as oil money and industry were taking off and making one of his hosts very wealthy. Iós would use the power of wealth and science from his hosts, and gain monopolized power to rule over all competing forces. There were so many genetic experiments he had to conduct, especially now that he had a small sample of the blood of one who was immune to his power. It was not a very big sample, but it would be a start, a start to understanding the blood of his beloved, and those of others immune to him.

It was not long ago, in fact only a decade, since Karl Landstiener and Iós discovered the Rhesus factor in the blood-typing system. There was a type of blood that interfered with the success rate in human breeding. This blood lacked a protein that collected on the surface of the blood cell, and it was not a common blood type. Together, they named it Rh negative, because it lacked the protein also found in Rhesus monkeys and positive blood types. Each blood type could either have the protein, or lack it.

This discovery really got Iós thinking about Neenah and Imi and Indra and their immunity, thus propelling his quest in science, to take it further than it had ever gone before. Iós needed to know why there were those who were immune to his power, and where they came from. Perhaps one day, he could prevent losing her the next time he found her. He would have solved the mystery and would have all the answers.

Izar was the first male who was immune to his power; this blood would be very important to their experiments. In the concentration camps in Germany, there were a few women that were also immune to his touch and invasion, but they lacked the silver eye color. When typed, those women had AB Rh negative blood. He had saved liters of their blood for further use in deep freeze storage. There were not many ways to use blood or test blood in 1947. Iós was making it his mission to propel science into forward motion, so that he could learn more. Perhaps in learning about the blood that was immune to him, he could learn more about himself.

It took nearly two weeks, but Iós made it to Germany. He arrived at the scientist' safe house in Leipzig. He tapped his beak on the window in a specific pattern, the single pane glass rattling in the quiet of the night. Mengele dutifully approached the window, as he knew that the master of darkness had returned. He had awaited the day the Iós would return and reside within him, as he had before and during the war. When together, they were an unstoppable force of creativity and power.

Joseph bowed after he opened the window; as his body was lowered his eyes caught sight of the leather strap and vial attached to the bird's leg. Moving close, he swiftly removed the items and then reached out to touch the bird gently on its head, tracing the tan heart-shaped mask on the face of the owl. Iós closed his eyes and felt the transformation ensue, currents of himself pouring into Joseph's body like electricity.

As if trying on the fit of a suit and coat, Iós stretched and slowly adjusted himself to the human form. Rolling his head from side to side,

Iós and Joseph opened their eyes. Much like Jushur, they were both aware when the other was in control. It was as if they were running the body in unison. Iós was fond of Joseph, and although his intentions were drawn from a darker well, he had the mind of a genius. There was no compassion or empathy, only logic and method in that man. His emotional blindness led him to make many of his greatest experiments, and even Iós would not be able to ever wash the horrors from his memory.

"Welcome home, Iós; we have been awaiting your return and further guidance," Joseph said as a quiet voice in his own mind.

"I had personal matters to attend to in western Europe. This sample is a rather important specimen; it is blood that needs to be stored properly for testing." Iós began walking towards a kitchen area and put the sample into the icebox.

"I have a plan for our team, a plan to travel somewhere far away, to be free of persecution and the consequences of war. We will go to North America, and I have already arranged to make the process smooth and trouble-free," Iós said with a grin, while he got himself a glass of water.

"I trust your wisdom, and tomorrow we can tell the others and create a plan; for now, perhaps, it's best we rest." Joseph's faint voice was eerie and emotionless.

They both walked down a narrow hallway, the old wooden floors creaking beneath their feet, soon reaching a door that opened to a room with a bed in it. Exhausted from the long flight, Iós removed his clothing, laid down, and covered himself with a few blankets to block the night's chill. It did not take long for sleep to arrive. His sleep was always dreamless, save for a few repetitive nightmares that plagued him.

The Sun was sharp in the early morning, highlighting dust motes that drifted across the room. Musty pink and cream wallpaper peeled at the corners, and the small twin bed with the metal frame creaked as Iós sat up. It was a new day, awaiting plans for the team's new life in the United States. Iós had traveled there and meddled with their political and religious affairs when the country was being founded. Those who traveled across the ocean to escape his monarchy didn't realize it was all still apart of his game. Iós helped instill fear into the men and women, and encouraged them to strip the natives of their power and connection to the land. He told them that the native people posed a threat to their industry and way of life and that they carried 'contagious' diseases. As the years passed, his plan for that country unfolded, especially when big oil came into play.

In the disheveled old room, he gathered his clothing and began dressing himself with methodical care, and chuckled as he thought aloud. "What a scheme, the freedom of the United States. There, I gave the souls enough power to imitate freedom, but disconnected them from finding their own inner light and sense of purpose. No uprising can take place when comforts and freedoms are given."

As he put his legs into a pair of trousers, he pondered how the native people were like the ones that he had lived amongst long ago. They lived simple lives, where technology and travel would have never ever advanced, a boring complacency with the experience at hand.

"How then, could I find her again? How could I solve her immunity to my power without science and order?" Nodding to himself, he justified the culture's dissemination with his own righteousness and hunger for full control. Ala, Neenah, Imi, and Indra were all souls and situations in which he could never control the outcome, but that was all about to change.

Iós was buttoning his shirt slowly and precisely during his mental pep talk, which was fueling his passion for all of the scientific discovery that awaited him and his team. They would sculpt the world into a place where the answers were tangible and documented.

As he bent over to lace his shoes, he thought, "I will not let her die again -- not ever." Iós bit back the tears when Indra's face flashed past his mind's eye, an image of her expression directly before she evaporated in the grenade blast. Smooth, glistening skin and features that displayed sorrow; her cold silver eyes wide with disbelief. He wanted to reach out and call to her, for her to comply and for their chase to end. But she could not hear words unspoken, and she disappeared.

Iós stood back up, his shoes laced tight. He straightened his spine in a confident posture, his chest and chin elevated. He stared at himself in the small, plain mirror that stood before him. His red eyes were leaking small tears as he combed his hair into greased perfection. Iós blinked the tears away and cleared his throat. He brushed back his feelings, and was now ready for his meeting and journey back to the United States of America.

Layer 28: Paesh - Old Artifacts

Tiago drove away and Paesh waved. She was relieved to arrive at Lu's house; it felt like ages had gone by without her seeing him, although Lu was in the dark about all that had happened. She figured there were some things she needed to tell him, and her body was shaking with the day's events. She wanted him to know the truth, before any further feelings unfurled... because right now, her life was heading down path she could not return from, and if Lu wasn't able to handle it, she needed to know.

Lu answered the door. With a look of surprise on his face, he moved in slowly for a hug. Paesh was gentle with his ribs, but moved in close. The envelopment of his arms was instantly soothing. "You're back so soon. I didn't expect you here," Lu said as he pulled back. "Is everything all right? Who dropped you off?"

"Tiago. Lu, can you take me to my house? There's something I need to share with you, but I need to be home to share it," Paesh stately clearly. Her serious face and frazzled hair made her look even more like the wild scientist she was.

Lu nodded with questions in his eyes, and walked inside. He came back with a set of keys and his wallet, and locked his door behind him. He handed the keys to Paesh. "Would you mind driving us there? I'm still on pain meds."

"Sure thing." She took the keys, and swiftly drove them to her house. Lu looked at her home appreciatively, and sighed. "Such a cool house... nice and tucked away from everything. You're like a Faerie or something," he said as he got out of the car, pleasantly enjoying the flowers along her driveway.

"Funny you say that," Paesh said, nearly laughing, walking through the gate. She walked across the yard to refill the cat's food and water dishes. Meanwhile, Lu wandered through the gate at his own pace, admiring her garden property.

"Your garden is marvelous! I absolutely love it here; your wisteria vine is so beautifully twisted, and coming back for a second bloom!" Lu said, reaching up to touch a bud lightly with his finger.

"Yes -- growing things is mostly what I live for, my true joy. It's slow and simple. Watching something take to life and wither to death is so fascinating," Paesh said, wistfully running her hand over the poppies, knocking loose petals to the ground.

"So, what is it you wanted to tell me? Should we take a seat in the garden?" Lu said, sitting on a cushioned swinging seat.

"It's a rather long story. I'll grab us some tea," Paesh replied, disappearing into her kitchen. She soon came out, two glasses in her hands, filled with sun tea and lemon. "For starters, what I'm about to share with you is going to sound crazy," she said, handing Lu a glass. "I'll start by showing you something I saw today, and then I'll explain why I have reason to." Paesh looked conflicted as she pulled out her phone. "Look at this picture." Paesh held up her phone, displaying the photo of the black electric car, like the one Lu had described that had run him off the road. "Does this look familiar? I saw this with Tiago today, in the parking lot at USC's Neurology Lab. The car is also familiar to me, from my own experience."

"That *is* the car, no doubt about it. I've never seen another car like it," Lu said, rubbing the stubble on his jawline. "Do you know who it belongs to?"

"Yes, a Dr. Jacob Allen -- and apparently he's the private investor of the lab that we work at... but I found that out just today. He's very involved in the scientific community here; have you heard of him?" Paesh said, reading Lu's face for clues.

"I *have* heard of him, but didn't know he owned our lab." Lu took a sip of tea and savored the taste, his eyes swelling with concern, as if focusing on a complex puzzle.

Paesh handed him the printouts of the brain scans they'd done on her today. "Tiago and I have been running tests on me, and today we did some brain scans. These are strange results, but I myself can't understand them. I'm not sure if you can either." Paesh took a deep breath, "Aw, shit. I don't know where to start with any of this!"

"Unfortunately, I don't know how to read them either," Lu said, squinting at the numbers and lines on the pages. "Maybe you can start with how you know Dr. Allen." Lu's voice was reassuring, easy and calm.

This was only the second time she'd told anyone what had happened that night, and it felt good to get it out. When she finished her story, Lu's face was blank, as if he were unsure how to respond. He closed his eyes, and when they opened, they gleamed a deeper silver than before. His face was angry, and he was confused; he took a deep breath and calmed himself.

"What a vile man. That's such an odd thing to do to someone... then to pay you off to keep quiet. What the hell? Do you know why he wanted your blood?"

"Not at the time, no, but over the last couple of weeks, it's become clear to me," Paesh said as she stood up. "I need to show you something." She walked into her house, and Lu followed. She headed upstairs into her room. Disappearing into her closet, she started moving boxes out, to make her way to the back of the small space. Eventually, she pulled out the big designer duffel bag full of cash and the dress. Lu calculated the evidence at his feet. Without a word, she then took her laptop from her desk and plugged a USB thumb drive into it -- one she kept hidden in her junk drawer.

She opened the video file of her at the lab with Jeff. She pressed play, and they watched the video together. When the clip ended, she played it again, and then a third time. Paesh sat quietly, and at the end of the third viewing, she let out a huge sigh. "I think this is why Dr. Allen wanted my blood. I know it's a lot to believe, a lot to take in, but that's why Tiago and I are doing tests. Tiago knows because he saw the surveillance footage. He also had to deal with the man who quit, who is the guy I terrified in the video," Paesh said, backing away from Lu, as if to give him space to take it all in.

She sat next to a few open cardboard boxes she had unearthed to reach the bag of cash. On the top of the boxes, there was a wooden box, ornately carved with small designs: the contents of the package that her mother had sent. She had only gotten it recently, but she couldn't open the latch on the wooden box. In her frustration, she'd set it aside. Likely getting distracted, she'd tucked it back with the other forgotten things.

Paesh didn't know much about the contents of the wooden box, except that there was a journal inside. The journal was among the few items her grandfather had left behind for Paesh's mother. Her mother was only fifteen years old when her father took his own life. He left behind an apology note, a journal, some personal affects, all his money, and the deed to his house in Basque country. Her mother likely read and reread that journal till the pages were soft; she was a sentimental and open-minded woman. This same wooden box had sat on his neatly-made bed; his body was found in the woods by the sheriff. He was a natural man, and loved being amongst the trees.

As a young, fatherless girl, her mother grew up fast, and didn't go to college. Instead, she decided to go visit the land the house deed was linked to. Her mother was brave, and traveled through Europe well into her mid-twenties, acquiring strange jobs while seeing the world. Her mother always landed on her feet, like a cat; she was never the type to let life weigh her down. That was how she met Paesh's father, when she was traveling across Europe. Paesh had heard stories of her grandfather many times, and was told that one day, the house would be shared between her sisters.

Paesh stared at the box, and felt the soft carved wood beneath her fingers. Her mind was straining to recall her grandfather's face. She had only ever seen one photo of him, so she couldn't conjure his face as if he were a ghost, lingering in the back of her mind.

Lu cleared his throat, and sipped some tea, "Paesh, forgive me for my silence. I'm processing all of this. It's— well, a lot."

This stirred Paesh from her fugue; she had nearly forgotten he was there for a second. She looked at Lu hopefully while he spoke.

Lu saw that she was listening and continued, "You know, I think that ordinarily, I wouldn't believe such wild claims... but there's evidence all around that connects the dots." He shook his head and inhaled, as if he had smelled something strange. "The most disturbing thing about all of this is how we're connected. The way you appeared in the surveillance video is strikingly similar to the way I see you in my dreams." He ran his hands through his hair and pulled at it slightly. His body was relaxed, though; he was not startled by Paesh's shapeshifting in the video, or by his uncanny dreams. Paesh saw his eyes move to the duffle bag, and she saw anger flash across his face. He was openly disgusted and angry that Dr. Allen had gotten away with hurting her and had likely run him off the road. Paesh could see him asking *why* in his mind, scrounging for reasons.

"The connections don't end there, either. I also know Dr. Allen... well, at least my body does. He was my doctor when I was in the hospital after my accident. Back when I was in a coma." His eyes dropped to the floor, and he inhaled sharply, puffing his chest out with a groan of pain in his throat. "He was only my doctor for the first few weeks, but still, it's odd. When my health was more stable, I was moved into a different part of the hospital, and along with the move, they paired me with a new doctor. I was told I was lucky, as Dr. Allen rarely takes on clinical patients, and that he was one of the best."

Lu rolled his eyes and looked over at Paesh, who was sitting crossed-legged on the floor with the wooden box in her lap. Her head was tilted. She was clearly intrigued and horrified that Lu had brought up being in a coma so casually. They sat together in a space strung together by silence, until Paesh made a remark in a monotonous voice:

"How did you know he was your doctor if you were in a coma?" Her gaze was far away.

"It's on my medical records. They record everything, so there's a list of the doctors who provided care. Their signatures are on all the documents. It's standard."

"Oh, duh, of course. I have more questions... two, actually. One, how did you end up in a coma? Two, why would he want to run you off of the road if he was the man who helped heal you?" Paesh asked, fidgeting with the latch on the box.

Lu nodded, "Well, this all happened just over a year ago. The accident itself I don't actually recall, but I was told that I was surfing on a windy, gray day. Chaotic weather compared to Santa Cruz's normal surf for the season. I had a big ego, and thought I could handle it. I was at a beach up off the 1 North, it's called Bonny Doon, a spot I surfed at routinely. Apparently, a wave sloshed me into some rocks pretty hard, and luckily someone was there to see me struggle and not resurface. It was Jon from the bonsai class... apparently he'd been my friend for years before the accident. Jon knew I had gone out that day, and followed me there. He saved my life..." Lu paused, and his eyes welled with tears.

"I'm sad that I can't recall my friendship with him from before, but he's a man I'm proud to know. It's a strange thing, but I don't remember much of myself from before the coma. Dreams, aspirations, personality quirks, my sense of humor, and all the other bits that make people themselves... I'm completely different now, or so I've been told."

He paused again, and a slight smile crept onto his face. "It was almost like being reborn. I retained a lot of my cognitive abilities pertaining to science, cooking, gardening, and building. It took me a few months to integrate myself into my community and work again, but intellectually, I'm relatively the same."

Paesh took it all of his story in and was astonished. "Wow, that happened really recently! I'm so glad you survived. How long were you in the coma?" Paesh asked, hoping it wasn't rude.

"One month, and then when I woke, I remained in the hospital to recover for a second month," Lu said, nodding, recalling memories that felt so far away now.

"Wow, that's a long time. Thank you for sharing that. It's very fascinating how your brain pressed the reset button when you woke up. I'm sure it came with so many challenges." Her palm was over her heart, and she thought of the strange boy from the library who gave her the ring, and how he had mentioned that he would "find a body." She became very quiet as her mind linked strange details that might not belong together.

"I've had a lot of time to process it, but thanks -- I'm glad I'm alive too. Sometimes, I feel like I have memories that weren't from my life as Lu. It's strange. I feel like after I met you, more of myself made sense. It's like an intricate puzzle, and somehow we're connected. A strange destiny has brought us together... and if you were wondering, I'm not afraid of you. Even though this is all crazy, I believe you fully. You can't go through all this on your own... it's too maddening." Lu finished speaking and nodded his head. He scooted himself to sit behind Paesh, leaning his back against the wall, and pulled her in close to him.

"Thank you," Paesh breathed. "Having your support makes a big difference. I don't feel as alone in all this chaos. I'm glad you didn't limp out of my house wishing you felt well enough to run." Paesh smiled, resting her head back on his chest. They both sighed at the same time, making the corners of their mouths turn upwards ever so slightly.

"What's in the box?"

"Oh, it was my grandfather's. He killed himself when my mother was still young. He left a diary and some things of importance. My mom shipped it to me recently; she wanted me to get to know him." Paesh tried to open the latch, but couldn't. "I haven't even gotten it open yet," she said, frustrated.

Lu's arms reached around with a groan of pain, but he moved his hands to the latch, and pried it open with his strong fingers. *Click,* the latch opened, and the smell of old leather and wood filled Paesh's nostrils. A brown leather book and a small box were the only contents of the container. Paesh opened the box and, eyes perplexed, took out a small wooden ring. When the wooden band touched her skin, she immediately began to feel her body shift. Her skin sparkled with golden light, and her senses became clearer.

The ring had golden symbols woven around the whole band. Lu watched from over her shoulder, and held his breath as he saw Paesh's skin change. "Whoa, the ring is affecting me; it makes my body feel more alive somehow," Paesh said, then handed the ring quickly to Lu, who took it carefully between his fingers.

Holding it immediately silenced him; he was dazed, and stared at it carefully. He was statuesque. All his focus was tuned into something else, and the surrounding sounds waned to a dull static.

While Lu sat quietly holding the ring, Paesh, unconcerned about his silence, opened the journal. Paper flittered to the floor from between its pages. Picking the paper up, Paesh saw that it was a glossy photograph, and the face of her grandfather stared at her. This was the same photo she had just been trying to recall. He was a handsome man, with a fine beard and olive skin. Paesh gasped aloud when she saw his large silver eyes; that were haunted by sorrow. She knew him, somehow, from somewhere!

The journal had a cover page that was titled *Remembering Eithar,* by Izar Kerbasi. Paesh turned to the next page and began reading. As she read, she was immediately captivated, and did not want put the journal down; why hadn't she read it sooner?

"Lu, look, this is my grandfather. I think we should read his journal together, if you're interested. Oddly enough, he looks a little like you..." her words trailed off as she spoke. Turning slightly, she waved the picture in front of Lu's face, but he was looking off in the distance, as if hypnotized.

"Lu, are you all right?" Paesh asked firmly, as she lightly shook his shoulder, being careful of his injury.

Lu stirred, and inhaled suddenly through his nose. "What? Hmm. I just had the strangest daydream when holding the ring. Wait -- is this him? Your grandfather?" he asked, grabbing the picture and trading it for the ring.

"Yes, this is him. He looks a bit like you, don't you think?"

The color drained from Lu's face, and he blinked a couple of times while examining the picture. "I, uh, I think I need some fresh air," Lu said, while moving both himself and Paesh so he could stand up.

"Oh, okay, totally --" Paesh said shuffling herself out of the way. She zipped up the duffle bag, and threw it back into the closet; taking the journal, she followed Lu back down the stairwell. Heading straight for the garden, he collapsed on a faded wooden bench in the sunlight, among the flowers. Paesh took this moment to use the bathroom and splash some water on her face. It was a damned astonishing day; in fact, the whole week was turned on its head. Whether Lu was ready to hear it or not, Paesh felt desperate to read her grandfather's journal. She wanted to flip through the pages and smell the sweet scent of old paper and aged leather. There was something within her that was adamant about reading the journal. It felt very important.

After patting her face dry, she left the bathroom and joined Lu outside. She left him to soak in the Sun and digest what they'd learned, while she took the swinging seat across the garden, adjacent to him. She sat crossed-legged, and opened the leathery journal, taking care with the pages. The text was in broken English, as well as Euskara. Using a pad of paper, Peash wrote down the Euskara to look up the sentences for translation, writing the English translation underneath it. In times like this, she was grateful for technology. Her phone had decent service, and she was able to use her translator app.

Izar's words immediately drew her in, starting with the story of his childhood in the Basque country. With all the translation, each page took some time to get through. The first sentence she needed to translate was foreshadowing somehow: "Hasieran, bidea ez zen argi. Urruneko amonek baino ez zekiten sekretuak sabelean harriak bezalakoak ziren. Bizitza osoan zehar eraman nituen zer ziren jakin gabe." It translated to, "In the beginning, the way was unclear. Secrets that only distant grandmothers knew were like stones in my stomach. I carried them around for most of my life without knowing what they were." Paesh was not clear on how direct the translations were, but she got the gist of his message.

She sat enraptured with the text for what felt like hours, when the journal took a turn: Izar visited the Irati Forest. Just as Paesh started to translate another section, Lu walked up, looking a little more refreshed, but still distant. Paesh no longer worried whether he believed her not; unexplainably, she felt safe, and patted the empty space next to her for him to join her. He sat slowly and cleared his throat; his voice sounded dry.

"We've learned a lot today, and I just want you to know, I'm here for you and I'm only more intrigued. With our details combined, I feel like everything, as abnormal as it is, makes more sense." He scratched his head, and turned his face to display a shy smile and a loving stare. His face displayed his thoughtfulness.

"Also, I'm extremely hungry. Maybe we can whip something up from the garden, or gather some stuff from the store? That is, if you're hungry too, of course. You look like you might be quite the cook by the way your kitchen was set up." He raised his eye brows and leaned in flirtatiously. "A proper witch with all your hanging herbs, bowls of fresh produce, the mortar-pestle, and jars of spices."

Paesh smiled and arched an eyebrow. "You would be correct; I take great pride in cooking. I'm starting to get hungry myself. I think I have enough ingredients to whip up a nice meal." Paesh used a slice of paper to mark the spot in the journal, and closed it. "This journal is really fascinating -- maybe we can read it together, and decode it over wine after we eat," Paesh said, standing and shaking her legs out. The hard wood from the bench was not forgiving on her tailbone.

"I think we might need whiskey rather than wine, but that sounds like an excellent plan," Lu said, groaning to stand as he followed her towards the kitchen.

"I'll brew you something for the inflammation, too. Maybe we can cut a little of that pain down. I even have a homemade salve for muscle pain that we can put on your ribs and shoulders," Paesh said casually over her shoulder as she crested the doorway. With Lu at her side, she felt comfortable sharing her true self and her magic. Thus far, he had accepted every peculiar part of her. Lu's eyes traced every graceful step she took with curious intrigue. His broad shoulder-span and height shielded her from behind.

A grin like a crescent Moon stretched across Paesh's face as she formulated a brew for Lu in her head. She was truly beautiful in her loose-fit jeans and simple peach colored tank top. She wasn't wearing a bra, and the full curve of her breasts moved lightly with ease as she did. Natural radiance oozed from her pores, and each step was poised and swift. Something had changed today inside of her; something magnificent within her was now awake. Confidence bloomed from her core, like a lion stretching its limbs after a long slumber, or a growing fire fueled by the wind.

Inside, Lu sat on a bar stool and kept his eyes following the soft sway of Paesh's hips as she selected a few jars of herbs and one of resin. Reaching a top shelf, she rose onto her toes, and seemed to grow just a few inches to reach the desired jar, her skin glittering with gold and lavender as she did so.

When her kettle was set to heat and she was blending pinches of everything together in a glass jar, she spoke clinically to Lu. "These will help with your cracked ribs, as well as the inflammation and tissue regeneration. It's a blend of opium, white willow, horsetail, skullcap, turmeric, cayenne, and ginger. Also, I have some salmon in the freezer we can cook up with some rice and veggies." Paesh moved around the kitchen, extracting a pot, a glass baking dish, and rice from the cupboards.

"Thank you, that sounds heavenly. What can I help with?" Lu's eyes were interested and intent, watching her methodically move about her kitchen. His body became more relaxed in her nurturing presence.

"Actually, I can handle it. In the future we can cook together, but I'm excited to dig into that journal, so I'm going to streamline this," she said as she reached deeply into her freezer to find the salmon.

After dinner was prepared and baking, Paesh disappeared and returned promptly with a small jar of salve. "Okay, Lu, would you like some of this muscle salve on your wounded ribs and bruises?" she asked, smiling, tilting her head, proudly holding up the jar.

Lu almost purred, and nodded. "Thank you -- yes mam. I would love some. But it's hard for me to reach over my head; you'll have to help me with my shirt." His eyes were sheepish.

Paesh moved slowly towards him and stood close, facing him, while he sat on the stool. She nodded; her eyes were caring and clinical once again, but she said nothing. She lifted his shirt slowly until it was past his shoulders. She then leaned in and lightly kissed Lu on his forehead, the tips of her breasts grazing his bare chest.

Paesh laid her palms on his shoulders and his upper back, gently reading his body, sending love to each wave-form that comprised him. She pulled away slowly to open her salve jar and gather some into her hands. Gently, she covered each bruise and the inflamed ribs. She was focused and thorough. She gently kissed parts of his broken body, and as she did, she began to shift and sparkle. Her body morphed and her hair turned white; her eyes became slightly larger and farther apart. She looked like an angel from the cosmos, glistening and abstract.

Lu opened his eyes and lifted his chin; he leaned back slightly, reaching his arm up to move some of her hair behind her ear, and trace the line of her jaw with his fingers. His eyes marveled with amazement.

"You are the most beautiful angel I have ever seen, fallen from space, gracing me with your presence and love. It's incredible -- my pain is dissolving. Each breath I take, I no longer feel the sharpness in my ribs. What is this healing magic?" Lu's baritone voice was pervasive. The vibration of his sentiment and question could be felt through his chest; and Paesh felt its resonance as she slowly pressed herself into him. Leaning in, she kissed him again. Like pupils dilating in the light, when their lips touched, her soul shrank into a slender point and shot somewhere else altogether.

It was quick when she left her body, whipped away like a rock in a slingshot. Her surroundings were a shifting blur until all came into focus, and she found herself sitting on a golden disc, like the one in her dream. She was holding a cup of murky liquid that sloshed at the rim. Next to her was a man, his skin dark and starry like the night sky; and he sat close to her. Her gaze was lost in the depths of his skin, which looked as if he were painted with space itself. He sat still, holding her closely. Paesh took a sip of her dark liquid, and again her surroundings began to shift and blur into another setting.

The new surroundings resembled a cave; the texture of the place was amorphous and fragmented, like that of a dream. She found herself standing face-to-face with herself. Their silver eyes met, and they assessed one another. Their matching lavender/golden skin shimmered, as if it were breathing, like light reflecting on the water.

"Where are we? ...Or who are we? Am I you?" Paesh asked, taking in the sights and smells of the cave.

"You are here. I am you, and you are me; a part of me fractured through time, I suspect. I was wondering when I would see you here, or if I would at all. I am Celosia, the Watcher of the Web that binds all things. As for who we are, I am not sure when I began or when I end, but I am, ' Celosia said, her face austere.

Paesh nodded lightly and raised her ear, waiting to hear more, as she were unsure if that made any sense or answered her question.

"We are in a dimension that is suspended far beyond Earth, that much I know. The waves of vibration are smaller here, fast and tightly arched together. Matter is not set in stone; it is flexible." Celosia said, shrinking and expanding herself and blinking into another part of the cave without moving.

Paesh nodded and laughed to herself. "Interesting... so how exactly am I part of you? How did I get to Earth as a separate slice? Am I a fragment? An echo?" she asked, her voice clear as a bell in the strange void of the cave.

Celosia gestured to herself with her hands, placing a palm where her heart would be. "I sent part of myself there, and in some sense, it's already over and has yet to begin. This is a realm beyond time." She raised her other arm, gesturing around them, her movements peculiar and robotic. "The universe is complex, and my soul seems to be in more places than I was aware of. I was contacted; summoned, if you will. Forces of destiny were calling me, leading me to Earth. I was summoned because of an infectious imbalance; Earth was seized by a virus, a dark energy. Surrounding star systems feared the darkness would spread. I volunteered myself to go to that perplexing little corner of the universe. So, I sent a small part of myself there, hoping to create balance somehow."

Celosia's face was taut, her internal struggle to translate these complicated concepts displayed in the ridges on her forehead. "I am a force of balance, but even I am surprised sometimes. Earth was denser than I thought, a prism I didn't know how to navigate or retract from once I arrived. Like a light off in the distance, your fragment became dim and hard to see. The fracture that is you was hard to feel. I had difficulties connecting through the thickness of space and time.

Despite this challenge, here you are; you made it back, but not for long, I gather."

Paesh stood for a minute, taking in all the information, her mind bending with the concept of a soul's journey. "Hmmm... like radios broadcasting a signal, the waves are bent and twisted through time and space, as if scrambled. It comforts me to learn this, as I've been having visions and dreams of places and scenes like this, of different lives. My life wasn't making any sense before; but what am I supposed to do as a force of balance, a mere fracture who has forgotten itself? Earth is crazy, and it is certainly dark. I wouldn't know where to start," Paesh said, her mind stretching to remember everything about Earth and viruses. Her thoughts were scattered and jumbled; she had so many questions she wanted the answers to, but didn't know how much time she had.

"All I have been able to see from my side is that the virus is not what you might expect. The virus is a man, *in* a man --something that can move from animal to human like a parasite. It evades death, and has over time gained control over Earth's energetic field."

Paesh was quiet, and thought about Earth: its wars, suffering, and death, humanity's never-ending pillaging of resources in the name of greed. She thought of kings, religious leaders, and the 1%. She connected how they had controlled the masses throughout history. Her mind's eye flashed an image of Jacob Allen, and chills ran down her spine. She wasn't certain of anything, but it made sense that there was a force behind all the darkness on Earth.

Celosia saw that Paesh was interlacing the information in her mind, and took her hand. Wordlessly, she guided Paesh to a staircase carved of stone that led to a giant, steamy basin. Celosia continued to speak while they ascended.

"All I know is, I have lived more than once on Earth. When I died the first time , I felt it reverberate into my core. I had visions of fire and fear. Everything was black and white. Part of my soul tumbled around, trapped in Earth's field, unable to return home to me. I gather that we were born again, as whoever you are now."

They had reached the top of the stairs, and Celosia stepped into the liquid gracefully. Paesh followed; the warm liquid was soothing, and immediately calmed her mind. Everything became sharp and clear. Her body relaxed.

Celosia continued, "The virus has created a net around Earth, keeping souls trapped, destined to recycle and incarnate again and again. We must restore the balance somehow, set them all free, bring light where there is shadow." Celosia's eyes were filled with both sorrow and hope.

Paesh was trying to soak in all of what was being said when she heard a very distinct *ding!* And just like that, her soul snapped back into her body. She was on the floor, the oven timer was sounding, and Lu was holding her in his lap. She had changed back into her human form, and inhaled sharply as she opened her eyes.

"Oh, thank God," Lu said, "I'm glad you're awake. Wait here, I'm going to turn the oven off so we don't start a fire."

The kitchen wasn't far from where she laid; she was covered with a blanket, and propped up with a pillow. When Lu sat back down, his face displayed relief -- and terror.

"What happened?" Paesh asked, her voice weary with confusion.

"Well, we kissed, and then you sort of slowly went limp, and I laid you on the floor. You were still breathing and your heart was beating, so I covered you up and waited. You were only out for about seven minutes, but in that time you slowly faded back into your more human self," Lu said rapidly, words tumbling over each other. "Has this happened before?" he asked, concerned.

"Yes. No... well, sort of, but this time it was different; I went somewhere. I met myself, the cosmic angelic version of me. I need to write it down while I still remember. Will you grab me a paper and pen from the drawer over there?" She waved an arm towards a desk. "I'll explain later." She closed her eyes, and sighing with relief, held onto the information.

She wrote down all that she could remember; it was a very clear experience, but she recorded it down in case her memory betrayed her later. She filled nearly a page, each otherworldly detail captured in ink. They then quietly enjoyed the dinner Paesh had prepared. Surprisingly, the food had not been burnt in the process. After they were satiated, Paesh poured them each a glass of whiskey and, along with a big ice cube, added star anise and orange peel to each glass. Unsettled yet comfortable, they sat on her couch, and it was then that she handed Lu the paper and was ready to share what had happened.

Layer 29: Iós - Power Struggle

I ós soared through the night sky, his white wings ghostly against the darkness. His mind was racing, thinking about the day. Why had Tiago brought Paesh into the neurology building? It was ironic, as the neurology lab was where he stored his freshly completed antibody serum. To his relief, it appeared to have been untampered with.

His wings caught a thermal pocket and he rose higher, gliding through the air, circling above the wooded nature preserve that surrounded Paesh's home. The Sun had set a couple of hours before, and the darkness would have been disorienting, but he knew the area well. He often slept in the trees near her house so he could keep watch on her. He missed her, and felt like it was the only time he could really see her as she was.

When Iós turned towards the side of the house, he noticed that Lu's car was in her driveway, and there were dim lights on in the lower part of the house. Iós was angered by Lu's presence, angry that he was alive and getting in the middle of all his efforts. Lu had been one of his patients just over a year ago. Lu's blood was responsible for a lot of his movement forward with his antibody research.

When Lu was delivered to his ward and placed under his care a year ago, killing him would have been easy -- as simple as pulling a plug from an outlet. A helpless man in a coma, lying vulnerably under his control. But one year ago, there was no reason to kill him. In fact, his rare blood was a helpful key for Iós' research into antibodies to his immunity, as Lu had AB Rh-negative blood. In all of his years researching genetics and blood, he had come to know that those with AB-negative blood were immune to his invasion. With new technology for genetic mapping, he had also come to know that the rare blood type came from the genetic blending of humans and the Fae, the beings who inhabited the realm that run parallel to humanity's.

Using ancestry mapping, with his advanced database collected from willing donors all around the world, he had been able to find those who carried the Rh-negative factor. In his long life, he had seen realms that other scientists had not, and experienced the otherworldly beings for himself. He was well aware that there were more conscious beings than just the humans. Although they rarely interbred with humans, due to various complications, there were in fact a few hybrids who walked among the humans unnoticed. The blood type AB-negative in particular had the strongest immunity to him, and could specifically be traced back to people of French and Basque descent.

Iós had also come to the understanding that he himself had contributed to these hybrids, all those years ago with Indra in the forest. He had intentionally placed his seed into Indra in hopes of making a child... although Indra held its existence as a secret for centuries, until moments before Iós destroyed her tree.

Despite the years of wondering, Iós had known deep down that she was keeping something from him. When coming back for Indra, he waited in the woods as a lingering and listening raven. Indra never came, though he waited for a protracted time. One day he crossed paths with a being from the Fae realm; a decomposing stench followed him as he sat near an animal long dead. Iós landed himself near the being, and asked him if he had any information on Indra's whereabouts. The being reacted oddly; he knew of Indra, that was clear. When he spoke, it was in the form of a riddle, and he disappeared immediately after he spoke. His riddle had stuck with Iós through time:

"I tend to the dead, so they may be reborn. Monsters live on, and hopefully will transform, through the helix of their heirs."

After that aberrant encounter, Iós was in an information limbo, but suspected he had a child somewhere.

A swell of laughter startled Iós from the memories of his past, and pulled him back to the present. Curious, he flew in for a closer look through the kitchen window. There she was, rinsing out glasses and washing plates. Her face was dreamy and glowing with the warmth that liquor brings. Despite her slight inebriation, she cleaned the dishes swiftly, and walked back across the kitchen, out of view from the window. Iós felt a great surge of jealousy and anger, as he could hear their light rumbles of laughter pouring from the living room. Paesh sounded so happy; she sounded like she was in love.

Iós thought back to when he had seen her again for the first time. He'd known it the moment he laid eyes on her: Paesh carried the same soul as Ala, Neenah, Imi, and Indra had. It was a cold winter's day in Santa Cruz, and Iós had just gotten out of a board meeting downtown. He spent very little time in Santa Cruz as Dr. Allen, but it was the best place to continue his research. As he was walking down the sidewalk to meet his driver, he saw her. She was closing up a storefront, locking a stubborn lock with a jangle of keys on a ring. It was uncanny, the sight of her; he nearly lost his footing. "Could it really be her?" he wondered out loud. Luckily, she was just out of earshot, and paid no mind to the well-dressed man on the sidewalk.

She was consumed with the stubborn lock and their battle for the key. She bore the same self-assured look of peace and openness as usual, and despite the delight and polite charm in her face, there was mystery just beneath her exterior. Iós fought himself to not assist her, to not introduce himself; instead, he memorized the name of the shop she was locking up.

Iós had learned that, ironically, she was a student of biology and science. She was living with many other students in a giant old house that wasn't suited for the royalty he believed her to be. Hers was a very modest life, given how lavish everything in the 21st century was; she was simple and unspoiled. Her ethics were strong by nature; as always, she was disciplined and hard-working.

He discovered she was a student when he visited the storefront she had locked. It was an herbal apothecary she humbly managed; it couldn't have paid much, and yet it required a lot of knowledge that she freely shared to help others. He challenged himself to keep his visits rare, so he only picked up small details about her once a month. He feigned incompetence, requiring her aid in choosing suitable herbs for his needs. Albeit brief, he cherished those small moments with her. The young woman was above all earnestly kind, and it was hard for him to hold any resentment from the past towards her. Her open energy towards him made it clear that she had forgotten Iós, as well as who she had been before. Although she was a little odd, she played the human part well.

All those lifetimes ago, when she had known who he truly was, she had loved and hated him as the fallen angelic monster that he was. But now it was all new, and they were two strangers in a small town talking about the weather and super-foods.

There was hope for a fresh start, and his science was nearly complete; finding her reignited his passion to drive his project home. He could finally cure her of the immunity! Naturally, when Lu arrived on the scene, his plan took a huge detour, and became littered with obstacles.

He knew that Paesh had fallen in love with Lu the moment they met. Now there was a competitor, and this made Iós' eyes red with anger. That was why he had tried to remove Lu from the equation as soon as possible with the anonymous accident. Upon checking the location the next day, he was certain he saw the crumpled motorcycle laying atop Lu in the ravine below. Iós was victorious, and his enemy lay defeated and forgotten! However, when he left that scene to follow Paesh to work, he was surprised to find that Lu had somehow survived the crash.

Iós followed Paesh that whole day, eventually to Lu's home, where he sat helplessly while they fell in love. It was like watching a plane crash from the airport windows: nothing could be done to stop it.

Iós was infuriated, but he was always a clever strategist; indeed, that was his entire life's work. Lu would actually be a proper candidate for the antibody, thus making his body a useful tool, as he already had a place in Paesh's heart. It might be a better plan than removing him altogether. As long as Paesh remained ignorant of his gift of invasion, he would be able to make use of Lu.

Iós waited outside on the porch railing; peeking in through the window, he saw Lu and Paesh sitting so closely there was not one millimeter of air between them. Paesh was leaning back onto Lu's chest, while they read a journal and referenced a paper of some kind. Their eyes were focused and squinting; their jaws hung open slightly, as if they were mystified. At one point, Paesh wrote something down and then used her phone for something else, and then wrote down more on the separate piece of paper. Iós did not know what they were reading, but being close, he listened for any implicit details of its content.

Paesh broke the silence. "Lu, listen to this translation. 'The Irati Forest opened the doors of a secret home to me, when I had eaten the dried mushrooms from Elenuta. I saw the Lady of the Forest that night, her body forged from oak and her hair from foliage. Indra."

Lu cleared his throat and sipped his whiskey. Paesh reread the translation again to herself, and then looked back into the old leather journal. "Your grandfather was having a psychedelic trip that enhanced some psychic skills he already possessed. Perhaps—?" Lu trailed off, scratching his head. "You *are* connected by blood, and perhaps you and he share some otherworldly connections. Maybe he could shape shift as well," he said pointedly, his eyes joining Paesh's on the journal's next passage.

Iós could not believe what he was hearing. What book would contain any details about Indra or the Irati Forest? His mind snapped to Izar, the post-war hitchhiker, the one who later led him to Indra's tree. He had thought Izar was killed with the blow to his head; he was bleeding profusely, and there wasn't help for miles.

There was nothing Iós could do as a bird. He wanted to rip that journal from their hands and burn it before they learned anything more. Iós did not know how much Izar knew of him, but surely Indra had told him *something*.

He quickly took flight back towards Dr. Allen's home; he needed a new vehicle to deal with this properly. As he was lifting off, he heard Paesh speak before elevation muffled the rest: "Tulsi, is that you?" she projected as she burst through the back door.

Paesh stood in the dark with a glass sloshing in her hand as she watched the small white bird fly away. Iós didn't look back, but he knew she was watching him leave.

Layer 30: Paesh - Fungi

aesh stepped back inside, her smile cheeky and disappointed. She dropped her shoulders with an emphatic sigh. She knew Tulsi would return again, and in all honesty she had enough company at the moment.

"Did your friend not care to join us?" Lu said, with a wide grin and tilted head.

"No, she flew away. I saw her watching us through the window, but she must have been startled or something." Paesh sat herself back down, snuggling close to Lu. She leaned in and lightly brushed her face onto his, as if she was leaning in for a whisper. Instead she just lingered, lightly pressing herself into him. Lu welcomed her in and wrapped his arms around her.

"We're going to figure this out. It seems like your grandfather left a lot behind for you. I feel like this is tying it all together," Lu said in whisper, reassuring Paesh. Even though she seemed like she had so much figured out, he knew she needed extra assurance.

"Wait a minute!" Paesh said, as if something had just clicked, "my dream journal and the ring! I'll be right back." Paesh slowly pulled away, then nearly ran upstairs. She promptly returned wearing a ring and holding a few journals. She sat down and displayed her hand to Lu.

"Look at this ring. It fits the description in my grandfather's story! The one that washed up from the ocean while he was out at sea with his father. The same ring he used to pledge his love to Indra!" Paesh sat down, placing the journals on the coffee table. She was feeling a little lightheaded with all the excitement and whiskey.

"How did you get that ring? It *does* fit the description. Uncanny!" Lu exclaimed, as he grabbed her hand and got a closer look.

"It was bizarre... a little over a year ago, a random young man gave it to me. He mentioned things about soulmates, and finding a body, and before he disappeared, he handed me this." Paesh rolled her eyes and turned to Lu. "And believe me, it was so weird I spent the whole day looking for him, but I couldn't find him. Since then, I've kept my eye out for him, and never once have I seen him again."

"I'm not surprised by anything at this point," Lu said in a monotone.

Sighing loudly, Paesh settled back into her seat next to Lu. They both sat in silence while Paesh started flipping through her dream journals, her eyes scanning the pages looking for something specific. Nothing but the sound of flipping paper filled the room. Her eyes brightened when, eventually, she found what she was looking for.

"Listen to this: *Waking at 2:44 02/22/2020*

I was a tree, an oak tree. Starting from a small sapling. I was inside of it and outside of it. I was a woman, and also a tree. There were many strange beings that I met, all welcoming me to the forest. There was a tall being, very androgynous, slender and stoic, named Beaudry. There were golden stones and the wind was a woman; I remember wanting to fly away like her. I remember the Moon; it was not Earthen and gray, but instead luminous and mixed shades of blue. Then I woke up.

"Weird, right? Oak tree and a forest," Paesh said, flipping through her journal. "I also remember that name, Indra... I've heard it before, besides in the contexts of Vedic Mythology in Hinduism... wait. Hold on, here it is.

Dream Journal at 02:22 8/26/2019: There was a warehouse I was wondering through; the floors were made of rivers, and objects I cannot recall were sailing past me. Suddenly, I was at a ceremonial burial or something on a cliff's edge; a woman lay on a stack of wood, her face pale and stiff with death, a single blue lotus flower sewn to her third eye.

I jumped off the cliff, and found myself underwater, which then became the galaxy. When I turned to see Earth, I saw that it was covered in an electrical netting. It looked like the geometric shell of a virus, actually... my scientific brain in the dream postured the question, "Is that a virus?" When suddenly, to my left there was a being, light green and blue silks covering her form. "They are all trapped in there. Do not forget your promise, Indra." I looked down at my feet, and wondered to myself what promise I had made. Then I woke up."

Lu breathed in and shook his head in disbelief.

"Wow, will we have to read all of those too? It's a relief that these threads are connecting. Let's keep reading your grandfather's journal, and if you remember anything, we can cross reference it," Lu said, grabbing the leather-bound journal.

Paesh nodded, and small tears of relief fell from her eyes. Lu looked up at her. "Do you want to take a break and sleep? Start translating in the morning? I apologize if I'm a little mad with curiosity. Once I get going, sleep may prove difficult for me, especially after a day like this."

Paesh laughed, and wiped her eyes with the inside of her tank top. "No, I'm fine, you're perfect. It's the whiskey; it always aids in animating my feelings. I'm touched, and relieved that you want to learn more, too. I am so grateful for the support. Should I make us something sweet to eat while we continue?" Paesh smiled and stood, already heading to the kitchen to put together some fruit, chocolate, and buttered toast.

The two of them munched and continued to read the journal. It got stranger and stranger. Izar did not spare any details; he wrote down the facts, and then wrote down his feelings about the facts. They were translating a section that was sharing Indra's story after Izar had gone into her realm of the Fae. Lu and Paesh were loopy at this point, with squinting eyes, but they were determined to learn more. Lu felt he needed to urinate, so went outside to find a dark place to relieve himself.

When he was just about finished, he saw car lights approach and then turn off. The quiet buzz of an electric car rolled closer towards the driveway. Lu strained to see in the dark, but his stomach lurched when he saw the familiar black expensive car: it was Dr. Allen's. He immediately ran back into the house and locked the backdoor.

"Paesh, pack the journals and translation! Dr. Allen is in your driveway, and we need to get the hell out of here, NOW!"

Paesh froze momentarily, her expression quickly sobering; then she scrambled to grab all the journals and papers. Lu picked up her grandfather's box and put on the wooden ring, then scooped his wallet and keys from the counter as they headed for the front door. Anxiety was swelling in Paesh's throat; she felt like she couldn't breathe.

Why is he coming now, so late at night? Paesh wondered to herself, while her shaking hands reached for the deadbolt on the door. Waiting in the darkness of her foyer for the proper moment, they saw Dr. Allen emerge from his car and leave his door open. As if he knew his surroundings well, he headed straight for the back of her house, through the garden. Paesh quietly opened the front door, and they both hurried to the Jeep. Paesh slammed the lock button while Lu started the car; they were in reverse before the engine had time to settle.

Lu backed down the entire street with competent precision. He was calm, but very focused on the task at hand. When they reached the end of the road, he pivoted the Jeep and threw it into drive.

"What the hell? Why is he there? It's nearly two in the morning!" Paesh yelled, her voice hoarse and elevated with adrenalin.

"I have no clue, but I'm glad we didn't stay to find out. I'm glad you were not alone," Lu said, rubbing his tired, disbelieving eyes.

"Maybe he saw me at the lab today. Shit. Where should we go?" Paesh asked, her mind racing.

Lu shrugged. "Not sure. Somewhere unsuspected... he could be close behind us. I'm glad I have my wallet, as I don't think we should go to my house. He probably knows where I live."

Paesh nodded, and tried to think of a good place to go. "We could always go to Harbon Hot Springs -- they take people in at all hours. We can rent an adobe cottage and finish transcribing this tomorrow. It's just a little over three hours away," Paesh said slowly. "There's WiFi and a cafe with a small store. I haven't been out there in years -- I don't think anyone knows I used to go there."

Lu nodded. "I've heard of that place. It's like a hippy Mecca out in Middle Town, off the 20, right?"

"That's the place. We can also relax and soak in the pools and untangle our thoughts in the sauna," Paesh said, rubbing her hands together, excited. She hadn't been able to go alone since the incident with Dr. Allen. She'd never even mentioned it to her therapist Genevieve, Tiago, or Milad; no one connected to Dr. Allen would know where she might have gone.

She needed to clear her head and escape town.

The Jeep rolled and weaved on Highway 17, heading east through the Santa Cruz Mountains, and then north. Lu put on some soft music, and despite the time, he drove like a champion. Paesh checked behind them periodically, and not once did they see Allen's black car, or any car that was following them. When they stopped for gas halfway to their destination, Paesh bought herself a hat to cover her lavender hair, just in case.

When they arrived, they were greeted by a very tired yet clear-eyed man with long, curly hair. He was wearing loose-fitting linseed clothing, and leaned forward in a silent bow inside the check-in station. It was nearly 5:00AM as Paesh and Lu stood securing their information and booking a cottage. They were both ready for sleep. Getting back into their car, they drove slowly up the small, winding road towards the cottages. Oak trees covered all the hills for miles, and they almost seemed to bend ever so slightly when they drove past. Paesh rubbed her eyes, certain she was seeing things at this point.

Once inside with their door locked, they collapsed onto the bed and slept deeply. Lu held Paesh closely as the slept, and for the first time, she was able to sleep comfortably while lying in a man's arms. But maybe she was just that tired.

Layer 31: Iós - The Hunt

Iós slipped quietly from his car; all was dark, except for the dim light coming from the back porch of Paesh's house. He did not even bother to close his car door, for he feared it would alert them to his arrival. He just needed to procure the journal and stop Paesh from learning anything more. Should the need arise, he had brought along the antibody serum in a prepped needle. In fact, he'd brought three, just to be safe.

Creeping around the back, he walked through the garden, and squatted low past the windows. He made his way up onto the porch and peered inside. He did not see either of them on the couch any longer. Perhaps they had retired. The thought of another man with Paesh made his blood run hot, and he gripped the door handle so fiercely he broke it. A loud clank filled the silent night, and Iós held his breath, hoping he had not just woken them. As he waited to see if there was any reaction or movement to the sound, he heard car doors shut, and a car start.

He stood straight up, and quietly walked back down the porch and back through the garden. When he made it to the driveway, Lu's Jeep was gone. *Did the two of them just leave? Or was it just Lu, in a stroke of luck?* Iós wondered.

He ran back around the house and forced the porch door open, which was easy since he had broken the door knob. He walked swiftly to the coffee table, where there was no sign of the journal or any of the papers they had been writing on. He looked around quickly, finding nothing, with one last place to look: upstairs.

He knew her house was old and creaky, but he still managed to ascend the old stairs with the quiet grace of a cat. He saw that her room was empty and dark except for a small lamp; it was clear that the bed was untouched. This brought some relief to him, but he brushed it aside. He had to think quickly, as both of them must have seen him and left in the Jeep when the moment was right. Just in case, he searched her room for the journal; she had very few belongings, so it was easy to turn everything over quickly.

Back in his car, shutting the door and turning it on, he breathed out heavily and screamed. They had both escaped! They could be anywhere by now! Either way, he had to try to find them, so he pulled out of the driveway quickly and zipped down the road.

First, I'll check to see if they stopped at Lu's house, Iós thought. He set the address in his car's navigation system, heading towards the coast, to West Cliff Drive. He broke all the speed limits, and made it there easily. When he passed the house, all the lights were off, and there was no Jeep in the driveway.

"Damn, they could be on their way to anywhere by now." A fear filled Iós, "I wonder if they went to the Neurology Center. After today, maybe they already know enough to go there and look." Driven by his paranoia, he made his way to the neurology lab, where he saw an empty parking lot, and a security guard on his phone.

He pulled up. "Hi there. Have any cars been in this parking lot tonight?" Iós called out from his window.

"Uh," the man's eyes peeled up from his phone and became startled when he saw Dr. Allen with his window rolled down. "No, Dr. Allen, not a car since everyone packed up and left for the day."

"Thank you, Michael," Iós said through clenched teeth as he rolled up the window. He was so angry that he had let them escape. *Hopefully they'll return, and if they don't... well, I've always enjoyed a proper hunt.*

Iós drove to his home, defeat hanging around his neck like an anchor. He used facial identification to open his front door, and immediately went into his office to do some digging on the little he knew about Izar.

Layer 32: Paesh - Understanding the Past

Paesh and Lu woke to the screech of a blue jay; the Sun was high, casting through the skylight above the bed. Their bodies were stiff with exhaustion, and they stretched and untangled themselves as they regained consciousness.

"Good afternoon," Lu said during a yawn. "I slept so well out here, like the dead."

Paesh laughed and rolled over to the edge of the bed, her legs touching the ground while she assessed the inside of the dome. She'd never actually stayed in an adobe dome before. It was earth-colored with cream accents. The decor was natural and simple. A small kitchenette and a bathroom made it the perfect self-sustaining getaway.

"Would you like to venture out to soak and find sustenance?" Paesh asked as she poured them both a glass of cold spring water. Lu nodded, and they drank their glasses effortlessly, dehydrated from the long night and drive.

The air was already hot, with the summer sun directly overhead. Once outside, they headed for a trail with light coverage offered by the trees. The small trail through the oaks would take them to the springs. They could also take the road, but it was far too hot.

The forest floor crinkled under foot, tinder-box dry. The hills of oaks and mulch led to a creek below, which had nearly run dry with the season's drought. Paesh couldn't help but think of Indra and Izar as they walked past the oak trees, wondering if she truly *was* Indra, and whether everything she was learning was in fact real.

Lu reached out and took her hand, tangling his fingers slightly through hers. Paesh felt something smooth and hard on one of his fingers. When she looked down to see, Lu looked down as well. "Oh, I forgot I was still wearing this! I'm so sorry. I grabbed it last night in the chaos when we were leaving your house. I think I put it on so I wouldn't lose it."

Paesh noticed that the ring fit him perfectly, and she liked the way it looked on him. She was also wearing her own ring from the bizarre night before. Truly, she thought, they looked divine together on their intertwined fingers. It comforted her somehow, and reinforced her suspicions that she and Lu had known one another in some distant place in time. Their connection was no accident; it was cosmically fated. Lu did look a lot like the men on her vision board.

"Are you bothered that I'm wearing the ring? You're awfully quiet," Lu said, hesitation clear in his voice. He tried pulling away his hand to remove the ring.

Paesh shook her head slowly while laying her other hand on top of his struggling one. "You should keep wearing it; it suits you. Think of it as a 'partners in secret' ring." She leaned in conspiratorially. "I have mine too," she emphasized, moving her fingers like a dancer, showing off her ring.

"I shall guard it and cherish it while I wear it," Lu promised, nodding his head once. "Speaking of Indra and Izar, when we slept, I had the most vivid dreams about them. It could be because we were reading his journal all night, but I feel like it was due to the ring too. I enjoy how it feels on my hand."

Paesh nodded. "Splendid. I think you should keep it on, and we can see what happens." Paesh's face expression moved the conversation, starting with a huge smile. "I am *so* excited to rinse yesterday off of me! The warm and cool waters await us."

When they made it to the resort side of the property, there were decks and chairs, pools and fountains. Fig trees shaded most of the water areas, and jasmine vines covered most of the arbors. Every plant was well-manicured. Wind chimes and low-volume chatter filled the soundscape. They undressed in the co-ed changing room, and left only their rings on. It was clearly a spiritual place; many different kinds of people gathered here to heal and tend to their inner selves. Silicon Valley CEOs and traveling gypsies alike came to the water's call. Without clothing, it was harder to know who was who, which equalized everyone in its own magical way.

After showering, they circulated from hot water to the cold spring pool and back again. They drank from the spring fountains, and let the water take away all the insanity that had crashed into their lives. The cold-water pool was at the top of a set of stairs; plant life surrounded the pool, and fresh water circulated into it consistently. The sound of trickling water was soothing. As Paesh stepped in, her skin became taut and her nipples hard, pulling her breasts up into a perfect plump shape. She stayed in the cool water for a long time, allowing the discomfort to shift into comfort. Her muscles eventually let in the cold, and her shoulders relaxed.

After that, she and Lu hit the sauna and steam room to finish their soaking session. Both of them were elevated and famished, as soaking and sweating can really build up an appetite. After they dressed and showered, they made their way down the winding paths and through gardens to reach the cafe and market. They both ordered salads and sandwiches, and devoured them easily. There was no conversation while they ate; rather, they focused on the nourishment and enjoyed the view and each other's silent company. It was nearly five o'clock when they finished, and they were already dreaming of another nap. On their way to the adobe cottage, they purchased some snacks, tea, and a candle from the lightly stocked market. When they felt properly insulated by creature comforts, they retreated to their little dwelling and laid down for another nap.

When they slept, they were once again entangled, in pure safety and comfort. Lu held Paesh, and they each slept a deep and comfortable sleep. No arms went numb; no one lay awake fearing to move and wake the other. It was truly the most compatible pairing of bodies, as if God themself had crafted their bodies for each other. Upon waking, they found that the Sun was setting, and Paesh felt alive; she felt whole and protected.

When they were ready, they went back to Izar's journal. They had the only dome with an option for WiFi, an Ethernet cable that plugged into a hotspot. This was intentionally chosen so they were able to translate the language, despite their location.

They read, they wrote, snacked, laughed, cried, and sat with their jaws hanging open at some parts of his story. They were four hours deep when they reached the part about James, and how he had destroyed Indra's tree. They had completed the core of the story.

"I cannot believe his ring was made from her tree. His ring came from the Fae!" Paesh marveled at the wooden band on Lu's hand. So much information was flowing through her. Paesh then furrowed her brow, addressing the elephant in the room. "This Iós has lived so long. He can mask his identity within another, so he could be anyone -- which is completely insane. The information coincides with the vision I had when I fainted, too." Paesh was now standing and rambling, while mindlessly devouring a raspberry muffin. Lu hadn't touched his;

he was lost in thought, reading back through the pages of translations and tapping the coffee table.

Paesh continued, "I mean -- okay, so did I reincarnate multiple times to eventually become who I am now? Meanwhile, my purpose is to stop the virus?" Her eyes were wide with disbelief. "I can't believe my Mom never told me about this in detail. I think she must have thought he was crazy... but little did she know it was all real." At this point, Paesh was just pacing around the dome asking herself questions and moving her arms as if she were a sign-language interpreter trying to keep up with a slam poet.

Lu sat straighter to speak, and used his arms to organize each thought. "Paesh. So not only is your soul connected to Indra, but your lineage is too. You and your grandfather are literal descendants of Indra and Iós. Your grandfather was immune to his invasion; Izar mentioned that James touched him in the truck, and appeared disappointed while his hand lingered." Lu shuffled through the papers until he found the passage he was referencing. When he found it, he reread it. "Yes, here it is. 'James was creepy; an eerie feeling swarmed my intuition. The man removed his glove and held my hand in a grip for longer than seemed necessary. His confusion was blatant...'" Lu ended the passage. "So does that make you immune, too? Something to do with your blood and your soul?" Lu asked, looking up at her.

"Hmmm. My blood type is AB-negative. It's rare."

Lu met her eyes. "That's my blood type as well! Maybe that's one of the threads that binds us," he mused. Maybe that had something to do with Dr. Allen.

Paesh's face went pale, an expression of horror and simultaneous epiphany on her face. "Dr. Allen founded the blood bank and genetic database -- he's in the .01% kind of rich. He took my blood by force, but didn't kill me -- but he tried to kill you. He's able to read minds; that I'm certain of. When he had me in his creepy lab closet, he displayed that skill. He also spoke to me as if he knew me, like he had done his research. Maybe it is a stretch, but stick with me..." Paesh cleared her throat and took another bite of muffin and swallowed hard. "If Iós can change bodies, then he can't die. What if Dr. Allen is Iós, and is researching our blood to *end* this immunity. It seems like he wanted to own Indra, to keep her; but if she was immune, he *couldn't* control her. I see the drive."

Lu rubbed his eyes at all of the facts stacking against them. "Indra didn't know how to stop Iós, and thus far he hasn't died, so how we are supposed to fix this?"

Paesh responded, her finger tapping on her chin. "I have no idea, but I'm sure there has to be a way. Fengári, the wind spirit from the journal, seemed to think there was. I have hope that we can figure it out." Paesh fell back onto the bed, sighing, but then suddenly shot back upwards. "Oh shit!"

"What!?" Lu said nearly jumping up from the couch.

"Tulsi, the white bird that was following me around! The damn bird could hear my thoughts -- I even have witnesses of that. I showed Genevieve. That bird followed me *everywhere*. It responded to my words; it could understand me. It was with us at the bonsai class, then on the drive home. What if Tulsi was Iós and was jealous of you, Lu? It's all making sense. What a psycho."

"Tulsi was in the window last night at my house. I saw her... or him, rather. We were decoding and reading the journal, reading it out loud. When I went to look, she was flying away; and then two hours later, Dr. Allen shows up. I bet he wanted this journal. He didn't want us to know the truth about him. I think he took form of the bird, and has been watching me." Paesh's face oscillated between anger and amusement.

Lu looked as if he had just seen a ghost, and it was clear that his mind was thinking the worst. His eyes moved to the windows, and darted around outside. He leapt up and closed all the curtains.

"This is all insane!" He lowered his voice, nearly whispering, "I mean, it makes sense in a way, but it's also crazy. What happens to Dr. Allen when Iós isn't in his body? Is he compliant or even aware? Until this ends, there will be no telling *who* he is. We can't live in fear like this," Lu said, joining Paesh on the bed.

"No, we can't. If we fail, we'll be trapped here reincarnating along with everyone else. We need to figure out a way he can be stopped, to free the souls." Paesh sat still and calmly while she spoke. She felt the intense weight of her soul's challenge; it was the weight that had been there all along, her whole life. It all felt fantastical, and yet made complete, sane sense.

"I think we should have another soak now that the stars are out. Rejuvenation awaits us once more. Let's clear our heads," Lu said, standing and reaching for Paesh's hand. He kissed her knuckles gently, and motioned with his head towards the door. "We should also hide the journals and papers, just in case. It makes me nervous leaving something so pivotal just lying about." Lu shuffled all of the papers together and stacked them to fit beneath the area rug.

Out under the stars, the ambiance of the soaking area had transformed. Lit candles and cafe lights decorated the already-enchanting gardens. Soft murmuring, wind chimes, the rushing of water, and light laughter filled the soundscape once more. In the dark, however, something about it felt more mystical, more magical. In the changing room, a tall, poised man smiled at the two of them; he stood confidently, not at all self-conscious of his nudity. He tilted his head, motioning for Paesh and Lu to come close; his green eyes were warm with fatherly energy. Despite this, Paesh was still hesitant, but walked close enough.

The man handed them both heart-shaped chocolates wrapped in pink foil and said, "Eat half and float along; eat the whole thing and dive deep into yourself. These are vegan magical chocolates, courtesy of Mother Earth." He giggled and winked, as if they were supposed to know exactly what he was talking about.

At first, Paesh was nervous; what if he was Iós? But something in her inner guidance let her know that this man was trustable. Something in his eyes was guiding and nurturing, so she received the chocolates and bowed by way of gratitude.

When he walked away, Paesh and Lu looked at one another and shrugged, shy smiles creeping onto their faces. "I think these have psychedelic mushrooms in them, like the ones Izar took in the Irati Forest," Lu said in low whisper.

Paesh nodded. She had eaten mushrooms before, small bites on camping trips, although this was an auspicious and timely way to be given them. They undressed, and decided to try half of the chocolate -- even though it's well known to not imbibe drugs or candy from strangers, which in this case made it a two-for-one risk. But an inner knowing led both of them, and they listened. The chocolate hearts were fated, and surrounded by the oak trees and healing water, they knew they were safe. The waters were protective and gurgling up from the Earth's center. The environment was pristine to take mushrooms, and floating along didn't sound too wild. The chocolate was also delicious, so it was hard to only eat half.

Lu looked serious and stoic, while Paesh was nearly giggling from the bottom of her belly. They began their soaking ritual, and found nothing was happening beyond the magic that already surrounded them. They spied the tall gentleman who gave them the chocolates, and he looked hypnotized in the distance. Yet as if he had sensed them, he looked over in their direction and gave a knowing nod and smile. He then turned and went back into his own world.

All of a sudden, small sensations began in Paesh's throat and in her visuals. It was just as Izar had described in his book, and like she had felt before. Paesh began breathing deeper, as if tasting the oxygen the trees were providing. The night-blooming flowers twirled, and even the water had its own display of fractals and rhythms.

Paesh noted that, even though Lu had exceeded many of her standards, this above all would be the test of character and connection between them. The mushroom spirit was taking them on a healing journey through the waters, suspending time. Things could get uncomfortable, or things could be comfortable, but likely it would be both.

Paesh and Lu had grins that seemed to stretch a little farther than normal, and they held each other softly in the hot pool. They were submerged in the water; their chins kissed the surface of the reflective liquid that was becoming more alive with each breath. Tea lights lined the wall where the water was flowing from. Steam refracted off the candles' flames, while the splashing of the water echoed in the adobe cover that surrounded the pool. It was much like a cave. Together, they faced one another, dancing flames challenged by the steam and wind, flickering potently. The staccato flashes of shadow and light were symbolic. Paesh saw Lu's face shapeshift several times with the light's dancing movements.

Holding one another's gaze, they were both scanning the depths of their own souls through the other. Sometimes their eyes would soften, focusing on the whole of one another's faces, which made it apparent both of them were shifting in the flexibility of the light's perception. These layers within them unraveled all that ever was, and all that ever would be. Paesh was grateful that no one else had come to join them in the hot pool, despite how moderately populated the springs were that night; this moment was gratefully undisturbed.

Before they both became overheated, Lu's face shifted into one last shape. His skin was dark in color, as if it were painted with the night sky. Paesh gasped out loud and reached out to touch his chest. When her hands met flesh, he appeared as the Lu she was familiar with. His eyes were silver and beaming in the darkness. Lu pulled her in and kissed her. It was a slow kind of kiss, one that she had never had before, a kiss full of memories and secrets. A kiss etched in stone. With the heat of the water and the magic from Mother Earth, this kiss sent them both temporarily to the stars.

The chocolate medicine was activated, and it made the sensation of touch so visceral, so meaningful. Paesh was reminded of what was important, and who she truly was. When they opened their eyes, they decided to cool down in the cold spring to offset their heat. Relief spread through their bodies when the cold water embraced them.

Time was like taffy, and they were not sure how long they had soaked for. But they had shed their stress and stagnation, and felt that a break was in order. They both sat wrapped in towels, tangled in two lounge chairs pushed together. The deck they chose was less lit and set away from the pools; it was perfect for viewing the night sky. They were content, no longer fearing the events that had just passed them; rather, they began to feel compassion, confidence, and an understanding of why it was they had fallen through lifetimes in conflict with Iós. There was no explanation as to why it was all okay, but they just knew.

Paesh stood, with a smile. "I'll be right back, with some water and..." she was already skipping off towards the locker room before she finished her sentence. Lu sat patiently, enjoying breathing deeply on the chair, the evening's cool air filling his lungs. Tears slowly rolled down his face, emotions releasing from him without his control. Beauty and insanity all at once. Lifetimes of feelings catching up with him.

Paesh returned promptly, with small balls of foil and two cups of water. "I would like to take the rest of mine. You do what you feel, but I brought yours just in case," she said with a Fae grin. Her eyes were mysterious, and even more beautiful than he had remembered. He was nearly paralyzed by his adoration for her. Like a statue, he stared at her wordlessly, as tears continued to stream down his face.

Paesh handed him his cup and foil; he grabbed the cup and drank, not realizing how dehydrated he had become. Sitting closely in silence, they both drank the water, truly enjoying the sensations of the human form. Sight, taste, touch, scent, hearing, and ESP were all so enthralling, so delicious. What wonder was the squeaking of the bats and the calls of the owls. What wonder was the scent of jasmine and lilies wafting from the garden. What wonder was the scintillating touch of flesh on flesh, its varied textures and sensation. What wonder were the stars in the sky, breathing and blinking down at them, telling their stories from the past. What wonder was the taste of Mayan chili chocolate with bits of ginger and mushrooms ground fine like powder. So many beautiful feelings to experience in the beautiful moment...

Paesh and Lu both unwrapped and ate the rest of their medicine from the tall man. Paesh thanked him in her mind, knowing full well he would hear her.

Eventually, they returned to the pools, and dried off for good, with slow movements, wide-eyed at everything. Everyone seemed to be on the same wavelength, loving and welcoming. In the locker rooms, they changed into their clothing and made to leave. They used the trail through the oaks. Lu brought a light, but neither of them felt the need to use it; they found that their eyes were just fine, acclimated to the darkness. The oak trees whispered as they passed through, and Paesh could have sworn they were saying, "Indra... welcome back." She leaned as she walked, straining her ears to hear more clearly, but the sound of mulched leaves under their feet was extremely loud. Paesh grabbed Lu's arm, and motioned for him to stop; she pointed to her ears, smiling, as to not alarm him. He stopped and listened as well.

It was quiet for some time, until they both heard it: "Indra, welcome home. The Queen of Quercus, from across the sea. All oak dryads know your story." Zipping lights moved quickly into the largest oak tree on the trail.

Paesh focused on that tree and spoke. "Thank you. It feels good to be home, at least inside myself, anyway." Her voice felt foreign coming out of her.

"It is your greatest gift to bring balance. There is a place devoid of love, flooded in power and darkness," the whisper said, a little more clearly than the time before.

"There is. I'm not sure how to bring love to such a place," Paesh said, exasperated, remembering the challenges ahead.

"The Earth medicine you currently embody is a wise spirit from our realm; that will be the greatest key. Use it wisely," the whisper said as a closing statement; the small lights that had gathered in the tree dispersed and zipped past them. One even landed on Paesh, moving right into her chest.

Lu's eyes were unblinking with wonder, as it was an extraordinary experience to see and hear. He held Paesh's hand while she closed her eyes, and used her free hand to touch where the light had gone into her. It was warm and filled her with love; a familiar feeling coursed through her body. A tear rolled down her face, and she crumpled at the knees and cried. She cried not because she was hurt or scared, but because she was beginning to remember everything, all the joys and fears together. These tears were so much more than sorrow or grief. They were necessary step to cleanse her overwhelmed nervous system.

When she could catch her breath, she stood, and Lu with her. They bowed at the tree and blew kisses as they walked away, towards their cove of a cabin. They were ready for a small snack, water, and cool, cozy blankets. When the candle, water, and snacks were situated near the bed, they huddled in the blankets. They laid and stretched together, sensually kissing small parts of one another. It was a tender swirl of feelings and movements, self-consciousness and insecurities left behind. Breathing played the largest role, and eventually, what little clothing they wore fell away.

They were rising and falling like hills, their bodies perfect for each other, fitting together like pieces of a once-broken plate. Paesh opened herself to him in all ways that were closed before. Energy like wind starting spinning at the sacral of their spines. It rose as their velocity did, building a torrent of gusts. It weaved up through their hearts as they were synced in abstract movements. They both were sounding out in low-toned pleasure when the wind reached their foreheads. As it burst through the crowns of their heads, they were both reborn in the height of unearthly pleasure. Sensation flowed through each wave of their bodies and into their souls. They lay on one another, listening to the symphony of music that their tempest created, and it danced around them and through them.

It was a song older than time, and they both recognized it. They had each mindlessly hummed their half of the tune during simple tasks throughout their lives, unaware of its origin. And now, both tunes were merged, like a woven spider's web or the mycelium beneath Earth's surface. So much felt clear in that moment, and they lay in ecstasy, revived. Then they both drifted off into sleep, Lu holding onto Paesh.

The next morning, Paesh lay awake, her eyes staring into the skylight windows. Overnight, everything had gelled; there was a strong inner knowing for what would come next with Iós. In that clarity, she laid silently next to Lu, listening to his slight snoring that resembled a cat's purr. She was calm, as she had never been more certain of anything in her life.

Layer 33: Iós - The Son's Perspective

Iós fell asleep at the desk in his study, drool pooling on its maple-wood surface. He awoke with a sudden panic and snapped upright, his eyes stunned by the early morning's light casting in from the east-facing window. Taking in his surroundings, he put together who and where he was, and what he had fallen asleep doing.

Iós had found little to nothing about Izar, only that he immigrated to the U.S. and had had one daughter, who presumably was related to Paesh, as she had his journal. He was not known for anything outlandish or loud; he had owned a plant nursery in Northern California until he committed suicide when he was nearly fifty. It all made sense, but it didn't solve the unrest in his stomach; instead, it tightened like a rag rung dry of water.

He stood and fixed himself some coffee with his copper espresso machine. Dr. Allen had acquired a luxurious life since Iós had entered into it. He was gratefully quiet and subservient. All he had to sacrifice was a week or two from any given month. He was a brilliant and undiscovered doctor that Iós had used to his advantage since back in the late 1980s. His body was now more youthful and healthy, and his wealth was astronomical. Dr. Allen was his loyal servant, and he was paid well for it.

He poured his coffee and steamed milk into a ceramic mug, and took it on his patio. Taking in the view, his gaze looked out over Santa Cruz from the high vantage point. He enjoyed the bitter flavor of his coffee, as he rarely added sugar. Sugar was an industry that he had propelled to gain favor many years ago, and he knew how terrible it was. It was highly inflammatory and addictive, not that it affected his body much; but he just didn't care for it like the humans did.

His phone rang, and rang, until he put it in airplane mode altogether. At times, the cacophony frustrated him and teased his wits. There was nowhere quiet in the city.

"Will I play these games for all of time?" he wondered, as he pulled a frayed thread on his pants. Iós had grown complacent in the world he had built around him, his mind heavy with the stories of time. Through all of his time here on Earth, he had played so many roles, compiled so many memories, accomplishments, and growth. Yet among all of his hosts, within every story, he was never truly at home anywhere unless he was with *her*. He was always the visitor, even though he nearly owned it all... and that was not satisfying. Blood no longer fulfilled him as it once had. Killing people was still sustaining, but it was a monotonous part of his life, like any simple task was. Like taking out the trash or weeding a garden.

The souls on Earth were all there recycling for *him*. Truth be told, initially he didn't even know it was a possible outcome; although when it happened, it ensured that his Neenah, his Imi, his Indra, would not be able to leave. When religious deities were worshipped, when wars were fought, each soul was actually participating in a mass ritual that sustained the grid that held them on Earth, like small individual beams of electromagnetic light, all set to broadcast on the same signal. Iós was pleased at the power funneled for his gain.

Collectively, the souls on Earth enslaved one another by buying into his format. All those years ago, the feminine balance withered and the Moon herself dissipated at the tipping point of darkness. It occurred in that singular moment when there were enough souls on the planet who were aligned with his program. Despite the fact that he was the cause and still believed in his way of leading, Iós missed the Moon and her once-sparkling shimmer. Even the wind blew with less luster, and the tidal pull had shifted.

There were now so many fragmented souls splitting into the recycling program. One hate crime could fracture a soul into three pieces; and after death, all the pieces were pulled back separately into the river of life. All those pieces would become more confused upon their next reincarnation. Like the momentum of an avalanche, these acts of fracture only reinforced the grid around Earth. It made Iós' head spin, thinking about and how quickly it happened. Despite this long-winded mess and chaos, all he truly ever wanted had yet to be obtained. However, he was close, and he could feel it. With his antibodies, he would soon have her, and she would see. She would live forever with him in his palace of souls.

Iós sat for hours, just staring into the view. He was watching a hawk swooping down for a kill when his smartwatch alerted him that a vehicle was passing up his driveway, towards his gate and camera. It was Dr. Allen's son, Bentley. He was driving his opalescent Tesla, his hair chin-length and wild, as if he hadn't brushed it in days. Bentley gave a crisp salute of a wave that was entirely mocking. He wore aviators that reflected back to the podium with the camera-and-call button.

Iós sighed out loud; he loathed when he had to deal with Bentley. Every time he visited, he was always proposing a business idea or needing a loan for his extravagant lifestyle. Over the years he had watched the boy grow into Peter Pan, now at the ripe age of 34. His trust fund didn't vest until he turned 36.

Regardless of his distaste, Iós buzzed him up, as Dr. Allen and he had an agreement. He stood to stretch his legs, which were tired from the sedentary nature of his afternoon. When Bentley arrived through the front doors, he was humming a tune, and headed straight to the kitchen's fridge for something to drink. He grabbed a bottle of fresh-pressed green juice and orange juice each, which Katherine, Dr. Allen's nutritionist, hand-pressed and delivered every morning. Bentley made a cocktail of the two, and spied his father on the balcony.

Bentley strolled out there with an eccentric confidence, juice in one hand and a single wildflower in the other. "Hello Father, thanks for buzzing me up!" Bentley said while making a small bow, extending the flower to his father with a wide grin across his face.

"Hello, Bentley. What will it be today?" Iós asked, sighing. He had grown tired of the handouts, but he had to oblige as per his agreement with Dr. Allen.

"Ah, I see. Today we have Mr. Hyde," Bentley laughed. "I'm glad I can tell the difference these days; it helps me not to take things as personally. Despite your coldness, you are correct and perceptive." He winked and pointed at Iós.

"Typically, your arrival is prompted by you needing money or legal help. So perhaps I'm not perceptive, but merely trained. I would rather cut the thoughtless small talk, so we can get you set and on your way. I'm rather occupied at the moment," Iós said, with his arms behind his back like an army general.

"Hmm, well then... okay, fair. You got me, I'm here for money. I need $20,000 to get me through the next two months. I won't even give you the long version of what it's for." He leaned in with a wink.

"Is that all you'll be needing?" Iós asked. "Let's do 40,000, so you won't need to come back as soon."

"Ouch, Father, that hurts me, but you know I'll never turn down a higher offer." He grinned, again satisfied, truly unbothered by the coldness.

Bentley had been born when Iós had already been in the picture, and grew up believing his father had Multiple Personality Disorder. There was a time he took Iós' coldness to heart. Luckily, the day he took psychedelics and went to therapy, he learned that his father was mentally ill. He knew that the cold version was someone entirely different. He did not know why, but he knew deep down that his *real* father would return another day.

Iós had left the balcony while Bentley finished his juice. He returned quickly with a check and cash, and handed it Bentley. The son smiled, bowed, and left as easily as he had arrived. Iós was left standing there, dumbfounded by the boy's lack of drive. And yet there was something about Bentley, something that Iós envied and had the chance to watch from a distance. Bentley was spiritual; he was aware of things that others were not. His perceptive nature was like a flashlight in the dark. He was kind, and had love in his heart for his father; he always knew when Dr. Allen was not himself. There was something about his open-minded carefree thoughts that gleamed from his green eyes. He didn't feed the machine or the planetary grid. His soul was not fractured -- it was whole, bright, and beaming. Even though he was reckless with money and had a tendency to party, for the most part he was giving it away to his friends and creating small foundations to feed children and fund community gardens. Iós wasn't exactly sure what he did with his time.

Iós saw potential in him to win and succeed, climb the latter and become someone -- a man of true meaning and substance in the world, successful and dominant, a go-getter in the corporate chain, as his inherited money could put him at the front of the line anywhere. Instead, he found his own way that seemed to fulfill him. In fact, he felt more fulfillment than Iós had ever experienced.

Deep down, Iós was jealous, although he would never admit it.

Layer 34: Paesh - Inoculation

aesh crept silently from the bed. Lu was out cold. Paesh scratched a small note onto a loose leaf of paper and tucked it under the water glasses. Without waking Lu, she successfully made it through the door, and closed it silently behind her.

She was on a mission, walking quickly towards the pools and market area. She did her best to be graceful and not draw too much attention to herself, but she was scanning every person she saw. She was looking for the tall man from the night before, the one with the special chocolate gifts. He should be easy to spot; it was only 8:11 am, and hopefully he was having breakfast or a soak before he hit the road. When she made it to the pool area, she was covert in her scanning, as she did not want to appear creepy or gawking. Instead, she admired the flowers until she was sure she saw everyone mill past her. There was no sign of him there. The cafe and market would be her last two options, beyond scouring the camping platforms that were scattered through the oak-covered hills.

Making her way down the path paved of small mosaic tiles grouped intentionally by color, she made it to the courtyard. Turning past the fountains and around statues, she descended on stairs towards the market and cafe. To her great relief, the man was sitting alone, drinking a green latte out of a ceramic mug. He would be sitting long enough to finish his drink, so she went in to order one as well. Paesh exhaled with deep relief as she went into the cafe, where she ordered a matcha latte with oat milk.

When she had her drink in hand, she made her way outside and over to the man's table, which was farthest away and in partial shade. "Good morning. Would you mind if I joined you?" she asked, hoping she wasn't coming on too strong.

"Good morning... uhm, sure, please have a seat," the man said, a little taken aback at first, and then open to the company.

"Lovely, my name is Paesh," she said, moving a rather loud and rattling metal chair, and settling into it across from him. The cushion was far too thin.

"I'm Oscar. Thanks for, uh, joining me," he said, winking as he lifted his mug to drink.

"Yes... it's not typical of my character to be so imposing, but I was lucky enough to receive one your magical gifts last night..." Paesh gazed off, her eyes zoning out into the background of lush green foliage.

"Ah, I see! They're rather nice out here; it seemed you two enjoyed yourselves. Such teachers, they are." Oscar spoke in a hushed voice, as if he were trading juicy gossip.

"We did. In fact, you have no idea how monumental it was for me and the healing of my soul... without oversharing the lunacy that is my life. Anyway, I came to find and thank you. I wondered if you had more, for sale that is?" Paesh said, lowering her voice and grinning widely, hoping that he wouldn't be alarmed.

"Mmm. You're welcome; it was my pleasure to share last night." He sipped his matcha, savoring the flavor. "It is sort of my..." he paused, looking for the words, "underground business, if you get my mycelium pun. I oversee the cultivation of the main ingredient, so I assure you it is a sterile, clean source. As for the chocolate, it is organic and mixed with other herbs for taste and adaptogenic purposes." Oscar looked side-to- side, aware that his business was not legal, but he smiled too, proud of his passion. Such a beautiful gift veiled by the asinine rules of the government; such a pity.

"Oscar, that is such a relief to know. I would love to support your cause. Can I PayPal you? I left all my cash at home in Santa Cruz," Paesh said with her phone ready in her pocket.

"I can take PayPal, certainly, and I have a stock with me, but it is in my private room. I'm staying in the small building with all the doors. After these lattes, do you want to walk with me?" Oscar asked, swirling his drink in the mug, trying to incorporate the foam stuck on the upper rim back into his drink.

"That would be most appreciated. I have so much clarity today; there's a spirit teacher within that fungi," Paesh mused.

"Exactly! You definitely resonate with the frequency. When I saw you and your partner last night, the both of you were the least human-looking creatures in the waters. I'm not exactly sure what I saw, but that was why I offered it to you both. I felt compelled," Oscar said, casually bewildered, taking a deep breath. "So, Paesh, what do you do for work?"

"... I have been told I tend to shift the way I look," she laughed. "I'm a biologist and I work in a lab." Paesh fidgeted with her cup. The thought of her real-world life was so stale and foreign at this point... she wondered if she would ever go back to work. She drank the last of her latte; it was cooler by now, and went down easily.

"Wow, how interesting. Anyway, I see that we have finished our drinks. Shall we go?" Oscar motioned, and grabbed their mugs to return them.

"Yes, and thank you," Paesh said, standing up as well.

When they were concealed behind the door of his private room, he opened a beautiful cooler case. Inside he had small, individual foiled hearts, and also labeled boxes that were white with gold labeling. She assumed that those were the bigger purchases.

"Beautiful!" Paesh gasped. "I love the labeling."

"Thank you; my boyfriend Bentley made them. He's an artist, and handy with tech stuff. I let him do all that for me -- he's an angel. All righty, then, each chocolate has 2 grams of Thai *cubensis*. The singles are $20, and the boxes contain 10 of those; I sell those for $170," Oscar said, holding up the box. "How many will you be wanting?"

"I'll take a box; that would be perfect. How can I find you on PayPal?" Paesh asked, handing him her phone so he could plug his info into her account.

"There you go. You can send me the $170, and be sure to pick the Family and Friends option, not Sale of Goods," Oscar said, sweetly and with slight sass.

Bling, the transaction made its beckoning tone.

"Here's a bag, just in case anyone sees you leave my room. Even though the boxes are beautiful, they're still illegal."

"That would be great. Thank you so much, Oscar. You have literally saved my world, and maybe *the* world."

Paesh wondered to herself as she wandered out his door and waved. She made her way back to Lu; hopefully he wasn't stressed that she had left him alone.

When she returned, he was calmly drinking some water, and reading over the notes they had taken decoding the journal. "Good morning, Lu," Paesh said as she came in; she set the bag down, and came to sit close to him.

"Good morning, Paesh, how was your walkabout?" he asked with sincerity.

Paesh explained what she was feeling -- her clarity, her plan -- and displayed the box of chocolates. She was cool and clear when she delivered the plan. Lu was patient and listened, nodded slowly, and took in her ideas. Although he was receptive, he was quiet when she finished, and looked back to the papers.

"I like that you've found a route and plan of action. I'm not sure I completely follow it, but maybe on the drive back we can go over it more. For now, let's finish the tail-end of this journal and complete all the translations before we leave the safety of this place," he proposed. He was encouraging and hopeful, even though there was something in him that felt slightly worried.

"I like that idea very much. We can check out tomorrow, since check out is in just three hours," Paesh asked, while she wrapped her arms around Lu. She kissed him on the cheek and held him, so relieved he was there with her and receptive to her plan.

"That would be great. I sleep like a king out here, away from the city and sounds. I really have enjoyed this place, and the fact that you've brought us here. After the week we've had." Lu praised, with his eyes sparkling and looking into hers. "Also, ahem," he cleared his throat, "I've never had a night like we did last night. It was by far the most—- natural connection I've *ever* felt with someone. I want you to know that I'm here with you, through it all. Whatever it takes to keep us safe and together, I'll do it." He kissed her hand and then smiled at her, his energy steady, like a warrior riding home from battle, like a sailor at sea with the wind behind him. He was a pillar of grounded energy.

"I too was amazed at the natural connection... You're my rock, Lu. Meeting you has been the best gift. Last night a door opened in me, something that had been closed for a long time, and I intend to walk back through that door."

Lu nodded, and they laughed a little. As they leaned in for a kiss.

"So, let's finish that journal," Paesh proclaimed with triumph.

They read, snacked, and read some more. The morning Sun quickly turned to afternoon heat, and the cicadas buzzed in the distance. Paesh yawned and stretched her arms up, her eyes squinting with strain on the translation.

Before they knew it, they'd finished the last translation, and it put them both at ease that the information was now solidly in their minds, where things could not be stolen. There wasn't much more information on Iós or Indra; after the explosion, Izar's encounters with them withered away.

"His life had so much build-up, and so much loss. It's interesting; I feel really connected to your grandfather," Lu said, scratching his head and lying back on the couch. "The vision with his father was interesting, when he went to say goodbye to his mother. Before we read this, I felt like I saw that memory when I first put this ring on..." he mused, as he held out the hand with the wooden ring on it.

Paesh reached out and kissed his outstretched hand. "You were lost in thought, I recall; it was hard to stir you from wherever you were. You were in a coma before, after all; maybe that has something to do with it."

Lu turned his head slightly, and took a deep, thoughtful breath. "Things did change after the coma. There was one thing the doctors couldn't explain in the follow-up appointments. My eye-color changed from blue to silver... which is, oddly enough, the same eye color that you have, and that your grandfather had," Lu said, pulling Paesh in to lie on top of him.

"It's a rare color," Paesh whispered. "I have a strange hypothesis; would you like to hear it?" she whispered, her eyes serious, one ear pressed into Lu's chest.

"Try me," Lu said, one arm wrapped around her and his eyes closing.

"What if, after Izar killed himself, his soul went searching to incarnate near me? Maybe he wandered until he found me outside the library, somehow utilizing that peculiar kid's body. Maybe he was an open channel or on psychedelics. He gave me that ring; how would anyone know to find that or have it?" She ran her free hand through her hair. "Bear with me. I know it's a stretch, but you had your accident the same week I met that guy. What if, shortly after he found me, he also found *you* on your way to the hospital. And maybe your old soul was ready to leave, so he stepped in."

After Paesh spoke, the room was silent. Lu didn't respond right away, although she could feel his body stiffen as his mind raced. It wasn't impossible with all that they had been experiencing, but maybe it was insensitive to suggest. Paesh was worried she had offended him. She held her breath without realizing it, nervous that she had taken her theories too far.

Eventually, Lu broke the silence. "You think I may be the soul of your dead grandfather... If I was, would it change the way you feel about me, in some sort of weird familial thing?" Lu asked timidly, his voice nervous.

"It wouldn't change the way I feel. I've been pondering this possibility since we opened the box and you told me about your coma. It wouldn't change a thing," Paesh said, sighing out a huge breath.

Lu cleared his throat. "Well, Paesh, I've also been wondering that, as many of the memories I inherited after my coma were in this journal, and only make sense now that I've read it. Wearing this ring has been like washing dirt from a window. My memories were murky before, unclear and distant; but now they're easy to access. I think I *did* come looking for you."

They let those words sink in, lying there breathing and feeling how their bodies responded to that hypothesis.

"I think you did too, and now we're together, and maybe we can solve this matter with Iós once and for all," Paesh uttered softly.

They fell asleep until the sky was dark. Then they both soaked again and enjoyed their last night in the comfort of their bungalow in the oak hills, where they were safe together. In the morning, they took their leave, heading back to Santa Cruz.

Layer 35: Iós - No More Running

A white bird sat quietly perched in a large, ornate wooden cage. The cage stood adjacent to a bay window that was inundating the room with sunlight. The light exposed the faint teal iridescence of the bird's plumage. Thick, healthy Pathos vines climbed throughout the room, reaching their tendrils to graze the arms of a large leather chair. The door opposing the bay window clicked open, and then shut.

Iós sat in the armchair near the birdcage, and reached for the latch. It was not long before his electric impulse took over the bird, and Dr. Allen was sitting in his chair, momentarily dazed by the familiar sensations of transition. He reached into a pocket and pulled out a note. It read:

Dr. Allen -- I will be away for a few days, but I will need to come back a little earlier than normal. I trust that you will be okay with that. We can adjust your schedule in the coming weeks; I may be out of the country for some time. Your son came by yesterday, and I sent him off with a nice check and some cash. He seemed chipper, as usual. Such a smart lad.

-Iós

Dr. Allen put the paper in the small metal incinerator next to the chair, and then opened the window and let Iós fly free. He propped the window open with a bar and locked it into place. Iós leapt out of the cage and stretched his wings; as he made his way out into the sky, Dr. Allen stood watching for a while before he left the room, closing the door behind him.

Iós first flew out of town; he wanted to clear his mind and sleep alone in the woods for a couple of nights to just escape the duties of man. He wanted merely to be a bird, and so he was. He flew to some forested areas just south of the city, and found himself a nice place to rest. In his time away from town, he reset himself, his focus, and his dedication to his plan. He thought of his extremely well-built safe at Dr. Allen's home, and it contents. His precious antibodies serum lay in syringes in the safe's temperature-controlled environment. Iós thought of all the people who had been sacrificed to get him to this next step.

After a few days in the forest with the clean air, free of WiFi and radio wave signals, he was ready to return to town, and complete this project once and for all.

On his way back home, he checked Lu's residence for occupancy, but it was vacant of light and life. He then flew to Paesh's home, and found that she too was still gone. Would he have to find her all over again? How far could she have gone?

Iós let himself in through the bedroom window that she had left open. All the items in the house were in the same places they had been the night she and Lu had left. He noticed her purse was still on her bedroom floor, limp and pouring out onto the carpet. Iós saw that her wallet, ID, and passport had been left behind. She wouldn't be getting onto a plane or train anytime soon. If they had skipped town, it wasn't for long; they didn't prepare well for it.

The waiting game was hopefully nearing its close. Iós went to her bed and roosted on a pillow to sleep. He felt a little closer to her, sleeping where she slept.

Hours later, he stirred when he heard car doors shut. He flapped to the window's ledge and looked below at the garden gate and path towards the driveway. He heard slow footsteps approach, and in the dim light of sunset, he saw that it was Lu, with Paesh held closely to him. Rage and jealousy burned through his veins, and his feathers ruffled in response to his feelings. When the two were on the back porch landing, he heard Paesh gasp. "What the hell happened to my door!" she grumbled in distaste while pushing the squeaking door open.

Iós had forgotten he had broken her door; well, now they knew someone had broken in. A small oversight that hopefully wouldn't affect much. Iós took the opportunity to fly when they were both inside the house, so they wouldn't see him soar into the trees. From there, he waited to see if the two were planning to settle there for the night. When they made no signs of leaving, Iós took flight back to Dr. Allen's. It was time to finish this; or rather, for it all to finally begin.

Upon arriving, he found that Dr. Allen was tired and reluctant to go back into dormancy, but he did as he was told. He sat in the chair and reached out for the bird. When Iós was in control, he caged the bird and headed for his safe. Equipping himself with the antibodies serum, he dressed and walked out to his car.

Layer 36: Paesh - Bottoms Up

What the hell happened to my door?" Paesh grumbled as she and Lu pushed it open.

"Clearly, Dr. Allen forced his way in; he was probably looking for the journal," Lu said, low anger forming a growl in his throat.

"Let's get some tea and food on. I want to feel nourished and charged up in case he comes soon."

"Paesh, I'm with you every step of the way. Your plan is wild and I trust in your intuition, but it still makes me nervous. This man tried to kill me a couple a days ago, and you want to willingly let him come in and take you? Is there another way?" Lu pleaded as they walked into the kitchen.

Paesh went a little stiff and looked frustrated. She took a deep breath and turned to face Lu, exhaling. "I'm sorry. You've been through so much, and I know this is dangerous. He tried to kill you because of me. He wants me. I know this sounds insane. I spent centuries in my last life running and resisting him. I had anger and hate built up in me at the atrocities that Iós was creating." Paesh's eyes welled with tears, and her voice was slightly elevated. Lu was watching her intently, and listening, his jaw tight.

"I want to have compassion for him. Even though he's not technically a person, I think he needs to feel the love inside the medicine. It has the capabilities of altering him, this fungus; it can polish him like a stone in a tumbler. It will take a massive dose, which is why I bought all of these," she said as she held up the white box with gold labeling.

"I'm going to eat five of them. It will be heavy. If I let him inside me while I'm on the medicine, he'll have nowhere to go; he'll be forced to take the journey with me. You by no means need to stay here with me. Please leave if you're uncomfortable or nervous. However, if you are here with me, I would ask that you eat them as well, in case he tries to enter both of us. I know it's a lot to ask, but something inside of me is so certain..."

Paesh paused and combed her hair back, tightening the skin on her forehead. "Something inside me is streaming in from far away. When we made love, it opened a door in me, and this feeling is coming from that door we opened. The answer isn't violence; it's not destruction of the enemy. Instead, I think it's transformation and compassion. I think that the medicine of the mushroom is calling to Iós. He can't hear the call. He's been so enwrapped in hate and possession of power, people, and places for so long that he's forgotten how to listen... or maybe he never knew how." Paesh closed her eyes, and felt all the cells in her body tingle. She knew that this was a lot to ask of Lu, but she hoped he dared to join her.

"This is all assuming he'll be bringing the antibodies with him. It's assuming he's already had success making them. Despite these potential errors, I won't leave your side, and I'll do my best to fearlessly join you. I've never taken that much of anything before. How do we get to him?" Lu said, his voice cracking but his eyes steady. He wiped his sweaty palms on his jeans.

Paesh was setting water to boil, and she pondered his question. She didn't know for certain that Allen had made the antibodies, though a kind of knowing inside of her gave clarity that he had. She brought two mugs down and set them by the kettle. She was facing out towards the garden, the Sun's light nearly faded. Looking out into the trees, she spotted a small white bird perched towards the top of one. She stopped and watched it for a quiet five minutes. Eventually, the bird moved and took flight; it was Tulsi. Her wing-shape was unmistakable.

"Paesh, are you all right? You've been staring out that window for a while now," Lu said, stepping in behind her.

"I know he'll be coming to us soon, because I just saw him fly off," she said. "He's been desperately waiting for us. He will be here soon." She turned to face him. "Will you prepare us some fresh snacks? There should be stuff in the fridge. I just need to freshen up, use the bathroom, and splash some water on my face."

"Sure..." Lu answered after she left the room. He rummaged around and made a small plate of fresh fruits and vegetables, and he added the hot water to the mugs on the counter, where the herbs inside would steep. When Paesh returned, Lu went up to do the same she had, to have a little time to center himself and freshen up -- to prepare for this risky plan.

They cleared a space in the living room, moving the furniture and bringing in blankets, pillows, and candles. They made a cozy atmosphere together and sipped on the hot tea. Lu suddenly looked like he was struck with an idea. "Isn't Iós telepathic? What if he reads our minds about our plan?"

Paesh had forgotten that detail. "Maybe we could wear tinfoil hats," she joked. "That's an oversight on my part; I suppose it *will* be a test of the mind. We have to think the thoughts that would seem normal and expected in the circumstance. Or maybe if we both wear headphones with loud music, it will help drown out our natural thoughts," she suggested, half-certain.

"The headphones might work. Do you have any?" Lu asked. Before he could finish, she was already halfway upstairs, and soon rummaging through drawers. She had a few pairs of Bluetooth earbuds somewhere.

She returned with two pairs of earbuds, and they put them in and set their phones onto the music of their choice, ready to hit play when Dr. Allen arrived. Paesh was planning on listening to Tool's *Lateralus*, as that album had always helped her block out thoughts. Lu, as his hair was short, borrowed a beanie from Paesh to cover the earphones, so they would not be seen.

Now that their plan was in place, they forced themselves to eat a few bites of berries and cucumbers, as their nerves had gotten to their appetites. Then, together, they opened the psilocybin box and counted out the chocolates, while sitting in their pillow-fort circle. They both ate five chocolate hearts, and it was a challenge to get them all down, but they managed. Anticipation was building, and Paesh tried to stay calm, as it was her plan. Doubts were slowly creeping into her mind, and fear was beckoning her. Attempting to wash it away, she sipped on the hot tea, also washing the taste of chocolate and mushrooms from her mouth. Lu's bravery was tangible, and he held her while they waited.

They held each other while lying down, waiting and listening to the sounds of the room as they become more vibrant and interactive. The sound of fabric moving against fabric was symphonic. The texture of their skin had changed ever so slightly. The medicine was kicking in, and it had only been fifteen minutes.

Suddenly, a sound like a spaceship roared somewhere outside the house, and then a car door shut. Footsteps sounded in the gravel... and then there was a figure in the doorway. Dr. Allen. Paesh knew she had to seem normal, so they both sat up and pressed play on their phones, starting their music. They both concentrated on keeping their thoughts contained and contaminated by song lyrics.

"Hello there. hope I'm not intruding on a slumber party," Dr. Allen said, eyeing the moved furniture.

"What the hell are you doing here?" Paesh leapt to her feet, putting on a shocked face.

Lu followed, standing up behind her. "Dr. Allen?"

"I'm here for you, Paesh. The blood you gave me a year ago has helped me quite a bit on my research project --"

"I didn't give you anything, you son-of-a-bitch. You *stole* it!" Paesh snarled, her body feeling strangely full of muscle and bone, her human form highlighted by the magic mushrooms.

"Either way, you and Lu, funny coincidence, have both helped me solve a puzzle, and I would love for you to be the first to try it." He pulled the syringes from his pocket and waved them around.

Lu leapt forward, swinging at Dr. Allen, clocking him in the jaw. Although unfazed by the blow, Allen pulled a gun from his pocket and struck Lu in the head with it. Lu went down, but he wasn't unconscious. He was crumpled, though, and sighing in pain.

"LU!" Paesh called out, and tried to move towards him.

Iós pointed the gun at Lu, and shook his head at Paesh. "Look, here we all are, just like last time, in the same format but a different setting. This time I have a gun instead of a grenade. I think this time I'll kill him; that was my biggest mistake last time." Iós pointed the gun at Lu and pulled back the hammer.

"Stop, please, I'll do what you want! I'll comply, please, just don't kill him!" Paesh moved in front of the gun, closer to Allen. All the while, her vision was completely altered.

"Fine. Lu, go outside or I'll shoot Paesh," Iós barked, his voice hot with command, veins in his forehead and throat prominent.

Lu looked at Paesh with knowing eyes and made his way outside, where he lay flat on his back, listening.

"It's been a long time, Iós. Just go on and get this over with. I'm done playing games with you," Paesh said through her teeth; she was grateful she could still build a coherent sentence without bursting into tears or laughter.

Iós pulled her arm close, and ripped her sleeve down. His eyes rolled with her scent flooding his nose, but he focused and injected the antibody serum into her arm. The needle was thick and it hurt; he was not gentle when he pushed the serum into her.

"What will this do?" Paesh choked, her eyes fixed on the amber liquid as it emptied into her arm.

"It will finally allow us to be together, Indra; at last you won't have to die, or run from me. It will allow me to enter you, giving you immortal-like qualities," Iós said, his hand on her throat now, testing her pulse. "What does it feel like?"

"Cold. My whole arm is losing sensation," Paesh said as she stumbled backward. "I feel dizzy."

Iós' eyes flared with concern as he watched her stumble backward. He reached out to stop her fall, gripping her arm firmly. She hit the ground on her side, and Iós sat on his knees next to her. He covered her with a nearby blanket, and turned her head to face upward. He sat and waited, watching her vitals and measuring her body's response to the serum. He knew it would take a little time to kick in, so he waited.

Paesh nearly lost consciousness from the mushrooms and the serum, and found herself holding onto reality by a single blue thread. Eventually, Iós reached out to her forehead, and he felt himself slowly sinking into her field, through her flesh and into the current of her lifeforce. He had finally done it! He was inside!

When Dr. Allen came to his senses, dazed and docile, he found himself kneeling on the floor next to a woman who seemed to be incapacitated. He leapt backward, saw the syringe on the floor, and gasped. He felt the weight of the handgun in his pocket. In the other, he found two syringes filled with amber serum. He left those on a nearby counter and ran for the door. He nearly stumbled over Lu, who was tripping so hard he did not react. Dr. Allen got into his car and drove away.

Meanwhile, Lu got on his hands and knees and crawled inside towards Paesh, who was lying on the floor, moving slightly, as if struggling in a dream. He crawled past the used syringe, and looking around, saw more on the counter. He reached for one, and injected himself on the inside of his right thigh. The serum felt cold and metallic as it took over his bloodstream. He made his way over to Paesh, who was still moving. He reached to her ears and removed her earphones, and then held her hand.

The medicine of the mushrooms was in full swing, and both of them could hardly move, as was the plan. Lu pulled Paesh in closer, and they lay forehead-to-forehead, his hand holding hers. Lu could feel that Iós was inside her, and he was forced to sit in on this journey with them both. Whether he was in Lu or Paesh, he had nowhere else to go.

Layer 37: Iós - Polished

As soon as Iós invaded Paesh's body, he realized that her inner atmosphere was different. There was loud music blasting in her mind, and all her body's sensations were lit with a fire he had never known before, a feeling he had never experienced. He felt nauseous and hot; he felt someone holding him, but his eyes were blind to the form. In fact, he wasn't sure if his eyes were opened or closed. There were colored fractals spinning across his field of vision, as if he were viewing flowers through a kaleidoscope, until the vacuum pulled him in deeply and he was on a ride he could not escape.

His mind and Paesh's were flooded with visions and sensations of death and darkness; there were flashes of horrific memories of the acts he had committed. There was fire and smoke. Rotting flesh and decomposition churned like rolling waves. They waded through the river of death towards the centers of their shadows. The medicine was pulling him on a journey, and Paesh along with him. Tears streamed from her eyes, wetting her face. Screams and moans of terror escaped her throat, until there was nothing but stillness and darkness.

Like dirty water sifting through a filter, the darkness was stripped from the source.

When the silence continued, and steady breathing began, there was peace, and soft colors surrounding them all. Iós saw the Moon spirit, and the grid around the Earth he had created and inspired souls to enforce. He felt emotional loss surfacing in waves as flashes of Ala, Neenah, Imi, and Indra came past his mind's eye. These rare emotions were soft and felt foreign when they were not accompanied by hate and anger. Iós experienced his feelings from a whole different perspective, and was able to reflect clearly on his own actions.

The visions were relentless, and filled with exhausting tears as well as physical movement. The body he was within was convulsing with nervous system cleansing. This happened for some time, until again, everything hushed to stillness and a darkness again surrounded him. This directed him towards his memories from before Earth, before they were veiled with confusion and amnesia. It was as if, again, he was floating along in space with nothing but his own company.

Meanwhile, Paesh and Lu were connected, keeping a live conduit open between them for Iós to travel. They shared the burden, and were so deep in the medicine it was unclear who was harboring Iós from moment to moment. They acted as joined reservoirs holding one circling fish. Paesh didn't know where she was amidst the chaos; it was as if she were displaced, and yet experiencing her body's sensations all at once.

Iós was still deep inside of his own vision. In the distance a light began growing, something big and swelling like a firestorm. He felt himself being sucked into the tumble of matter and light, until he was stretched and strained. Another flash of white, piercing light boomed, and he found himself whole, somewhere else... a place where he was not confused about who he was or where he was.

He was Eithar, orbiting a black hole with Althea, awaiting their plunge into the unknown. He remembered it all; he was uneasy, and did not want to go into the black hole. He was internally fearful and reluctant. Conversely, Althea, who was next to him, was calm and radiant. Everything about her inspired him to be brave and follow her anywhere, despite his own unresolved fears. Together, they shared the same soul, bound by love. Their union had created this galaxy he was visiting in his vision; it felt as if he were waking up from a terribly long dream.

Iós realized that what he had become through the black hole was only a fraction of himself, merged with parts of his own creation. Iós was the sliver of fear and doubt; he was the resistance of control and the runner from death. When he was pulled through the black hole, that sliver of himself attracted elements of the Kitsune to merge with him, as like attracted like. He had journeyed through space as an aspect of himself that needed polishing. In his connection to Althea, he was always searching for her, desperate to control all that he could not.

Within a simple blink, Iós was back in a body, lying on a hardwood floor. He was aware of the form, but was still unable to move with any success. Memories of Althea stayed with him, and he could feel her presence like the warmth of touch. He felt her smile radiate light, and her ghostly form reached out and touched his chest, in whoever's body he was within.

Something cracked open, like bud flowering. He felt breath in his proverbial lungs, and he could taste the love in each breath. He laughed and breathed deeper, tapping into a feeling he had never felt here on Earth as his fragmented self. It was as if he were becoming whole again. He was fully remembering and embodying Eithar.

This caused Paesh to cry; tears were falling from her eyes, and she could not control them. She Let go of Lu, and held Iós inside of herself. He was like a raw stone fresh from the Earth, being tumbled to a smooth polish. She had given him a chance to see where he was from, why he was so lost. He was healing within her mortal walls, reforming himself.

He knew now why he was so drawn to Indra and Paesh, as she was Althea. He just couldn't see it before.

A voice sounded from somewhere within them both: "You have somewhere else to be; you are free from this form." Iós breathed deeply and let go, allowing himself to fall into wherever he needed to.

Lu opened his eyes and looked at Paesh, who was glowing brighter than he had ever seen. Her eyes were closed, and her body was vibrating lightly. She made a sharp inhalation, drinking in the air -- then a being as dark as the night sky sat up out of her body. His skin had the depth of galaxies and star systems. He looked around the room, his silver eyes gleaming in the low light. Then he stood and walked out of Paesh, her body relaxing as he exited. The being bent down and touched her on the forehead, and kissed her gently. He was Eithar embodied, polished from Iós, liberated from his limited perspective.

In remembering his true nature, he knew that he had somewhere else to be.

Eithar looked around the room one more time, and slowly dissolved while lifting up into the air, through the ceiling, space, and time. When he surpassed the atmosphere of Earth, the gridlines surrounding the globe followed him like a cape. The farther he sailed away, the more the cape dissipated and scattered amongst the stars.

He held onto the feelings and memories of Althea as he transported himself elsewhere. Like a magnet through spacetime, he felt himself drawn somewhere specific. When he landed, he found his feet grounding onto a metallic landing; it was a golden disc with symbols on it. He was kneeling and dizzy.

When his vision cleared, he was face-to-face with a familiar form, a woman with lavender skin and silver eyes. She peered down at him curiously. She circled him, assessing his form and features. She eventually introduced herself as Celosia.

He was not back in his own galaxy, but in yet another place. Celosia was familiar to him; it was the name of one of Althea's creations in their home galaxy. Perhaps, as Iós was a fragment of Eithar, Celosia was a fragment of Althea...? They must have been scattered throughout the universe, like shrapnel meant to be lost and found.

After they stared at each other for a long time, he spoke. "Do you remember me?" He stood to take a step forward and pushed his hair back from his face. Celosia did not respond to his question; she only stared at him.

Layer 38: Fengári - Release

Like a baby's first breath after birth, Fengári woke to life and strength, small tendrils of her soul reassembling from across the planet. The grid was lifted, and there was room to stretch and move once more. She headed straight for the Sun to find Ílios; it had been so long since she had seen him properly.

When she entered the Sun, she was greeted with the longest embrace, a merging so passionate it could break time itself. Iós was gone, and their prism was now set free. The once-trapped souls were free to exit when their Earth bodies perished, each soul able to travel back to wherever it had come from. Souls could stay on Earth, too, but it was unlikely that many would. Now that Iós, the influence of darkness, had been transformed, those who still inhabited Earth would slowly wake up to the atrocities that they blindly followed for so long. It would not happen overnight, and certainly not in one lifetime, but those who choose to stay could build a cleaner and more loving future.

"That, my dear, was an unexpected detour for our project," Ílios sighed as he released Fengári from their embrace, standing back to take in the sight of her.

"I learned more about darkness and the potential shadow of a soul when I locked myself down there. Thank you for coming down with me and finding me. It was a much-needed hope." Fengári spoke with her gaze fixed in Earth's direction. Bewilderment splashed across her face as she recalled all the bizarre events of her lives. "Time can feel so eternal when you're down there, and I did not expect that."

"Time is so illusive. When I would come back up here without finding you, I was angry with the place we had created. Its limitations felt so real when there was no way out for you. Time just kept creeping along. Fengári, when you dissolved, I was flooded with fury and anguish; it was such an impulsive choice, and yet I know why you did what you did. It was brave, and it was selfless." Ílios eyes were also fixed on Earth. They sparkled green and were filled with theatrical passion as he recalled his experiences. "Despite it all, it is still a wondrous place, but what to do is next? What shall we do with Earth?"

Fengári turned to acknowledge Ílios, and then looked back towards the blue plane, glimmering at its peaceful distance. "I will relight the Moon, and may it serve as a deep-seated reminder to all the lost souls, so they know that they can leave if they so choose. Perhaps we will suspend the prism, and keep it running until these souls are finished with their stories. I know Celosia is down there, and has finally fulfilled her promise. I'm sure she will want to finish her story naturally before moving on."

Ílios nodded. "We will keep it running, then. I would love nothing more than to see the Moon alight again; it has been gray far too long."

Fengári reached out and held the side of Ílios' face, and blinked at him slowly. Her piercing blue eyes smiled at his, while her whole essence moved backward towards the Moon. Like wind and dust, she swirled around its spherical landscape. Reclaiming her orb, she sank into its surface, inoculating its dull gray-brown surface with millions of tiny diamonds. When she reached the hollow center, all parts of the Moon pulsed with light. Seafoam green and pearlescent blue swept over the loamy dullness of all that was dusty and gray before. Once again, the prism was fully functioning, and Fengári was connected to all the souls who remained on Earth. From her layered pages of time, she could lightly influence these souls towards more balanced choices, sending them messages in dreams by inspiring creativity in art and technology. She could influence those who remained in power to shift their perspectives now that Iós was no longer there to manipulate them all into hatred.

Balance was finally underway. Of course, when the people of Earth noticed the Moon's new colors, there was initial panic, and scientists everywhere speculated and spoke of Doomsday. However, when most of the souls looked up, they had a strange sense of deja vu.

Layer 39: Paesh - Clarity

Paesh opened her blurry eyes to a dimly lit room that was shifting and breathing; the mushrooms were still working through her system. But it was obvious the climax of the trip had ended, and that it would get easier from this point forward. She turned to see that Lu was watching her, his eyes wide and streaming with tears.

"Paesh..." he struggled to get words out, "Are you... you?" He scooted closer to hold her hand.

"Yes, I think so. Are you you?" she countered, propping herself up on her elbows, blinking repetitively to see if that helped her vision.

"I'm me. Did you see what came out of your body? There was a man made of the galaxy..." Lu said. His words were slightly slurred, and his timbre was childlike.

Paesh sat up fully, and the directional shift of her blood made her temporarily lightheaded. When she felt the dizziness fade, she turned her head to look at Lu. "I felt something lift out of my body; it felt like I was a giant banana being peeled. When I opened my eyes, I saw him, and he kissed my forehead. At first I thought it was you, because of the silver eyes, but then I could see you next to me out of the corner of my eye. I've seen this man before from my dreams, the one painted with stars." Paesh recounted the sight of him. She was blown away by what had just happened, and she was parched from all the tears shed. Her eyes scanned the room until she spotted her mug of herbs from earlier. She grabbed it and drank from a mug that felt foreign in her hands. The now-cooled brew revived her, its taste strong and distinct.

"Iós transformed into that star being. Something happened to him when he was forced to take the medicine, and it must have shifted something inside him. I wonder where he went," she mused, her head feeling heavy on her neck. "The dose was so potent I felt glued to the floor with the weight of it. I don't think I'll ever need this much again." Paesh laughed as she reached over to Lu and held his hand. "You okay, bud?"

"I am. I feel lighter, but I'm definitely still tripping pretty deeply. Let's go outside... I think it will help. Let's bring some of these!" he exclaimed while he struggled with an armful of blankets, his dexterity limited.

Paesh laughed, and helped him. They made their way outside, where they spread the blanket on the ground near rows of flowers and herbs. They triumphantly laid back. The stars were prominent in the sky, and the night air was still warm. The Moon was slowly rising above the edge of Paesh's house, and they both strained their eyes when it did. The Moon was altogether a different color; it was teal and seafoam green, and it reflected light like a gemstone. The traditional craters upon its surface were no longer visible.

"Does the Moon look... way different to you?" Lu asked, while he scooted closer to Paesh.

"It does. Why is it green and blue? It's glorious, but maybe we're still tripping harder than we thought," Paesh said, laughing, while the wind blew the stems of the flowers near their heads. Moths flitted around in the air, while crickets and frogs sang them a song. Paesh and Lu giggled and cried. They experienced so much love for the planet and each other, just as they had back at the hot springs, their level of coherence returning.

The two of them fell asleep beneath the stars, as the Moon was now sparkling a whole new brightness up above.

The colorful dawn woke the both of them, their bodies stiff with the awkward positions they had fallen asleep in. "Good morning," Lu moaned, his hair wild with sleep's design. "God, you're beautiful."

Paesh shrugged and curled into him. "Thank you," she whispered.

"Did we accomplish what we were trying to?" Lu asked. "That was a night beyond belief."

"It was the wildest thing I have ever experienced. I felt him transform in me; I felt his anguish and darkness, but then I felt realization and lightness," Paesh said, her throat strained and dry from the laughter and crying the night before. "I think we did it..." Paesh trailed of as she stood, "I'm going to make some tea. Do you want some?"

"I would love some," Lu said, his throat also dry.

They enjoyed their tea while the insects and birds started their morning rituals. Paesh pulled a sweater over her head, and Lu wrapped himself in a blanket. Their heads leaned in together and they laughed a little at the insanity of it all. Something felt lighter in the world; something felt free.

PING! Lu's phone went off. It was still in his pocket from the night before. He moved to get the thing out of his pocket, and saw a news banner on the top of the screen. It read:

Moon changes color; astronomers are hard-pressed to find a cause. NASA advises that citizens remain calm.

"Holy shit, look at this!" Lu clicked the link and opened the page for her to read.

Her eyes went from annoyed to amazed as she read the headline. She scrolled down to see a picture taken of the Moon. It was seafoam green and teal, just as they'd seen night before. "Okay, so we weren't imagining that last night," Paesh said, taking a slow, measured sip of her tea, mulling over the information.

"Maybe Iós leaving has something to do with it? Perhaps the souls really are free to leave now." Lu postulated, taking a sip of his tea as well.

Paesh closed the phone. "Well, I'll take NASA's advice and remain calm." She laughed sarcastically, and set Lu's phone down.

"Now that we've completed our mission, what do we do?" Lu wondered, in a slight mocking tone.

"Well, I do have a closet full of cash. Maybe we can go on a trip to the Basque territories, and then down to Portugal for some surfing," Paesh joked, but she wasn't entirely kidding.

"I like that idea," Lu replied, his eyes far away. "I suppose we should see as much of this place as possible while we're here. Who knows if we'll have to stick around for the next life?"

Layer 40: Althea - Elastic

Althea closed her eyes as they walked into the blazing pressure of the black hole, to be stretched and shattered along with pieces of their creations from their joint galaxy. The pressure fractured her awareness in more ways than she had thought it would. She felt a part of herself merge with particles from her favorite creations, like attracting like. Reassembled, she floated away from the memories of her galaxy and the identity of Althea. She fell softly across the universe, like a feather in the wind. This part of herself landed in a place outside of space and time, a place that was hers and hers alone to create and to manage. There was a cave, a tree, and a nebulous sea surrounding her.

Like a dream within dreams, she lived there, observing the galaxies far and wide. In this plane of existence, she had simply forgotten everything until the time came for her to wake up, when the stories she was invested in were closed and balance was achieved.

The perception of existing in her plane outside of space and time felt infinite, until it didn't.

SNAP! The stretching and tumbling began again; a soft feather landed, now pulled back like elastic. There was, like before, light and heat. Intense sound boomed and chilling quiet blanketed. Althea found herself whole again, no longer segmented with amnesia. She was once again orbiting the black hole with Eithar, as they had been in the beginning. They seemed to have come out the other side almost as quickly as they had entered. As quickly as a cosmic breath, they were inhaled and then exhaled by the mysterious glow of the singularity.

Althea looked around, and to her dazed surprise, their once-destroyed galaxy was intact again. The pressure and vacuum of the dying Sun was lessening its grip. She could feel its implosion dimming, the light at the center beginning to fade into an amber glow.

Althea and Eithar shrank backwards, collecting themselves away from the old star. Althea was filled with stories and dreams of places and experiences far away, a journey that consisted of layers upon layers of lifetimes. Upon walking through the hole in the star, they had both emerged feeling wiser.

Althea's once-sharp edges softened, her once-cracked layers filling in. Her longing for transformation and autonomy brought her perspective. These lessons made her honor her Union with Eithar all the more.

There was a reverence in her that reverberated outward; both Eithar and herself were quiet with reflection. Where had they just been, and why did it feel so long, and yet so quick? They had spent eons away, and yet it was but a moment. The black hole took them into its belly, its fine-tuning portal, exposing the quirks of their souls, allowing them to explore their faults amongst victories, and enjoying the symphonic harmony between them.

The black hole was a mystery that they would likely never solve, but its ability and offering to fine tune their souls changed them both forever.

THE END & PERHAPS THE BEGINNING

About the Author

I am Maja Fagras, a woman with varied musings. A solo traveler, gardener, healer, and entrepreneurial creative. In 2018, I gathered my courage to share my story with the world.

The story, Celosia's Web, which fell into my mind, with the gravity of a falling stone, needed to be told. Initially, like any persevering artist, writing was tailored around a full time job; needless to say it required a heap of diligence. Halfway through the process, I left alone for the island of Bali, to finish writing the novel on a sabbatical, where my mind could truly surrender into the story completely. I finished in January of 2020 just before this world tock a turn on its head.

I am currently working on a second novel, They Were Dowsing for Water, as well as a series of short stories. Keep an eye for them in 2025.

Follow me on @majafagras.author